TITLES BY LORI ANDREWS

FICTION
The Silent Assassin
Sequence

NONFICTION
Genetics: Ethics, Law and Policy
(with Mark Rothstein and Maxwell Mehlman)

Future Perfect: Confronting Decisions About Genetics

*Body Bazaar: The Market for Human Tissue
in the Biotechnology Age*

*The Clone Age: Adventures in the New World of Reproductive
Technology*

*Black Power, White Blood: The Life
and Times of Johnny Spain*

*Between Strangers: Surrogate Mothers, Expectant Fathers, and
Brave New Babies*

Medical Genetics: A Legal Frontier

*New Conceptions: A Consumer's Guide to the Newest Infertility
Treatments, Including In Vitro Fertilization, Artificial
Insemination, and Surrogate Motherhood*

Birth of a Salesman: Lawyer Advertising and Solicitation

EDITED BY LORI ANDREWS
Assessing Genetic Risks: Implications for Health and Social Policy
(co-edited with Jane E. Fullarton, Neil A. Holtzman,
and Arno G. Motulsky)

THE SILENT ASSASSIN

Lori Andrews

St. Martin's Paperbacks

This is a work of fiction. All of the characters, organizations and events portrayed in this novel are either products of the author's imagination or are used fictitiously.

Grateful acknowledgment is made to East Coast USA Vietnamese Publishers Consortium for permission to reprint "My Poem" by Nguyen Chi Thien.

THE SILENT ASSASSIN

Copyright © 2007 by Lori Andrews.
Excerpt from *Immunity* copyright © 2008 by Lori Andrews.

Library of Congress Catalog Number: 2007007879

ISBN: 0-312-94648-1
EAN: 978-0-312-94648-7

Printed in the United States of America

St. Martin's Press hardcover edition / May 2007
St. Martin's Paperbacks edition / June 2008

St. Martin's Paperbacks are published by St. Martin's Press, 175 Fifth Avenue, New York, NY 10010.

10 9 8 7 6 5 4 3 2 1

For the 58,249 and those who loved them

Those who know do not say, and those who say do not know.

—Lao-Tzu, *Tao Te Ching*

PROLOGUE

THE TANK that ended the Vietnam War over thirty years earlier by crashing through the gates of the presidential palace provided cover for Huu Duoc Chugai as he strode to the War Remnants Museum in Ho Chi Minh City. At 2:00 A.M. the few people on the street were drunks or lovers, probably with little interest in the tall forty-year-old, but Chugai fell into a routine of keeping in the shadows, his head down. His pace picked up on Vo Van Tan Street, then slowed as he wove through the arsenal of captured American planes and bombs outside the museum. He swore under his breath as he clipped his shoulder against the rocket launcher attached to a rusting American helicopter.

He glanced around as he reached the door of the main building, saw no one, and let himself in with a key. Chugai was a man who made the most of opportunities. The ministry that previously employed him oversaw the park system, including the museum. He'd hung on to a key to the museum, not knowing at the time how he would use it. His life was like the construction of the tunnels at Cu Chi. He believed in stealth, in collecting and manipulating information, in winning at all costs. Sometimes he couldn't tell if it was his birthright or the two years he'd spent in the United States that had honed his resolve. But his planning was about to pay off.

He locked the museum door behind him, congratulating

himself on his choice of a meeting place. When the general arrived, Chugai planned to walk him past the photo of American soldiers posing with the severed heads of two North Vietnamese soldiers. It would remind the man of his debt, of how Chugai's father had saved his life during the war.

Chugai moved into the room that held a tiger cage for prisoners of war. He lit a cigarette, thought about the warm bed of his mistress he'd just left, and smiled again at his own cleverness. He'd arrived a half hour before the proposed meeting time and was keeping watch so he could let the old North Vietnamese solider in. Or maybe he would move back through the museum, so the man would knock and wait for a few moments, just to show him Chugai was running the show.

His thought was abruptly interrupted by an arm reaching around his neck and grasping him in a choke hold. His cigarette fell to the floor as his assailant spun him around. Chugai looked down in embarrassment at the general, who was three inches shorter than he. How the hell had he gotten in and crept up so silently?

The older Vietnamese man grinned, with a touch of madness in the corners of his eyes. Chugai was sufficiently chagrined that he forgot his grand plan to walk the general through the museum to seal his loyalty. Instead, he thrust an envelope into the general's hand. The man didn't even open it. Instead, he held his pointer finger up, signaling *one*.

Chugai knew what he meant. He'd kill once more and then he would consider the debt repaid. Chugai opened his mouth to speak, but the man was no longer listening. Instead, the general had moved over to the French guillotine that was on display.

The old man placed the envelope on the wooden bench at the bottom of the guillotine and let loose the weighty blade that had been used to kill prisoners of war. The crushing thump severed the envelope in half, shredding and scattering the Vietnamese and American currency it held. As Chugai rushed over to see if the airline ticket was still intact, the general disappeared out of the museum.

Screw it, thought Chugai. If the general wants to do it his way, so be it. Chugai put the mangled currency and plane ticket into his pocket. He didn't care how the general got to Washington, D.C., as long as he killed the bastard.

CHAPTER ONE

LUKE KNELT on the hand-loomed rug next to the bed and started zipping his guitar into its traveling case. The loud crackle of the industrial-sized zipper brought Alex in from the next room. Her long, wavy blond hair cascaded over her black turtleneck and she still looked flushed from their lovemaking. She walked up behind him. "I heard the zipper and thought it was your pants coming back off."

He turned toward her, still kneeling, and faced the fly of her jeans. He reached his hand up to the snap at the top. "Dare me and I'll have you back in bed in twenty seconds flat."

She thought about how that might make him late for his flight to London, and how she'd probably lose her favorite parking spot at work. Then she smiled down at him. "Dare you," she said.

A flurry of clothes streaked across the room like the streamers from a New Year's Eve popper. She fell back on the bed and he joined her, licking her mischievously down her body, a favor she promptly returned. Then he moved up over her and they made love tenderly, gingerly, his face down close to hers, nose to nose, their sighs turning into gasps. As they were about to climax, they rolled across the bed, so that she was on top of him, almost seated, lifting herself up and down. Her hair shook like a horse's mane.

She came first and the rolling motion caused him to climax and groan. She flopped over next to him and buried her head in the crook of his arm. Brushing her hair back from her eyes, she noticed the wristwatch she'd failed to remove before lovemaking. "Yikes, Luke, we'd better hit it."

She got out of bed, but Luke feigned exhaustion. She bent over to shake his shoulder and her cell phone rang. A tune by Luke's rock band, the Cattle Prods.

"Oh, Luke, you didn't reprogram this again, did you?" She was glad it hadn't rung like that in some high-level meeting.

"Alex Blake," she said into the receiver, as Luke continued to simulate a coma.

The familiar voice of Major Dan Wilson said simply, "You've got a date with a corpse at eleven hundred hours."

She hung up and addressed the body on her bed. "Up and at 'em, Luke. You're not my only stiff today."

A few minutes later, Luke and Alex had packed the trunk of her battered '63 yellow T-Bird and were racing to National Airport. She couldn't bear to refer to it by its new name, Ronald Reagan International Airport. Hadn't they named enough stuff after him? Was it true that every big city now had a Reagan Street, a Reagan School, probably even a Reagan Prison? Was anything safe from the creeping Reaganisms? She could imagine a day when they would start renaming people's body parts. Yes, my Reagan bone broke just above the Coca-Cola cartilage.

At the United terminal, Luke lingered to say good-bye. He handed her a CD of songs he'd recorded for her. She looked at this almost handsome man as he shouldered his guitar case and gripped the handle of a meager duffel bag of clothes. He loved playing and writing lyrics so much that he'd do it for squat—and, in fact, earned only slightly more than that. But the music did provide him an excuse to see the world. When an old bandmate in London offered to put him up in exchange for Luke helping the guy move his piano to his new flat, Luke jumped at the chance and the Cattle Prods Second World Tour was born. After London, there would be gigs in Spain, France, and Denmark.

"I haven't taken any vacation. Maybe I'll meet you in Barcelona," Alex said.

Luke looked down at the ground, then back up at her. "That's not so great," Luke said. "I'm staying with Vanessa."

Alex's mouth gaped before she could hide her feelings. And then the curbside skycap told Luke he'd better haul ass if he wanted to make the flight.

Luke stepped forward. "It's nothing. She's just a friend. I'll e-mail you once I land." He bent over to kiss her, but she turned her face and the smack landed on her cheek.

Luke ran into the terminal and Alex started the old T-Bird. As she sped toward the George Washington Memorial Parkway, she pumped up the heater to chase away the chill she felt, a combination of the unseasonably cool December day and the icy thoughts running through her mind. Who the hell was Vanessa? Probably someone he'd met on the First World Tour, last year, after he and Alex had broken up.

The parkway was more like a parking lot that time of day. Alex used her time in traffic to pick up her messages at work. One from Dan, left before he reached her at home about the autopsy, and another ordering her to meet with the head of the Armed Forces Institute of Pathology, Colonel Jack Wiatt, at 2:00 P.M.

As a civilian working at the AFIP, she bristled at the term *order*, especially when it came from Wiatt, with whom she'd tangled on more than one occasion. When President Bradley Cotter had appointed him head of the AFIP a year earlier—and not head of the FBI, which he'd wanted—he'd practically gone postal. But it turned out the AFIP suited him. Overseen by the U.S. Department of Defense, the compound functioned like a city, with its own fire department, police station, and hospital. The facility sat on 113 out-of-the-way acres in D.C. near the Maryland border, four acres larger than the Vatican. Like the Vatican, the AFIP had a surprisingly wide reach, often working in mysterious—or at least sub rosa—ways. It oversaw forensic investigations in the United States and abroad involving the military and the Executive Branch—all without the close scrutiny that the public and Congress gave other institutions like the FBI and CIA. A high-testosterone soldier who'd led men in every war, incursion, altercation, and conflict since Vietnam, Wiatt was a man for whom rules were flexible. Running an institution where they could be bent suited him. But he and Alex often butted heads as she tried to do her job using genetics to create biowarfare vaccines and he pulled her into activities that took her away from her work.

Once she reached the compound—a frustrating forty-five minutes later—Alex nosed her car toward her favorite parking spot, but, of course, it was now occupied. The only space left was across the base from the main AFIP entrance. She walked to the door of the National Museum of Health and Medicine, which was connected by tunnels to both the AFIP, where she worked, and the Walter Reed Medical Center, where she often provided second opinions for prominent patients.

As Alex approached the museum, she was surprised to see twenty or thirty people outside, some holding placards. The museum was usually a sleepy place, with tours of third graders staring at the microscopes and medical oddities like the stomach-shaped hair ball from a teenage girl who constantly chewed (and swallowed) her curls. This was a much different crowd. Elderly Vietnamese couples in cream-colored flowing pants and denim-clad college students carrying signs with phrases like LET THEIR SPIRITS REST IN PEACE. A thin white guy in his early twenties with a megaphone blocked the sidewalk. He shouted into the mouthpiece, "Give back the Trophy Skulls."

He looked straight into Alex's blue eyes, at her beguilingly sweet heart-shaped face. His gaze traveled down her body, noting her beat-up brown leather jacket and jeans, nicely taut over her lean, athletic curves. He handed her a placard to carry.

"No, thanks," she said. "I work here."

ON THE way to her lab, Alex stopped at the office of her best friend, Navy Lieutenant Barbara Findlay, the African-American lawyer who was the AFIP's general counsel.

"So, what's with the crowd outside?" Alex asked. She folded her legs under herself in the comfortable chair across from Barbara's desk and reached into the cut-glass candy bowl that was Barbara's way to get secretaries and generals alike to stop in and chat.

Barbara, poised and feisty in her crisp Navy uniform, leaned forward and pushed a *Washington Post* across her desk toward Alex. "Didn't you see yesterday's newspaper?"

Alex shook her head. "I was busy having good-bye sex with Luke."

"Breakup sex or tour-schedule sex?"

Alex thought for a moment. "Not sure yet."

"Frankly, Alex, your taste in men—"

"At least I'm taking a swim in the dating pool. You haven't even put on your suit."

Barbara laughed. "A teenage daughter and parking lot full of protestors keeps me busy enough."

Alex looked down at the front-page photo of a small hill with a pagoda-shaped pillar of five carved stones on top of it. She read the caption. "The Ear Mound?"

"Yes, the Korean Ear Mound in Kyoto, Japan. A five-hundred-year-old pile of ears that Samurai warriors cut off of Korean soldiers."

"Why ears?"

"The Samurai generals got a bonus for each soldier they killed in Korea. At first they sent back heads, but when the ships got too crowded, they started dispatching just the ears."

Alex looked at the mound of dirt as high as a house. "They must have killed tens of thousands."

Barbara nodded. "Recently, a group of Korean monks placed fifty Korean flags on top of the mound and began to negotiate for a return of the ears, at least spiritually, to Korea. That's what provoked the Vietnamese Ambassador to the U.S. to contact us. Some U.S. GIs kept skulls of North Vietnamese soldiers. Most of the skulls were confiscated when they tried to bring them back through U.S. Customs. And the skulls ended up here. We've never displayed them, though, because the soldiers shouldn't have taken them out of Vietnam. We just stuck them in a drawer."

"So what's the big deal? Give them back, let them rest in peace."

"It's not that simple," Barbara said, getting up from her desk chair. She motioned for Alex to come with her.

As the two exited the office, Barbara walked with the dramatic posture of a soldier, her body forcefully and efficiently slicing down the hall. The kinetic Alex commandeered more space.

They approached the storage area of the museum, and Barbara said, "Wiatt wants me to see if I can find a way to delay their return, some legal maneuver."

Alex wondered why Wiatt would care about sending back a drawerful of skulls. Sure, he'd fought in Vietnam, but hadn't the whole nation moved on?

"What's his problem?" Alex asked as Barbara approached a cabinet in the storage room.

"Well," Barbara said, "the U.S. soldiers added a few touches of their own."

Barbara pulled open a drawer, and Alex peered in. The skulls stared back at her. Some had grotesque faces painted on them; a few had their craniums lopped off so that they could serve as ashtrays. A half dozen had been painted neon colors and covered with graffiti, with holes drilled through the top and candles jammed in.

Alex's eyes grew wide and she shook her head. She'd seen

bodies and bones in all states of decay, disease, and disfigurement. But graffiti on someone's superciliary arch? This was chilling and demeaning. "Who would do something like this?"

"Now you see. We can't let them go back like this."

CHAPTER TWO

AFTER LEAVING Barbara and the skulls, Alex donned a gown and gloves to enter the autopsy suite. It was nearly eleven. Through the glass wall, she could see it was quite a party in there. Thomas Harding, the Chief Pathologist, was peering intently into the open chest cavity of the corpse. Given his wire-rimmed glasses, lean body, and short, thinning red hair, the sixty-year-old might have been nicknamed "the Professor," were it not for the ropy muscles and heavy tan he'd acquired working on his sailboat. Like Alex, he was a civilian working at the AFIP. In his free time, he competed in regattas and Scrabble matches. In the taglines of his e-mails to Alex, he always included a new word of the day. Yesterday's was "ludic: relating to, or characterized by, play." Harding had explained that psychologists in the 1940s invented the term as a more academic-sounding way to describe children having fun, "ludic activity." Between the skulls and the corpse, Alex could see her ludic days were numbered.

At Harding's side stood thirty-five-year-old Captain Grant Pringle, back rigid, right shoulder forward, posing in his annoying Mr. Universe style, as if to show off his bulging bodybuilder muscles. Alex couldn't help but think of an article in the journal *Science* by geneticist Jon Gordon about a genetically engineered bull whose chest was so enormous that eventually his legs couldn't hold him up. A few more bench presses and Grant might topple over.

Grant playfully leered at Alex through the glass and licked his upper lip. Growing up in Vegas, he'd internalized the warped, fanny-slapping view of women that city fostered. Which was why Barbara, in her role as the AFIP's general counsel, repeatedly sent him to gender-sensitivity training.

"What have we got?" Alex asked as she approached the body.

"John Doe, found in a Dumpster," Harding said. "Killer started the autopsy without us."

Alex glanced at the hole in the torso and noticed the heart was missing. "How'd he end up here? Seems like an ordinary D.C. street crime."

Grant smiled at her, lips twitching at the corners. He thrust out the photo he was holding, a detailed close-up of the entry wound. "We got him because of my WOW program."

It wasn't bad enough that Grant posed like Popeye. His projects had acronyms like something out of a comic book.

Harding knew she had zero tolerance around Grant. "Weapons of War," he explained.

Alex nodded thanks and thought about how different Harding was from Grant in attitude and appearance. She could imagine the thin, balding Harding a century earlier with an old-fashioned doctor bag in hand. Grant she could picture a century in the future as a genetically engineered cyborg. Their work reflected their differences as well: high touch versus high tech.

Harding consulted on patients at Walter Reed and performed autopsies in forensic cases. Grant ran a futuristic gee-whiz lab at the AFIP that designed new body armor, weapons, and intelligence-gathering devices for the military. Congress practically gave him a blank check to pursue whatever loony idea he came up with. But, Alex thought grudgingly, one of his crazy designs had saved her life in a recent case.

Harding used a surgical knife to extend the wound into a Y-shaped incision from shoulder to shoulder and down to the pubic bone.

"D.C. cops turned him over when someone recognized the wound's bayonet shape," Grant said. "We're comparing the wound to weapons in our collection to figure out what the perp used."

Harding pulled his protective goggles over his eyes, nodded to Alex and Grant to stand back, and used the electric Stryker saw to cut through the sides of the chest cavity. The pathologist made a series of cuts along the vertebrae to enable him to remove the internal organs. As he examined and weighed them, Alex looked at the corpse's face. He was good-looking, well kept. She moved closer and lifted one of his hands. "White-collar worker for sure," she said, examining his nails. She turned the arm this way and then that. "No drug marks, not the kind of guy who usually ends up in a Dumpster."

"No sign of struggle, either," said Harding.

"I'll run what's under his nails just in case," Alex said. She took a small knife off a tray and scraped under the nails. "Did you notice the red stain on his forefinger?"

Harding nodded.

Alex brought the finger up near her nose. "Smells like some sort of spice. I'll sequence it."

"Spices have DNA?" asked Grant.

"All plants and animals do. Whether I can recover it depends on how processed this spice is."

Harding was using a small set of tongs to pull a few tiny brownish-yellow swatches from the gaping hole in the dead man's chest.

"Fabric?" Alex asked.

Then Harding pulled out a bigger something yellow, curved, and about two inches long. "Looks like a rose petal," he said.

Alex, who'd earned both an M.D. and a Ph.D. in medical genetics from Columbia University, had joined the AFIP to design vaccines to stave off biowarfare. Occasionally she was pulled in on forensic cases, and sometimes she bridled at the time it took away from her work on toxins. But she admired Harding and was learning about how each subtle action of a killer indicated something about him—or her.

Tracking a killer was like doing psychoanalysis from a distance, putting together a puzzle of someone's personality when most of the pieces were missing.

She thought about the rose, the empty chest. "Female troubles?" Alex wondered aloud. "Someone making a point about how heartless he was?"

"Chicks don't usually wield a bayonet," Grant said.

Alex rolled her eyes at Grant. "Don't you remember that 1980s Barbie board game, 'We Girls Can Do Anything'?" she asked.

Harding turned the body over, so his buttocks and back were faceup. Grant moved closer to the corpse. "Looks like he plays for the other team," Grant said.

"Slight abrasions on the anus, lots of semen inside," Harding confirmed. "Looks consensual, though."

"Still, it's easy enough for a lover to become a killer," Alex said. In fact, she'd felt a fleeting desire to strangle Luke when he uttered the word *Vanessa*. She used a syringe to extract some semen from the corpse. Maybe she'd find a match to his lover in the FBI DNA database, CODIS.

"You know, I'm against gay marriage . . . ," Grant said.

Alex and Harding looked at him as he cracked a smile.

". . . Haven't they suffered enough?" Grant winked.

Alex shook her head. It was no secret that Grant hated the institution of marriage, or rather his former partner in it. The way he told it, quoting a country western song, Debbie got the gold mine and he got the shaft.

Alex swabbed the red powder from the dead man's finger. Harding looked at his upper arm. "He's got a bit of an induration here," he said, touching a raised area. "Maybe a recent vaccination."

"If it's a live vaccine, I might be able to identify it in his blood," Alex said, as she put the swab into an evidence tube. "We could get Chuck to check it against the Centers for Disease Control list of suggested travel vaccines."

"Okay," said Harding. "I'll have someone take a photo so Chuck can run facial recognition software against recent passport records."

Alex thought about the matter-of-fact way Harding dealt with the dead. Her training hadn't given her the same distance from the deaths of her patients. She'd known them as people, when they were alive. She'd met their families. Each death she'd encountered as a doctor was personal to her.

Alex took one more look at the John Doe, trying to get a sense of him as a person. Young, good-looking, and well-off—judging by the tailored slacks he'd been wearing in the Dumpster. A Mr. Right for some lucky guy, for sure. Alex wondered what had gone so wrong that he'd gotten himself killed.

CHAPTER THREE

ALEX HATED it when her gene sequencer let her down. The four colors of the chemical bases on the screen usually presented a pleasing, artistic vision, but this particular run seemed jagged and jarring. Red, for adenine. Blue, for cytosine. Green, for guanine. Orange, for thymine. Each of the squares symbolized a link in the chain of the spice's DNA. But they didn't match any common cooking or medicinal spices. She looked at the quilt of colors, trying to make some sense of it.

She entered the command that transformed the colored squares into their respective chemical letters—*ACGT*—as if, by that flick of the switch, she could magically will the evidence to give her more information. No such luck.

She fared better with the vaccine run. The John Doe was protected against malaria, hepatitis A and B, typhoid, and Japanese encephalitis. He'd even had the new inoculation against avian flu, H5N1. Probably had been out of the country for quite a while, so he wasn't your average tourist. He'd had a hit of the flu vaccine at least six months ago and then a booster in the past month, which was what had caused the small red bump that Harding had noticed.

But the spice was eluding her. It was plant material, yes, but it was not in any of her databases. Didn't match up with the known pleasure drugs—hashish, magic mushrooms, and so forth. Plus, he looked too polished to be a druggie, too much a member of the working well. Certainly not from the neighborhood where his body had been found.

She turned on her heels and walked past her three gene sequencers—over a million dollars' worth of hardware in twelve feet of lab space. She entered the glass-walled cubicle that housed her desk and computer. She'd had a hand in designing the space and had located her office in the inner recesses of her large rectangular laboratory, rather than down the hall, to be close to her scientific experiments. She chose two glass walls for the square in the far corner that was the inner office so she could glance over to see how far along her machines were in their sequencing efforts.

As she peered from a distance at the unfamiliar sequence of the spice, the fingers of her left hand tapped out a rhythm on the desk. She was like a concert pianist who could recall long strings of notes in his mind, but she was tapping out a different kind of tune. Pinkie, pointer, pointer, ring finger, middle finger. When she tapped, each of her fingers represented one of the four letters of the genetic alphabet. A few seconds later, she realized what she was tapping. *ATTCG.* It was the beginning of the sequence of the cystic fibrosis gene. Her unconscious was giving her an idea.

She signed on to a genetic Listserv and posted part of the spice sequence, putting out a query to see if anyone knew what it was. There was a remote possibility this would yield something. In 2004, Michael Caplan, a Yale professor who cooked with curry, started researching its beneficial effects with an eye toward treating cystic fibrosis. Soon other biologists began playing with all manner of spices in their quest for cures. Nothing new about that. Back in England in 1775, Dr. William Withering discovered that digitalis in the foxglove plant could treat heart disease, a treatment still used today.

As Alex logged off, she heard a knock on her laboratory door and saw Barbara enter.

She got up. "Don't trust me, huh?"

Barbara laughed. "You've missed more than one meeting with the colonel. I wanted to make sure you didn't forget this one."

As they walked down the hallway, Alex said, "There are some perks to being a civilian around here. Wiatt might fire me, but at least he can't court-martial me."

"Don't tempt him. You know he always finds a way to get what he wants."

Barbara started opening the door to Wiatt's office. Alex's first glimpse of the man was disconcerting. The colonel was sitting on a desk chair in the middle of the room staring at something or someone. As the door swung open, Alex's eyes focused on what held Wiatt's gaze. The skulls.

Alex's eyes were drawn to them as well. They were out of their ignoble drawers—transferred instead to two rows of a library reshelving cart, ten per row, each carefully held in place now on a foam base. The one on the far left looked particularly menacing. The face painted on it was a howling banshee, like the Edvard Munch painting *The Scream*.

"Colonel?" Barbara said as they entered.

Wiatt looked at the two women. "I can't let them go back like this," he said to Alex. "Can you clean them up?"

Alex walked to the library cart. She pulled on a pair of latex gloves from her fanny pack, picked up the Screamer, and brought him up to eye level. When she was in medical school at Columbia, a guy had run a store, Maxilla & Mandible, on the Upper West Side. The thriving boutique sold skulls and bones to people who wanted to decorate their apartments in a style known as "Dead Tech." The owner prepared the specimens, describing his work as "Boil, boil, boil, scrape, scrape, scrape." But Alex could see that no amount of boiling or scraping would remove the color here.

"I'm afraid I can't help you here. Bone is porous. The color's been absorbed."

"Besides, sir," Barbara said, pulling up a chair next to the colonel, "the Vietnamese Ambassador to the U.S. has photos of three of the skulls. He'd know they'd been tampered with."

"For Chrissakes, how did he get ahold of pictures?" Wiatt asked.

Barbara looked sheepish. "Actually, one of our own scientists published an article about them in the early 1980s. I'm afraid he came up with the title, too. 'The Vietnamese Trophy Skulls.' "

Wiatt's eyes flared angrily and his voice turned thunderous. "Nothing like this happened on my watch in Nam." Then he quieted. "But I can imagine our men doing this. They were just boys there. No, *we* were just boys. Angry, desperate boys."

The way he spit out those last three words pierced Alex. Her father had been one of those boys, an Air Force sergeant in his twenties when he'd served in Vietnam. Not just served, given his life there, killed by a Viet Cong bomb when Alex was five. He was a fog now, a mist that she tried to capture in her memories, but she didn't know which images of him were real and which she'd made up to give herself comfort. She couldn't picture his face anymore, the face that was from memory rather than photos. But she could recall the smell of his Irish Spring soap and the feel of his rough cheek when he scooped her up in a hug. She could relate to people with Alzheimer's disease, as she cursed her own failure to hang on to her memories.

Wiatt got up, walked over to his desk, and held up a book. David Lamb's *Vietnam, Now: A Reporter Returns.* "I just started reading this and I realized how little we knew back then. We knew nothing about the culture, about how they had a university, Quoc Tu Giam, in 1076, a hundred years before Oxford, six hundred years before Yale. We thought they were savages, vermin. But this . . ." He glanced at the skulls. "Who were the real savages?"

He sat back down at his desk and transformed himself back into the penetratingly competent commanding officer they were used to. "Okay, Blake. The color stays, but scrape away the wax. We don't need to advertise that our boys were using some of them as candleholders."

"And, Lieutenant Findlay," he said to Barbara, "arrange for us to give them back to the Vietnamese Ambassador in the quietest ceremony possible. No press, no fanfare. Tell everyone we are trying to respect the spirits of the dead."

CHAPTER FOUR

ALEX WHEELED the skull-laden library cart down several long hallways, back to her lab. She ran into a half-dozen people on the journey, most nodding politely or saying hello without even looking down at the contents of the cart. One good thing about working at a place with *Pathology* in the name, Alex thought, nobody gets too upset no matter what goes wheeling by. Only a cafeteria worker screwed up her face as Alex rolled on.

She pulled a table into the middle of her lab so she could work on the skulls with the candle wax, thinking she could steam them to loosen the wax, then peel it off. She picked the most difficult one to start—one with an intricate pattern of psychedelic flowers on it and two taper candles, only half burned down, extending through holes in the skull. That was her usual mode, plunge in where the water was the deepest. She positioned it in the center of the table, and then gingerly dragged the library cart with the remaining skulls to the back of her glass office at the rear of the lab. Not many folks ventured into the lab and, because of most mortals' fear of the bioterrorism bacterium she studied, far fewer stayed more than the few seconds necessary to conduct their business. But she still wanted to give the rest of the skulls their privacy and keep them out of sight of any visitors.

Alex quietly approached the first skull, bowing her head

slightly, a gesture of respect. Looking for a way to remove the grit, she took the compressed air can she used to clean her keyboard and aimed it inside the skull. The air pressure dislodged dust from eye sockets and tooth rims. But it also released some of the smells of war that the skull had been hiding. A light scent of gunpowder surrounded it like a halo.

Using the Bunsen burner, she heated a beaker of water and then aimed steam from a flexible tube at the skull. The dripping wax candles dislodged and she was able to pull them out. She stared, half-admiringly, at the eye sockets, which were the centers of sketched neon pink and green daisies. She took a step back and tried to imagine what he had looked like in life. He was tall for an Asian man, but had the distinctive low nasal bridge and short, broad dental arcade. She was viewing him so intently that she hardly heard the door open. When she looked up, she let out a yelp. It was as if the skull had come to life. A full blown Vietnamese man was standing right in front of her.

He stuck out his hand, and she held up her gloved palm to show him why she wasn't shaking back. "I'm Dr. Troy Nguyen," he said.

"And this is a classified project," she replied, walking around the table to shield the skull. "I'm afraid you'll have to leave."

"I certainly will not. Didn't you read the memo from the director of the National Institutes of Health?"

Alex looked over at her garbage can, where she routinely dumped, unread, all the paper she received in intraoffice mail. Working for the government was a junk mail nightmare. Every day she got inches of paper. A copy of each new drug approval from the Food and Drug Administration, new wage and hour laws from the Equal Employment Opportunity Commission, the lists of updated mail drops for each Armed Forces unit stationed around the world.

The Vietnamese visitor followed her gaze and angrily began rooting around in her trash until he found what he was looking for. He pulled out a piece of paper and handed it to her. A Starbucks stain ran through it like the Mississippi, but she got the gist of it. This jerk was some kind of "grief counselor" who would accompany the skulls on their return to the Vietnamese consulate.

He shook his head. "Didn't you read it? I've been detailed to AFIP."

Alex had no idea what that meant. She'd worked for the government for nearly two years and hadn't mastered—no, hadn't cared to master—the endless jargon.

He looked annoyed and started talking to her slowly, as if she were a child. "That means my big boss, the Secretary of Health and Human Services, loaned me to your big boss, the director of the AFIP. Until the skulls are returned, I am part of the AFIP team."

Alex fluttered her eyelashes like she imagined a bimbo would. "I never take gifts from strangers. I'll write a nice little thanks but no thanks to the Secretary of HHS. Please leave my lab so I can get back to work."

Troy Nguyen gave an exasperated look, and turned sharply on his heels. He took two steps toward the door, and then pivoted and walked back toward her. "Let's try this again," he said. "I don't like it any better than you do. I'm not even trained in grief. I'm just the highest-ranking Vietnamese-born guy at the National Institutes of Health. Can we just get a cup of coffee somewhere to talk about how we are going to get through the ceremony?"

She looked at her watch. It was now 4:00 P.M. and she had a briefing in the John Doe case at 5:00 P.M. "I'm tied up until six at least."

He shook his head. "I've got a Little League game to go to. How about tomorrow morning? The Starbucks across the street at eight A.M.?"

She nodded and he thanked her. He left and she realized she was a little disappointed about the Little League game. She wasn't quite ready to head home to her Lukeless apartment.

CHAPTER FIVE

MAJOR DAN Wilson smiled when Alex entered the L-shaped conference room that served as the Task Force center for whatever high-profile case they were investigating. He stood from behind his desk, with its chaotic mounds of case folders and evidence, and joined Alex and the already-seated Grant at the conference table. When they'd been working round the clock on the Tattoo Killer case, Dan had moved his desk in there to be closer to his team—including computer tech Corporal Chuck Lawndale, whose desk occupied the small arm of the L, along with a couch and espresso machine. Dan liked being in the center of the action, and had never bothered to move back to his office. Alex noticed that the corkboard walls were only lightly covered now—she counted just three investigations ongoing, none with the heat of the previous serial killers or political crimes that kept Dan's adrenaline high.

"Let's go," Dan barked in his Brooklyn accent. In his early forties, his bushy salt-and-pepper hair dipped down over one eye. He motioned Chuck over to the conference table and the young corporal from South Carolina took center stage, standing next to a laptop at the table's end, projecting data to the Plasmavision screen on the wall.

"We fed in the vaccine information from Dr. Blake's lab—"

"Please, just call me Alex," she interrupted.

"—and we found that the vaccine pattern matched those the Centers for Disease Control recommended for a trip to Vietnam."

"Vietnam?" she said quietly. The country that haunted her as a child now seemed to be haunting the AFIP. Protestors, skulls, a corpse. Like Wiatt, she was learning how much she didn't know about that small, distant country. "I couldn't identify the spice, but Vietnam certainly has a lot of plants and animals that are unique and not yet catalogued."

"Did you run his photo against customs photos?" Dan asked the young corporal.

The military men Alex worked with at the AFIP were notoriously good at stone faces that hid all emotion, but she could see a flash in the young man's eyes signaling that he was hurt that his boss had insinuated that he wasn't doing his job.

Chuck clicked onto another screen. "These are all the U.S. citizens who returned from Vietnam in the past month." Names ran by in a hallucinogenic torrent. "More than ten thousand."

Alex was astonished. "When did Vietnam become so popular?"

"Surprised me, too," Chuck said. "Turns out it attracts ecotourists."

"What the hell does that mean?" asked Grant.

"Environmentalists," Alex said.

"Tree huggers," Grant said. Grant was wearing a rubber glove on one hand with strange electrodes on each finger. Probably related to some virtual reality project he was working on, Alex thought. He often brought gadgets to meetings and dangled them tantalizingly in front of people, waiting until their curiosity overcame them and they asked their purpose. Alex decided not to stoke his ego. She ignored the flashing glove, even when Grant starting aiming the rays in little annoying circles across her breasts. What a putz, Alex thought, but she wouldn't give him the satisfaction of starting a fight. Without interest or anger from her, Grant let his gloved hand fall to his side.

Chuck continued, ignoring Grant's comments and gestures. "Since 1990, Vietnam has created seven national parks. In the past few years, three new species of large mammals were discovered there—more than anywhere else in the world. They've got a thousand islands off their 3,200-mile coastline. More than half the people coming through customs had been on an ecotour, but none of them had stayed long enough to meet the profile of Dr. Blake's vaccines. So we focused on the fifteen hundred Americans who had gone to Vietnam on business."

Grant pulled off his magic glove and used his hands to repeatedly stretch it, then snap it back. His arm muscles moved in waves as he stretched. Grant got nervous if he wasn't showing off his body in some way.

Chuck clicked again and brought up the Web site of the U.S. Chamber of Commerce. Alex was astonished by the number of companies doing business in Vietnam—mostly big names like General Electric, Target, Best Buy, Bristol-Myers, Eastman Kodak, and dozens more.

Of the businessmen entering any U.S. airport on itineraries originating in Vietnam, the recognition software pulled up three passports. The three photos appeared on-screen. They were slightly younger than the man they'd autopsied, but passports were good for ten years and at least two of the photos were taken six years earlier. "They looked like possibles, and we followed up. All three men are alive and accounted for," Chuck said. "I'm wondering what you want us to check next, sir."

Dan didn't hesitate. "Check all the arrivals from Paris, London, and Amsterdam in the past month. Maybe he was the type of guy who might want to chill for a while if he's spent the past few months in Southeast Asia."

Alex admired the way Dan gave directions, the intuitive way that he created leads to follow. She was tied to concrete data, like the forensic DNA matches that spit out of her computer. Her work was logical, mathematical, rational. Maybe that's why, in her personal life, she was often drawn to dreamers.

Dan turned to Grant. "Drop the glove and tell me what you've got on the MO."

Grant set the glove down on the table in front of him. A menace to women, Grant fell in line to male commands. Alex wondered if she should practice talking with her voice an octave lower.

"Gay or straight," Grant said, "no similar MOs, with a missing heart. If you count other missing body parts from gay stiffs, Williard Pergamore had his tongue cut out last week in a murder near Capitol Hill."

"They get the guy?" Dan asked.

"Nope."

"Follow it up for other similarities. And show the John Doe's photo to anyone who knew Pergamore."

Dan turned to Alex. "Any luck on the semen?"

"No match to anyone in CODIS. What about missing persons?"

"We tried that," Dan said, "but he's only been dead for a day. If he travels a lot, his neighbors wouldn't think anything of his absence."

Alex knew that finding his identity as soon as possible was crucial. Most murders were solved in the first few days, if at all. Longer than that, people skipped town; witnesses' memories faded. "The Dumpster where he was found. Any trace of DNA from the assailant?"

Dan shook his head. "As soon as we find the primary crime scene, I'll page you for DNA collection."

Alex ran the odds in her head. In a city with hundreds of thousands of apartments, storefronts, parks, and Lord-knows-what other places where a murder could take place, it was like searching for the one stutter in the thousands of base pairs of a cancer gene that caused the illness. Scientists were cowed by such odds, but Dan didn't pay attention to probabilities.

She considered the man for a moment as he thought about what they should do next. Barbara had told her that in his first forensic case Dan investigated the death of a sergeant major when his Jeep exploded. Dan initially suspected murder, but when a second Jeep exploded, killing an Army wife and her three-year-old son on a different base, he unraveled a defense contractor scandal, with faulty parts and kickbacks. That led to the much-publicized court-martial of a Pentagon-based general. After spending so much time with the military acquisitions staff in that case, Dan tried to use as few military gadgets as possible. Close enough for government work was not good enough for him, particularly since he liked to maintain more than a passing relationship with danger. He carried a weapon he bought himself—a Beretta .45 model 1911—and had started to drive his own gray Chevy Malibu rather than the Jeeps, Hummers, and Ford Tauruses that the Army offered up. Gray because his spook friends told him that was the most difficult car to trail.

"Let's try to find out where he picked up his honey last Monday night," Dan said. "Grant, I want you and a date to check out the Flying Dutchman."

"Well, Alex," Grant said, snapping the glove in her direction, "put on your dancing shoes."

Dan smiled. "It's not that kind of club. Chuck here will act as your date. And leather is more the ticket."

A cloud came over Grant's face. He took a deep breath. "Okay," he said, turning to Chuck, "but no hand-holding."

"What's to say he went out at all that night?" Alex asked.

"Odds are it was a pickup," Dan said. "Nobody has that much sex with someone they see all the time."

Obviously, he didn't know about partners like Luke, the Energizer bunny of the bedroom. But Alex could see his point; part of what fueled the lust between Dan and his Israeli photojournalist wife was that she was always on her way to—or back from—some exotic locale. No getting bored when you and your partner rendezvous on erratically timed furloughs.

Alex looked at Grant and Chuck, both in uniform. She'd thrown herself into the D.C. club scene with Luke and knew how much they'd stick out. "You're not sending them like that?"

Dan shook his head. "I'll requisition some black jeans and black T-shirts from the Gap."

"You've got a line item for club clothes?" Alex asked.

Dan smiled. "You'd be surprised what I can conjure up when a killer's at large."

CHAPTER SIX

ON THE drive home, Alex thought about the John Doe. The killing was obviously not about money. He was found wearing a Cartier Roadster watch, worth at least five grand. Nor did drugs seem to be the motive. Tox screens showed he wasn't a user and he didn't seem the type to sell. And there was that other gay murder. Could a serial killer be targeting gays? Maybe Dan's club hunch would pay off.

She expertly jammed her T-Bird into a microscopic parking space a mere block from her apartment. The parking gods were smiling down on her tonight. She grabbed her briefcase—an old saddlebag, actually—from behind the seat and locked the car. Before she'd left the office, she'd printed a few things that she wanted to read. Top among them was the scientific article on the Trophy Skulls.

Ahead she saw the familiar neon sign, CURL UP AND DYE. When Alex moved into this former beauty parlor, she left almost everything as it was. Dryer chairs and three walls of mirrors in the large linoleum-floored room that served as her living room. Posters of hairstyles, circa 1960, covered the fourth wall.

Only the bedroom—the former beauty parlor's room for bikini waxes—was entirely redone. A worn hand-loomed rug in gold and turquoise that her mother, a cultural anthropologist, brought back from Burma. A photo of the delicately curved back of a twenty-two-year-old Asian woman over the bed—snapped by a former boyfriend, a professional photographer who'd run off with the model. And tonight, she thought as she entered the bedroom, the evocative scent and carelessly wrinkled sheets of an afternoon, night, and morning of sex with Luke. That man sure knew how to say good-bye.

He could also cook, which made him even more appealing than the usual stream of artists, musicians, and poets who made pit stops in Alex's love life. Alex opened the fridge, put the remains of Luke's white bean chicken chili into the microwave, poured wine in a water glass (neither she nor Luke was that great at doing dishes and the wineglass supply had bottomed out), and opened her laptop to check her e-mail while she ate.

She hated herself for already checking to see if Luke had e-mailed an explanation about Vanessa. Her heart sank when she realized that his return address was nowhere in sight. Then she remembered that he wouldn't even have hit London yet. A poor musician couldn't afford to fly direct. He'd been catching a flight to Boston, then on to Reykjavik, enduring a four-hour layover, and continuing on to London. He wouldn't make it there until at least 4:00 A.M. her time.

Between savory bites (at times like these, Alex loved the idea of having a househusband), Alex checked her other e-mails. Nobody from the genetics group had a clue about the spice, but a few men she'd met at American Society of Human Genetics meetings had penned greetings to her. One told her how attractive she looked in the newspaper photos after the capture of the Tattoo Killer. Annoyed at Luke, she almost e-mailed a flirtatious response, but she knew her dating limits. No scientists, no doctors. No matter how hip they seemed initially, they eventually wanted her to settle down with them. She couldn't imagine it. *Settle down.* Even the term was hideous. It made her think of *settling,* making do with less than you deserve.

After dinner, Alex tackled the Trophy Skulls article. The author traced the history of spoils of war, noting how white men's scalps were traded by natives in North America and shrunken heads were bartered in Africa. He speculated that the Vietnamese skulls had a similar role. He'd interviewed the men who'd been caught bringing them into the country. One boasted that he'd killed the man whose skull he decorated, but the others insisted they'd acquired them in other ways, such as by winning one in a poker game, taking one from the possessions of a dead buddy as a way to honor him, or just plucking one from the piles of skeletons that littered the many battlefields. The connection between a particular skull and a particular GI was as foggy as mist over a rice paddy.

Alex walked into her bedroom and flicked on the television at the foot of her bed. She caught the end of a Barbara Walters interview with the Vice President's wife, Abby Shane. Abby had been a blond-haired West Virginia television weather girl when then–trial lawyer Tommy Shane dumped his first wife for her. But she was shrewd and had crisscrossed the state in a miniskirt, with a Charlie's Angels–like group of her friends, showing up at car washes and bowling alleys to get her new hubby elected governor. When Bradley Cotter, the blue-blooded Senator from Connecticut, sought a running mate to capture what the *New York Times* called the Southern vote and the *New York Post* called the White Trash vote, Cotter reached out to this almost unknown governor who, from his days as a trial lawyer, brought along a gaggle of unions and a closetful of god-awful brown suits. "West Virginia?" the pundits snorted. "Isn't that the state that was invented to make Alabama feel good about itself?" But the blue blood and brown suit had eked past the other guys and been sworn in the previous year. Abby, who at thirty-two was half her husband's age, had traded her long Dolly Parton blond curls for a short brown Jackie Kennedy hairdo. And now that she was a heartbeat away from the First Ladyship, she'd even begun wearing pillbox hats.

Barbara Walters quizzed Abby about the diplomatic trip

she and the Vice President had recently taken to China. Alex had to give Abby credit. She correctly pronounced the names of the Chinese president and his advisors and launched into a discussion of an upcoming economic summit.

Walters probed more personal ground. "Isn't the age difference between you and the Vice President a problem sometimes?"

Abby's features rearranged themselves, donning the girlish mask that Walters seemed to desire. "My husband's awfully romantic," she said.

They cut to some footage of Shane doing a not half-bad job of playing "The Shadow of Her Smile" and Abby looking like some femme fatale leaning on an antique piano in his White House office. Alex hoped Shane's ex-wife wasn't watching. All that syrupy romance would probably make her puke.

Abby's image dissolved to the nightly news, and Alex saw they were leading with a photo of the John Doe, asking for information. The photo revealed only the corpse's head, which had not been marred in the attack. That struck Alex as odd, now that she thought about it. The MO pointed to a crime of passion—the rose, the missing heart. But people who killed in a jealous rage usually mutilated the face.

Alex mulled that over as she removed the traces of Luke from her bedroom sanctuary. He'd been staying with her for the past two weeks, ever since he'd put his stuff in storage and sublet his Arlington, Virginia, apartment so that he could take off on tour. She pulled off the sheets, mentally humming "I'm going to wash that man right out of my hair." Where did that come from? Probably some old musical that she watched with her grandmother. She yanked off the bottom fitted sheet and a multicolor fabric snake seemed to fly across the room.

She bent down to pick it up and realized it was Luke's lucky guitar strap, the one they'd bought at a flea market near the Capitol one Sunday. She opened the nightstand next to the bed. She didn't want to see any reminders of Luke, but it might be nice to have a little luck in her bedroom now that he was gone.

CHAPTER SEVEN

ALEX MET Troy Nguyen at Starbucks the next morning. She sprung for his chai tea and ordered her indispensable dark roast. They hadn't even made it to a table when he began to quiz her. "What can you tell me about the Trophy Skulls?"

Alex winced. "We don't call them that anymore. Aren't you supposed to be comforting the recipients?"

"What term do you like: *Spoils of war? Candleholders? Ashtrays?*"

Troy had raised his voice and people were staring.

"Shh," Alex said, as they sat down. "And what are you bugging me for, if you know all that already?"

"I'd like to know if you could get enough DNA from them to make identifications. I've got to figure out whether we will just be giving them back to the government, or if we should start trying to trace families."

Alex considered his question as she sipped her coffee. "DNA testing would be a dead end," she said finally. "How would we figure out whose DNA to compare the skulls to? Do you know how many people were killed over there?" She immediately regretted the question. This was his country she was talking about, his relatives who had died.

"Two million Vietnamese were killed," he said in a clipped tone. "More than thirty times the American body count."

Neither of them spoke. Each was lost in his or her own tie to those deaths.

"It is a challenge," he said. "But you didn't run from identifying the ashes at the World Trade Center."

Alex sighed. "In that case, we began with the names of the missing people who worked in the Twin Towers. We knew whose DNA we were looking for. Relatives brought hairbrushes and other items for us to test and compare. Besides, how'd you know I was at the WTC?"

"I Googled you. I like to know about the people I'm dealing with."

"Stalker," she said.

"Five minutes with a person reveals more than any Web site could," he said. He tipped his chair back and began reciting, "You have a gratingly independent streak that I would take to indicate an absent father, yet you have occasional touches of seeming compassion, probably from taking care of a withdrawn mother as a child."

"Thank you, Dr. Freud. Let me guess, you put yourself through med school as Nancy Reagan's psychic?"

"And you probably slept through your psychiatric rotation," he said. "Otherwise you would know that your childhood preordains your behavior as an adult."

"Don't you believe in free will? Like, I *chose* to meet with you this morning?"

Troy laughed. "It wasn't a free choice at all. You feel compelled to dress and act like you are spitting in the face of convention, but you nonetheless are one of the most responsible people you know. Your mother was probably some sort of counterculture type, the kind that's hard to rebel against, because they're much further out there than you are."

Troy had nailed enough truth about Alex's life to make her uncomfortable. "Enough getting your jollies as the Peeping Tom of my psyche," she said. "I've got to get to work. I'll see you at the Vietnamese Embassy when the handoff takes place."

"Didn't you get that memo, either?"

"Which?"

"The one that says the ceremony is now going to be full tilt, at the White House, on New Year's Day."

So much for Wiatt's idea of a quiet handoff.

"Say it ain't so, Joe," Alex said to Barbara. Today, the candies in Barbara's office were Butterfingers, a definite step up from yesterday's Smarties.

"Wiatt is about to jump out of his skin," Barbara said, nodding.

"Whose idea was it?"

"Believe it or not, it came from the Vice President. He had the brilliant idea that we should use this as an opportunity to ask the Vietnamese government to turn over any POW/MIAs they still have."

"Does he actually believe there are Americans still alive over there?"

"Vice President Shane is a shrewd politician. For someone who pulled a George W. Bush with his National Guard service, he's milked that war for all it's worth. He was one of the first state governors to travel to Vietnam once the borders opened up again. Made two trips with MIA groups, which got him a lot of support from the NRA types who don't usually back Democrats."

"Can't Wiatt do something about this?" President Cotter had been his Yale college roommate.

"Not likely. After the Vice President made his suggestion yesterday to the *Washington Post,* both Shane's and Cotter's popularity rose fifteen percentage points."

"Great."

"There's a silver lining to the Vice President's maneuver. Both sides—the Vietnamese government and the White House—want to make political hay with this. Since we've got a couple weeks, we can think creatively about damage control. Wiatt's already decided you should preside over the return of the skulls."

"Why me?"

"Seems more humane to have a doctor than a soldier.

He's scheduled a meeting for you with the White House protocol chief late this afternoon."

"You coming with?"

"Can't. I'm picking up Lana at school this afternoon and driving up to the Bronx for my mom's birthday."

"What about the actual ceremony?"

"Sure, I'll be there. Not to mention a member of Vietnam's equivalent of Congress—the National Assembly—their current Ambassador, and so forth. So will a psychiatrist from the NIH, Dr. Troy Nguyen. Have you met him?"

Alex rolled her eyes. "He hasn't got much of a bedside manner."

"Yeah, he was pretty curt with me, too. Waiving some stupid memo around and ordering me to find him an office."

Alex slammed her hand down on the desk. "We're going to be stuck with him here? Didn't Wiatt raise hell about that?"

"Nope, Wiatt actually asked Sergeant Major Lander to help him move into room one-sixty. Wiatt's anxious to stay out of the limelight and this Nguyen character will deflect some of the heat."

"One-sixty? Did you have to put him right down the hall from me? Why not at that AFIP outpost in Maryland?"

"I know how you feel. He acts like the general counsel's office is some glorified secretarial service for him. This morning he stormed into my office demanding I get him his own secure fax line. What the hell kind of grief counselor needs something like that?"

"So why don't you try to get him 'detailed'—or whatever it's called—back to NIH?"

"Just think of him as a kind of insurance. . . ."

"Insurance?"

"His language skills will make a big difference. When Robert McNamara visited the National Cathedral in Saigon during the war, he tried to say, 'Long live South Vietnam,' in Vietnamese. But he screwed up the intonation. Instead, he informed them, 'The Southern duck wants to lie down.'"

Alex laughed, then reached for another candy bar. "Dr. Nguyen strikes me as stubborn, opinionated—"

Barbara smiled. "That sounds a little like a certain geneticist I know."

Alex shook her head in exasperation.

"Alex, the Vietnamese government is hammering us in the world press over these Trophy Skulls. If Dr. Nguyen is the price we have to pay to save a little face, we'll just have to ride it out."

Alex considered it. "Three whole weeks?" she asked.

Barbara nodded. "But as soon as the skulls go back, he goes back to NIH."

As she left Barbara's office, Alex's mind wandered to her first trip to the White House two years earlier. On a Saturday morning tour, Alex had made love with Luke in the cloakroom. Somehow, a visit to swap skulls just didn't have the same appeal.

CHAPTER EIGHT

BACK AT her lab, Alex found a package outside her door. It held a book from Troy: *Customs and Legends of the Vietnamese*. His note said, "Less than a month to prepare."

Alex took the book into her inner office, sat down, and flipped through it. Lucky numbers. Lucky colors. And a series of pages with Post-its that indicated what treatment was owed the dead. She looked up from her reading at the remaining skulls.

The smallest one was blackened from smoke, with a chubby candle jammed into a hole on the top and four hand-rolled cigarette butts sticking out of its toothy grin. Alex moved the skull to the table in her laboratory. With her gloved hand, she removed the cigarettes. They had traveled with this person thousands of miles from Vietnam more than thirty years ago and it seemed wrong to just ditch them in the trash. She didn't have a plan yet for what to do with them, so she stuck each one in its own evidence bag and put them on a shelf in the cabinet that housed the chemical reagents essential for running the DNA sequences.

She used her proven technique, directing steam at the skull. The wax readily disassociated itself from the bone. It was like removing a wig from a head, except for a large cylindrical plug of wax—the bottom part of the fat candle that had been stuck in the center of the skull. She set it aside on the table, and stepped back to look at the skull. The face area was dark, but the part of the skull formerly under the wax glowed an eerie white, evoking a 1920s flapper, a platinum blonde with close-cropped wavy hair. That's when Alex realized something was terribly wrong. These were supposed to be skulls of enemy soldiers. But looking at the rounded chin and the slight supraorbital ridges above the eye sockets, Alex realized this skull was from a woman.

She walked around the table and tried to tell herself it was okay. Hadn't women and even young children wielded guns in Vietnam? This one probably had dressed like any other soldier and someone just shot her, at a distance. Yeah, that must have been it.

Alex came full circle and stood in front of the skull once again. She reached her gloved hand inside and felt a set of pebbles. She peered in and saw that they weren't stones, but instead were tiny neck bones. So much for the killed by mistake theory. This woman had been strangled, up close and personal.

Alex pulled a wheeled stool out from under her lab bench. She sat down for a moment in front of the skull to catch her breath. She dealt with the remains of the dead all the time in her lab, but they were almost all killed by infections or toxins. There was something random, providential, and, of course, natural about death from a disease. Murder, during war or during peace, seemed like a slap in the face of the world.

She tried unsuccessfully to rub off the rest of the soot. Below the white caplike area where the wax had been removed, a dark layer covered the eyes, nose, and chin. The skull looked like a Middle Eastern woman wearing a veil, a shrouded lady who'd met a horrible death.

Alex bent down to bring herself eye level with the skull and tried to visualize the woman in life—smiling, talking. But instead she could only imagine the shrouded lady's grim last moments.

She replaced the skull on the library cart in her inner office, then cleaned off the table in her lab. She was about to toss the wax and candles that she'd removed when she noticed something embedded in the wax cylinder from the woman's skull. It looked like a piece of paper.

She opened a cabinet drawer and took out a small pick, the one she'd used to excise tiny pieces of lung tissue from a century-old corpse when she sequenced the Spanish flu genome. She started to pick away at the wax surrounding the paper. It freed easily. A letter had been stuffed in the skull after one candle had burned, before the other was added, as if someone were trying to hide it.

The handwriting was uneven and there were holes in the paper. Alex looked at it and guessed that whoever wrote it was balancing the paper on a surface that was relatively soft and not at all flat. Maybe his own lap or leg. The words, messy letters in a thick red pencil, were like wounds on the page, and it took her a while to decipher them. "I'm bit up bad and got the breakbone fever, the Lord's revenge for what we did. Nick throwing gas on the four hootches. Us shooting the six burning gooks who ran, sitting ducks. Lord, have mercy, lord. S.F."

The letter ended abruptly.

A cascade of questions flooded over her. Who was the writer? Who was Nick? What had they done?

She reread the letter, hoping it would take on a different meaning. Then she looked directly in the eye sockets of the female skull, made a silent promise to the woman, and walked down the hall to Wiatt's office. She laid the letter in front of Wiatt on the desk and sat in the chair across from him. "I found this in one of the skulls."

She helped him decipher the messy text, and watched his reaction carefully. A flare of anger, then sadness. He shook his head. "There's no way to tell what this means."

"Sounds like another My Lai," Alex said.

Wiatt thought a moment. "Blake, why is it that whenever I give you a simple task, you manage to turn it into something that requires major damage control?"

She knew he was alluding to her actions in the Tattoo Killer case, where a DNA test gone wrong led to a high-speed chase and the arrest of a prominent federal official who happened to be innocent.

"I guess now is not the best time to ask you to get Dr. Troy Nguyen off my back."

"At this point, we need all the Vietnamese allies we can get." He nodded toward the door, then returned to his work. "Just turn over the letter to Lieutenant Findlay. She knows the drill for possible court-martial. And let's hope it doesn't come to that."

Alex left his office and turned a corner toward the office of the general counsel. It was locked. Of course. Barbara had left for her visit to the Bronx.

She wasn't about to shove a thirty-year-old letter under her door. Instead, Alex wandered back to her own office, e-mailed her friend about the letter, and put the wrinkled paper back on the shelf.

At 4:00 P.M., Wiatt stopped by her laboratory. "I'm riding with you when you meet the protocol chief. I need to talk to her boss."

Alex marveled at the casual way he could propose to drop in on the President. Those bright college years must have created quite a bond. Maybe they were in Skull and Bones together, or Fish and Chips, or whatever those secret societies were called at Yale.

A soldier from the transportation detail met them in front of the AFIP in an armored town car. Wiatt opened the door for her and she scooted across the backseat. A wall of glass separated the driver from the backseat. Soundproof, Alex guessed. On the way to the White House, Wiatt said, "Who have you told about the letter in the skull?"

"Just you."

He rubbed his chin. "I'll handle it with Lieutenant Findlay from here on without your participation. Consider the whole matter confidential."

"Is that *confidential* with a *c* like in *cover-up*?"

Wiatt looked at her coldly. "No, we'll do the right thing. Just not in the public eye. The American soldiers in Vietnam were the most honorable men I've commanded. In the entire war, only two hundred and fifty of our men surrendered—and none of them fought for the other side. In World War II, whole platoons surrendered, and took up arms with the Germans. Yet Vietnam veterans get blamed for everything." He knew what he was talking about. The previous year, the President had planned to make him the director of the FBI, but his Chief of Staff advised against it, telling the President that too many medals from that war blew up in people's faces.

"My father fought in Vietnam," Alex said quietly.

"I bet he didn't come back as some out-of-control killing machine."

"No," she said, "he didn't come back at all."

Wiatt bowed his head. "Sorry, Blake. I didn't know."

COLONEL JACK Wiatt had no problem getting in to see the President, taking the flabbergasted Alex along with him. Alex had never expected to be in a two-on-one meeting with the attractive former Senator from Connecticut, President Bradley Cotter. Barbara would be so jealous. Ever since she was a young girl, Barbara had followed the activities of politicians like other women followed movie stars or British royalty. She might not know who took home the latest Oscar or Grammy, but she knew the birth dates, voting records, and extramarital affairs of the entire Executive Branch. To Barbara, D.C. was one riveting soap opera.

The President held up the French newspaper *Le Monde*. The Screamer skull stared out from the front page. "This isn't exactly helping my international reputation," he said.

"Why return them here at the White House, then?" Wiatt asked. "Doesn't that put you in the middle of it?"

"That was my initial reaction, but Shane talked me out of it. And he's got a point. We need to take the high ground. When the communists in Laos began to return the remains of American GIs, they shipped them back like dirty laundry, in old suitcases. I want to show that we're better than that."

As the President and the colonel talked, Alex looked over at the fourth person in the room, a Marine major standing ten feet from the Commander in Chief, with a briefcase handcuffed to his wrist. Alex thought he looked like one of those currency couriers in the drug lord movies.

President Cotter noticed Alex staring at the Marine. "The codes change every day," he told her. "Every morning I get a card with a list of numbers—not just for the nuclear weapons, but for things like rerouting Air Force One. I keep them in my wallet. I used to just keep them in my suit pocket until Jimmy Carter told me he once sent them to the cleaners.

"Do you want to say hello to Sheila?" the President asked Wiatt. Cotter looked at a screen on the wall, with multicolor dots. The Executive Resident Usher's Office had a digital locator box that showed the location of each member of the First Family—as well as the Vice President and his family—wherever they were in the White House.

"Secret Service makes each one of us wear a tracking device," he said to Alex, pointing to a tiny flat-tipped pin stuck in his lapel. "With one hundred and thirty-two rooms, they can track my family or the Shanes if there's any emergency."

Alex stared at an architect's schema of the White House with hundreds of numbered dots. The gold dots apparently belonged to the President's family. Number "one" was the President, in the room she was in. Two must be the First Lady, Sheila Cotter, and three, their son. The red ones must be the Vice President and his wife. They were both in an office in the West Wing—awfully close together, Alex noticed.

"Matthew's fighting it," said Cotter, referring to his sixteen-year-old son. "Pinned his to the pillow one night so it looked like he was sleeping, then snuck out to see a movie with his friends."

"Don't get too mad at the boy," Wiatt said. "Think what we were up to at his age."

Cotter laughed. "I don't even want to go there. Plus Sheila tells me my ratings would be in the toilet except for Matthew." The President's sixteen-year-old son was a heart-throb for the *Seventeen* magazine set. He had dark curly hair, a tanned athletic body (baseball, soccer, skiing, hiking—he'd find his way outside in any season), and an easy manner in public. The previous summer, he'd convinced some philandering European royals to work with him on four continents building houses for Habitat for Humanity. The princes and princesses treated it as a publicity stunt—but he'd hammered and sawed his way through the entire summer. Everything Alex had read in the press about Matthew was favorable. Either the Cotters had the greatest publicist in the world or Matthew was a genuinely nice kid.

A thin woman with a stiff cotton candy arrangement of gray hair entered the room. Beatrix Graham, the protocol chief. She glared at Alex's jeans and sighed. Shaking her head, she said quietly, "There's only so much I can do."

Wiatt and Cotter went off to say hello to the First Lady, who would miss the return of the skulls because she was taking her son to visit colleges that week. As they left the room, Alex heard Wiatt say to the Commander in Chief, "There's been a development I'd like to talk to you about."

Beatrix shut the door behind the two men. She motioned Alex to a chair, and Alex sat down.

Beatrix explained that the ceremony would take place in the East Room. "It has the right gravitas," she said. "Seven presidents have lain in state there, including Abraham Lincoln and John F. Kennedy."

She gave Alex pen and paper and told her to write down everything she said. An hour of instructions followed. Alex's hands were cramped from taking down the dos and don'ts. She couldn't wear pantsuits, flip-flops, Hawaiian shirts, or any item of clothing that could be construed as supporting an enemy's military. She could not bring a camera or recording device. She would be bound by Letitia Baldrige's etiquette manual. She could not take out any item of makeup in public, nor wear a skirt shorter than one inch above the knee.

As Beatrix droned on, Alex felt trapped. Clearly, the protocol queen couldn't use this spiel on the foreign dignitaries, movie stars, or sport stars who alighted at the White House. They dressed however they damn pleased. But as a government employee, Alex was under her heel. Alex zoned out as Beatrix launched into a monologue on what silverware to use when. She looked over at the dots and saw that the dot for the Vice President, the red number one, was now in the room with the gold one. The First Lady wasn't there at all. The Vice President had now joined whatever discussion Wiatt and the President were having. And she could see red number two—Abby Shane, she assumed—lingering just outside that room.

Beatrix Graham clapped her hands together to get Alex's attention.

But Alex was anxious to get back to her lab and away from this protocol nightmare before Beatrix got it in her head to teach her to curtsey or something. "I hope you aren't planning to wear that suit to the gathering."

The older woman looked down in stunned silence at the black silk suit she was wearing; it hit her legs perfectly, mid-knee. She brought her right hand up to her pearls, and rubbed her fingers over them as if they were a talisman. "Whatever can you mean?" she asked.

Alex handed back the pen. Then she flipped the notepad into the trash bin. "I don't know whose etiquette books you're following, but they aren't multicultural. Black is a bad luck color for the Vietnamese."

Beatrix Graham put her hands across her suit jacket in alarm.

"Tell Colonel Wiatt I'm heading back to the AFIP to do some real work," Alex said, turning toward the door.

"But the ceremony—," said Beatrix.

Alex looked back over her shoulder. "There's a wonder-fully charming Vietnamese gentleman named Troy Nguyen. Perhaps you can get him detailed over here to instruct you on the matter."

Alex smiled as she headed for the Metro. Maybe she had just killed two birds with one stone.

CHAPTER NINE

BACK AT the AFIP, Alex bought a Coke and a peanut butter and banana sandwich in the cafeteria for dinner. She noticed Troy sitting alone in the far reaches of the room, a good thirty feet from the nearest occupied table. She decided to join him, feeling slightly guilty that she'd sicced Beatrix Graham on him.

He wasn't making camaraderie easy. He'd chosen the only table with just one chair. She grabbed one from another table and pulled it with a screech across the floor, causing heads to turn.

"Looks like you've got the attention of the primates here," he said, nodding toward Grant, who was looking their way, along with several bodybuilder buddies. "Doesn't it get you down spending your days with so many alpha males?"

Alex stifled her urge to quip and decided instead to take his question seriously. "To tell the truth, what bothers me are their poker faces. It's hard to judge what anybody's thinking." Alex gestured with her hands as she spoke, raised her eyebrows, smiled, and crinkled her nose.

"A far cry from you," Troy said. "You've got a symphony of facial expressions going on, even just between your nose and your chin."

Alex nodded toward the occupied tables. "I take it you're not doing any male bonding in your new assignment, judging by the space between you and the nearest soldier."

"Didn't like American soldiers when I was a child in Vietnam, not going to start now."

"Why'd you accept this assignment then?"

"No choice. The NIH director insisted."

Alex noticed that he'd positioned his arm over whatever he had been working on when she sat down. She looked at it and he quickly moved it to his briefcase.

"No need to hide it," Alex said. "I can't read Vietnamese."

Troy glanced up at her, then pulled a stack of letters out of the briefcase next to his chair. "We've received nearly two hundred letters from families wanting to know if the skulls belonged to their husbands, their brothers, their sons. They're all asking the same question—a question of you. Will you help the corpses speak their names?"

Alex nervously tapped her right foot. "There just isn't any way we can start identifying those skulls."

He finished the bologna sandwich he'd packed from home and folded up the bag for reuse. "I'm sure you'll think of something," he said.

He got up, leaving Alex to finish her sandwich alone.

WIATT HAD told her to steer clear of the letter, but it was the only thing she could think about when she got back to her lab. She absentmindedly tapped her fingernails on the counter, then realized that she couldn't think of a genetic sequence to focus on. She paused, her lab quiet except for the hum of the glistening refrigerator that held the samples of the toxins she studied for her work on biowarfare vaccines.

In the peace of the lab, Alex realized there was one link to the past that might help her track down the events in the letter. The early Trophy Skulls records, computerized by the researcher who wrote about them in the 1980s, indicated the name of the soldier that each skull had been confiscated from.

In her glassed-in office, she plugged in the description of the skull and the terms *black smoke* and *thick candle*. A name popped up. Private First Class Michael Carlisle had brought the skull into the country on April 24, 1972.

She switched to a military records database she'd used in previous criminal investigations. She typed in "Michael Carlisle" and found two identically named men from the Vietnam era. Only one had a discharge date in 1972, though. From West Virginia, he'd done two tours of duty, the first in 1969. He'd been a PJ, a parajumper, trained in parachuting, scuba diving, combat medicine, and helicopter-borne fire-fighting. He'd flown three hundred rescue flights and earned an Air Force Cross for a mission in which he'd descended from a low-flying, cumbersome HH-43 Huskie helicopter on a cable and winch, used an M16 to fire on the enemy, and hoisted three downed pilots, one by one, up to safety.

As to the skull, he said he'd won it in a card game. Was that believable? she asked herself. Or had Michael Carlisle strangled this woman—maybe in a lovers' spat?

Follow the evidence, Alex told herself. What did she know so far?

The Samurai may have chopped off heads in war, but was it likely that an Air Force parajumper had pulled such a stunt? She swallowed hard as she tried to visualize it. The transformation from head to skull wasn't easy. Could Michael Carlisle have strangled a woman, then hacked away the skin or boiled it off? Secretly? In front of other men? Maybe in some Thomas Harris thriller, but not in the midst of the bullets and bombs of a war. Most likely, the skull had been collected from a battleground or a bombed-out house days or weeks after the woman died by someone other than her killer.

It was more difficult to distance Michael Carlisle from the letter inside the skull. She didn't know how often platoons in the Vietnamese jungle crossed paths with other American units, but wasn't it likely that, if he'd won the skull playing cards, it was from someone in his own unit and that the letter discussed the atrocities committed by that group?

Alex looked again at the letter, focusing on the name "Nick" and the initials *S.F.* She started running cross-checks in the database to get the names of the other airmen in the two units he'd served with. The first platoon had no Nathan,

Nick, Nicholas, or Nate, or anyone with the initials *S.F.* Ditto with his second unit.

Then she noticed another entry in his records. He'd served with his second unit until February 1972. When all but three of his platoon died, he was reassigned. He joined the USAF's 302nd Aerospace Rescue and Recovery Squadron. The same one as her dad.

She took a deep breath and looked up at the female skull. Could her father, the man she'd idolized for decades, have been part of a group that killed civilians in cold blood?

Back on the computer, she pulled up a list of men who'd served alongside her dad in Vietnam. Her chest was tight and a sharp pain was pressing against the back of her eyes as she played Russian roulette with the names from her dad's platoon, more than fifty men in all. But none exploded off the page. No Nick. No S.F.

Alex felt better. Like the Trophy Skulls article had said, these skulls were traded like baseball cards. Just because Michael Carlisle had the woman's skull in his possession didn't mean he and his unit killed innocent villagers. And, she told herself, it certainly didn't mean her dad was involved.

But a wisp of doubt remained. From Dan she'd learned so much about the fallibility of the Armed Services. Who's to say that the records were accurate? There were a lot of guys over in Nam. Maybe a couple of units met up.

She sat down at her desk and put her head in her hands. Her father had died when she was in kindergarten. At that time, she didn't have the emotional repertoire to go through the traditional stages of grieving. But now—faced with this new link to her dad—she felt an irrational rage about his deserting her. If he could abandon a five-year-old girl, who knew what else he was capable of?

She nervously paced her lab, wishing she smoked. Wasn't that what people did in old movies when they wanted to think more clearly? But Alex had never even tried cigarettes. Her mom had enough bad habits for both of them. Cuban cigars, all that moving around when she was a kid as her mother tried to outrun the memory of her husband's death.

In medical school, Alex had learned all she could about Vietnam Stress Syndrome. It didn't just affect soldiers. Her mother suffered as much from the war as anyone who'd been over there. Alex remembered the days following her father's death when she'd felt she had no parents at all since Janet spent most of her time weeping in bed. Then came the years when Alex was nine, ten, and eleven and her mother would move them from state to state, wrenching Alex away from each new set of friends, as she tried to find a spot with better vibes.

Janet might have ended up off the grid, in some Montana survivalist enclave with the other burnouts from the war, if it hadn't been for graduate school in cultural anthropology. Now a professor at Oberlin College, Alex's mother made a living from her obsession, teaching courses about social movements.

Well, Alex couldn't argue with that. Wasn't she working out her obsessions in her job as well? She'd gone into medicine to study diseases and disasters that cut down people in their prime.

She walked back over to the charred skull. She put on a latex glove and felt the ridge above the woman's eye sockets as if, through touch, she could discern the secrets of the woman's last hours. She wished Barbara were at the AFIP tonight. She needed someone to reassure her that her world had not shifted off its axis, that her father was still the man she remembered.

She removed the glove and tapped the keyboard to enter another database, seeking more information about Carlisle. After Nam, his records showed a couple of visits to the VA hospital in West Virginia for treatment of migraines and emphysema. Although he enlisted while in high school, there was no record of his going to college on the GI bill after his discharge. No military-related records at all after 1974.

She printed out the sheet of information. She thought of calling the VA hospital for his phone number, but it was unlikely he'd still be living at the address he'd given the hospital thirty years earlier. She stared at the page, then picked up a pen and drew a red circle around Michael Carlisle's Social Security number.

She glanced at her watch—nearly 9:00 P.M.—picked up the printout, and headed to the conference room. She did a double take when she saw Corporal Chuck Lawndale dressed in black. He looked more like Luke's drummer than a soldier.

"I'm sorry I'm out of uniform," he said. "We're trying a few other clubs tonight, ma'am."

Alex cringed. "Chuck, I'm not that much older than you. Can you just call me by my first name?"

He shook his head. "It doesn't seem right, ma'am."

Alex decided not to get in a discussion of protocol now, when she needed a favor. She passed him the paper. "I've got a guy's Social Security number and I'm looking for a phone number, current address, anything you can get me about him."

"Is this about the John Doe?"

She shook her head. "No, it's another matter Wiatt is working on." Well, that was pretty much true, wasn't it? Although Wiatt seemed to be working on burying any information about the fate of the woman's skull and the letter within it.

"No problem," Chuck said, minimizing the whirring figures on the screen and pulling up a national database of drivers' licenses.

"He's a local," he said a moment later. "Lives about forty-five minutes from here in Maryland."

Alex peered over his shoulder, and copied down the address.

"Want the phone number, too?"

Alex nodded. But this was too important for a call. She was going to pay Michael Carlisle a visit.

CHAPTER TEN

WITH MICHAEL Carlisle's address on the passenger seat beside her, Alex eased her T-Bird onto Georgia Avenue. She punched the car radio, hoping she could summon one of the two stations that usually worked, but her efforts were met with a stoic silence. Maybe she would splurge and buy herself a new radio for Christmas.

Alex fell into her usual approach to driving—speeding, feinting, and weaving around the slower cars. In her rearview mirror, she noticed a Jeep seemed to be following her—no mean feat considering her fearlessness at the wheel.

As she left the main roads, she decided that she didn't want the company even if it was just some car jock having a good time keeping up with a blonde in a sports car. She overshot the entrance to Highway 27 and flew through the last bit of yellow at a stoplight, leaving the Jeep behind her, then turned down a side street, backtracking and speeding down the highway's on-ramp.

She drove a dozen miles down Highway 27, the tail car nowhere in sight. She exited into a wooded, rural part of Maryland. The trees—probably spectacular in daylight—were eerie and annoying at night, branches covering street signs, impeding her search for Rampart Road. It had been a mere flicker on the map, a thin hair of a road about ten miles off the main highway.

The mailbox where Lompoc Road met Rampart was a large high-tech rectangle, with a single name: CARLISLE. She turned down the dirt road, only to find her way blocked two hundred feet farther on by a metal gate. As she got closer, she also saw a keypad and video camera. She pressed the button and a man answered. He asked her to look directly into the camera and state her business.

"I'd like to talk to Michael Carlisle," she said.

There was a moment's hesitation and then the gate moved smoothly inward. She wound along the road to a spectacular house, a contemporary glass and concrete series of cubes at odd angles. A man in a low-to-the-ground wheelchair held the door open for her. He took a long look at her heart-shaped face, then lowered his glance to the rest of her body. "I don't know what you're sellin'," he said, "but I'm buyin.'"

He waved her in and asked her to follow him. He used his muscular upper arms to spin the rubber wheels quietly across the polished maple floor. At the end of the hall, they entered a cavernous living room with a ceiling that slanted upward to the top of a thirty-foot-high wall of glass. Candlelight in the room created a soft glow, and the bright moonlight outside gave the illusion that there was no division between the forest and the room itself.

Alex looked around and noticed there was no couch, nor chairs. Of course. He didn't need them.

He swerved his chair abruptly to turn and face her. "I don't get many pretty girls surprising me out here," he said. "What do you want?"

Alex shifted her attention from the forest to the man. She tapped her foot nervously, then guiltily stopped, aware of the functioning of her limbs, the deathly stillness of his tanned feet peeking out from under the hems of his jeans.

He seemed to relish her discomfort. He was strangely fearless, given that he was confined to the chair.

"I just want to ask you some questions," she said.

"Odd time of night for someone to roll in, taking a census."

"No, it's personal. It's about Vietnam."

He stiffened in the wheelchair. "Take off your coat," he

said. He stared at her fiercely, his words ambiguous. She couldn't tell if it was his way of inviting her to stay or he wanted to make sure she didn't have access to a weapon. She stripped off her coat and dropped it to the floor.

He stared at her blue jeans and black turtleneck, the fanny pack around her waist. He seemed satisfied.

"Can I get you a drink?" he asked.

She noticed a half-empty glass on a granite table. "What are you having?"

"Bourbon," he said.

Alex nodded. "The same. With ice."

He pointed her toward a large set of pillows near the fireplace. "You'll probably be comfortable there," he said. Alex watched nervously as he wheeled over to a wet bar on the side of the room. Her eyes stayed on him as she arranged a few pillows into a more chairlike formation. With a few pillows underneath her, and even more as a backrest, she'd be almost at the height of his lowrider wheelchair.

He rolled up in front of her, a cut-glass tumbler on the chair balanced in front of his crotch. His wheelchair was no muss, no fuss. It didn't have armrests, or a drink holder, or a motor, or a computer. Just a set of wheels and a canvas back and seat. Alex wondered what that was about. From the looks of the house, he could have afforded the best, a voice-activated do-anything-you-ask Rolls-Royce of wheelchairs. Maybe this one made him feel less disabled. It was just a slight extension of his body.

Alex took the glass he handed her and sat in the plush cushion chair she'd created. She nervously ran her left hand over the sumptuous pale gold velvet and burgundy silk, then nodded toward the wheelchair. "Were you hurt in Vietnam?"

Carlisle looked perplexed a moment, then said, "No, I was in my element there. Most guys don't want to admit it, but Nam was the best thing that ever happened to me. Taught me what I was made of. And I came back on my own two feet.

"This," he continued, pirouetting the wheelchair around, "some asshole truck driver did to me, on good ole Interstate

79 in West Virginia. Luckily I had a damn good lawyer. Got a major jury verdict."

"Must have been good, if it set you up here," Alex said, looking at the vast land visible through the window.

"Used it as seed money for a couple of businesses. Now I've got a venture capital firm in Chevy Chase, Carlisle and Sons."

"How old are your sons?"

He smiled. "Haven't got any. But one thing I learned is that the big boys don't want to invest unless they feel you've been around for quite a while. Sounds a lot more reputable to have that extra generation in there."

He sat back, calmly sipping his bourbon and not pressing her about her business. She watched him for a few minutes as she thought about the many questions she had for him.

She downed another gulp of bourbon and stared at his strong arm muscles, poking out from the sleeves of a dark gray T-shirt. She raised her gaze and noticed how his light brown hair highlighted intensely aware black eyes. He seemed vaguely amused by her nervousness.

"I'm part of a group at the Armed Forces Institute of Pathology that's working on the return of Vietnamese skulls to the government of Vietnam," she said. "You've probably read about it in the *Post*."

Was she imagining it or had his shoulders tightened?

"Yeah, what's it got to do with me? I talked to some old guy at the AFIP years ago. Told him I'd won the skull in a card game."

She nodded. "That's what the file says, but he didn't log a date for when the card game occurred."

He looked at her like she was crazy. "Excuse me, but my calendar had a habit of floating away whenever I'd cross some hellhole river in Nam. And my social secretary had his head blown off."

Alex smarted from the harsh words. She looked behind him at the stone sculptures lining the wall. Some sort of Hindu dancers, she guessed. As the trees outside swayed in front of the moon, the shadows of the sculptures moved, performing elaborate dances. Then she faced him again. "We don't need an exact date. Just, did you get it with your early units or the last one?"

She realized she was holding her breath. She desperately wanted him to have won the skull before joining her father's unit. That would mean her dad had no possible role in a massacre.

"What do you think? We lived on what was on our backs. I had to carry food, medical supplies, ammunition, ropes, you name it. No room for a skull. I picked it up a few days before I came back."

She scrunched her face to hold back tears. What had she accomplished? She'd just made things worse. In her botched investigation, she'd now placed the skull—and the letter inside it—within reach of her beloved father.

She stood to leave.

"You're going, just like that?" he asked. "Without even introducing yourself?"

She held out her hand and he shifted his bourbon from his right hand to the left to shake it. His palm was slightly cool from the cold glass.

"Alexandra Blake," she said.

"Alex Blake, did you say?" He looked her up and down. "The sergeant's runt?"

She nodded. Her heart raced at this odd link to her father. Since her childhood, she'd been consumed with curiosity about her dad. At the Vietnam Memorial, the Wall, she'd sat on the grass and studied the chiseled set of twenty-four letters—*Alexander Northfield Blake*—that was her only remaining connection to her dad. Her mother would not answer questions about him. His death, at the height of their love, was unbearable for her to talk about. But now she was in the same room as someone who had served alongside him.

He balanced his drink between his legs and grasped her hands in his. She was standing and he was seated, but he had such a strong presence that he seemed to tower over her. "My condolences," he said with a solemn formality.

He wheeled over to a granite table, opened a drawer, and pulled out two items. One was a joint, which he proceeded to light up with a battered Bic he fished out of his pocket. "The sergeant was a good man. Didn't play favorites. Didn't lose his dignity. Had this infuriating habit of talking with his hands, like this."

He waved his arms wildly about, dropping ashes from the joint. Alex teared up. It was exactly the way she herself spoke.

Carlisle handed her the item in his other hand. It was a business card. "Carlisle and Sons." A Chevy Chase address.

"I keep all my valuables in a safe at work. I have some photos of the squadron there. Maybe even one with him. Stop in one day and I'll pull them out for you."

Alex took the card, and nodded.

"And come back to my forest sometime." He smiled slyly, and looked her up and down in an obvious yet somehow flattering way. "If you're anything like the sergeant, you might just get off on the danger."

CHAPTER ELEVEN

The pager on Alex's nightstand went off that night at 1:00 A.M. Her heart did that crazy flop it did whenever adrenaline coursed through her sleep-deprived body. She untangled herself from the sheets, called Dan's cell phone, and wrote down the address he barked out. "We've caught a break in the John Doe case," he said.

The Georgetown street was an upscale residential one, pillars and bricks that sparkled in the moonlight, well-appointed lawns. Mostly large houses, and a building of six fancy town houses, recently constructed.

Alex entered Unit C, the crime scene. Dan, Grant, and Chuck were already there. Streaks of blood flooded the white carpet, the walls of the foyer, and the edge of the front door. The harsh track lighting spotlighted a broken bouquet of decaying yellow roses with obscenely long stems. A burgundy leather briefcase was propped upside down, its papers fanned out around it.

Grant handed Alex a business card. She could tell from the black dust on it that it had already been fingerprinted. "M. Ronald Gladden, C.P.A., Ernst & Young," with office addresses in the District and in Ho Chi Minh City. Alex looked up from the card to a slick original Mapplethorpe photo of a man's glistening naked back in the entryway. Not the poster version, a signed edition. "Not my grandpa's accountant, for sure," she said.

Alex turned over the business card. On the back of the card, the dead man had written his home phone number.

"The major was right," Grant said. "A guy at tonight's poetry slam at My Left Hand had picked up the stiff—I mean before he was the stiff—last Monday night. Recognized him from the photo we were showing around."

"Why didn't he come forward when the photo ran on the news?" she asked.

"Doesn't own a television set," Chuck chimed in. "Says it interferes with his art."

"The poet said he had just met the guy, was supposed to join him at a movie Tuesday night," Grant said. "When the guy didn't show, he called him twice from the phone in the box office, then assumed Gladden was just one of those, quote, fuck and run guys."

Chuck had followed up. "I plugged into Southern Bell records on my laptop. Sure enough, three calls to this number from the theater, ten minutes apart on Tuesday. Reverse directory got us this address and then we paged the major."

Dan broke away from the man in the robe he'd been interviewing, the John Doe's neighbor, who'd told him that Ron Gladden had spent the past six months working in Vietnam. He joined Alex and began to fill her in. "I like this as a crime scene, there's enough individuality to it—the roses, removal of the body through the front door. There's a signature here. I've just got to figure out what it is."

Alex was drawn to the kitchen. An airline ticket on the counter—and an open tin of foie gras in the refrigerator—confirmed what Dan had predicted. Gladden had spent a few days in Paris on his way home. She opened a kitchen cabinet with her gloved hand and eyed a row of spices, all with labels in Vietnamese. The one nearest the front had a reddish tint. She opened it and took a whiff. The smell was hard to place—part cinnamon, part hibiscus, part clove.

When she returned to the living room, the photographer

had finished and Alex could concentrate on her search of that room. She aimed her blue light in concentric circles beyond the pool of blood to see if she could find any hint of the assailant's DNA. Dan told her it was unlikely she'd find anything. Judging by the smudged marks on the delicate, silky paper the roses were wrapped in, the killer had been wearing gloves.

"We're in luck with the paper, though," Dan said. "These aren't grocery store roses, or the kind you buy at the side of the road. Paper they came in must have cost a fortune itself."

Alex cocked her head at him.

"Spent time in the doghouse," he explained. "Personality and work schedule like mine, you end up buying a lot of apology bouquets. I'll check high-end florists in the morning."

So far, the blue light was turning up almost nothing. Usually, an inhabited apartment was loaded with DNA from the owner—hairs, flakes of skin, evidence of amorous encounters. But this guy must have had the place industrially cleaned before he came back from his trip. There was hardly a trace of Ron Gladden here, let alone an assailant.

It was frustrating. It looked like a bloodbath in here, but there hadn't been a struggle. At the autopsy, there had been no defensive wounds on the body, no DNA from anyone else under his nails.

After fifteen minutes searching, a faint glow caught Alex's attention. A little blood on one of the rose thorns. Any luck, the killer had been imperceptibly pricked through his gloves, unwittingly leaving a trace of himself behind.

Alex was bagging the rose when Grant came out of the bedroom. "Lot of jewelry, two thousand in cash on the dresser," he said. "He's also got a great shoe organizer in the closet."

Alex shook her head. "What's with you, two nights at the clubs and you turn into *Queer Eye for the Straight Guy*?" She looked over at the expensive stereo, the forty-two-inch plasma TV filling most of one wall. "We already knew robbery wasn't the motive. Not many robbers drop off their dead in a Dumpster."

Chuck entered the living room, his gloved hands carrying

a sleek black computer tower, with the side panel removed. He showed them the empty ribbon connector. Someone had removed the hard drive. The computer was useless to them.

"Here's how I think it went down," Dan said. "Gladden opened the door for whoever was delivering the flowers. Judging by this stain here," he pointed to a blood splatter a few inches from the door, "the guy whipped out the weapon from behind the bouquet and slammed it full tilt into him before the door even closed behind him."

Alex looked at the blood pattern. "The body was still standing when the heart was removed," she said. "That means . . ."

Dan nodded. "Our victim's last vision on earth was a guy sticking a hand into his chest to remove his heart."

CHAPTER TWELVE

AT 6:00 A.M., after just four hours' sleep, Alex woke up wondering if her doubts about her father had just been a dream. She clicked on CNN on the set at the foot of her bed to ease herself into the day. There was a clip of the President's speech the night before, vowing to lessen the United States' dependence on Arab oil, to seek reserves in other parts of the world, and to offer tax credits for new technologies for oil exploration. Alex noticed that the harsh television lights made him look a little more wooden than he did in person.

She rolled out of bed to shower, as CNN moved to the next story. She bent down to turn off the set, only to come face to face with the image of the Screamer skull and a report on the criticisms from around the world of the GI who had stolen it. *Kín nhu' bu'ng,* the Vietnamese called it. The secrets of the grave. Or, more angrily, the grave-robbing incident.

Alex showered and put on a different set of jeans and another black turtleneck. As she walked through the linoleum-floored living room at the Curl Up and Dye, she noticed the red light flashing on her answering machine. A call must have come in while she was in Ron Gladden's town house. She pushed the button and heard Luke doing a riff on an old song: "The way you wear your hat, the way you sip your double espresso Carmel Macchiato, the memory of all that, no, no, they can't take that away from me. . . . Hey, Alex, did you give up on me already? It's two in the morning your time. A record exec from Amsterdam caught my show last night and invited me there for a few days. I'm on my way to the airport now. He's got a few friends he wants me to meet."

Alex sat down in one of the hair dryer chairs when the message ended, feeling the same push-pull she always did in her dealings with Luke. Closeness, joy at the little songs he created for her. Jealousy and foreboding when he was three thousand miles away and about to meet someone's "friends," which usually included some leggy model or sexually aggressive groupie.

But, Alex thought, can those women dissect a fruit fly in twenty seconds flat or clone a gene? She laughed out loud at her further thought: Who would want to?

She tried to convince herself she probably wouldn't have taken time off to meet Luke in Barcelona anyway. Why spend nights in a series of smoky clubs listening to Luke play the same tunes over and over? Besides, she'd uncovered a connection to her father, with Michael and the skulls, and she was determined to find out where it led.

AT THE AFIP, she typed Ron Gladden's name into the sequencer. That simple act of identification made her feel that some progress was being made. She called up the forensic analysis of Gladden's genes on the computer monitor hooked to the Applied Biosystems gene sequencer. Her first step would be to compare the makeup of five genes of the blood on the rose to the analogous genes from Gladden to see if it was the dead man's blood. She put the blood into a cocktail of enzymes to break down the DNA, then used a polymerase chain reaction to amplify the small amount of DNA from that blood. This would provide enough to run her tests and still have some left over to give defense attorney experts if a guy was brought to trial based on her DNA work.

She then dotted her portion of the DNA sample onto a microchip and inserted it into the sequencer. Ten minutes later, the five genes in the sample had been sequenced, compared to Gladden's DNA, and declared not to match. That was a great start. It meant that the DNA could belong to the killer. Of course, it could also be the blood of the florist who had arranged the bouquet. Once Dan's men tracked down the florist, she could obtain swabs of DNA from the flower shop employees to rule them out.

Alex held her breath as she began the next step, comparing the thorn blood to the DNA profiles of convicted felons in the CODIS database. Maybe the genome gods would be smiling down on her and she'd nail the suspect even before Dan got hold of the dead guy's boss. She didn't put much stock in that happening. Usually it was the stupid criminal who got caught and ended up in the FBI database—like the guy who wrote a holdup note on the back of his personal check. An hour after he robbed the bank, the cops tracked him down at his home address, which was imprinted on the check. Not like the cool precision she imagined Gladden's killer had.

While she was waiting for the CODIS comparison to run, she considered other tests she could employ. The angle of the bayonet wound suggested that the assailant was shorter than Gladden. She scrutinized the sex chromosomes in the crime scene sample to see if the blood on the rose was that of a woman. Nope, it was XY. Whoever pricked himself on the rose was a man. She left a message for Dan, saying not to bother collecting DNA swabs from any female employees of the flower shop.

The CODIS results took an excruciatingly long time to correlate, as the DNA profile from the thorn was compared to ne'er-do-wells across the country. A rapist in Kansas, serial killer from Colorado, white-collar felon from Delaware, man who'd drowned his girlfriend's child here in the District. Hundreds of men were convicted of vile, unspeakable crimes each day, and, within a few days, their DNA profiles were entered into CODIS. In fact, in the twenty minutes since Alex had started running her comparison, four more killers and six armed robbers had joined the database.

At last, the CODIS results appeared—no matches. Whoever pricked himself on the rose wasn't a convicted felon—at least not in the United States. Frustrated, Alex considered how she might get more from that database. The CODIS data could be linked to some demographic data about offenders, including what the felon considered to be his race. For the next hour and a half, she threw herself into creating a computer program to see whether a DNA sample could be used to determine the race of an assailant. This was a hotly contested issue in genetics. With all the mixing and matching, the intermarriage and melting pots, it was hard to figure out a person's race by the genes he or she inherited.

Alex might be able to get a rough approximation. As she did the calculations, she thought of a genetics class she took in medical school. She remembered her professor cautioning: "There is more genetic variation within races than between races." In other words, blacks sometimes differed more from other blacks than they did from the local Ku Klux Klansman.

She worked the rest of the morning trying to apply her new protocol. It was nearly lunchtime when she got the results. The blood from the thorn had a 6 percent likelihood of being from a Hispanic, 3 percent likelihood of being from a non-Hispanic Caucasian, 15 percent likelihood of being from an African-American, and 76 percent likelihood of being "other."

Great, she thought. What the hell kind of other? There were only about five thousand ethnic groups in the world—from Pima Indians to Samoans. Her next step would be to go through the National Library of Medicine database to see what recessive genetic diseases distinguished one ethnic group from another. African-Americans had a higher rate of sickle cell anemia, and Ashkenazi Jews of Tay-Sachs disease. Perhaps she could identify the ethnic background of the assailant by analyzing hidden disease genes in the blood.

As her computer started identifying disease mutations in the blood from the thorn, Colonel Wiatt strode into her laboratory, a determined look on his face. Alex's body tensed as she prepared for a dressing-down. Was he here to chastise her for leaving the White House early? Had he found out about her journey to Maryland to see Carlisle?

He was holding something in his hand—a black-and-white photo. He thrust it at her and she glanced at the image—a head shot of a soldier, midforties.

"Colonel David Braverman," he said, as if that would mean something to Alex.

She stared at the photo and then up at the tall man in front of her.

"The highest-ranking MIA in Vietnam," Wiatt continued.

Still no clue about where he was going with this.

"The Vietnamese Ministry of the Interior found his remains. They will be returning them at the White House ceremony."

"That's great," Alex said.

"You don't seem to understand, Blake. Now it's our turn. You've got to find out who these people are." He pointed with a precise, curt gesture over to the library cart.

"That's impossible," Alex said.

Wiatt glared at her, signaling that her response was unacceptable. "The President himself asked that at least one of the skulls be identified by next Friday when he meets with the Vietnamese Ambassador to finalize plans for the exchange."

"But—"

Wiatt held up a stern finger to silence her. "That was not a request, Dr. Blake. It was an order."

Then he turned and strode out, his long limbs covering the length of her office and lab in just a few steps.

MIFFED BY the unreasonableness of the task assigned to her, Alex left her lab to look for sympathy—and chocolate—in Barbara's office.

"How was the birthday?" Alex asked her.

"Lana didn't want to leave. I forget about how much family means to her, how she craves the interactions I left home to escape."

"Such as?"

Barbara smiled. "She spent the whole weekend helping my dad put together a one-thousand-piece puzzle of *The Last Supper*."

Alex peeled the wrapper off a KitKat as she tried to imagine Barbara growing up in a home like that. She was about to launch into a tirade about Wiatt's tyranny when Barbara motioned her to the computer screen.

"This thing with the letter in the skull doesn't look good," Barbara said.

"What do you mean?"

Barbara pointed to a Web site simply titled: "War Crimes."

"After Bosnia, some law students from Chicago-Kent College of Law set up a database about incidents of genocide and other war crimes."

Alex looked at the links. You could search the Web site by ethnic group (atrocities against the Kurds, for example), by type of war crime (rape in Haiti), by date or place of incidence (Abu Ghraib prison), and by any number of categories. There were photos of victims, a chilling gallery of people beaten, burned, tortured, starved, electrocuted, knifed, castrated, and beheaded.

"Believe it or not, the Justice Department tried to shut down this site," Barbara said. "X-rated sexual pervert sites all linked to it. Some guys were getting off looking at the pictures of people who had been tortured, women who had been raped."

There were some days when Alex learned more about her fellow man than she wanted to know.

"Amnesty International sued to keep it going," Barbara continued. "Mainly the victims of war crimes and the witnesses write about recent events in places like the Middle East or South America. . . ."

"Let me guess, there are reports from Vietnam."

"Yeah. They aren't contemporaneous, like the ones from Bosnia, so you don't know how much weight to give them. The Web site wasn't set up until 1992. But take a look at this."

Alex read a description, entered in broken English, of the burning of a village outside of Qui Nhon. The words were ominously similar to those carved with red pencil onto the paper in the skull. "Gas." "Four hootches." The description gave the same body count as well—six Vietnamese civilians.

"There's no date on the description, so it will be hard to track down which American troops were in the area at the time. But maybe Amnesty International will know how to get in touch with the person who entered this."

"We know the incident occurred before 1972," Alex said. "That's when the letter in the skull entered the country."

Alex read further. The village was described as being a two-hour walk west of Qui Nhon. "The witness was a boy, seven years old at the time. He saw his father shot in front of him."

The two women sat in an uncomfortable silence for a moment, feeling the horror of the image wash over them.

Alex, who knew every word of the letter by heart, knew the description on the Web site was precisely in line with what the soldier had accused "Nick" of doing. "What if this is the same incident?" she asked.

"Then we handle it like any other criminal investigation, and we court-martial the bastards who did it."

Alex sat frozen in her chair. She wondered if a court-martial could reach into the grave. And—if by some remote chance her father had been involved—she wondered if her mother could survive the revelations.

CHAPTER THIRTEEN

ALEX JOINED Grant and Chuck at the conference table for a noon update on the Gladden case, but Dan was nowhere in sight. At 12:15 P.M., Dan finally arrived, looking exasperated. "It's not enough I've got an investigation to run," he said. "Now I'm hand-holding the mayor."

Alex looked at him quizzically.

"D.C.'s had a god-awful crime rate for decades," Dan said.

"Coke-snorting former mayor didn't help," added Grant.

"Yeah, but D.C. politicos could always point to the crown jewel, Georgetown," Dan said. "Safer than Palm Beach. Safer than Grosse Pointe. Safer than Palo Alto."

"Way safer than Manhattan," Grant said.

Alex could see where this was heading. "But now some upstanding citizen gets killed in his Georgetown home . . ."

Dan nodded. "Upstanding citizen who lives on the same block as two Senators, an Ambassador, and a running back for the Redskins. Hizzoner was on the phone with Wiatt an hour after we found Gladden's body. Told him he wanted the crime solved pronto."

Alex couldn't imagine that Wiatt took that well. "Wiatt told him to shove it, I suppose."

"Not that simple," Dan said. "Turns out there's an AFIP plan to buy some adjoining property—owned by the District—for additional lab space."

Ah, D.C., Alex thought. Politics as art form.

"So, with that cheery prelude, what've we got?" asked Dan.

Grant reported that his Weapons of War program had identified the bayonet. He didn't have this particular model in his collection (a fact he noted with a disappointed pout, like a kid whose parents won't buy him the latest Grand Theft Auto video game), but, with Chuck Lawndale's computer help, he was able to use VA hospital records to show that this particular wound came from a Soviet bayonet, a Moisin Nagant, used by the North Vietnamese Army during the war.

Alex reached out for the photo of the weapon that Grant was waving about. She thought of her father in Vietnam. Bombs and bayonets. The daily risks he faced. The schizophrenia of the dangers of war speckled with the memories of a wife and young daughter at home.

Alex returned the photo and heard Chuck report that the poet's alibi had checked out. At the time Ron Gladden was murdered, he was visiting his grandmother in a nursing home, as he did every Tuesday night. Plus, there was nothing to indicate he'd ever entered Gladden's town house.

Finding the florist was easy—a Virginia flower store attached to a greenhouse had been broken into Tuesday after closing time. The owner reported it, even though only one bouquet was stolen, because she needed a police report to have her insurance cover the broken window. It wasn't until Dan showed up at her door that she realized the truck had been taken out for a joyride as well. She'd been the only one who'd handled the bouquet before it was stolen, which meant that the blood on the rose, with its male DNA, was indeed the killer's.

Alex's tests for ethnic-based genetic diseases showed that the killer had a mutation in his hemoglobin gene, a form of Hemoglobin (Hb) E/beta-thalassemia. It wouldn't affect his health, but would create a 25 percent chance of having a child with a serious thalassemia if he had a child with a woman with the same mutation. That information was of interest to Alex not because she was concerned for the killer's reproductive future, but because it suggested that the killer was from Southeast Asia, where that mutation was fairly common.

All leads seemed to point to a Vietnamese connection, but it was unimaginable what the connection could be, and how it could reach nine thousand miles to a town house in Georgetown. Dan put the conference room phone on speaker and called the home number of the head of the Ernst & Young office in Ho Chi Minh City, as Saigon was now called. Gregory Ramsey knew nothing about Gladden's personal life in Vietnam, couldn't imagine that he actually had one. "Ron was often still at the office when I left at nine or ten at night," his supervisor said. Ramsey was reluctant to divulge any details about the exact transactions Gladden had been working on. But he gave Dan an earful about the role of the accounting firms as fixers in Vietnam. "We're hired by companies from around the world to smooth their entry into Southeast Asia," he said. "In Vietnam, the rules change every few minutes. Getting approval to do business here takes standing in line at a dozen different agencies. We know the system and can get people through it."

"Why are companies hot to do business in Nam?" Dan asked.

"It's the thirteenth largest country in the world, with more people than any European country and almost any South American one. So, the market for new products is huge. Plus, it's got the highest literacy rate in the world—over ninety percent—and one of the cheapest workforces. People get by on a buck fifty a day."

Alex felt humbled. That wouldn't even keep her in dark roast Starbucks.

"With the type of work you do, you have access to a lot of confidential information about people's future business plans," Dan said.

"The best. But part of what we are paid for is our discretion. What one client tells us never enters the ears of another client."

"Any chance that Gladden crossed that line?"

"So far, no client has taken any out-of-character actions. If one of them had the scoop on another, we'd see some movement. A push to move a product out faster, or seek oil near the other's drilling area. Nobody on my end is behaving like they know something big."

"Who was the last client that Gladden worked for?"

"I can't tell you that," said Ramsey.

Alex, Grant, and Dan looked at each other. They could hardly threaten him with a subpoena. The D.C. courts didn't reach all the way to Ho Chi Minh City.

"Listen," Dan said. "How confidential could this be? You have a list of clients on your Web site."

"I'd like to help, but confidentiality is company policy."

"Well, how about this? I read the names one by one off the Web site and you say no if it wasn't his last client." Dan didn't leave time for a response. Instead he started in.

"General Electric."

"No."

"Intel."

"No."

"Procter and Gamble."

"No."

"Westport Oil."

There was a silence on the line. For a moment they thought the connection to Vietnam had been severed.

"Are you still with us, Mr. Ramsey?"

"Yes."

"Thanks for your help."

"Sure, let me know if there is anything else I can do. Ron was a good kid, a little flamboyant for my tastes, but he went the distance at the office."

Alex wondered how a good kid—an accountant, no less—had ended up with a bayonet in his chest.

AS SHE and Grant left the conference room, she heard a husky woman's voice saying, "Why don't you come up and see me sometime?"

They were alone in the hallway. "Don't tell me you've added ventriloquism to your bag of tricks?" Alex said.

"No, check this out." He pulled a cell phone out of his

pocket and pushed some buttons. The voice changed to French, then Russian, and then changed to a male's voice in a language that Alex didn't understand.

"Vietnamese," he explained.

"What's the point?" she said.

Then she heard her own question played back in Spanish. *"¿Que significa?"* she heard her cloned voice asking.

Grant showed her the phone, which looked a bit like a BlackBerry. "For our soldiers and diplomats abroad. It can convert English to forty-five different languages, and vice versa. It can also translate written text, such as enemy documents, into written or spoken English."

Slowly an additional potential use dawned on Alex. "Can it translate typed English into spoken English and back?"

"Piece of cake."

"Need a beta tester?"

"Haven't you got a lot on your plate already? Murder, biowarfare, the D.C. music scene." When Grant had run into her in a club in Arlington at one of Luke's concerts, she got to utter the words that few thirtysomething M.D.'s say, "I'm with the band."

"Not me. It would be great for Lana, Barbara's daughter. She's deaf. It would let her stay in touch when she's away from home."

"Sure, what the hell, we've got a version, one iteration back, that has text-to-voice, but no translations. She's welcome to it."

Alex followed him back to his lab, where he rifled through a mass of computer chips and wires in a drawer, finally uncovering a sleek black phone. He handed it to Alex. "Barbara's daughter, is she cute?"

"For God's sake, Grant, she's fifteen."

He grinned. "It never hurts to ask."

BACK IN her laboratory, Alex realized she was at a dead end on the Gladden case. She turned her attention back to the library cart, and picked up the woman's skull. She wanted to get closer to her, to learn something about her.

Unlike her efforts to identify Gladden's assailant, she couldn't do standard DNA testing on the skull. The type of DNA her sequencer generally used was DNA from the nucleus of a cell like blood, saliva, or other tissue. That DNA—nucleic DNA—contained 30,000 genes, half inherited from each parent.

A skull could offer up another type of DNA, though. Mitochondrial DNA, inherited only from the mother, contained only 37 genes, which were responsible for powering the cells. In Argentina, geneticists had used mitochondrial DNA to identify the bones of protestors who had been killed by the military junta. The bones of the young, idealistic college students were returned to where they began life, to their mothers.

She scraped some bone from the inside of the skull and put it in an enzyme solution to break apart the DNA for sequencing. When she saw the *A*'s, *T*'s, *G*'s, and *C*'s of the woman's mitochondrial DNA, Alex felt better, like they had been formally introduced. This DNA was the first step to identifying the woman. All it would take would be to find one living relative from the mother's line—the mother herself, a grandmother, or the dead woman's brother or sister—and Alex could figure out who the skull belonged to.

Around 4:00 P.M., Alex's lack of sleep caught up with her. She realized she needed a break to clear her thoughts. She told Dan he could reach her on cell phone for the next two hours, then pointed her car toward Chevy Chase.

She dropped the T-Bird with the parking valet in the bowels of a newly built ten-story office building. The kid looked at the car with a certain lust. She could picture him taking it out on a spin, Ferris Bueller–style, while she was upstairs. "Don't leave town," she said. "I'll be at Carlisle and Sons for just a short time."

The elevator had a peach-colored marble floor and dark wood paneling. According to the building directory on the first floor, Carlisle's little venture was on the top floor of the building. Not bad for a high school dropout from West Virginia.

When she knocked on the Carlisle suite, a female voice told her to come in. Inside, an intense woman in her early forties with prematurely gray hair, stylishly cut, was speaking emphatically to a Fed Ex driver. She was emphasizing how important it was that the package arrive in Phnom Penh within two days.

Alex held back as she took stock of the woman. She'd pegged Carlisle for the type who'd have hot and cold running girls in his life and use his power to hire a Playmate of the Month to work for him. But this woman seemed competent and driven. Alex would have to watch herself. She was getting as bad as Troy Nguyen in making flash judgments about people with insufficient data.

"And you," the woman asked as the driver exited, "what's your business here?"

Alex held out Michael Carlisle's business card. "I'm here to see him."

The woman reached out to shake her hand. "You must be Alex," she said. "I'm Ellen Meyer."

She led Alex down the hall. They passed what must have been Michael's office. Alex could see a fancier wheelchair there, with a computer screen and keyboard attached. They kept walking to a twenty-by-thirty-foot room, with books on shelves starting at floor level up to about the height of Alex's head, putting all the books within reach of a man in a wheelchair. Michael welcomed Alex and introduced Ellen to her as his business partner.

"I had the good sense to hire her away from DuPont, where she was the Vice President for International Markets."

"And I had the momentary lapse of judgment to walk away from a great pension to this roller coaster ride of a job."

"Was it me or the miles? Admit it, you're having a great run here."

Ellen turned to Alex. "I spend a hundred and fifty days a year on the road. The last thing I want to do is take a free trip on my frequent flyer miles. But he's right, I love this job."

Alex scrutinized the way Ellen looked at her "partner" and wondered if she loved not just the job, but also the man.

When Ellen left them alone, Alex took a closer look at the shelves of books. The volumes on history, economics, and political philosophy looked like they'd been consulted many times. At least a dozen were open on the table at the moment.

"You're a surprising man, Mr. Carlisle," Alex said.

"Always worked to my advantage."

"Your house wasn't what I expected last night, and now this . . ."

He motioned her to sit in one of the comfortable chairs in front of the one wall without books, a floor-to-ceiling glass picture window. "You've been watching too many made-for-TV movies," he said. "Crazed Vietnam vet . . . ," he rolled his bare bones wheelchair around behind her and put his hands softly around her neck, ". . . mistakes beautiful doctor for Viet Cong and strangles her."

His hands released his mock choke hold, and, for just an instant, his fingers brushed the soft skin below her throat. Then he took his hands away and wheeled in front of her. "Vietnam Stress Syndrome. What bullshit."

She looked at his soft gold turtleneck under an expensive beige suit. He was an attractive man whose tanned face sported lines that made him seem interesting, rather than old. Robert Redford as a successful pillar of the venture capital community. Not, Alex tried to convince herself, a man who could massacre civilians in cold blood.

"I can't imagine being one of those vets holed up in rural Montana, off the grid," he continued. "I'm much too addicted to being in the heart of the action."

"Why'd you leave the military, then?"

Michael laughed. "I could do the same sorts of things privately for a lot better pay. At least until my accident."

"And why the business world now?"

His eyes twinkled. "Lets me wreak destruction on a larger scale. And on the corporate battlefield, it doesn't mean squat that my legs aren't what they used to be."

He nodded up at the shelves out of his reach, above the bookshelves. They were lined with what investment bankers called deal mementos—plaques and sculptures to commemorate major financial transactions in which companies were acquired or spit out. And Carlisle had quite a set of these souvenirs—tiny oil derricks, airplane fleets, silicone chips, even a miniature pint of Ben & Jerry's. He'd certainly been involved in some major corporate finagling.

"All you need is a toy train and you'd have a whole city."

"Actually, that's the deal we are working on now. Putting a train like the Tokyo–Kyoto bullet train on the run from Phnom Penh to Hanoi. Seems like everyone wants a piece of Vietnam these days. And to get it they have to go through someone who knows the ropes like me."

"If that's the case, sounds like the Americans won the war after all."

Carlisle smiled, then wheeled over to a shelf of political philosophy texts—Aristotle to Machiavelli—and moved a few volumes aside. He entered a few numbers on a keypad and opened a safe door with a flourish. Peering inside, Alex could see a revolver balanced on what looked like a passport, some small boxes of the type that usually held jewelry, a pile of cash, and a few thin manila folders. He rifled through the folders for a few moments and pulled out a photograph. After locking the safe again, he held the picture in front of his eyes, where he could look both at the photo and at the woman sitting beyond it.

"You look a lot like him," he said.

The wonders of recessive genes, she thought. She had her daddy's blond hair and pale skin, looking nothing like her gypsy-colored mom, whose grandmother Ava had emigrated from Hungary.

Michael Carlisle rolled his wheelchair closer to her and dropped the photo in her lap. She picked it up and stared at her father, whom she'd last seen three decades earlier. Memories flooded back. The times they'd quietly cooked pancakes for breakfast, sharing an hour or so before her mother woke up. The way he marveled at each new trick she showed him—a ballet pirouette, a firefly in a jar. She'd seen other photos of him, but never this one. She pored over it ravenously, trying to memorize every nuance. The way he was crouching, gun on the ground next to him. How the sun made his eyes squint, like they sometimes did when he was laughing. The way the man on the far right looked at him, with a combination of fear and respect. That man was Michael Carlisle.

Alex looked up at Michael. "What was he like?" she asked quietly.

He thought for a moment. "A decent guy. Which wasn't easy over there."

"Can I keep the photo?" Alex asked. "It would mean a lot to me."

A smile crossed his face. "Only if you agree to dinner next Friday."

Alex considered the invitation. There was so much more she wanted to ask about her father. "Fine, but my treat. What type of food do you like?"

"Anything but rice," the handsome man in the beige suit replied. "I had enough rice in Nam to last a dozen lifetimes."

CHAPTER FOURTEEN

BACK AT the AFIP, she stared at the photo of the twenty-five-year-old blond, her father, with his broad shoulders and his sparkly eyes. This was the man she'd adored as a child. It was odd to view him in frayed combat gear, with battle fatigues, a rifle, and dusty boots. In the middle of the jungle, with death around each bend, the spit and polish of boot camp had been replaced by a battered weariness. The squint in his eyes from the sun as he stared out of the photo made it seem like he was trying unsuccessfully to see Alex.

She sighed. That was pretty much the case. She still looked to him in her heart and imagination and he knew nothing of her. Unless, of course, you believed Troy's book, which described the way the spirits of our ancestors lived among us.

She gazed at the photo, wondering if she should forward a digital copy of it to her mother. Then she realized it might upset Janet too much. She would wait until she next saw her to broach the subject. She propped the picture up against a large bottle labeled "Thioglycollate Medium" on her laboratory shelf.

She took a step back. For her whole life, she'd looked up to him, even though he'd died when she was just in kindergarten. But this photo underscored what Wiatt had said: They were just boys.

As she waited for a page signaling a breakthrough in the

Gladden case, she returned to the library cart. She picked up another skull to work on. It hadn't stood out as much as the other skulls because it had been painted in light beiges and greens. Up close, Alex could see that the artist was quite talented. He'd forged a painting of a rice paddy in tiny Impressionist dots.

The skull radiated a different aura than the ones she'd cleaned previously. Whoever the GI was who'd decorated it, he'd done so with respect and a sense of honor. This skull never served as a candleholder or an ashtray. The painting seemed to speak to the ability to hold on to one's humanity, to find beauty, to move beyond the paralyzing fear of being a boy in a faraway war.

Around 9:00 P.M., Dan called to say the D.C. police had caught the guy who'd killed the other gay victim. "Drug deal gone south."

"Can we rule out a serial killer?"

"Yeah. D.C. cops linked it to Colombia and we're focusing on Vietnam."

Alex thanked him for keeping her in the loop, hung up, and wandered down to the snack machine to grab something to eat. Dr. Troy Nguyen was pulling a knob on it, causing the last bag of Cheetos to drop out of the slot.

"Shit," Alex said. "That was going to be my dinner."

He opened the bag and tipped it toward her. "Help yourself," he said.

She reached inside the bag and felt the crunchy orange flakes gather on her fingers, then popped a Cheeto into her mouth. "How come you're not at home having dinner with your family?" she asked.

He hesitated for a moment. "No family here."

She let that sink in. "What about your kid?"

"Huh?"

"Little League, the other night."

"Oh, that's a Big Brother thing I'm involved in, for the Vietnamese-American Youth League."

As he spoke, she reached into the bag, grabbing a handful of Cheetos.

"Here, take the rest of them," he said. "I don't want to be responsible for you passing out from hunger in your lab." He handed her the bag, but she hesitated. "Better yet," he said, "let me take you out for real food."

CHAPTER FIFTEEN

THE THAI King was jammed, mainly because few restaurants near the AFIP were open this late. As Alex and Troy waited in the bar, the news anchor on the wall-mounted television reported on the President's new policies to find other energy sources. But this initiative got less time on the air than did the exploits of the Vice President's wife. Apparently, Abby Shane had returned on her own to China, where she joined Lil, the daughter of Chinese president Wang Hui Yu, for a massive shopping spree in Shanghai. The anchorman spoke of Abby developing a maternal interest in the girl, but the photos showed a different story. She and Abby were exiting a boutique, laughing, in similar tight leather pants and designer pastel leather jackets. They were just a handful of years apart in age. The anchor concluded by saying the Second Lady had reached out to the youth of China and Shanghai, which, judging by the photos, consisted of heading to a number of discos with a crop of Chinese bad boys, all of whom had perfected the gesture of shielding their faces with their jackets when the camera approached, just like in a perp walk.

Alex sipped her second gin and tonic—a really bad idea, she realized, on a day with little sleep and even less food. She was beginning to feel a dizzy buzz.

On the adjoining stool, a college kid with earphones was

kicking the bar in time to the music, causing Troy's Samuel Adams beer to slosh in its mug. After forty-five minutes of waiting and no table in sight, Troy threw some tens on the bar, and grabbed Alex by the arm. "I've got a better idea," he said.

He walked her to his car and drove her ten minutes to a four-flat on a quiet side street. They climbed the stairs to the top floor. He offered her another gin and tonic, but she opted for a jasmine-scented tea from a delicate porcelain canister on the kitchen counter. He sat her on a stool on the dining room side of the kitchen pass-through, where she could watch him cook.

"This will just take a few minutes," he said. He'd planned to eat salmon that night, and didn't have enough for two. So he broiled it and mixed it into Soba noodles, sweet pea pods, and white corn. He tossed a salad with gooseberry dressing and served it to Alex in the dining room.

"God, this would be great even if I weren't starving," she said.

"I like to eat well, even if I'm alone," he said. "I'm sure it's from a childhood of never having enough."

Alex thought about it. She'd always had enough food, but there were huge gaps in other ways in her childhood. Sort of like a Norman Rockwell color-by-number painting, with only half of the numbers colored in.

She looked at a photo on the credenza behind Troy. A Vietnamese woman in her thirties and a young Amerasian toddler. The woman in the picture made her think about the shrouded lady. Wiatt certainly had closed off further discussion of that skull and the letter within it. She wondered if she should tell the colonel she'd spoken to Michael Carlisle, the man who brought the skull into the country. No, not yet, she thought. She needed time to assure herself of her father's innocence.

Troy followed her gaze and reached for the delicate bamboo frame. "This was my mother, when I was eight, the day I left Vietnam."

"She didn't come with you?"

He shook his head and a look of sadness turned down the

corners of his mouth. "Two years after my father died, my mother took comfort in an American soldier. Right before Saigon fell, she sent me to live with my uncle in Jakarta. He eventually moved me to the United States with him, to Minnesota. She never left Vietnam, kept waiting for her GI Joe to return."

His sadness turned to bitterness and he raised the pitch of his voice, mimicking his mother. "He promised he come back."

"I'm sorry."

He pointed to the girl in the photo. "My half sister, Lizzie."

Alex looked at her pale hair, her gangly long legs. Obviously the soldier's child. "Where's she now?"

"Well, the guy never came back for her, or for my mom. Lizzie's been trying to get to the United States for years."

"Child of an American, what's holding it up?"

"Well, there's no proof of that."

"Anyone can just look at her." Alex thought about the early paternity cases, in the 1800s, long before DNA testing could link a particular dad to his kid. They used to just hold a crying baby in the courtroom and figure out whether he looked like the accused dad. She bet a lot of bald, red-faced guys were erroneously held to owe child support.

"There's a loophole in the law," Troy said. "Any child of an American mother, no matter where in the world he or she is born, is a U.S. citizen. But the child of an American father is only a U.S. citizen if he acknowledges the child in a legal action."

"That doesn't seem fair."

"There's even a U.S. Supreme Court case on it. The dad was an American soldier stationed in Vietnam during the war. He brought the child to the United States when he was six to raise him. The boy got into trouble in his twenties and the U.S. immigration service deported him. It meant nothing that his father had raised him here for over a decade. Since the father hadn't *legally* acknowledged paternity under the federal statute, they were out of luck."

"There's got to be something you can do."

He shook his head. "It's really bad for Lizzie now. Everyone assumes all those cute little half-American kids got out after the war, on boats and planes. But there are hundreds of them in their thirties now who have no country at all. Vietnam doesn't want them. The U.S. shut its doors. For the past five years, since my mother died, she's lived in a displaced persons camp near the Chinese border. She's persona non grata—she's about a foot taller than most Vietnamese women and she's got tattoos and a stubborn streak, not exactly marriage material there. So she was dumped in a camp with few supplies, horrible sanitation. I can't tell you how many lawyers I've paid—here and in Vietnam—to try to rescue her. Nobody wants to try to overturn a U.S. Supreme Court case."

Alex thought of Barbara, who'd managed more than her share of legal miracles. "I may know just the person for you."

A flash of anger crossed his eyes. "That's such an *American* affectation. Thinking you can just fix something thousands of miles away." His voice silenced to almost a whisper. "My father believed in you, that the Americans meant to help the South Vietnamese. Look where it got him."

She followed his gaze to another photo. Her breath caught when she realized it was a photo of a run-down cemetery.

"We were lucky," he said. "We got his body back almost intact. Except where his face was blown off from a bullet through the skull. But the cemetery for Southerners, where his bones are interred, is completely in ruins. The widows of the soldiers in the North got pensions, beautiful burials in the Truong Son cemetery near Dong Ha in Quang Tri. Their husbands were *liet sy*, martyrs. My mother got nothing but derision. The families of the South Vietnamese, the people you Americans were supposedly trying to help, have been paying for your generosity ever since."

Alex looked down at her lap, then up at Troy. "I'm sorry. I don't know what to say."

Troy raised his voice. "This is why the Trophy Skulls are so important. You Americans don't give a moment's thought to the war anymore, except when there is some embarrassment for one of your political candidates. Did he serve or duck the draft? Did he shoot a few gook women and children on the way to becoming a decorated war hero? In Vietnam today, the most-watched television show is a thirty-minute program that tells what is known about the final days of Vietnamese MIAs—to help their relatives find their bones.

"The dead are members of the family. We worship them each day and offer paper replicas of things that they need in the afterlife—it could be clothes, a washing machine, a piano, anything. If a person's death date is unknown, or their bones cannot be found, their souls wander aimlessly and they can't be taken care of properly."

Alex looked again at the cemetery photo and noticed that next to it was a white paper cutout of a house. "This represents a home for your father?"

He nodded and she looked at it more closely. "Why is the paper folded up on all the windows?"

He shifted in his chair, then put his hands serenely on the table in front of him. "That is how Vietnam views itself, as a house with all the windows open. We have been attacked by outsiders for a thousand years—the Chinese, the French, the Cambodians, the Americans. But we held firm in our culture and our beliefs. All those outsiders were nothing more than ill winds that blew into our house and then out the other side."

Alex thought about her father's death and wondered what she would offer to him. It tugged at her heart to realize how little she knew of him, except for his love for her. Did he have hobbies? Did he like to read? All that the five-year-old Alex had known about his life took place in the warm circle of his arms around her small body.

Alex realized that Troy was staring at her, waiting for her to speak. She pulled herself out of the cloud of memories. "And you," she said, "what cutout would you want offered to make your afterlife easier?"

He answered without hesitation. "A motorcycle. I've always wanted to try one."

His comment broke the tension. They rose to clear the plates and Alex offered to wash the dishes.

"No, thank you," he said. "I'll drive you back now. You have important work to do on the bones of my countrymen."

Alex wondered, Can the dead become more important than the living? Here Troy was turning away her offer to help his sister, but pressing her to help identify some strangers' skulls. She thanked him for the dinner and then they drove back in silence to the AFIP.

CHAPTER SIXTEEN

THE NEXT morning, Alex rolled over in bed and reached for Luke. When she touched an empty pillow, she opened her eyes with a start and remembered that he was three thousand miles away.

She eased herself out of bed and put on an oversized man's robe, which hung loose even on her five-foot-seven frame. She padded into her home office, opened a desk drawer, pulled out the handwritten note from Luke, and began to dial the London phone number on it.

A message machine clicked into service on the other end. "'Ey, mates!" the voice said. "We're the Tuttles. Leave us your thoughts on our latest song." A guitar swelled under the voice and other singers joined in. She listened to the first stanza and realized that Luke's voice was not on this particular track. She kept the line open for a second stanza and then felt silly paying transatlantic rates to listen to bad rock. She'd call back some other time to try for a live Luke.

As she got dressed, the morning news showed the latest in what Alex was dubbing Abbygate. Apparently, day two of Abby's Chinese visit was going to be much different. Visits to hospitals, watching a school play at a junior high. The Administration had clipped her wings big-time. But they hadn't cut her off from her new friend. She'd invited the Chinese president's daughter, Lil, to the White House for the tree-lighting ceremony the following week.

AT THEIR 10:00 A.M. meeting, Dan told his team what he'd learned from the president of Westport Oil. "The Vietnamese government is going to sell exploration rights to an oil field in the Phu Khanh basin off their southern coast," he said. "In 2006, when they did that with the fields off the northeast coast, six companies put together a joint venture that scored over a billion barrels."

Grant whistled under his breath. "Way to fuck the camel jockeys."

Dan nodded. "Ron Gladden was supposed to have an inside track on information about the new oil field's potential so Westport could circumvent the option phase and make an outright offer for drilling rights. That way the company would scoop Shell, British Petroleum, and the governments of China and Holland. Small company like them might have ridden away with a major haul. But Gladden was the only guy who had information on the report. The company paid Ernst and Young a two-million-dollar retainer and—poof!—their report went up in smoke when their guy got killed."

"He must have given them some preliminary stuff by phone or e-mail," Chuck said.

"Nope. E-mail from Vietnam isn't safe. Too many government snoops on their end. Plus, it's unreliable. Government closed it down entirely for months earlier this year."

"What about backups on his office computer?" Chuck asked. "I could check the hard drive if you get them to send it to me."

"Once Gladden was posted back to the United States, they wiped the drive clean for the new guy."

The break-in at Gladden's was starting to make more sense to Alex. The upended briefcase, the missing hard drive. The killer had probably been after that report.

"The trail's pulling us to Nam," Dan said. "We can catch a Navy transport plane to the Philippines this evening, with a charter to Ho Chi Minh City. Who's up-to-date on vaccinations?"

Alex knew Dan was. He'd often celebrate the close of a case by jetting off to whatever backwater country his photojournalist wife was working in. Famine in Biafra. A revolutionary leader in Ecuador. The latest Nobel Peace Prize winner in the Sudan.

"Not me." Chuck shook his head with a sense of loss. This could have been a big break for him, trailing leads outside the United States.

Grant answered in the negative as well, but with a blanched look that big men sometimes got at the thought of needles.

"Shit, guys," Dan said. "Didn't you join the service to see the world?"

Slowly an idea formed in Alex's mind. She raised her hand. "I can go. With my infectious disease work, I've taken every vaccine in the book. Even if Chuck and Grant got their shots today, it would be a week before the vaccinations took effect."

Dan blew out a deep breath, a semiwhistle, while he contemplated the pros and cons of taking Alex along. "You're not trained for this," he said.

"I can at least sit in on the interviews you do and verify what went down if it later goes to trial." Then again, she thought, maybe it was better if Dan's interrogations took place without a witness. He had a reputation for unorthodox tactics. "Plus I've got some business with the skulls that would be better handled over there. I'll need maybe an afternoon there to deal with that."

"Okay," Dan said. "But one whiff of danger, and you're back at the hotel or on the next plane home, get it?"

Grant shot Alex a bemused look. See, it seemed to say, you're just a girl.

"Dan," Alex said, "I work with toxins every day where, one wrong move, one mix-up in vials, one pinprick-sized hole in my gloves, and I'm a dead woman."

"Yeah, Alex, that's your business. But I'm not going to have you die on my watch."

Before she went home to pack, she stopped in room 160.

"I might be able to identify one of the skulls," she told Troy.

His usually serious face brightened. "How?"

"I'm pretty sure it's from a village west of Qui Nhon. And I was able to get some mitochondrial DNA from the bones."

"So you can trace the maternal line?"

Alex nodded.

"What makes you think you can find the mother?" he asked. "There will be so many who lost their sons, even in a relatively small geographic area."

"This skull is different. It's a woman's."

Alex read the shock on Troy's face.

"Listen," she said, "I don't want to provoke some sort of international incident. We need to find a way for me to collect relatives' DNA in Vietnam without blabbing to the world that we've got a woman's skull here."

Troy's eyes widened. "You're going over there?"

She nodded.

"We could solicit the blood on the weekly MIA show in Vietnam."

Alex was vehement. "Way too public."

Troy thought for a moment. "I know a lawyer, Mr. Kang, from that province. He tried to help me get Lizzie out. His brother's a doctor."

Alex nodded. "That's good."

"West of Qui Nhon, you said?"

"Yes, two hours walking."

Troy opened a drawer and unfolded a map. "About here. Probably around Lo Duoc." He pointed to an area slightly inland from the sea, then looked up. "Do you have any idea how old the mother might be by now?"

Judging by the woman's back teeth and the strength of her

skull bone, she was in her early twenties. Assuming her mother was between fifteen and forty when she gave birth, in the 1950s, she'd be anywhere from seventy to ninety-five years old. "Seventy or older," Alex said, "but, if the mother isn't alive, another of her children would do. They'd all have the same mitochondria."

Troy was excited. "I'll call Kang at home right away. It's eleven at night, but I might be able to rouse him."

He refolded the map and gave it to her. "Take this. I appreciate your caring about the spirits."

She felt guilty as she left the room, map in hand. Finding out more about the shrouded skull was only part of the motive for the trip to Vietnam.

Alex left Troy's office hoping that she was doing the right thing. She felt a sense of kinship and responsibility as the caretaker of the young woman's skull. But she didn't want to open a diplomatic wound that would be impos-sible to heal—or learn things about her dad that were better left in the shadows.

CHAPTER SEVENTEEN

ALEX HAD never been on a military transport plane before, and she'd been prepared for a small, rusty jet like something out of an old movie, particularly when Dan had referred to the aircraft as a C-40A Navy clipper. When it came time to board, she was surprised that it looked like a familiar Boeing 737 reconfigured to carry more cargo than passengers. The supplies and equipment the plane was carrying, she learned from Dan, were for a project initiated by President Cotter. In 1992, the United States had closed its Subic Bay Navy Base in the Philippines, a base the size of the San Francisco Bay area. After nearly a century occupying that base, the military had left behind unexploded ordnances, chemicals, petroleum supplies, and hazardous wastes. Soon after taking office, Cotter had spurred a joint U.S.-Philippine Task Force to clean the base up. The four other passengers on board—sitting a good dozen rows away from Dan and Alex—were the former base commander, a senior official from the Army Corps of Engineers, and two researchers from the Environmental Protection Agency.

Dan sat on the aisle and Alex sat next to the window. While the plane was waiting on the runway, he was leafing through a pile of annual reports from Westport Oil. A routing slip showed that the Securities and Exchange Commission had messengered them over. One thing she had to say about working for a federal agency—it was amazingly easy to get information from other branches of government. Big Brother definitely was not only watching, but gossiping to its siblings.

"I don't think of West Virginia as an oil company hotbed," Alex remarked.

"Think again," Dan said, handing her the 1999 annual report. The cover showed an 1869 stock certificate from the Ritchie Mineral Resin and Oil Company of West Virginia.

As she flipped through the report, she saw a photo of a younger Tommy Shane, trial attorney. Dan looked over her shoulder. "According to Westport Oil's president, Shane's been on the board for years. Had to put his stock in a trust since he assumed office. Something about federal laws on conflict of interest."

She flipped a few pages further and stopped at another photo. It showed the Westport Oil president talking to an attractive secretary at a desk. "Is that Abby Shane?" she asked. She wasn't sure since the woman in the photo looked too young.

Dan nodded. "Way before she was a Shane. Bennett Anderson—the guy who runs Westport—told me she's smarter than she looks. Smart enough that, after a little over a year at the company, she sweet-talked one of our board members, the program director of the CBS affiliate down there, into giving her a stint as a weather girl."

First CBS. Then Shane. So Abby climbed the ladder of success one board member at a time, Alex thought.

"How'd Westport Oil decide to do business in Vietnam in the first place?" Alex asked. "From what that Ernst and Young guy said when you called him in Ho Chi Minh City, it's not easy."

"Anderson went over with Shane on an MIA trip when Shane was governor. His wife's uncle was among the missing."

The takeoff was slightly rocky, but as soon as the plane leveled off, Alex took off her jacket and placed it against the window. She wanted to sleep as much as she could on the flight so she'd be alert when she landed. She drifted off easily, and came to when Dan shook her shoulder.

She opened her eyes in surprise, not comprehending her surroundings. The men in the back of the plane were staring at her.

"You cried out," Dan said. "Some sort of nightmare."

Alex thought about where her unconscious had taken her. "I was dreaming of spiders, rats, and Mr. Glover."

"Mr. Glover?"

Alex shook her head. "He was the principal of my grammar school in Cleveland."

Dan laughed. "What's so scary about him?"

Alex thought back to her kindergarten year. "The way he looked and spoke. My mother described it to her friends as 'Alfred Hitchcock without the warmth.'"

"Now that you're up, do you want some food?"

She shook her head. Her dream involved everything that had scared her most when she was five years old. She had regressed back to the time her father had died in Vietnam.

She closed her eyes again, to ward off further interactions with Dan while she explored her feelings. She thought of the plane that had taken her father to Vietnam on his first tour of duty, back in 1971. Just twenty-four years old, younger than Alex was now, he'd been sent off to the jungle. Like so many men of his generation, it was the first time he'd left the country. He'd been forced to say good-bye to a young wife and his one-year-old baby. Was he scared? Pumped?

He'd already been in the military a few years by then. Maybe on the flight he'd joked and played cards with the younger men, hoping to ease their fear. Maybe they spoke of their girlfriends or families back home. Maybe they silently prayed. As at so many other times in her life, Alex felt an empty wave roll through her. So much she wanted to ask her father, but never could.

She opened her eyes and unfolded the map of Vietnam Troy had given her. She drew on it with blue and red pencils, in a formation that looked like a children's connect-the-dots game. The blue dots represented every place her father's unit had traveled in Vietnam, the red dots, Michael Carlisle's earlier units.

When she first discovered the letter in the skull, she had no idea where the incident had taken place. But after seeing the description on the War Crimes Web site, she was fairly sure it had taken place outside of Qui Nhon, in the village of Lo Duoc.

Alex's chest was tight and she realized she'd been holding her breath as she tracked the two men's movements. She breathed in deeply, with relief, when she saw that neither had ever been stationed near Lo Duoc.

In response to her sigh, Dan looked up from his reading and saw the paths she had drawn on the map. "You planning a bigger tour of Vietnam than you told me?"

"No, I'm just tracing the route my father took when he was there." She pointed to the blue route. "He spent a few days in Ho Chi Minh City, but never went to Lo Duoc, where I'll be collecting blood."

Dan glanced at her map. "War isn't exactly like an American Express tour. Those copters flew all over. Plus, the whole damn country is only the size of New Mexico. The distance from one place to another just isn't that great. Your dad could easily have gone to Lo Duoc."

CHAPTER EIGHTEEN

THEIR SECOND plane landed at Tan Son Nhut airport, on the northwest edge of what used to be called Saigon. In the late 1960s, it was the busiest airport in the world in terms of the takeoffs and landings. As the plane set down, Dan took Alex's hand and said a soft prayer for Alex's father and his fellow soldiers who'd died in that part of the world. His action surprised Alex. Dan wasn't at all religious and he was too young to have served there. He'd been deployed as a well-decorated Marine in the Gulf. But the deaths during the Vietnam War loomed over even today's generation of soldiers.

They'd arrived after twenty-six hours of air travel. It was 9:00 P.M. Sunday by Alex's body clock, but 10:00 A.M. Monday local time. In the streets of Ho Chi Minh City, Alex was shocked by the dizzying throngs of people riding motorbikes, perilously crisscrossing in front of each other. She chided herself for how little she knew about a country that loomed so large in her life. When she heard "Vietnam," she thought "jungle." Instead, she was in a thick diesel fuel–drenched motorcycle equivalent of the Indy 500.

They dropped their bags at the Majestic Hotel—along with Alex's liquid nitrogen tanks to bring back the DNA—and then, after showers and breakfast, took a cab to the Ernst & Young branch in Ho Chi Minh City.

When Gregory Ramsey escorted them into his private office, Dan laid out what he'd learned from Anderson. "I need to know what would happen with an oil deal on this end. Who decides on drilling rights?"

"The last big deal, it was the Vietnamese Minister of the Interior, Huu Duoc Chugai."

"What do you know about him?"

"Odd guy. Fairly big in the Communist Party, but he went over to the U.S. for an MBA from Harvard. Came back and ran his Ministry like a Fortune 500 company, handpicked his successor, then moved over to the Qui Hoc."

"The what?" asked Dan.

"The National Assembly—their equivalent of Congress. Chugai's still got a lot of sway at the Ministry, and now politics figures more strongly in the mix. He's aiming to be elected president next July, challenging the favorite son, an Assembly member favored by the current president."

"When will they decide on the Phu Khanh basin deal?"

"Next week. Our ass is on the line unless that missing report shows up soon."

Alex looked at Ramsey. "Isn't it odd to have just one copy of something so important?"

He shook his head. "Corporate espionage beats tourism as the fastest-growing sector of the economy here. We never copy sensitive documents. Obviously we weren't planning on our guy ending up dead."

When Dan asked him about Gladden's personal life, he passed them on to the Vietnamese receptionist. According to her, Gladden typically had a late dinner at Blue Ginger, an expat friendly restaurant in a former journalists' club. The restaurant had banished pumpkin soup from the menu; that was the main dish served to American POWs during the Vietnam War. Gladden would work late, then go over to the extravagantly decorated restaurant, eat seared tuna, and listen to live music.

He hardly ever broke that habit, but once the receptionist had seen him in an unusual spot. She was walking to the opera and, on a side street two blocks behind the opera house, she'd noticed the tall blond Gladden sticking out among the dark men on the crowded street of cheap restaurants that served dishes like sparrow and steamed silkworms. She was about to call out to him when a Chinese man swept toward him, took him sharply by the elbow, and pushed him into a restaurant, as if he was trying to keep them out of view. She was worried for Gladden in that neighborhood and was relieved when he showed up at work the next day.

"Did the man seem like a lover?" Dan had asked her.

She looked confused. "No, he showed no fondness toward Mr. Gladden."

"Did Gladden seem worried the next day when he came to work?"

"No. In fact, he seemed . . ." She searched for the right word. "He seemed proud."

The receptionist gave him the name of the restaurant that Gladden had disappeared into. Xiao Xiong. Dan asked if he could use a scanner, computer, and printer for a few minutes. She was shy and uncertain at first, but he said it would help in tracking down Gladden's killer.

He would follow up on the restaurant while Alex went to Lo Duoc. Perhaps there was more cooking at Xiao Xiong than steamed silkworms.

CHAPTER NINETEEN

WHEN ALEX landed at the Qui Nhon airport, Dr. Kang met her in a wheezy old Jeep. They could hardly carry on a conversation over the noise of the carburetor and fan belt as they traveled down the pocked roads to Lo Duoc. When Kang swung widely to avoid a hole in the road from a wartime mortar blast, Alex grabbed frantically for the liquid nitrogen tank in the back, steadying it so it wouldn't bounce out of the Jeep.

With her mother's nomadic life, Alex was familiar with the rhythms and odors of dozens of cities and towns, but the village of Lo Duoc was nothing like the places she knew. The smells were still close to the land, voluptuous plant scents, whiffs of emotion from the sweat and strains of the passersby.

Kang had arranged for Alex to collect blood from families whose daughters, mothers, or sisters had gone missing around Lo Duoc during the war. Scores of them lined up to be pricked by Alex. She was humbled by their dignity as even the young children ambled up to her, stuck out their arms, and, without a sound, turned over their lifeblood. She chastised herself for coming here only to take, with nothing to give. There were pregnant teenagers here, whose bellies protruded over sadly scrawny legs. She should have brought them vitamins. A man with a fever raised his arm for her, but was so dehydrated that her needle couldn't find fluid in his body. His leg was infected from a farming accident. What had she been thinking to come here without antibiotics?

Dr. Kang noticed the concern in her eyes. "We don't know where to begin. The people need so much and the health care is so sparse." His English was good. From 1963 until 1975, a New Zealand surgical team had treated civilians in the provincial hospital in Qui Nhon. Kang had been fascinated by them as a young boy, and after medical school in Vietnam he'd gained a New Zealand internship.

"I feel ashamed not to have brought drugs or supplies to help you," she said. She opened her kit. She and Dan had both been issued malaria pills, one bottle of antibiotics, and—in case an emergency brought them to a hospital in Vietnam—clean needles so they wouldn't risk hepatitis or AIDS from the needles that were reused from patient to patient. She showed Kang what was in it and then gave it to him.

He solemnly nodded thanks.

Since he'd lived in this area during the war, she longed to ask him if he knew anything about a nearby massacre. A moment came when they paused to rest in the shade and quench their thirst. Alex had brought a chicken sandwich and some banana chips from the hotel, but didn't feel right eating it in front of the malnourished crowd. She had slipped her lunch to one of the pregnant girls, urging her to get enough nutrition while the baby grew inside her.

An older man had proudly given Kang a piece of goat cheese. He'd brought the goat to the blood draw to show her off. In the shade, Kang shared the cheese with Alex, then cut into a large spiky fruit and offered Alex some of the yellow pulp he scooped out. She wrinkled her nose at the odor, but it tasted as sweet as ice cream.

"*Durian* fruit," he said. "We have a saying, 'Smell like toilet, taste like heaven.'"

Alex smiled and licked the last bit of the pulp off her fingers. "I thank you for your kindness," she told Kang. A deep breath, then she continued, "You've lived through many tragedies with the Americans, no?"

He nodded.

"I am told there was perhaps an incident where innocent people were killed, not far from here."

Kang's eyes turned into tiny dots. "People do not go there anymore. The spirits are too angry and no crops will grow on that spot."

"What do you know of it?"

"We were living in Qui Nhon and refugees from that village and others were pouring in. My mother died shortly after that and, in my dreams, I sometimes confuse her death, in our home, with the killings there."

"That must have been terrible for everyone. How old were you when it happened?"

"It was 1969. I was fourteen."

Alex breathed a quiet sigh of relief. Nineteen sixty-nine was a full two years before her father ever came to Vietnam.

Kang seemed lost in thought. Alex looked at the rolling fields of a rice paddy off in the distance. She had lost her father in Vietnam thirty years ago and again, this week, when she read the letter and began to doubt him. But here today, she had gained her father back.

CHAPTER TWENTY

THAT NIGHT, Alex met Dan at a riverside restaurant back in Ho Chi Minh City. Her uniform of black turtleneck and jeans had no place in this tropical climate, so when she'd arrived back from Lo Duoc she'd bought a white dress with a soft, draping neckline. For about four dollars more, the shopkeeper had thrown in a pair of graceful leather sandals.

"You look amazing," Dan said.

She knew it was not just the dress but the cloud that had been lifted. Now everything around her seemed doubly vibrant. Her nostrils were tickled by smells of fish she couldn't identify. She wanted to rush down to the dock and leap on one of the covered wooden boats or dash into the street and pedal a bicycle cab.

It was all she could do to contain herself and pay attention to Dan's description of what had happened that afternoon. He'd made his way to the Xiao Xiong restaurant with a stack of flyers with photos of Gladden, thinking a Chinese man and a blond might have stood out. But there wasn't a Vietnamese person in sight. The entire restaurant was filled with Chinese men in their twenties and thirties. The man behind the bar said he didn't recognize the photo, but he seemed nervous and kept looking out of the corner of his eye at a large man surrounded by others at a corner table.

Dan had moved toward the hulking man. The other men at the table stopped eating and looked to him for direction. Their leader clapped his hands in front of him, indicating that they should all settle down. He took the photo from Dan's hand and, without looking at it, said, "I've never seen him."

"That's funny," Dan said. "I heard he was your boyfriend."

One of the men at the table stood up and threw a punch at Dan. The Marine sidestepped it and the hulk said something to his henchman in Chinese. The guy sat back down, fuming.

"What happened to the man in the photo?" the leader asked.

"He was murdered," Dan said.

"Southeast Asia can be a dangerous place for Americans. I thought they'd learned that."

Dan turned away from the man and started passing out flyers to the other customers, pointing out the international toll free number on the bottom. "No questions asked if anyone calls with information about the guy. Who knows?" He looked around the room and rubbed his fingers together like he was touching money. "It just might be worth your while."

When Dan had paid his tab, the bartender had looked him straight in the eye when he handed him his change. Dan then added an American twenty-dollar bill to the tip.

Dan told Alex, "Two blocks from the bar, I looked at the bills he'd given me in change."

He handed Alex a five-thousand-dollar dong note. On it, the bartender had written: "Ly Chinh. Phu Khanh."

"Is Ly Chinh a person? Someone related to the drilling project?" Alex asked.

"That's what I thought at first, but it turns out that it's a bar. A bar where a murder took place a few days before Gladden came back to the States. We've got an appointment with a local cop there tomorrow. He wouldn't say much over the phone, other than that the killer hasn't been found yet."

Their food arrived and Dan asked Alex how her project had gone that afternoon. "Great," she said, thinking about her father. Then she added, "I'm hoping that when I get back to my lab, I'll be able to link one of the families to a skull."

THE NEXT day, Dan and Alex took a small plane to a run-down landing strip in the Phu Khanh province, then a bus to the harbor near the offshore oil field that Westport Oil had planned to bid on. The bar and police station were both within a mile of the harbor. Dan and Alex began walking to the address that Inspector Ngoc Heip had given Dan. The men smoking and sneering along the way looked like they ran these streets. Dan unconsciously patted under his arm where he usually wore his holster. But of course, his Beretta wasn't there. A visit to some accountants hadn't warranted all the paperwork for taking a gun through customs.

The grimy men who were scoping him out showed a little more respect after he'd patted his jacket. They didn't realize that he wasn't packing. But they started swarming together in a larger group. Alex began to consider how she and Dan might repel these scaggy men. Dan put a protective arm around her, ready to firmly push her in whatever direction was most safe.

A couple stumbled out of a bar a half block away, catching the men's attention. Perhaps that couple looked like easier pickings or maybe they were deterred by Dan's "gun."

"They're like cockroaches in New York," Dan said to Alex. "No matter how hard my mother cleaned our Brooklyn apartment, those glistening brown blobs would skitter across the floor. In some places, it's not so easy to get rid of the vermin."

Alex followed Dan into a run-down wooden building that matched the address Inspector Ngoc Heip had given him. The inspector kept them cooling their jets in the reception area, sitting on a wooden bench. A cop behind the desk pretended to know no English, but Alex could see that he had a British law enforcement manual on his desk.

The inspector came out a half hour later. He saw that Dan was in his forties, like he was, too young to have fought in the war. That seemed to break the initial hostility that Ngoc Heip had expressed over the phone. But Alex's presence seemed to make him uncomfortable.

"And what is your interest in a barroom brawl in some run-down port city?" Heip said in formal, British-accented English.

"We're investigating a murder in the U.S. that could link to the murder in the bar," Dan said.

"I find that highly unlikely."

"Humor us," Dan said.

Heip walked over to a file cabinet and pulled out a file. He kept it close to his body as he looked inside. "What exactly do you want to know?"

"Our guy—an American—may have been killed as an act of vengeance. He left Vietnam a few days after your murder. We're trying to find a connection."

Heip showed a photo to Dan. "This might be too much for the young lady."

Alex tensed. "I'm a doctor."

"Suit yourself," Heip said, shoving the photo in front of her face.

Not a Vietnamese man, as she'd expected. A Brit, whose face had been beaten to a pulp, blood soaking down over a white oxford cloth shirt.

"What was he doing here?" Alex asked.

Heip shuffled through some pages of the file. "Cameron Alistair. Geologist on some sort of assignment."

Alex turned to Dan. "Are you thinking maybe Gladden killed him?"

Heip chortled. "A Chinese man killed him. We haven't found him. But these alcohol-fueled spats happen all the time."

"This Alistair character doesn't strike me as a big drinker," Alex said. His face had none of the signs of chronic alcoholism.

Heip looked into the file and grudgingly agreed. "Bartender said he just had two beers."

"Who threw the first punch?" Dan asked.

"Ly Chinh isn't the sort of place where anybody admits to noticing anything. Most everyone had scattered by the time we got there. Bartender claimed he was in the back getting more glasses when the fight broke out. Came back out when he heard the crash, saw a Chinese guy run out with the dead man's overcoat."

Dan thought for a moment. "His coat?"

Heip looked at the frayed raincoat that Dan was wearing. "It was an old overcoat, the bartender said. Probably not any better than yours. I'm not sure why he'd want it."

"Did DNA tests tell you anything about the killer?" Alex asked.

Heip chortled. "You're as much a dreamer as Officer Duoc here." He nodded over to the man at the front desk, who was avidly reading the British forensics book. "We've barely got money for guns, let alone lab equipment. Unless someone gets killed right in front of us, our investigations pretty much go nowhere. We're paper pushers most of the time. Send the reports of the crime on to the Central Party. Shoot a few—how do you say it?—villains if we can catch them in the act."

"What about a search of Alistair's apartment?" Dan asked.

Another laugh. "It had already been rerented. Mr. Alistair was due to fly home to Cambridge that night. His work here was over."

"Surely you must have some lead," Alex said.

"The assailant was Chinese. That means we've narrowed it down to one of the 84,000 Chinese who live in Vietnam— unless, of course, he was a Chinese tourist."

This was not leading anywhere, Alex thought. Dan must have agreed, because the next minute he was thanking the inspector and they were back out on the street.

Back at the port, Dan called the receptionist at Ernst & Young. When he hung up, he said, "Gladden met with Cameron Alistair about Westport Oil earlier in the day that Alistair was killed."

"Where do we go next?"

"Home. I'll get a Chinese-American MP from the Philippines to track down leads at the restaurant in Ho Chi Minh City. We can pick up the trail back in the U.S."

CHAPTER TWENTY-ONE

BY THE time they landed back at the Norfolk Navy Base, it was 8:00 A.M. Friday. Dan told Alex to go straight home, but she headed to her lab instead.

Once there, she opened the liquid nitrogen tank, waving aside the vapor as she used tongs to transfer the samples to a tank in her lab. Troy dropped off tea and some spring rolls. "I want you to be able to concentrate on the blood and not leave your lab," he said.

"Well, then, let me get started."

On his way out of the lab, Troy stopped to look at the woman's skull, which was resting on its side.

Troy noticed the jagged neck area, where the bones had been broken. He said nothing when he left, but his eyes turned to angry slits.

He disappeared before Alex could react. She wasn't sure how anyone could make things right with the woman's family. But she was convinced that the first step was to analyze the samples in the tank. Since the massacre had occurred in 1969, and the woman was dead by that time, she only analyzed blood from families whose daughters had gone missing by that date. By noon, she'd worked her way through twenty families without a match. She was beginning to feel like a bit of a dolt. Had she gotten dozens of people's hopes up for nothing?

She looked at the woman's skull overseeing her activity. She took another sample from the tank, used the Gentra machine to pull DNA out of it, then began to coax out the sequence of the sample's DNA. While the sequencer ran, spurting out a chain of chemical letters one by one, like the beads of a necklace, she logged the family's name and address into her computer. The sample had been donated by a missing woman's mother, Binh Trang. She returned to the sequencer just as it was finishing its run.

The squat machine, like a silent square Buddha, had smiled with favor on this sample. The mitochondrial DNA was a match to the woman's skull.

Alex felt proud of herself. She'd identified the skull within Wiatt's ridiculous timetable. The White House could arrange for the woman's family to attend the handoff.

She called Wiatt, then Troy. Troy picked up on the first ring. The excitement in Alex's voice when she said his name conveyed the discovery even before she began to speak.

"I'll be right there," he said.

THE TIME was midnight in Vietnam. Troy made the call. He may not have had training as a grief counselor, but he knew that telling Binh Trang that she would be getting her daughter back would help lift some of the darkness of grief the woman had felt for more than three decades. Troy covered the receiver and filled Alex in while the woman continued to talk to him. "She says she always knew she'd get her daughter back. The mother's name, in Vietnamese, means peace."

Troy went back to his conversation. Alex couldn't tell what he was saying.

She watched him closely as he spoke. He was ecstatic about being able to make this call. But then his voice became hushed. Even though he was speaking in Vietnamese, Alex sensed disbelief in the expression on his face.

When he hung up the phone, Troy was quiet. "I had thought one of the American soldiers did this to her," he said, pointing to the ridges on the bottom of the skull. "I apologize for thinking that. She hung herself."

Alex, too, had leapt to the wrong conclusion.

Troy continued, "Before she could be properly buried, fighting broke out in the area, and when her family was able to return, the body's head was missing."

Alex felt odd accepting Troy's apology. Maybe the young woman's death wasn't caused by the soldiers. But the letter inside her skull was evidence of an incident of destruction on an even larger scale. And identifying the skull was the first step for Alex in identifying the soldiers who may have killed innocent citizens.

AFTER HER success with the skull, Alex felt emboldened to try her hand at another problem. She visited Barbara's office to ask how Troy's sister Lizzie might immigrate to the United States.

"Sounds like you've reached a détente with the annoying psychiatrist," Barbara said.

"It's less about Troy than it is about his sister. I know what it's like to grow up without a father." As does Lana, Alex thought, but she didn't want to offend her friend by saying that.

"How about dinner with Lana and me tonight?" Barbara asked.

"I've got plans."

Barbara raised her eyebrows. "Plans you haven't discussed with Mama Findlay here? Business or pleasure?"

Alex thought for a moment. "Both, I guess."

Then she headed home for a much-needed nap before her dinner.

CHAPTER TWENTY-TWO

FINDING A nonrice restaurant for Michael Carlisle was more difficult than she'd expected. Cuban ones had black beans and rice. Italian ones were riding the risotto wave. Japanese, forget it—even the sushi came atop rice. Southern food had jambalaya.

Alex finally settled on the trendy Fare Restaurant, which boasted high-end American food—burgers with foie gras, club sandwiches of filet mignon and lobster. The décor was interesting—contemporary video art, wide spaces. Enough going on there to keep the conversation moving, but accessible for a guy in a wheelchair. As if Michael needed accessibility. He struck her as the kind who would wheel his chair up over a table like an all-terrain vehicle rather than be deterred from going where he wanted.

He'd arrived early and managed to snag the best table, one that was farthest from the others, in its own enclave. On the wall across from him was a towering video of a lipsticked blonde seemingly conversing with a video version of a kindly looking older man on the wall behind Michael. Alex sat down and he pointed to four buttons on their table. Two allowed you to change the features on the man or woman; the other allowed you to change their mood. Imploring woman and haughty man. Violent woman and angry man. Erotic woman and uncertain man.

"In case we run out of things to say?" Alex asked.

He leaned forward in his wheelchair. "Somehow I don't think men get bored around you."

"Actually my boss was expressing that very sentiment last week. He's longing for the years B.A. Before Alex."

"What did you do, clone a sheep?"

The wine steward walked their way. Like all the employees, he was wearing a bowling shirt with decals from an American state on it. His was Texas, with lassos threaded across his chest. He brought a silver tray with a bottle of amber liquid and two crystal glasses.

"You ordered?" Alex asked.

"Saw a twenty-year-old bourbon on the menu."

Mr. Texas poured two glasses, and Michael raised his in a toast. "Here's to the skull that brought us together," he said. "May he rest in peace."

"It's not a he."

Michael seemed surprised. He whistled under his breath. "What a fucked-up war."

She nodded. "Actually, a lot's happened since I saw you last. I went to Lo Duoc."

She looked at him for a response, some fear or guilt. But instead, he smiled. "Now that you've seen the country, maybe you can understand why I go back every chance I get."

She thought of the rice paddies and water buffalo in the countryside, the vibrant smells, the abundant plants.

"There's an elegant rhythm to it," he continued. "Practically everyone gets by on less than a dollar a day. They live off the land, live in the country where most people have never used a flush toilet. Truth is, I've learned I don't need to live in a place where I can buy thirty brands of deodorant."

"Don't your trips remind you of," she struggled, not able to directly address the war, "of your first time there?"

"When I think back, what I try to remember most is women in slim boats and white dresses collecting armfuls of lotuses growing in the shallow waters. Seeing them purifies those other memories, the jagged ones that appear without warning. Like a pile of bodies from a bombing of my first squadron. My buddy Andy and I pulled them all in a row and then covered each of them with a tarp, thinking we were honoring them. But it made them seem so anonymous. Identical lumps with their feet sticking out from under the tarp. 'Cept for a guy who'd had his left leg blown off. I can still see his one boot, the right one, sticking out."

Alex shuddered at that unsettling image. Then the waitress arrived in a bowling shirt with Colorado on it. She locked in on Michael and bent slightly so that he could see the cleavage between her Rocky Mountains. Michael ordered a maple pork chop. The waitress turned to Alex, almost as an afterthought, and grudgingly recorded her request for an asparagus and herb omelet.

"During the war, I operated using every cell in my body," he said. "It's like having ten extra senses and then coming back here and only getting to use the usual five. It's like being a fully developed human organism there, and coming back here and being plankton."

"That's an odd way to think about it," she said. "I would think most people would be relieved to be out of danger. It almost sounds like you miss it."

"It's hard to explain. There was nothing to stand in my way, nothing about my ninth-grade education, who I knew, how much money I had or didn't have. All that mattered was how I used those extra senses."

Michael reached into the briefcase next to his wheelchair. "I found another photo. One of the donut dollies took it."

"Donut dollies?"

"Yeah, women from the Red Cross who flew in with supplies, games. Sometimes even donuts."

Alex took the photo. It was a side view of her father, his youthful short hair capping a face with a faint trace of a smile. He looked wistful and much younger than in the other wartime photos she'd seen of him. There was also an emotion to the composition. The photographer obviously had cared about her subject. "Where was it taken?"

"A village near Khe Sanh," he said. "The day before, we'd

been involved in an aggressive firefight in a nearby hot combat zone. We'd been told it was a routine rescue mission of a downed pilot, but we were badly ambushed by the Viet Cong. Your dad was yelling orders, but the gunfire, the screams of the villagers, were drowning them out. Four of our men were killed. The next morning, your old man was on the radio chewing out the guy who'd sent us in with no backup. Afterward, we felt that rush of being alive. That combination of pure joy and dark guilt that you've survived."

But ultimately, Alex's father hadn't. "I've never really been able to put the Vietnam War behind me," she admitted. "But that was personal. It's odd to be involved in something professional that focuses on the war as well."

Her eggs arrived. "Breakfast for dinner?"

Alex put some of the omelet on her fork and lifted it to his mouth. "Tell me I've made a mistake."

He reached over and touched her wrist sensuously as the fork neared his mouth. "No, you haven't made a mistake," he said. She knew that he was referring to more than her food choice.

"What do you remember about a guy named Nick?"

His eyes narrowed slightly and he seemed far away. "That's an odd question. Didn't know anyone by that name. Why do you ask?"

"A letter about him was stuffed in the skull you brought into the country."

"Oh? Anything dramatic?" He started casually clicking the buttons on the table, switching the videos while listening for her answer.

"We're looking into it."

"That was a long time ago. So many of the boys sent to war were nothing but cannon fodder. Chances are this Nick character is dead and gone."

"There were also four cigarettes in her mouth. Do you know anything about that?"

"God, I hadn't thought about it in years," he said. "They were from one of my last days in Vietnam, after the firefight I told you about."

"Why four?"

Michael was quiet for a moment. "One for each of our men who were killed that day near Khe Sanh. Condemned men get a last cigarette, but our troops didn't even get that. It was a little ritual we had. Four of us were taking their last puffs for them."

Troy had enlightened her about Vietnamese death rituals, but Michael's words brought home the fact that every culture tries to do what it can to ease death's passage.

For the next half hour, their conversation ranged wildly. He was energized by her impressions of Vietnam and she was grateful for every little detail about her father. She told him about Troy's sister and the unsympathetic Supreme Court case. They ordered dessert, and both played with the buttons on the table, creating a curious assortment of video couples mouthing silent words to each other across the table.

"Pick your favorite woman," Alex said.

He clicked on the first one, obviously enhanced across the chest. "Not smart enough," he said.

The second one, a brunette with glasses, didn't measure up, either. "Not interesting enough." A series of clicks followed, accompanied by a series of rejections. "Way too neurotic." "What an ego!" "Too scared." "Looks too much like our waitress."

Then he reached over to the plug next to the table. He pulled it out of the socket and the video screen behind Alex went black. Her long, curly blond hair was now silhouetted against the dark screen behind her.

"Now, this woman, she intrigues me," Michael said.

Before Alex could respond, the manager rushed over. "I'm sorry about the video," said the young man, a map of California across his shirt. "I'll get our tech guy over here in just a minute."

Alex and Michael shared a conspiratorial grin. When the manager left, Michael said, "Nobody ever suspects someone with a disability of acting badly." He plugged the video back in. "Anyone in a wheelchair could get away with murder."

When the video woman flickered back on, the relieved

manager nodded in their direction from across the room. Alex excused herself to use the ladies' room. She was looking forward to the chance to learn more about her father—and, truth be told, about this man as well. Could she be interested in him? She'd always run with younger men—musicians, artists, actors, poets in their late twenties. This guy was old enough to be her, well, father.

On the way back to the table, she gave her credit card to the waitress as she passed her. She was determined to pay. The waitress looked at Alex's jeans, and then across the room at her attractive older dinner companion.

"Honey, a man like that can afford you," she said. "Don't kill chivalry for the rest of us."

"He can afford ten of me," Alex said, "but I still want you to charge my card."

When she returned, Michael was just hanging up his cell phone. "My latest deal is going a little sideways, and I've got to handle it."

Alex flicked the button until a biker appeared on the video screen behind him. "Guess I'll have to go back to my old boyfriend here."

He took her hand. "Don't give up on me yet. Why don't you come by the house Tuesday night, I'll make you dinner."

She liked the slight thrill of danger she felt at the idea of being back in the forest. "Sure, why not? What time?"

"Eight o'clock. I'll pick up food from A to Z . . ."

"Artichoke to zucchini?"

". . . so that you can have whatever your body craves."

CHAPTER TWENTY-THREE

THE VALET outside of Fare brought Michael's ride—a Volkswagen EuroVan at least a decade old with West Virginia plates. He smiled at Alex's reaction to what he was driving. "Buddy of mine outfitted it for me after my accident."

He opened the passenger door and Alex peered inside.

"*Outfitted* hardly does it justice," she said. The interior made the van look like a Space Shuttle posing as a mild-mannered Beetle. The passenger seat had been taken out and the push of a button caused a ramp to descend so that Michael could wheel up into the van. As he maneuvered into it, he ascended to the point where his face was level with hers. He reached behind her head with his right hand and brought his face toward hers and kissed her. She smelled his aftershave and breathed in the blend of pear and pepper aromas that she recognized as a Nino Cerruti cologne. His caress at the back of her neck excited her and she returned his kiss with a verve that seemed to amuse the valet. Then she stepped back and caught her breath.

She noticed the backseat of the van was filled with a sleeping bag, a duffel bag, and a small camp stove. "Planning a trip?" she asked.

"Always, darlin'," he said. He used his muscular forearms

to move himself effortlessly off the wheelchair and over into the driver's seat. "That song 'Ramblin' Man' was written about me. Next time, I want you along for the ride." He handed the valet a twenty-dollar tip and took off.

Alex hadn't called for her car because she'd decided to walk through the neighborhood around the restaurant where the boutiques and galleries were open late to lure in Christmas shoppers. She'd planned to spend at least a few more hours with Michael that evening and couldn't rewire her brain to go back to the AFIP when he'd abruptly changed those plans.

A gallery featuring women artists was hosting an opening, serving hard cider and delicate Swedish Christmas cookies. Alex stopped and admired the work, listening to the artists explain how they chose to work in paints or fabrics or ceramics. A luminescent shawl in teal, rose, and deep purple asserted itself as the perfect Christmas gift for her mother. The gallery owner wrapped it in handmade paper, tied a ribbon around it, and finished off the package not with a bow but with a pin made of an old Mahjong piece. Janet would love it, Alex thought. Emboldened by a successful purchase, she went into a record store to get a gift certificate for Lana—her first item for the Christmas stocking she was planning to jam with goodies for her fifteen-year-old friend.

En route to the cashier, Alex saw an end bin of CDs labeled "Local Talent." She couldn't help herself. She rummaged through in search of Luke's band, the Cattle Prods. She found one of theirs, *Wasted,* and flipped it over to stare at Luke's intense eyes, so much at odds with his relaxed grin. Always a supporter of his work, she moved a dozen of his CDs to the front of the bin, where they would be more apt to be purchased. Then she went to a computer, typed in the name of a song, and left the store with the gift certificate for Lana and a CD for herself.

At home, she poured herself some Old Weller and put on her new CD. "Ramblin' Man" blasted through her living room, followed by Willie Nelson's "On the Road Again," and Bob Seger's compelling traveling song, "Turn the Page."

When she fell asleep that night, her right foot was pointed downward, as if on the accelerator. Maybe it was time for her to move on down the road.

CHAPTER TWENTY-FOUR

IN HER nightmare, Alex was drowning. The water around her was chilly, and the blue doom of her fuzzy thoughts seemed to prick her back to a cloudy consciousness. Ice. She must have fallen through the ice. She couldn't move, couldn't catch her breath because of the heavy weight of the ice above her.

She could feel pressure on her windpipe and realized it wasn't a dream. A heavy figure in a ski mask was sitting on top of her, his hands squeezing her throat. She kicked him through the sheets, but the way he had her pinned, she couldn't knock him off of her. She worked her left arm back and forth until it sprung out from under the sheet. She clawed wildly at his face, pounding, swiping. But all she managed to do was to twist the ski mask so his eyes were covered. His fingers lightened their touch for a split second, but he didn't bother to reach up to move the mask back in place. Instead, he arched his back so she could no longer reach his head and pressed harder on her throat.

She leaned her face to the right and bit his left wrist, the only part of his body within reach of her teeth. A second later, she spit out the taste of leather. She punched her fist into his chest. He grabbed her wrist with his right hand and slammed her fist into her nose. She could feel the blood trickle out of her nostrils.

The fingers of his left hand pressed further on her throat. His right hand was cupped over her fist cutting off almost all the air to her nose. He bent forward as if he were going to say something, but no sound emerged from his mouth. Only the slight odor of fish, like at the restaurant in Ho Chi Minh City.

The pain and light-headedness were pushed aside for a moment by her anger. I'm not done yet. Not finished with love, with work, with life. She pressed her body forward, butting his head. Her right arm released from the sheets and lashed over toward the nightstand. In a haze of losing consciousness, she pulled open the nightstand drawer. She grabbed Luke's guitar strap and whipped it over the man's head like a noose. She pulled it abruptly and then shifted her body hard to the right when he lifted his hands up to pull away the strap. She jerked her body upward, sliding out from under him, still pulling wildly on the cord that tied their two sweating, panting bodies together. She jerked farther to the right and fell off the bed. The cord bit into his skin, silencing his breath, snapping shut his movements. She continued to pull with all her might much longer than necessary. It was as if her only purpose in life were to hang on to the guitar strap. As if the whole universe revolved around this one act.

Eventually, the adrenaline that fueled her faded and she realized that her throat hurt and that her shoulder muscle was cramping. She smelled the stench on her bed from where the man had soiled himself in his last moments. Still she could not give up, could not believe she was out of danger. Instead, using her feet against his body as leverage, she continued to pull with her right hand as she reached up with her left hand to feel for a pulse at his neck.

When she verified that he was dead, she burst into tears, fueled by a combination of rage and incomprehension. This sort of thing didn't happen to her. She was an investigator of cases, not a victim. Suddenly, she wanted a gun in her home. She needed weapons; she needed alarms. Maybe she even needed a man. For the first time in her adult life, Alexandra Northfield Blake felt vulnerable.

She lay on her carpet, naked and shaking. Then she began to pull herself together. She stood up, rubbed her throat, and ran her right hand through her long blond curls. Still feeling light-headed and dizzy, she turned to the corpse. "Well, buddy, you have the right to remain silent."

Then she collapsed back on the rug. She had taken another person's life. The enormity of it chilled her.

Sure, she'd previously been in the presence of people whose life had ebbed away. She remembered each of them like a Greek chorus who stood on the edge of her day-to-day life. The bullet-ridden seventeen-year-old Puerto Rican kid who'd died in the ER of New York–Presbyterian when she couldn't wheel him to surgery quickly enough. The thirteen-year-old girl from the Upper East Side who couldn't face telling her parents she was pregnant. She'd birthed the baby into the toilet of the guest bathroom of their Park Avenue apartment, then hemorrhaged to death moments after reaching the hospital. Three people's souls had escaped while she was on her surgery rotation aiding attendings who'd done all they could. But each of those people had died from circumstances beyond her control. Violence. Disease. Perhaps even, as some would suggest, retribution of the gods.

She stared down at her hands. This man died because of her.

She pulled off the intruder's stocking cap, expecting to see a kid on drugs, the usual D.C. street scum. Instead, she saw a Vietnamese man in his fifties.

She picked up the phone next to the bed, dialed Dan's home number, and whispered into the receiver, "Somebody just tried to kill me."

IN THE autopsy suite at the AFIP, Alex grabbed for the counter as the room swirled around her. Dan swiftly shoved a chair under her, then gently laid a hand on her shoulder to help stabilize her. She croaked a thank-you that unleashed the pain in her throat. As she sat, she examined at length the Latin sign on the wall, common to many such morgues. HIC

LOCUS EST UBI MORS GAUDET SUCCURRERE VITAE. *This is the place where death rejoices to teach those who live.*

Those who live, Alex thought. Her hand went up to her neck, touching the tender raw place where he'd tried to squeeze out her essence. A wave of nausea washed over her, and she leaned her head forward to bend it down toward her knees. After just a few inches, though, she yelped in pain.

She sat up straight and focused on the activity around her. She was comforted to see Thomas Harding make the Y-shaped incision in the man's chest. He caught her watching him and nodded at her, giving her a solemn look of empathy. After a few gulps of air, she walked unsteadily toward the autopsy table and looked down at her assailant's body. He was a little man, not more than her height, five seven or so. During her attack, she would have sworn he was six five or taller. Maybe this was why eyewitness testimony, so favored by jurors, was sometimes dead wrong.

Hers was a hazy state legally. She was the victim of a crime, and she was now a killer herself. She wouldn't be allowed to participate in the autopsy. But Dan could see the toll the evening had taken on her and was willing to cut her a little slack. When she told him she would only talk to him about what happened if he let her do it in the autopsy suite, he broke several pages of regulations and allowed it.

Alex knew it was silly and stupid, but she wanted to continue to assure herself that he was actually dead, that this wasn't some Hollywood thriller where the bad guy would get up time and time again to send the audience into screams of fear and the heroine into a further fight for her life. Alex blinked rapidly, fighting back tears.

She'd been unwilling to go to the emergency room, but now she wondered if she should at least get an X ray. She listened to her own breath for a moment, but did not hear any of the telltale signs of stridor, the audible sound of a rapid turbulent airflow through a narrowed air tube in the upper trachea.

She swallowed, then coughed. Everything felt raw, but she was pretty sure she wasn't blocked. Another wave of dizziness came over her. Maybe she needed a second opinion. Was she getting enough oxygen? Was it a piece of bone blocking her trachea? Or was she just plain scared?

"I never should have taken you to Nam," Dan said. "This has got to be related to that trip. Maybe the cops, the oil prospectors, the people in the bar. Or even whoever the hell you saw in Lo Duoc."

Harding interrupted Dan's self-flagellation with some additional data. "I just got the lab work back on his blood and stomach contents. The guy couldn't have trailed you back from Vietnam. Judging by what he's ingested, he's been in the country a week or more."

"It doesn't make any sense," Dan said. "What would killing Alex accomplish?"

High heels clicked into the room and an attractive black woman answered the question, "Make the world safer but less interesting for men between the ages of eighteen and eighty?"

Alex fell into the hug that her friend Barbara was offering. "Now that your apartment is a crime scene, you're coming home with me."

Alex didn't argue.

CHAPTER TWENTY-FIVE

ALEX OPENED her eyes to see Lana signing frantically, then dropping her hands to her side and saying, "Are you all right? What happened?"

Alex sat up in the bed and looked at her reflection in the dresser mirror. Her image was surrounded by the tchotchkes hanging off the mirror that chronicled a fifteen-year-old's life. A necklace with half a heart, Lana's track and basketball ribbons, a dusty Camp Fire girl sash.

Alex rubbed the bump above her right eyebrow and looked at the shiner underneath it. The night before, hanging on to the guitar strap, she barely noticed when her head nicked the corner of her nightstand as she fell off the bed. But now the sharp pain in her temple was making her feel woozy. She tried to focus her eyes to check her neck for swelling. She remembered what she'd learned in medical school. Visible injuries may seem mild, but death from internal injuries may occur between thirty-six hours and a few weeks later. There was some mumbo jumbo medical term for it—*decompensation of the internal structures*. She would have to watch herself closely for any signs of trauma.

She faced Lana directly so the girl could read her lips. Alex was grateful for Lana's particular expertise today since speaking above a whisper burned her throat. "I'm okay now,

Lana," she whispered. "Someone tried to hurt me last night, but I'm going to be fine."

Alex looked at the Princess Jasmine clock, a holdover from this child's infatuation in second grade with the movie *Aladdin*. Alex suspected Lana kept it because, as a young African-American girl, she encountered few movie heroines of color with product tie-ins. The clock said 7:30 A.M.

Barbara entered the room. "Lana, I've made pancakes."

"But, Alex—"

"She'll be okay. She just needs rest."

Lana left the room, a little shaky from confronting Alex's injuries.

"Now we can talk," said Barbara. "How do you really feel? Can you breathe okay? Should we go to the hospital?"

"Whoa, slow down." Alex got out of bed. Her knees buckled and Barbara grabbed her elbow to keep her upright.

"Back to bed with you."

"But Dan—"

"I already called him. There's nothing new to report. Get some more rest, then, if you feel good enough, we can head over to the AFIP."

Alex knew Barbara was right. If she wanted to be able to help in the investigation, she'd need to get back on top of her game. Alex lay back down in the twin bed. As she glanced around Lana's room, she realized that Barbara had given her daughter the larger bedroom, a corner room with two sides of windows, one of which looked out onto the apartment courtyard. Ah, the sacrifices of mothers for their daughters, Alex thought guiltily. Maybe when this whole skull thing was over she'd invite her mom to D.C. The image of her mother—a much younger Janet—tucking her into bed when she had measles eased Alex's journey back to sleep.

WHEN SHE woke up that afternoon, she sat up slowly, dangling her legs over the side of the bed before she tried to stand. She walked unsteadily to the bathroom and drew a hot bath. In the calming warmth, she raised her knees and slid the back of her head under the water to wash her hair. Her vigorous strokes with shampoo were her attempts to wash away any scent of her attacker.

Drying herself off, she realized she was exhausted just from the small task of taking a bath. The red marks on her neck were flowering into bruises, and her throat hurt like hell, but she felt calmer and more rested.

She got dressed and walked into the living room where Barbara sat at the square wooden table that seated four. The kitchen was too small to eat in, and this table served as both the dining area and Barbara's study. Her laptop was open in front of her.

Alex walked over to the seated Barbara and squeezed her shoulder in a hug. "Thanks."

Barbara patted Alex's hand as it rested on her shoulder. "Pshaw," Barbara said. "You're practically family."

Alex sat in the chair across from Barbara. It was true. Neither of them had relatives living close by, so it was to each other they turned for advice—and sometimes comfort.

"Where's Lana?"

"Sent her to visit a friend. I wasn't sure where we'd end up today."

Alex conserved her voice, since speaking hurt her throat. She fell into an easy silence with her friend. The apartment had a lovely family feel that she hadn't experienced in her own childhood. The décor combined Barbara's neat, clean lines and muted colors with Lana's whimsical embellishments. A sideboard in the living room housed twenty or more multicolored candleholders, some of which Lana had crafted herself. It was a collection of sorts. Almost every holiday, Lana would pick one out for her mom, but, of course, they reflected Lana's own interests. A carved wooden bear candlestick from when Lana was nine. A multicolored twisted glass one from the previous Mother's Day. Maybe Alex would get them a silver one for Christmas.

Barbara asked Alex if she wanted to call Luke. Alex thought about how Luke may have gone the way of Karl the sculptor, Skip the photographer, and other extinct species of men in Alex's life. He'd been in Europe over a week now and still no word from him about the mysterious Vanessa. "Nah, but I'd like to go in to work now."

The women walked slowly down the block to Barbara's Subaru. Alex asked her to stop at a drugstore so that she could pick up a stronger painkiller. Her fanny pack might be small, but the essentials she carried included a syringe for collecting DNA from suspects, gloves for handling evidence, and a prescription pad for any number of contingencies. She looked at gargles on a shelf and picked the one that would most anesthetize her throat. She needed to be able to talk if she was going to aid in the investigation.

Barbara told Alex to put on a little lipstick before approaching the pharmacist, an exceedingly handsome blond man. "He'd be perfect for you," she said.

Alex rolled her eyes. And she couldn't help notice that, despite the fact that her face was practically crying out for attention—with the broken capillaries, mangled nose, and a large gash above the brow—the pharmacist was looking at Barbara, with her long legs and lovely figure. Alex popped a painkiller into her mouth, swallowed, and then whispered to her friend, "It's not me he's interested in."

ALEX AND Barbara nodded at the guard on the way into the AFIP, signed their names, and used Alex's key to enter the main hallway. They stopped in the rest room so that Alex could soothe her throat with the gargle. Then they continued down the corridor to Alex's lab. She used another key on her ring to open the door.

Alex was looking back over her shoulder as she swung the door open, teasing Barbara about the pharmacist, when Barbara's expression changed dramatically. Her mouth gaped open and she pointed inside Alex's lab.

Alex turned her head and saw cabinets and drawers open, papers scattered on the floor. She gasped. Her laboratory was her sanctuary, the calming home that she never had as a child. To see it this way was almost as much a violation as a killer in her apartment. Before Barbara could stop her, she rushed into the laboratory and opened the refrigerator where she kept the tissue cultures of lethal infectious diseases. Nothing seemed to be missing, but she'd need to go on her laptop to make sure the number and type of samples she'd recorded matched those in the refrigerator. Alex took a step farther into her lab, instinctively wanting to put the whole upturned place back in order. But Barbara called her back into the hallway.

"We've got to page Dan," Barbara said. "How the hell did this happen in a guarded military facility?"

DAN WAS still on-site, processing evidence about the Vietnamese man who'd attacked Alex. He had not gone home or slept since learning of Alex's attack. He met Barbara and Alex at the lab. Sensing the toll the recent events had taken on her, he put his hands on Alex's shoulders. "You're going to get through this," Dan told her. "I'll make sure of it."

To Barbara, he said, "How about taking her down to your office to wait?"

"Don't talk about me as if I weren't here," Alex said, the combination of adrenaline and painkillers fueling her aggression. "It's my lab and I need to know what's going on."

Barbara shrugged at Dan. She wasn't going to go against Alex's wishes at a time like this.

"Okay," Dan said. "Let's see if we can figure out what happened."

Dan opened and closed the lab door several times, then bent down and examined the lock. "Whoever let himself in had a key," he said.

They discussed timing. The night before had been a blur. Dinner. The attack. The autopsy. Alex tried to remember whether she'd been in her lab after the autopsy. Barbara reminded her that she had. Alex had stopped in her lab for her gym bag, which held a change of underwear, a T-shirt, and shorts. She fretted that she might not have relocked the door after she picked up the clothes. Lord knows, she was more than a little preoccupied.

"Okay," Dan said, "that puts the time of the break-in at

sometime between three A.M. and now. Let's assume he's not going to come at a busy time, like after six A.M. and let's look at the video on the door from this morning."

At the main entry to the AFIP, the guard nodded at Alex. "Heard you made a clean kill on the guy who tried to off you."

Alex shivered. Being a killer, which was what she was, even if it was in self-defense, seemed nothing to be proud of. Yet the guys around the building were already treating her with a little more respect. "It's not an experience I'd care to repeat," she said.

"Amen," said the guard as he ushered Barbara, Alex, and Dan into the small room behind the guard station and started running the surveillance tapes beginning at 3:00 A.M.

Barbara noticed that the way the camera above the guard desk was angled, it pointed down women's shirts. "What happened, did Grant position the camera?"

Alex made a mental note to watch how she stood when she came in wearing a tank top.

"Speak of the devil," Barbara said as the video showed Grant approach the desk and sign out. Alex thought he was posing for the camera; then she realized he always stood in that position to show off his muscles.

Dan looked at the sign-in book and noted the time that Grant left. "Three thirty," he said.

As Grant was walking out, someone in uniform with a general's stars was walking in. On the far side of Grant, the man's profile was just a blur in the dim fluorescent lights. Grant saluted, and the image of the man was partially blocked as Grant walked by. Only the man's tight, curly dark hair, with a dipping gray forelock, was visible above Grant's head. Dan looked down at the name on the sign-in sheet. "John Joseph Persh—" The signature deteriorated into a straight line. It was impossible to know what the whole name was. The video showed the man's back as he used a key to enter through the interior door of the AFIP.

Few other people entered the building between 4:00 A.M. and 6:00 A.M. Dan fast-forwarded through the comings and goings of another dozen people, stopping as their images passed the camera to figure out which name went with which photo. Most of them were associated with Dan's own team, in the AFIP in the middle of the night to deal with evidence from the attack on Alex.

Alex looked on as Grant reappeared on the screen a little after 5:00 A.M. He was carrying a large transparent evidence bag with a pillow from her bed and Luke's guitar strap. Alex's heart sank. She hadn't thought about the fact that people like Grant would be tramping through her apartment, seeing the personal side she did not bring to the office. She'd imagined that evidence would be collected by some anonymous person she'd never met. How many people now knew the four-letter access code for her apartment? Two weeks ago she'd changed it to *L-U-K-E,* so that her occasionally dyslexic musician lover wouldn't forget it. Now she felt like a hapless schoolgirl whose teachers had discovered a note about a crush.

Cafeteria workers arrived, with special key cards that allowed access only to the mess hall. Other video cameras recorded their work there. None of them were unaccounted for longer than an occasional bathroom break—certainly not enough time to get to Alex's lab and trash it.

A few other soldiers entered and left, people who were part of the massive eight-hundred-person AFIP workforce but were not personally known to the three of them in the guard's office. Troy arrived around 6:30 A.M.

Barbara looked at Alex. "What's a grief counselor got to do at the crack of dawn on a Saturday?"

CHAPTER TWENTY-SIX

A BREAK-IN at the AFIP was serious enough that the Secretary of Defense had to be notified. Wiatt arrived mid-afternoon, cutting short a meeting at the Pentagon. When Alex and Dan entered his office, he came out from behind his desk to look more closely at Alex's bruised face and battered neck. "When was the last time you went to target practice?"

Alex squinted her eyes. "I never learned to shoot a gun, period. I came from a teaching job, remember? It wasn't exactly open season on molecular biology professors."

Wiatt turned to Dan. "Get her started," he said. He walked behind his desk and sat down. "What do we know about the attacker?"

"Vietnamese, early fifties," Dan said. "Harding says that the condition of his teeth and the contents of his intestines indicate that he arrived in the U.S. recently, a week or so ago. He's a little out of shape for a professional killer, with a touch of arthritis. . . ."

Wiatt looked at Alex. "Probably what saved you."

Dan laid a piece of paper on the table. "Here's the kicker."

Alex recognized it as a pair of DNA profiles, run by the FBI crime lab, since Alex couldn't handle her own case. One was labeled "Gladden scene," the other "Blake scene." They were identical.

"Why would he want to kill Blake here?" Wiatt asked. Then he graced them with one of his rare smiles. "Not that I haven't thought of it myself from time to time."

Dan shook his head. "No clue why he'd go after Alex. The real question is why'd he go after Gladden. We solve that crime, and we'll learn how Alex got in harm's way."

"But what about the break-in?" Alex said. "My attacker was already dead by then."

"Speaking of the break-in," Wiatt said, handing her a slew of incident reports. "You had biowarfare toxins in that lab and now we've got to assure the government that none of them have gone missing."

"Shit," said Alex. "I just realized I'll have to test the contents of each petri dish to make sure somebody didn't take the culture with the toxin and replace it with something harmless."

"You mean someone might have stolen the makings of a bioweapon?" Dan asked.

Alex nodded. She'd have to repeat a month's worth of experiments to re-create the cultures she'd made from bird flu victims. "I'm going to have to get rid of everything that's in there. Even if the guy didn't switch samples, he could have added something to the cultures. If he did, all my future experiments on those cultures will be unreliable."

Wiatt turned back to Dan. "How'd an outsider breach security?"

"Almost everyone here last night checks out," Dan said.

"Almost?" Wiatt asked.

"There's a general who signed in. We can't make out his face on the tape. So far, we don't know why he was here."

"Christ, it could be anything," Wiatt said. "Supply issues, quality control oversight on the pathology lab, a tour through the Weapons of War for funding purposes. We've got inspectors coming in here all the time. What's his name? I know most of the guys at that level."

"The handwriting on the sign-in is a mess," Dan said.

The flash in Wiatt's eyes told everyone in the room that the officer who'd been working the desk would soon find himself in a less cushy assignment. Latrine duty came to mind.

Dan pulled out a photocopy of the page the general had signed. John Joseph Persh—

Wiatt said, "Black Jack Pershing?"

"You know the guy?" Alex asked.

"It's the name of the general who commanded the U.S. troops in Europe in World War I. He's been dead since 1948. The guy signed a fake name."

"How did you make that connection so quickly?" Alex asked.

"I served in Vietnam with his grandson, Army Second Lieutenant Richard Warren Pershing. He's buried at Arlington right next to Black Jack."

Dan said, "When someone chooses a fake name, it's usually an inside joke or represents some delusion the person has about who they want to be. I'll get Chuck on it right away—digging up old records about where John Joseph Pershing was born, what units he served with, what weapons he mastered. It might help us track down the fake Pershing."

"Still won't tell us how he got in here," Wiatt said.

Dan turned to Alex. "Have you loaned your keys to anyone?"

"No, I always carry them."

"Always?"

Alex tried to picture a typical day in her mind. The keys were in her fanny pack, except when she took them out to open various doors. When she went to the gym, she locked the fanny pack in her locker.

"Shit," she said. "Sometimes I leave them with a parking valet."

Dan and Wiatt looked at each other.

"I never thought about it," she said. "There's nothing on the keys to link me with the AFIP."

"If that was the weak point," Dan said, "our guy spent some time figuring out how to get to you. Where have you valeted the car since the John Doe showed up?"

"Last night, Fare Restaurant, the keys were out of my

control for maybe an hour and a half. Before we left for Vietnam, they were with a valet at an office building in Chevy Chase for about forty-five minutes."

"I'll need addresses for both," Dan said.

BACK IN her lab, Alex noticed she had a phone message. "Thanks for the mighty fine company last night," Michael's voice said. Alex wondered why he was calling her here, but then she remembered she'd given him her AFIP card that first night and hadn't given him her cell phone number or the home one, either. "I'll make sure I've got everything you want when you come by Tuesday night. No interruptions this time, I promise."

Alex knew she needed to cancel their upcoming dinner. But she was in no shape to deal with Michael at the moment. She'd call him later.

The barely recognizable surroundings of her lab made her feel all the worse. The evidence techs had disturbed it more than the original intruder. All the cabinets were open. The sequencers had been moved away from the walls and were covered with black fingerprinting dust.

She walked around, taking stock. There had been no damage to any of the elaborate equipment. The intruder hadn't been out to trash the place, but to find something.

Since the AFIP was on the same base as the Walter Reed Medical Center, she was sure that she could borrow a cleaning crew from the operating room there. She called Dan. "Can I start cleaning up?"

"Not yet," he said. "We've got squat about the guy who broke in. No fingerprints, other than yours."

"How do you know it was a guy?"

"Educated guess from the size of the glove prints. Either a guy or a taller-than-average woman. The unaccounted-for general was a guy."

Alex looked down at the floor, wondering if she'd already started contaminating the evidence. "What about shoe prints?"

"Can't pick up much on that floor. It's not like an outdoor

crime scene. Why don't you go back to Barbara's and get some rest, let us take a last sweep through the lab, and we'll meet Harding tomorrow morning to see what else he's got on the corpse."

Truth be told, she was feeling a little fuzzy again. "All right," she said.

But when she hung up the phone, she decided to try to retrace the burglar's steps. If he'd been searching for something other than biotoxins, where would he look first? Probably her desk.

She walked carefully back through the lab to her glassed-in office at the rear. She bent down to open a desk drawer, but realized that it would have been more efficient for the guy to sit on her chair, fan through the papers atop the desk, and then open the drawers on either side of the chair. She rolled her desk chair back and found a tiny sliver of a rose-colored fiber stuck to one of the wheels. The evidence techs hadn't found it because they hadn't moved the chair.

She walked back into her lab, put on gloves, and grabbed a pair of sterilized tweezers which she used to pluck the fiber off the chair's wheel. It probably dropped off the intruder's clothes, then the chair ran over it when he pushed the chair back in place.

She glanced at it more closely. Too bad the surveillance tapes weren't in color. Maybe this would match someone's sweater or shirt. But then she realized that didn't make sense. Most everyone who entered the building had been in uniform, particularly during that 3:00 A.M. to 6:00 A.M. stretch. The only exceptions were Troy—who she couldn't picture wearing rose—and the cleaning people, who were mostly men.

The fiber seemed thick, probably too thick for the type of sweaters people wore in the temperate D.C. winters. More likely it was a carpet fiber. She'd drop it off with Dan before she left the building to head back to Barbara's.

She opened a cabinet in her office to find a small evidence bag like the ones in which she'd stored the cigarette butts from the mysterious shrouded skull. As she plunked the fiber into a bag, she realized that something was missing from the shelf. She'd been so focused on assuring that her biotoxin work hadn't been tampered with, she'd just now realized that the letter from the woman's skull had been stolen.

Had Wiatt taken the letter to cover up the massacre? Alex rushed down the hall to his office. "Colonel, did you take something from my lab?"

"What could I possibly want that you've got?"

"The letter from the skull. The one about the massacre."

"Our Commander in Chief is about to meet the Vietnamese. And you've lost a letter that could blow up in his face?"

"Who knew the letter was there? Just you, me, and Barbara. Unless you told someone at the White House."

"Miss Blake," he said, dropping the *Dr.* off of her name as he did when he was angry. "You were sloppy with your keys and now I've got a potential national emergency on my hands." He pointed to the door of his office. "I hope you liked academia. Because as soon as you finish with the skulls, I'm kicking your ass right back there."

CHAPTER TWENTY-SEVEN

ALEX TREKKED to the conference room to drop off the pink thread she'd found on her floor. Grant was standing behind Chuck, reading the computer screen about the real John Joseph Pershing, an 1866 West Point grad who'd chased Pancho Villa, served in the Spanish-American War, WW I, and then was the Army Chief of Staff.

Alex joined them. "He was born in Linn County, Missouri," she said.

"Look at this," Chuck said. "When he was in his eighties, during World War II, he lived right here for three years in special-built quarters on top of Walter Reed Hospital."

"Sounds like my kind of guy," Grant said, pointing to a line in the report about him.

Alex looked down and read. Apparently this octogenarian had been a live wire. The prettier nurses would come out of his room rubbing themselves where they swore they'd been pinched.

"That was in the 1940s, Grant. Pinch a nurse today and she's likely to deck you."

Dan walked in and Alex motioned him back in the hallway, where she could speak with him alone.

"Wiatt just told me six ways to Sunday that you are off the Gladden case," Dan said.

"Son of a bitch," Alex said. "He might be hiding something." Quickly she filled Dan in on the missing letter.

Dan's shoulders tightened. "I've got a dead accountant, an attack on one of my investigators, and now missing evidence of a war crime. What the hell is the link between them?" He looked at Alex's bruised face. "Is there anything suspicious you remember? Have you been followed, gotten phone calls?"

Alex shook her head.

"Okay, get some rest. I'll deal with Wiatt."

She thanked him, handed over the thread, and grabbed her coat from her lab. Maybe by getting away, she could figure out who was targeting her and why.

CHAPTER TWENTY-EIGHT

THE NEXT day, Sunday, Barbara announced she would work at home while Alex rested. Alex protested mildly, but her banged-up body was desperate for the rest. Alex took a long bath, dressed, and then joined her friend in the living room for coffee. Lana had spent the night with her friend.

"All right, get in the car," Barbara said. "I've got a surprise for you."

Twenty minutes later, they pulled up into the parking lot of a building with a sign, JANE'S HOUSE.

Alex opened the door, expecting to enter a restaurant for a late lunch, but instead, she was encountered by the acrid smells of a shooting range.

"No, I can't," Alex said.

"Don't be silly. *Can't* hasn't been in your vocabulary in the past. Don't start now."

They were greeted by a solidly built short-haired woman in her late forties. "You're Jane?" Alex asked.

The woman exchanged glances with Barbara. Then she stuck out her hand to shake Alex's. "Denise," she said.

"She taught firearms at Norfolk when I was stationed there."

"Lieutenant Findlay here was one of my best students," Denise said. "She's quite a sharpshooter."

"Remind me not to get on your bad side," Alex said to Barbara.

Someone else arrived at the door and Denise moved to let her in. Barbara took Alex farther into the building.

"I don't get it. Who's Jane?"

"Jane was Denise's sister. Her boyfriend beat her up one too many times and she bled to death. Denise left the service and founded this private club to teach self-defense to abused women."

A woman in a tae kwon do uniform entered the hallway from a locker room. She'd been beat up almost as badly as Alex. She nodded at Alex. "Take care of yourself," she said.

"Thanks," Alex said as the woman disappeared into another room, where a dozen other tae kwon do students were already in position.

"Don't worry," Barbara said. "We're going to ease into this."

She led Alex into an empty dance studio, with a floor-to-ceiling mirror on one wall. They stood a few feet back from the mirror.

"Now," Barbara said, "assume the position you think is right for shooting a handgun."

Alex stood up straight and spread her legs apart with her feet parallel, just like she'd seen in police dramas on television. "How's this?"

Barbara pushed her palm on Alex's shoulder, easily knocking her off balance. "You need to be more stable for shooting. Here's what you do."

Barbara stood with her legs apart, then moved her left leg farther back than the right one. She bent slightly forward. "Use a fighter's stance to shoot. Your center of balance is better."

Alex followed her instructions.

"Not bad, but your left leg needs to be just a bit farther back. Your pelvis should be at a forty-five-degree angle from the target."

Alex complied. "You're right. This feels a lot steadier."

"Now tip your shoulders slightly forward. Nose over toes, we call it. This will help cushion the recoil."

Once she was satisfied that Alex was in the proper position, Barbara used a key to open her briefcase, and pulled out a semiautomatic pistol. She double-checked to make sure it was not loaded.

"Holy shit," said Alex, shifting out of her fighter stance. "You keep that in the apartment with Lana?"

"I know what I'm doing. It's in a locked case that requires both a combination and a key. I keep it out of reach on my bedroom shelf."

Still, Alex was surprised by this new information about her friend. Growing up with an antiwar mother, Alex had certain stereotypes about NRA types. They didn't fit Barbara.

She passed Alex the gun and said, "Back in position."

Alex's right hand dipped with the weight of the gun.

Barbara said, "You need to remember two things about holding the gun. Grip it hard and hold it high. I want you to feel like you are crushing this sucker. Now look through the front sight."

Alex put pressure on the cold metal and peered through the sight. She saw herself in the mirror, an incongruous vision. A black-and-blue face and a shiny gray gun.

"Okay, sister, let's try it out." Barbara took the pistol back and led Alex into a larger room where three other women were practicing shooting. As Barbara chose goggles and earmuffs for her, Alex looked at the woman at the far end of the range. She couldn't have been more than four foot eleven, a little wisp of a woman, but her aim was impeccable. If she could do this, maybe Alex could as well.

The women put on the equipment, but Barbara moved Alex's earmuffs back a bit so she could still talk to her. She guided Alex to lane 4 and loaded the gun.

"Point it only toward the target," she cautioned. "Focus the front sight on the target and pull it back in one smooth motion, like this." Barbara got off a shot, straight to the target's heart. She made it look easy.

"Your turn," she said, moving Alex in front of her. Alex got in position, her mouth dry. She took the gun from Barbara, who showed her how to web the fingers of her right hand around it and then steady the grip with her other hand. "One fluid slide of the trigger," Barbara said. Then she pushed Alex's earmuffs back over her ears and stepped back.

Alex looked at the paper target, already wounded from Barbara's shot to the heart. She got off a shot and was startled by the kick of the gun and how the muzzle seemed to bounce for a split second after she fired.

She'd aimed for the heart, but the bullet hit low, closer to the target's testicles. The little woman in the far lane looked at her and smiled.

Barbara pulled back Alex's earmuffs and said, "You had your hand a little low on the grip, and that's what caused the recoil and the low hit. But," she said, looking at the new hole in the target, "you at least made our guy there pretty unhappy."

AN HOUR later, back at Barbara's house, Alex tried to reconcile the morning's events with the quiet peace of her friend's apartment. She was happy to see Lana again and show her how to use the phone that she'd cadged for her from Grant. When someone spoke to Lana on the other end of the line, the words appeared on a computer screen so that she could see what he said, and she could answer back. For the friend on the other end, it would seem like any normal phone conversation.

Lana christened it with a call to her grandmother in the Bronx. Right before dinner, Alex challenged Lana to a game of gin rummy. The girl was relishing time with her surrogate aunt, but Alex noticed that she dealt with her mom in monosyllables. Barbara tried to pretend that nothing was wrong, but she was clearly grateful to have someone else spending time with her daughter.

After dinner, Alex put *Amélie* into the DVD player. She loved watching foreign movies with Lana. It put Alex on an equal footing with her deaf friend since both relied on subtitles, with the sound off.

Other than the occasional giggles and "ooh," they were relatively quiet, allowing Barbara to work on her laptop a few feet away on the small table. She filled out some paperwork about the break-in and did a little research about getting citizenship for Troy's sister Lizzie. When the credits came up, Lana bounced off to call her friends on the phone Alex had given her.

Barbara turned to Alex. "It doesn't look so great for Troy's sister." She had the U.S. Supreme Court's opinion on her screen. "The justices seemed more interested in protecting male soldiers' right to screw than the child's right to have a dad."

"Great. All power to the sperminator," Alex said.

"This boy was born during the Vietnam War to a Vietnamese mother and American father. The dad brought him to the U.S. when he was six and raised him as a permanent resident. But when he got into trouble in his twenties, the U.S. deported him. He wasn't a legal citizen because the dad didn't think to follow an obscure statute and acknowledge paternity under oath when his son was a child. If the roles had been reversed and the mother had been an American, the child would have had citizenship automatically."

Alex started reading the opinion over Barbara's shoulder. The justices seemed wary about opening up citizenship to the thousands of children of American GIs. The court opinion said that in 1969, the year this kid was born, there were 1,041,094 American military personnel stationed abroad. The court also seemed concerned that with modern travel, more than 25 million Americans went abroad each year. Alex threw up her hands in disgust. "So the Supreme Court just gave American men a license to screw foreign women and not live up to their parental responsibility."

"Seems like it," Barbara said.

"So that's it?"

Barbara sighed. "Afraid so. Troy's sister stays in Vietnam."

CHAPTER TWENTY-NINE

WHEN SHE entered the AFIP the next morning, the guard said, "Colonel Wiatt wants you in his office right away." Wiatt greeted her by shoving the *New York Times* into her hands. On the front page was a photo of Mymy, the Vietnamese woman whose skull Alex had identified. Alex turned the page and it got worse. Dr. Kang had appeared on the weekly MIA show in Vietnam. He'd described Alex's efforts to identify the woman—and disclosed that her skull had disappeared in an unprovoked attack on civilians in 1969. The reporter had even managed, through old customs records, to learn that Michael Carlisle had brought the skull into the country back in 1972.

"What have you got to say for yourself?" Wiatt asked.

"I didn't think . . ."

"Of course you didn't think!"

Alex stood her ground. "Is there anything about the letter in the paper?"

"No, it hasn't surfaced yet."

"Maybe now you'll start investigating what happened over there."

"I don't need you telling me how to run my outfit. You've done enough damage."

Alex's response was cut off by Dan and Grant, who came in to report on her keys. The manager of Fare had been vehement that her keys had remained untouched, and he was credible. So fearful of a Jag or BMW being stolen, he didn't allow the keys to be left on a wooden board outside of the restaurant like most valets in the District, but kept them on a board in his office.

The office valet at the building that housed Michael Carlisle's office was a different matter. Five in the evening, when Alex had arrived, was peak time for people retrieving cars. The valet worked alone, running up and down the parking structure, pulling out people's cars. It was a nightmare Rubik's Cube of a parking lot, a testimony to the value of real estate. Often he had to move one or two cars aside to get to the car he was actually seeking. The keys were unguarded for long stretches of time.

"What were you doing there?" Wiatt asked Alex.

"Seeing Michael Carlisle."

"The guy the *Times* wrote about?"

Alex nodded.

He turned to Dan. "Did you know about this?"

Dan shook his head.

"I checked the other building tenants," Grant said. "A health care clinic and a few law firms. Some retail on the first floor—a Starbucks, a bookstore, and a vitamin store. No reason for any of those tenants to be tied up in something like this."

"That's one way to prevent a court-martial," Wiatt said. "Steal the evidence." He seemed almost relieved to think the letter was safely being hidden.

"Wait a minute," Alex said. "You don't honestly think Michael Carlisle broke into my lab? There's no link between him and the events in the letter."

"What are you, his lawyer?" Wiatt asked. "Let's bring him in so I can talk to him."

"But—"

"Isn't an investigation exactly what you wanted?" Wiatt demanded.

"THAT RAINBOW of medals across your chest is pretty impressive," Michael said to Colonel Wiatt. "I reckon you left a piece of your soul in a lot of places."

"Okay, Corporal Carlisle," Wiatt said. "I don't need any shit here. We're just going to have a little debriefing about where you got the woman's skull."

"My corporal days are long past," Michael said. "I haven't had to kiss any military ass since 1972. In case you haven't noticed, I'm a cee-vee-lian." He stretched out the syllables and smiled.

Alex peered through the one-way mirror at Michael. She was standing alone in a dark, closet-sized space next to the interrogation room. Wiatt had asked her to watch the questioning in case Michael told him something that contradicted what he'd told her.

Alex had begged Dan not to join her. She didn't want to be distracted as she took the measure of the man.

"A war crimes prosecution doesn't care if you're wearing Air Force camo or a three-piece suit," Wiatt said. "Check the Code of Military Justice. For purposes of a court-martial, even a civilian is treated as if he were still a soldier."

"A court-martial? What the hell are you talking about?"

"There was a letter in the skull about soldiers setting fire to four hootches and shooting innocent civilians."

Alex watched as a somber look crossed Michael's face. His hands, resting on the top of the wheels of his wheelchair, moved slightly so that he rocked back and forth when he spoke. "Here's what I remember: I was playing poker with my third unit. Jeeter bet everything he had on a hand that I won easily. When he offered me the skull instead of the dough, I took it. Hell, I used to watch *The Addams Family* and *Dark Shadows* after school when I was a kid. Skull with a candle in it brought back memories."

"And where did this Jeeter say he got it?"

"Wasn't the sort of thing we talked about."

"Anybody around to back up that story?"

"Talk to the Wall. That's where they all are now."

Alex watched Michael's sadness as he uttered that line. So many deaths, including her father. So far, as she watched the man, there was nothing that raised her suspicions.

Wiatt switched his tactic. "Who'd you call from the restaurant Friday?"

Michael moved his chair forward slightly, a confused look on his face. "What's that got to do with anything? My call related to one of my financial deals. What's it to you?"

"Dr. Blake's keys were stolen—and probably duplicated— while she was at your office building. Her lab was broken into the night you had dinner. Certain information about the skull was stolen."

Michael chortled. "Sounds like a big chunk of your evidence went AWOL."

"I'm glad you find it funny. Dr. Blake wasn't laughing when someone did this to her." Wiatt dropped a photo of Alex in Michael's lap. It showed her, moments after Dan had arrived at her apartment, face pale, blood gushing from her head, the impression of handprints around her neck.

Alex hadn't even remembered that the photographer had shot that photo. She looked at the photo in Michael's hand and realized how close she'd come to being killed.

"Who did this?" Michael's hands tensed into fists.

"We thought maybe you would know. It happened after you placed your call."

"Are you crazy? Why would I want to hurt Alex?"

"Maybe you didn't think a court-martial would fit in with your current business strategy. Just turn over the letter and we can make a deal."

Michael looked down at the photo of Alex and then up at the calming picture of Frank Lloyd Wright's Fallingwater home on Wiatt's wall. "I don't have any damn letter and I had nothing to do with the war crime you described. But you were there, Colonel. Didn't every one of us do something that was culpable? We decimated their countryside, slaughtered millions of their people. We dropped fifteen million tons of munitions, more than twice what we dumped during the so-called good war, World War II—"

Wiatt interrupted. "Leave it to your lawyer to tug on the heartstrings. If we find you had anything to do with that incident, you'll be confined to more than a wheelchair."

"It'll get pretty crowded in that cell. Because if I get put away, all four branches of the military are coming with me." Michael swerved his wheelchair through Wiatt's doorway and rolled out with the unhurried grace of a man who owned the place.

CHAPTER THIRTY

THAT AFTERNOON, Alex started putting her lab back in order and tried to get her thoughts straight about Michael. He'd seemed upset that something had happened to her. She didn't find it credible that he was behind her attack or the break-in at her lab. Yet he'd brought the skull into the country. He did business in Vietnam. Not to mention that he was from West Virginia, home of Westport Oil. In fact, hadn't he gotten his start in business with the settlement from an auto accident there?

Alex called Barbara. "How do I find out about an auto accident case?"

"That's easy. Check the jury verdict reports from that jurisdiction. Most of them are on-line in Lexis."

Alex tried that, but since she didn't know the year the accident had occurred, it was painfully slow to go through each issue of the West Virginia jury reports. And they read like a chronicle of disaster. People turned into quadriplegics by the wrong anesthesia. Babies with mental retardation after a screwup in labor. She decided to try a different approach. She switched to the Lexis news database and typed in Michael Carlisle's name. He'd said the jury verdict was huge. Maybe it had been reported in the newspaper.

Sure enough she found the story, dated ten years earlier.

The colorful trial lawyer, Tommy Shane, had won a $2 million judgment for his client, Michael ("Mick") Carlisle.

She moved closer to the computer screen to make sure she'd read it correctly. Then she closed her eyes and tried to recall the writing on the letter. She'd been sure that the perpetrator was named Nick. But could she have been mistaken? Maybe what she'd read as "Nick" was really "Mick."

Could Wiatt be right? Had Michael—Mick—stolen the note to avoid a scandal about his service? A guy doing a booming business in Vietnam might lose it all if it became known he'd slaughtered civilians.

She knew Wiatt would now be letting out all stops tracking down information about Michael. Maybe he'd even put the White House and Secret Service on it.

She couldn't picture Michael ordering a massacre. But what did she know about war? Probably less than any of the soldiers in the building.

She went to find Dan to see if he'd learned anything about the thread. Chuck told her he was in the autopsy suite.

When she arrived there, Harding touched her chin and stared at the fading bruises. "You're looking much better," he said.

Harding had a drawer pulled out. She peered at the man on the slab. The man who tried to kill her. Maybe she was regaining her strength, or maybe the memory of what had happened in that bed was fading, because the man in repose seemed older and more fragile now. Perhaps this last glimpse of him would replace his potent appearance in her nightmares.

"As soon as I identified him as a Vietnamese male who recently arrived in the United States, the Vietnamese Embassy stepped in to arrange transport back," Harding said. "The corpse is being flown back to Hanoi today."

"Have they identified him?" Alex asked.

"No," Harding said. "He's got no tattoos, no birthmarks, no identifying marks. Nothing but a bullet lodged near his trachea. From its position, it probably caused him to be mute."

That new bit of information triggered Alex's memories. The man on top of her hadn't spoken. She remembered now his firm fingers on her throat and his quiet, calm breathing, even as she tried to fight back.

"Recent injury?" Dan asked.

"No. From the way the tissue grew over it, the bullet's been in there for a couple of decades at least." Harding walked over to the counter and picked up a tiny vial with a piece of metal inside. He brought it back and passed it around the group.

Grant, the czar of the Weapons of War program, recognized it immediately. "It's an M16 5.56 millimeter American bullet. He was shot during the Vietnam War."

"Or the American War, as they called it," Dan said. "Maybe his visit here was a lot more personal than we thought."

Barbara entered the room with Troy in tow. "Embassy called Dr. Nguyen. They've been dealing with him on the skulls and asked if he could help with the return of the body."

Troy didn't even notice Alex and her battered face. His eyes were immediately drawn to the corpse's sunken chest. He looked up at Harding with a hint of anger in his eyes. "Where are the internal organs?"

"Standard autopsy procedure," Harding said, glancing over at a set of jars, slides, and trays that held parts of the dead Vietnamese man.

"You can't send him back like that," Troy said. "We believe the body should be buried whole."

Harding let that sink in. "Ah, like Orthodox Jews."

"Precisely," Troy said.

"You mean we might have a Kohn case on our hands?" Barbara asked. She realized no one knew what she was talking about. "The Army did an autopsy on Marc Kohn, an Orthodox Jewish soldier who died under suspicious circumstances. When the Army removed and retained certain organs, his parents sued on the grounds that this violated their religious beliefs. They won $210,000 in damages."

"Un-fuckin'-believable," Grant said. "This guy tries to kill one of ours, and we might be sued by his family?"

Troy looked at Alex, carefully assessing her black eye. He offered her no comfort but instead addressed the group as a whole. "I'm just as sorry about Dr. Blake as the rest of you, but he can't be personally blamed. He was fated to take the actions he did and Alex was fated not to die yet."

Alex didn't like the sound of the "not . . . yet."

"Fate had nothin' to do with it," Grant said to Troy.

"All that's beside the point for the law," Barbara said. "No matter how you cut it, the family's not at fault for the murder attempt. The court in the Kohn case said his parents had a legal claim of their own for emotional distress on the grounds that their son wouldn't have a proper afterlife since his body wasn't buried whole."

"Let's just stuff some newspapers in his chest so it looks like the organs are still in there," Grant said.

"Why don't you just use his skin for a lampshade while you're at it?" Troy snapped. "Do you think it's only appearances that make a difference in the religion? You are not a smart man."

Troy stepped toward Grant, who shifted in position to pummel him. Dan pushed Grant back.

"Okay, okay," Dan said, "there's an easy fix to all of this. None of the organs have any evidentiary value; they're not linked to the crimes in any way. Harding can open him back up and return them."

"Like putting a packet of giblets back in a turkey," Grant said to Troy's scowl.

"But we're keeping the bullet," Dan said.

THE VIETNAMESE hearse driver spoke little English. Troy accompanied the body to Dulles to help cut through the red tape of getting the casket on the flight to Hanoi. When he returned to the AFIP, he found Dan and Alex in the conference room.

"The Vietnamese government knows more about the corpse than they were letting on," he told them. "The body is being sent to the Truong Son cemetery."

"Which means?" Dan said.

"It's the burial grounds for people who fought for the North Vietnamese. And the bill of lading for his corpse suggests his flight is not being billed to the embassy, but to the Ministry of the Interior. And the draping on the casket indicated that the man had been a general."

Dan nodded. "Thanks, I'll look into it."

Troy looked dismissively at Dan. "I tell you this because I want to help Alex."

He turned to leave, but he paused to look at the black-and-white photos tacked to the wall from the Ron Gladden crime scene.

"What part do the roses play?" he asked.

"Before the general attacked me, he killed a man in Georgetown with a bayonet hidden in a bunch of roses," Alex said.

Troy straightened up abruptly. "What color were the roses?"

The question surprised Alex. "Yellow. Why?"

Troy began to pace. "The color of betrayal," he said. Then he turned and left the room.

CHAPTER THIRTY-ONE

DAN MET Alex at her lab the next day. "This morning the head of Westport Oil got a CD-ROM in the mail. It has the company's name on it and Ron Gladden's signature."

"Sent before he died?" Alex asked.

Dan shook his head. "Postmarked from D.C. last Wednesday. A week after the murder."

"That doesn't make any sense," Alex said. "Why steal a report and then give it to the person who was supposed to get it anyway?"

"We're trying to figure out what was done with the CD-ROM after it left Gladden's possession," he said. "Anderson says it contains trade secrets, so he's not about to send it here, but Chuck got on a plane to West Virginia right after I heard. He says it's in an encrypted PDF form that can't be changed. So no one could have added information. The most that could have happened was that it was copied. The only odd thing about the CD was that it smelled like roses."

Alex thought about the upended briefcase at Gladden's apartment, the scattered rose petals. "Stolen when Gladden was murdered?"

Dan nodded. "Most likely. Chuck's swabbing for DNA and I'll want you to run it when he comes back."

"Of course," Alex said.

"I know you can take care of yourself, Alex, but watch

your back. There are too many pieces in play right now. The skulls, the oil deal. Do you want me to put someone on you?"

"What do you mean?"

"I could free up an MP for security detail on you."

Alex shook her head. Then she thought about her situation. She was staying with Barbara and Lana. The last thing she needed was to put them in danger. She should probably move back home in the next few days, as soon as she could face it. "I'll be okay," she said.

Dan took a long, full look at the tall blonde with the bruise and bump on her face. He smiled. "I'm sure you will," he said. "But for the moment, stay out of trouble. I've got all the investigations I can handle."

MICHAEL LEFT a message for her that afternoon. "Your colonel told me what happened. Are you okay? I'd like to strangle the guy who did it to you."

She listened to the message twice, going back and forth in her mind about whether she should return the call. Then she decided against it and started processing the DNA that Chuck had recovered from the CD.

Within an hour, she was able to report to Dan that the DNA on the disk was tied to three people—Gladden, the man who had killed him and attacked Alex, and the recipient, Bennett Anderson of Westport Oil.

"Here's how it could have gone down," Dan said. He waved the cheap blue Bic pen that he'd been writing with. Alex smiled as she watched the pen bob left and right through the air. The military ordered Parker pens. Dan so distrusted the way anything worked that was funded by the DOD that he even brought in his own pens.

"Gladden received the confidential report of the nature of the oil reserves from Cameron Alistair for his client Westport Oil. But before Gladden delivered it, he leaked it to a competitor—maybe, judging by who he was meeting with, a Chinese company or the government of China itself. For some reason, that didn't set well with the guys from the Vietnamese

Ministry of the Interior—maybe they stood to gain personally if the Westport deal goes through."

"So they settle the score by sending someone to kill
Gladden—yellow roses for betrayal—and get the deal back
on-course by mailing the disk to Westport?"

Dan nodded.

"Why come after me?"

"Good question. Your DNA work could finger the guy,
but all he needed to do was get back on a plane and he'd be
safe."

Alex tried to think of why he might have wanted to kill
her. Any rational investigative thought she might have had
dissolved into the feel of the man's hands around her neck.
Like a lawyer who represents himself, maybe an investigator
who tries to solve her own crime has a fool for a client.

Dan's pen stopped in midair. "Maybe this doesn't relate
to the murder at all. We can't rule out that it's about the letter
in the skulls."

"But why?"

"If the Ministry—or someone connected with it—is
counting on a deal with Uncle Sam, the last thing they need
right now is evidence of a massacre."

"Seems far-fetched to me," Alex said. "How would they
even know about the letter? Couldn't it just have easily been
taken by someone closer to home, someone trying to protect
the White House? There seem to be a lot of people around
here trying to convince me that, personally and politically, a
court-martial right now might be too dangerous a move."

Secretly, though, Alex was relieved by the idea that someone thousands of miles away had ordered her attack. The
idea softened her suspicion that Michael had something to
do with it.

"Just watch your back. I'll get you a gun that nobody
needs to know about."

"So I can be a liberal by day, NRA member by night?"

"I can't quite picture you hiding anything you're involved
in. It'd be more like you to start some kind of social
movement—Feminists for the Second Amendment."

"Great," Grant said, walking in. "I'll get one of my guys to design the logo. Instead of tits and ass, how about guns and buns?"

Alex shook her head at both of them. "Aren't I lucky to have well-evolved colleagues like you?"

Then she headed down the hall to Barbara's office. "I just want to let you know I'm going back to my own apartment tonight," she said.

"Are you sure, honey?" Barbara asked. "It's only been a few days. You might want to get a little more distance before you go home. You can stay with Lana and me as long as you want."

"Barbara, you're the best," Alex said. "But I've got to face the music sometime. The longer I'm away, the more threatening the whole thing seems. A few more days, and I'll be too scared to ever live alone again. I've got to plunge back in."

"Do you want me to come with you? I can give you a hand with the cleanup and, Lord knows, you could use some decorating tips."

"Nah, Lana will be happy to have some time alone with you after an overdose of Auntie Alex."

"Are you kidding? Seems like I'm the last person she wants to see these days. She's gotten so furtive and touchy with me."

To Alex, Lana seemed to be as sweet as always. "Maybe she's finally testing her wings, feeling a little independent."

"Yeah, it's probably just some teenage thing. But the next time you take her to dinner, put in a good word for me. I think we're entering that phase where Mom can do no right."

CHAPTER THIRTY-TWO

ALEX PARKED her car in front of the Curl Up and Dye, thinking that it was fitting that, now that the body of the man who tried to kill her was back in Vietnam, she was going back to her home as well. She tapped in the four-letter code to open the gate, and then thought about how that little security measure had done her no good. She walked down the inner corridor to the door at the end and hesitated before putting her key in. Maybe she should have taken Barbara up on her offer to accompany her. She wasn't sure that she was ready to face her apartment alone.

She leaned against the wall of the corridor. She passed through that hallway every day on the way in and out of the building, but never paid much attention to it. The paint was peeling—maybe she should give it another coat sometime. And add a plant, perhaps, or maybe a piece of art.

She giggled. What odd little twists a person's mind takes. The intruder in her apartment had frightened her, transformed her into a killer, and now the whole incident was turning her into Martha Stewart.

She jabbed the key into the lock, pushed open the door, and strode into the apartment.

The first thing she noticed was the smell. Not the smell of defecation and death like she expected, but a light combination of disinfectant and lemon. Bless his heart, Alex thought,

Dan must have had the place professionally cleaned after the evidence was collected. She looked around the main room, with its hair dryer chairs with plastic see-through bonnets. In the corner stood Luke's guitar stand and the amps his band used when they rehearsed here. Not a speck of dust on them. She bent down. No dust bunnies under the chairs, either. Ironic, Alex thought. The room never looked this good before.

She peeked into the kitchen, where the window had been replaced. She saw a thin wire leading from it to the adjoining wall. Dan had told her he'd arranged for an alarm to be installed. No more chance of someone coming in through a window.

Alex returned to the living room, sat in one of the dryer chairs, and played her messages. The first was from Luke.

"Man, don't you ever stay home anymore, Alex?" He sounded annoyed. "I'm calling to wish you a Merry Christmas a little early. I've got a chance to play at a benefit in Khasistan and I'm not sure what the phone link will be like. It's really a big break for me."

Alex could hear an impatient male voice in the background. "C'mon, mate."

"Well, love you, Alex," Luke said. Then he hung up the phone.

She wondered about a career boost in Khasistan, as the next message started.

"Aunt Alex, stay safe. And thanks again for the phone. I'm a real menace now that I can call anyone. I'll miss you tonight even if you sometimes snore."

Alex smiled and stood back up, her image reflected from the three walls of mirrors. She had some shiner, all right. Looked like she was KO'd in an early round of a featherweight boxing match.

She inspected the crisp white man-tailored blouse she was wearing, with the tailored darts nipping the fabric in around her waist. It was a flattering look, making her realize that some of the double takes she got from the soldiers at the AFIP the past few days were not just related to her shiner.

But it wasn't her look. Barbara had loaned her the blouse and Alex was glad to get back to her own apartment, her own clothes, and her own bed.

Oh, the bed. Alex walked into her bedroom, feeling a tension in her chest and a flop of her heart as she returned to the scene of her attack. She stared first at the gold and turquoise hand-loomed rug her mother had brought back from Burma. There was a brown, twig-shaped spot on it, three inches long. It matched the pattern of the gash above Alex's eye, where she had hit her head on the nightstand as she pulled on the guitar strap to save her life. She thought for a moment about how she felt about the imprint of her blood on the rug. Was it a sign of her vulnerability (the attack) or her strength (the harsh last pull that took her assailant's life)? Either way, Alex decided she'd keep the rug. There was something poetic about her blood being mixed with the sweat of those Burmese women who'd woven this fabric masterpiece.

The bed, though, was a different matter. With the memories of what occurred there, she'd never get to sleep. Plus, the mattress had been taken for evidence, leaving only a hand-me-down headboard from her landlord in medical school and a set of box springs. She and Luke had experienced a rainbow of pleasure on that bed (as had a few of her other lovers, in a methodical monogamous row), but Luke seemed as out of the picture now as the missing mattress.

Alex sat on the rug. She traced the pattern of the bloodstain with the tip of her finger while she considered the matter of a bed. Where was she going to get one at nine at night? And bed-choosing was a big responsibility. There was the issue of size, queen or king. And the matter of style—sleigh beds, four-posters, wrought-iron trellis beds, carved wooden antiques, slick Danish moderns. She wasn't sure she was up to this Rorschach of bed choices just yet.

She walked into the kitchen and opened a bottle of wine to celebrate her return home. The Cabernet bit at her still-sore throat as it made its way into her system. She flipped through the Yellow Pages and started dialing. Eventually she found a futon store that was still open and convinced the owner to deliver a mattress and take away her old bed that evening. She was content to sleep on a futon on the floor for a while—almost at eye level with the rug—until she decided which bed was right for her.

CHAPTER THIRTY-THREE

THE NEXT morning, Troy knocked on her laboratory door. He was carrying a tray with a porcelain teapot and two delicate cups.

"Ah, jasmine tea," she said. She led him to her inner office, glancing around to make sure there were no documents about the confidential court-martial question, and then helped him set the cups and pot on her desk.

"You look horrible," he said as they begin to sip.

"Actually," she said, "I had trouble sleeping. It's harder than I expected to be back in my apartment."

"Unhappy spirits linger."

Alex thought for a moment. Was it the apartment that had changed—with a mourning spirit—or had she herself been transformed? She felt an odd new kinship with the military men among whom she worked. She tried not to believe that by killing a man she'd gained entry into some exclusive male club.

Troy bowed his head in a disconcertingly formal gesture. "I want to thank you for identifying Mymy's skull. Your kindness will be recognized by her spirit."

Alex felt uneasy discussing part of a skeleton as if it were a human being who was passing judgment on her. She also didn't like the way Troy was making her feel ill at ease in her laboratory, the one place she always felt sheltered and comfortable.

Alex finished the last of the tea and said, "I need to get back to work. But we never did get that Thai food dinner. I know a great place in Adams Morgan. . . ."

He looked down. Alex remembered that he usually brought his lunch to work. He was obviously economizing.

"My treat," Alex said.

He considered it a moment, and then said yes.

"THE SMELLS are exactly right," Troy said as they entered the restaurant that night. The place served authentic Thai dishes, not the sweetened, plumped-up Americanized versions. The tables were like picnic benches, seating ten people. Troy and Alex were led to one with six seats already filled. Troy was intrigued to see their tablemates drinking *laukhaaw*—a fermented rice whiskey—from big buckets through two-foot straws. "My uncle and his friends spent many evenings in Jakarta drinking *laukhaaw*."

Overhearing him, the group at the table asked the owner of the restaurant for two more straws and invited Troy and Alex to join in. Alex sipped. "Not bad," she said.

The owner chimed in. "That's why Thailand has the fifth-highest alcoholism rate in the world." He ticked off the other four on his fingers. "After South Korea, the Bahamas, Taiwan, and Bermuda."

"How come it isn't a problem here?" she asked.

He pointed to a sign by the cash register saying you had to be twenty-one to buy liquor. "We card. We card!"

The potent liquid seemed to loosen some of Troy's memories and he began to tell Alex about his immigration to Jakarta.

"Do you ever go back to Indonesia?" Alex asked him.

He shook his head.

"What about Vietnam?" she asked.

"Twice. But you've got to understand—those who stayed resent those who left, no matter how much we try to do.

Vietnam lost a lot of its professionals. There are more Vietnamese M.D.'s working outside of Vietnam than there. More than three million people left for political or economic reasons."

"Or because they were too young to have a say in the decision, like you," Alex said.

He nodded. "When we go back, we even look different. Because we haven't been raised on a diet of rice, we are taller, heavier. In the hotels and marketplaces, we are charged higher prices than those who stayed and we are called a disparaging name—Viet Kieu. Never mind that the Viet Kieu send back over a billion dollars a year through the banks—and double that in cash, transported in suitcases or sent through less official channels."

Alex realized now why it was that Troy lived so modestly, for a doctor. From the level of resentment in his voice, she realized where his money had gone.

"It makes me think of the Cubans in Miami," she said.

"Somewhat the same, but at least they are in a place where there are enough of them to have some political power. We're scattered all over the country. What angers me most is that the postwar generation in Vietnam is more smitten with America than I am, yet feels holier than those of us who live here."

"What do you mean smitten?"

"When President Bill Clinton visited Hanoi, he was met by thousands of young people. One in four Vietnamese watched his speech on television. And for Tet in the year 2000, the magazine called *Youth—Tuoi Tre*—asked young people who they admired most. Hilary Clinton got as many votes as our Prime Minister. She was more popular than anyone in the politburo."

"Ouch. That must have pissed off the Administration there."

"Enough so that state censors destroyed the print run of 120,000 copies within hours of the magazine's release."

Alex tried to imagine a youth poll in the United States. Would a politician even make the list? Not while there were rock stars and basketball players to admire.

Troy continued, "Vietnam is still obsessed with the United States, and Americans never even think of her. Let alone all the Lizzies they left behind."

Alex bristled. "I think about Vietnam, my father there, all the time. And won't the event at the White House bring Vietnam back to the world stage? With all the media coverage the handoff has already gotten, they're even teaching the Vietnamese New Year's traditions in grammar schools this month."

Troy slurped the last bit of their neighbors' drink, then bowed to them. "Perhaps. Maybe the event at the White House will make, what's the expression? A big bang."

He flagged the waiter and ordered another huge vat of *laukhaaw* for the table. He began telling Thai jokes to everybody—a charming, bold side of Troy Alex hadn't seen before. She wondered what other aspects of himself he was hiding.

A cute brunette at the table asked how Troy got his first name. "It doesn't sound Vietnamese to me."

His expression turned serious. "When I came here, they took away my name. It was *P-h-u-c,* which means 'luck' or 'blessings,' but my sixth-grade teacher in Minnesota must have thought it sounded too foreign, or too much like 'fuck,' so she named me after some blond actor."

"Troy Donahue," Alex said. She'd always assumed Troy's name was more mythic, like the ancient Greek city.

"Yeah, I got ridiculed as a kid for that name. Somehow I think that being named Fuck would have given me a lot more power."

As the evening proceeded, their tablemates drank more than their share of the second *laukhaaw*. Troy and Alex were saved from getting totally wasted and could concentrate on the mango sticky rice dessert delivered to their table about twenty minutes later. Troy offered to drive her home, and Alex merely giggled. "Isn't the designated driver supposed to refrain from drinking?" she asked.

He grinned sheepishly. "I'm fine. I actually started drinking this when I was nine years old. I'm sure I've built up immunity."

Alex wasn't buying the immunity, given his flushed face. But it was fun to see him this animated, this open. "I only live a few blocks from here," she said. She thought about the deserted apartment, still tainted from the night of her attack.

As if reading her mind, Troy said, "Then I shall walk you home."

CHAPTER THIRTY-FOUR

TROY WAS taken aback by the dozens of reflections of the two of them in the walls of mirrors in Alex's apartment. "Some of my countrymen put a mirror on the outside of their door to scare away a dragon," he told her. "With this many reflections, you could scare the entire Iraqi army plus a cartel of Colombian drug lords."

Alex spun the round, layered lazy Susan of nail polishes and motioned for him to sit down in one of the hair dryer chairs. Troy seemed confused. "This is your *house*?" he said. "Or do you have a second job cutting hair?"

"Nope, I live here." She took his hand to lead him on a tour. "This is the kitchen," she said as they entered the next room. She pointed to the rooms beyond that one. "My bedroom and office are over there."

"Ah, more like it," he said, sitting down at the kitchen table. "Those other chairs look like something from a San Quentin execution."

"Troy, I think I like you under the influence of *laukhaaw*. You're a lot funnier."

He looked offended, as if she had accused him of being frivolous.

She sat down across the table from him and they both were silent for a moment.

"This is where you were attacked?" he asked.

"In the bedroom," she replied.

"By a Vietnamese man like me," he said.

"No, not at all like you."

"But you seem afraid right now."

Alex put her hands on the table and began tapping nervously. *GGATC CTCAC,* the beta-thalassemia gene. She realized it was the beginning of the DNA code of her attacker.

"It's difficult to be back in the apartment, yes," Alex said. "It has nothing to do with you. I've thought a lot about my feelings. Barbara tells me everybody is afraid of something. I guess I've been lucky. I hadn't really felt vulnerable before."

"Your friend is right. Everyone has something to fear— and something to hide."

"What do you fear?" Alex asked.

"I fear that my life will be irrelevant, without meaning." He was once again the serious Troy.

"Surely you can't mean that," she said, surprised. "Look at all the people you help in your psychiatric practice." Alex felt bad that she had slighted him with her earlier comment. She wanted to see him relaxed and joyful again.

"Why do you think I decided to cut down on seeing patients and take a straight research job at NIH? I'm mismatched with my patients. How can I help the sort of patients who can afford a private shrink in a city like this? A bunch of guys with midlife crises. What do I know that can comfort them? How can I even bring myself to care? I've seen so much worse. I want my life to mean something bigger than being a sounding board for some bored G-14 government official. I want to be significant."

"But the boys, you help them. The time you spend as a Big Brother."

He looked down at his hands, then up at Alex. "A small thing, still. But I can understand them. I can also understand your nightmares. Come, I will put you to bed."

He got up and walked into her bedroom. She followed him, wondering what she was about to get herself into. He stared at the futon, the stain on the rug. Then he knelt at the side of the bed.

"Get ready for sleep and I will tell you a story," he said.

Alex took a nightgown from her closet, slipped it on in the bathroom, and brushed her teeth. When she came out, Troy had pulled back the blanket on the futon, but was still kneeling on the floor.

She climbed into bed and he turned out the light. A sliver of moonlight illuminated the room from the half-closed blinds.

"I am sure," Troy said in a whisper, "that the nightmares will stop tomorrow."

"How can you know that?"

"Because today they buried your attacker. His spirit will be at peace and will not meddle with you."

Troy reached over and stroked her hair. What he said was surprising: *Dúa bé xinh xắn.*

Alex started to cry. The words had triggered a memory that went back decades, long before her attack. "What does that mean? When my father came home on leave, he called me that." She wondered how she had even remembered. It had not reentered her consciousness until this moment.

"Ah, he might have heard a song that we sing to children. It means 'a pretty child.' "

Troy started to sing, ever so quietly. Alex took it to be a Vietnamese lullaby. She listened to the soothing cadence of his song. She would try to remember the sensation of his lyrics drifting through her bedroom like a thin whiff of incense. She sensed that the memory would comfort her in later days, would banish the image of the masked man with his sturdy hands around her neck.

Alex looked at Troy. His eyes were heavy with sleep and he was obviously drunk. In no condition to drive right now.

She sat back up in bed. "It's so late. Why don't you stay here? You can take the futon and I'll sleep on the floor in the other room."

Troy looked over at a quilt that was draped over a chair in the corner of her bedroom. "I'll take the quilt into the mirror room. Wake me if you have a nightmare."

Alex nodded, but she doubted she would need to disturb him. Her body already was floating off into dreamland.

THE NEXT morning, Alex opened the door to her bathroom. Troy was standing in front of the sink in his boxers, hair wet from a shower, swishing some of her toothpaste in his mouth.

"Oops, I didn't realize you were in here," she said. In his reflection in the mirror, she could see ladderlike scars up the length of his arms.

He caught her gaze and turned to face her. "When I first came to this country, I felt so deadened. The American boys seemed to have a spirit, an energy, that I lacked. I used to cut myself so that I could show myself that I could feel something."

Alex touched his right arm, using her finger to trace one of the scars. He pulled his arm sharply back.

"You know what they say about psychiatrists," he said. "They go into that business because they are troubled themselves."

He walked out of the bathroom and started dressing in the living room. She gave him his privacy until she heard the footsteps that indicated he had his shoes on. Then she entered the living room. "You're not going yet, are you? I was about to offer you one of my world famous Gorgonzola cheese omelets," she said.

He walked over to her and stuck out his hand for an awkward handshake good-bye. "I was raised to never have eggs in the morning when I had something important to do."

He thanked her and was out the door before she could ask what he was doing that was so damn important.

CHAPTER THIRTY-FIVE

AT LUNCH in the cafeteria the next day, Alex unzipped her fanny pack and handed Barbara three envelopes from the Pentagon City Mall. "You and Lana were such sweet hosts, I wanted to thank you."

Barbara opened the gift certificates—from Macy's, Champs Sports, and Victoria's Secret. When she'd stayed with her friend, Alex had noticed that she could use a few things, like some new towels.

"This way you can get something for the house, something for Lana, and something for you," Alex said.

"Hmm, I wonder which is which?"

"Here's a hint—I just appointed myself the fairy godmother of your sex life."

Barbara laughed. "Judging by the way you run yours, I might be in for a wild ride."

As they were finishing their meal, Dan walked over with a newspaper and a bottle of champagne. He pointed to the *Financial Times* article reporting that Westport Oil had won the bid for the Phu Khanh oil reserves.

"Anderson thinks our unparalleled investigative skills were what led to the CD-ROM being returned to him," Dan said, "so he sent us this."

"If the information was leaked, how did Westport win?"

Alex asked. "Both bidders would have had the same information about the value of the reserves."

"The U.S. could throw in something the other bidder couldn't—the ceremony for the return of the skulls."

Barbara stared at Dan as he began to peel the foil off the cork of the bottle. "You know that, as government employees, we can't accept a gift worth over twenty dollars," she said.

Dan showed her the bottle of Champagne Cuvée Dom Perignon Vintage 1973; then he popped the cork. "I'm sure he got it on sale," he said.

Despite Barbara's stern expression, Alex let him fill her glass.

"You know who really owes us?" asked Dan. "Vice President Shane. His Westport Oil holdings are in a trust, but when he leaves office, he'll be eight million dollars richer."

Barbara thought it over and put her glass forward. "If he can make that much on the deal, I guess I can take a little sip."

AFTER LUNCH, Alex followed Barbara back into her office and closed the door behind them. "We need to talk about Wiatt. He's dragging his heels on the massacre," she said. "He questioned Michael Carlisle, who I'm convinced had nothing to do with it, and stopped there. I'm worried he'll try to cover it up entirely, now that the Vice President's company entered that oil deal."

Barbara nodded. "The colonel hasn't told me to back off yet, but now that a new oil source is involved, he's started talking about the whole incident as involving national security."

"Bullshit," Alex said. "Wiatt doesn't want to rock the boat for his friend in the White House. Is anybody investigating the allegations in the letter?"

Barbara shook her head.

"I know how we can figure it out," Alex said.

"Are you sure you aren't just trying to assure yourself that Michael wasn't involved?"

Alex wasn't sure of anything these days. Her home, her

lab—everything she'd taken for granted—had been turned inside out. "Just hear me out. We know that incident took place near Qui Nhon. We also know the letter writer was sick, from dengue fever."

"How'd you figure that out?"

"That's what the soldiers called break-bone fever. It's a virus transmitted by mosquito bites. There's no vaccine or treatment and the joint pain is excruciating—it feels like broken bones."

"Is it fatal?"

"Sometimes. The person starts bleeding through the nose, then the mouth, then the intestinal tract. Pretty soon the bleeding is uncontrollable and they just bleed to death. You can't even put an IV in them because that starts a flood of blood. But here's the rub that can help the investigation. I can match the medical records of the soldiers with dengue fever to the troop logs that show what unit was where. If we find a troop with a Nick and a guy with dengue near Qui Nhon whose initials were *S.F.*, we could figure out who caused the massacre."

"Opening up old medical records could be tough."

"Not as tough as the life of that poor boy who saw his father shot."

Barbara considered the matter. "I can think of one way to angle at it. I could say that we needed them for your biowarfare work."

"Brilliant as usual," Alex said. "And not necessarily false. It just might turn out to give me some ideas there, too."

CHAPTER THIRTY-SIX

BARBARA MADE good on her word. She was able to get Alex access to the medical records of men in Vietnam who had dengue fever prior to mid-1972, when the skull entered the country. Alex cross-checked them with the service records. But the cases of dengue fever near Qui Nhon were more numerous than she'd expected.

She walked out of her office into her lab. She fussed a bit, rearranging reagents on the shelf. Although most traces of the break-in—and of the later forensic crew—had been removed, the lab was not quite back to the pristine order that she depended on.

As she moved a beaker a few inches to the left and closed the top of a box of pipettes, she wondered if Troy was right about the angry spirits of the displaced skulls. Her troubles had begun immediately after the Trophy Skulls entered her life. She wondered what she could do to make peace with those particular ghosts.

It was late that night when Alex finished working her way through the endless combinations of data about Lo Duoc. She learned which soldiers and sailors had been in the vicinity. She found a couple of Nicks, Nathans, and other names that might be relevant, but none of them had served in a unit with a guy with the initials *S.F.* who fell ill with dengue fever. So much for her great theory.

As she sat at the desk in her office, considering what to do next, she wondered if all this focus on the Trophy Skulls in the past few weeks was a way to avoid thinking about the people in her life—Luke, her mother. She picked up the phone and dialed.

"Alex!" her mother said with surprise. They usually communicated via e-mail. Both their schedules were so hectic that they often sent messages in the middle of the night. More than once, they both were e-mailing each other at 3:00 A.M. and had a digital conversation at that time.

"Hi," Alex said. "I was wondering what you are doing for Christmas. Would you like me to fly to Ohio?"

"Oh, Alex, you know I'm not one for holidays."

It was true. While other kids' moms embroidered Christmas stockings or baked gingerbread men, Janet had treated holidays like any other day. It was her dad who bought her a blond-haired angel ornament each year. Alex had moved them with her from place to place her whole life. "We could just hang and go to the movies," Alex suggested.

"Oh no, I'm tied up already. A bunch of us are riding horses into the Grand Canyon to the village where the Havasupai tribe lives. The Bureau of Indian Affairs is trying to screw them out of their land, and we're going to have a helluva protest."

Ah, Janet. Still trying to change the world. Never met a cause she didn't like. "Sounds interesting," Alex said.

"Is everything all right with you?"

Alex thought for a moment. Getting attacked in her apartment and having her lab broken into seemed minor compared to the issues her mom dealt with. Genocide. Poverty. "Yeah, I'm still liking the job."

"Are you seeing patients again?"

Alex hesitated, knowing that her mother would not like the answer. "Rarely. I'm doing some interesting research on infectious diseases, though."

"Ah . . . ," said Janet, with a hint of disappointment in her voice.

Alex was remembering why she preferred e-mail as a

way of communicating with her mom. No pregnant pauses. No unspoken rebukes.

"Well, have a great holiday," Alex said. "Give the government hell."

"You, too, honey. Take care of yourself."

Of course Alex would. She'd been doing it since she was five years old. "Well, bye, Mom."

"Love you," Janet said, and hung up before Alex could reply.

ON THE way home late that night, the moon was a perfect circle. That sphere seemed to urge Alex to break out of her rut—to bounce around in zero gravity or eat green cheese. Alex smiled to herself and decided to let the moon redirect her tides. She stopped to hear music at the Galaxy Hut in Arlington, where Luke performed when he was in town.

Alex didn't even look at the poster on the door to see what that night's offering was. Sometimes it was country, often rock, occasionally folk, but tonight it didn't matter to Alex. She knew that she'd been away from music too long, the way that she sometimes realized, after a string of melancholy gray weather days, that her body needed the healing rays of the sun. Yes, music was what she needed. She was definitely lacking in Vitamin M.

The wall of sound that caressed her body as she entered the crowded room was definitely rock. The deep vibrations of the bass gave her a giddy jolt. This was a great idea.

Mac, the bartender, knew her well and had an Old Weller with ice waiting by the time she pushed her way through the crowd from the door to the bar.

"You lookin' or listenin' tonight?" Mac asked. He nodded his head toward a nice-looking man in a brown leather jacket at the end of the bar who was checking her out. Alex was touched that Mac was concerned about her well-being.

"I came for the music," she said.

Mac nodded. Alex knew that he'd do his best to discourage men from hitting on her and let her just enjoy.

Soon she was clapping and foot tapping with the rest of

the room. It made her realize how quiet her apartment had been without Luke and his band practicing in her living room. Plus, a typical week with Luke meant that they'd go out one or two nights to listen to a new band or an old favorite.

Alex watched as the drummer erotically pummeled the Gretsch drum set, with an occasional tickle of the Zildjian cymbals. The lead guitar player echoed the drummer's intense rhythm on his strings. Then the guitar player walked behind the drum set and, without either of them missing a beat, the guitar player took over the drumsticks and handed his guitar to the drummer. They both continued rocking on, to thunderous applause, each mastering the instrument of the other.

There was an energy about the performance—a linear drive—that Alex could identify with. When all was going well with her biotoxin research, she felt no hesitation about what steps to take next. It was like being a musician or poet to whom a song or poem appears full blown. But she envied the fact that, unlike a scientist or poet, a musician interacts with other band members and the audience. She rarely thought about it, but sometimes when she took a moment to breathe amidst all the activities and pressures of her life, she was struck that she was very much alone.

This was not one of those moments, though. Tonight she was part of the protoplasm of the crowd, with the music from the stage rewiring her neurons. She stayed until 2:00 A.M., but rather than feeling tired she felt refreshed. Maybe it was just having tangible evidence that there was a world outside of the boundaries of the AFIP investigations.

She was flying with energy when she arrived at the Curl Up and Dye. The information she'd been reading about dengue fever had inspired some new ideas for a vaccine project. There was still no treatment for break-bone fever and it was running rampant right now in Thailand. The Trophy Skulls would go back to the Vietnamese government soon and she would no longer be their caretaker. But maybe their legacy would be a vaccine for a deadly disease. Troy had taught her that the spirits of the dead needed things like

houses and food in their afterlife. But maybe they would also
like to be part of a social enterprise that aided the world.

As she opened the door to her mirrored living room, Alex
giggled at herself. She said to her slightly ruddy-faced (three-
bourboned) reflection, "Lighten up, girl." She leaned closer
to the glass to see if her eyes were bloodshot. Out of the corner of her eye, she noticed an awkward shadow in one of the
dryer chairs.

She turned sharply, holding her breath, fearful it was an
intruder. Instead, she saw a wreath of dead flowers, the kind
you see on a grave. The banner had the traditional RIP. But
stapled to that ribbon was another note, "Don't forget Lo
Duoc."

SHE RAN into the kitchen, grabbed a knife, and then
checked out her bedroom and its closet. She opened the
bathroom door and peered into the shower. Whoever had left
her the wreath was no longer in the apartment.

She bolted the door to the outside and looked at the
wreath more closely. With a pair of latex gloves on her
hands, she carefully turned over the note to see if there was
anything written on the other side. There was a pinhead-
sized brown dot of blood where the note had been stapled.
The author had probably nicked himself slightly with the
staple.

It was tiny, but it was enough. "Gotcha," she said.

Alex took two swabs of the dot. One she would give Dan
and one she would keep.

She sat in the dryer chair next to the one the wreath was
in, trying to decide what to do. This wasn't like the Vietnamese intruder. No windows had been broken; the lock had not
been picked. Someone had let himself or herself in.

But who had keys beside Luke?

Then she felt like an idiot. Whoever copied her keys and
let themselves in her lab could have copied her home keys,
too.

Had the person who'd broken into her laboratory now
broken into her home? But that didn't make sense. The lab

intruder made the evidence about Qui Nhon disappear. The person who broke into her house wanted her to make it public.

Who else might have had access to her house key? She hated herself for her suspicions, but she thought back to the night Troy stayed there. He woke up before she did. He could have easily grabbed her keys off the kitchen counter and headed out to copy a set.

She called Dan. He told her to leave the apartment and wait for him someplace secure nearby. "It's not safe for you to be there right now."

But she'd be damn if she were going to be kicked out of her own house, just when she had gotten up the courage to move back in. She double-checked the bolt, which would keep out even someone with a key, and called a locksmith. Dan could get whatever evidence he could find, but then she was going to change the lock.

"It's a new one on me," Dan said when he read the note. "I've seen plenty of attempts to warn off investigators—but to break into someone's house to tell them to stay on a case?"

He verified that whoever it was had let himself in with a key, looked around the chair for trace evidence from the intruder, and took a photograph of the wreath.

He tried again to convince her to go someplace else for the night, maybe even to stay with him and Jillian, but she held firm. In all, Dan was there less than fifteen minutes, and it took the locksmith another half hour to change her lock. Once she was alone again, Alex took a swig of bourbon to calm down. Forcing herself to take steady breaths, she thought about this new break-in. Who would gain if she pursued the investigation? Wiatt wanted to see it buried. But Troy had been ready to make the United States pay when he thought a soldier had strangled Mymy. Could he have found out about the letter somehow?

She went into her bedroom and carefully unfolded the quilt that Troy had slept on. She was rewarded in her search. There was a black hair, with a follicle attached. She put it in an evidence envelope and tucked it into her fanny pack. Then she rechecked to assure herself that the new lock and old bolt were fully engaged, took off her clothes, lay down on the futon, and fell into a fitful sleep.

CHAPTER THIRTY-SEVEN

WHEN THE DNA run came back assuring her that Troy's blood was not on the wreath, Alex felt foolish for having suspected him. Even though—or maybe especially because—she hadn't asked his permission to do the test, she felt that she'd crossed some line, invading his privacy in a fundamental way.

With her first theory deflated, she wondered who else would gain by her pursuing the court-martial investigation. Wiatt was sure that Michael was the key suspect, even though neither of his squadrons had been listed in the printout of units in the vicinity of Lo Duoc and neither had a soldier with break-bone fever.

But maybe Wiatt's continuing suspicion was a reason to suspect Michael, not of the massacre, but of depositing the wreath in Alex's apartment. If someone else was identified, he'd be in the clear.

Alex looked at her reflection in the lab refrigerator, comforted that she was still a blonde in blue jeans. She was beginning to feel a bit like the pop vampire Elvira as she prepared to find and test the DNA of yet another man in her life.

She opened the cabinet and found the four evidence bags with the cigarettes that had come from Mymy's skull. Michael had told her that he and three other soldiers had smoked them to honor four men who had been killed.

She picked up the first cigarette to determine if its DNA matched the blood from the wreath. She searched for the discoloration that meant dried saliva from thirty years ago, extracted DNA from it, and tapped it into the PCR machine to replicate enough of the DNA to enable her to analyze it. Fifteen minutes later, she transferred the DNA to a chip and ran it through the gene sequencer. She repeated this for the second and third cigarette, but none gave her a match to the wreath.

She began the sequencing run on the fourth cigarette. The sequencer ran for a few seconds, then started behaving strangely, the screen turning to a bright blue with the words *INVALID RUN* on it like it did when she'd contaminated a sample with her own DNA. She was about to rerun the fourth cigarette, carefully taking DNA from another spot on the cigarette, when she realized that the similarity between the DNA on the fourth cigarette and her own DNA was understandable. The fourth cigarette contained her father's DNA.

She felt a flash of awe. This was the closest she'd gotten to her dad, to his flesh and bones, in thirty years. She now understood why people in the 1300s established reliquaries, carved boxes holding pieces of skin or hair or teeth from deceased saints. It was humbling to feel this close to someone's essence. She had an odd feeling—it was him, but not him. She stared at the red, blue, green, and orange patterns on the screen of the sequencer. She couldn't remember the exact color of his eyes anymore, but here she was, facing the color of his DNA. For a geneticist, it was almost a religious experience. She saved a digital version of the sequence run. Then she put this fourth cigarette back in its evidence bag on the shelf. She understood better now what Troy was talking about. The remains of the dead still held power over the living.

CHAPTER THIRTY-EIGHT

THE NEXT day, Christmas Eve, Alex couldn't think of what to do besides going into her lab. In fact, as she sipped her coffee that morning, she realized she was looking forward to it. In just a week, the Trophy Skulls would be on their way back to Vietnam and she could concentrate full-time on her biotoxin work. Dengue fever was a new puzzle, too. Her involvement with the skulls might actually led to a break in her ongoing research. She guessed there was a silver lining even to the menial tasks that Wiatt assigned her. And, truth be told, he didn't bug her with things to do very often.

Hmm, she thought. Had she just had a charitable thought about her boss—the very man who had threatened to fire her? The Christmas spirit must be infecting her big-time.

On the drive to work, she listened to an NPR segment on the growing popularity of Vietnam's former Minister of the Interior, National Assembly Member Huu Duoc Chugai, and how he was inching toward the presidency of his country. The election would take place in July. He was going to use the Trophy Skulls ceremony at the White House and the Westport Oil deal to forge a different relationship with the United States.

She expected the AFIP to be deserted, except for the guard at the entry station, but, as she slammed the door of her car, she saw Grant getting out of his.

He walked over to her and, making a gesture with his hand as if he were tapping his fingers on an alarm keypad, said, "How's L-U-K-E?"

"Grant, give me a break, can't we pretend the break-in didn't happen?" she said. Then she continued quietly, "Luke's in Europe on tour." Probably with Vanessa by now, she thought. "How come you're not off celebrating?"

"Debra got all the ornaments in the divorce action. Along with everything else of value."

"You can start a new collection, you know."

"Yeah," he said, serious for once. "But I'm not quite ready."

After they signed in, Grant led her down the hall to his lab. Once inside he opened a cabinet and said, "Check out what Santa left for you."

"Oh, you know I'll never make the good girl list."

He laughed. "Yeah, that's why I like you." He handed her a box.

Alex was surprised. "You shouldn't have."

"I didn't," he said. "You can thank Uncle Sam—or, rather, the Senate Appropriations Committee, which is far more generous than old St. Nick."

Alex opened the box and found a phone, similar to the one that Grant had given Lana. Grant excitedly pointed out its features. "Here's the button that allows you to tape things, in case you have some bright scientific idea and want to record it," he said. "And here's the real reason you're getting this—the matrix that allows you to translate to and from Vietnamese."

Alex usually regarded Grant's projects as a waste of tax-payer funds. But she was grateful for this one. She wanted to be able to say something to Mymy's mother. She pushed a button and said, "I'm pleased to meet you." An instant later, the phone gave what apparently was the same sentence in Vietnamese.

She had a sinking thought. "Grant, you haven't pro-grammed this as some sort of joke, have you? I don't want to think I'm saying hello to the Vietnamese Ambassador at the

White House and later find out you've rigged it so that I've told him his fly is open."

"Nah, you'll get through New Year's without a hitch," he said. "But you might want to be careful how you use it on April Fools' Day."

In her office, Alex started reading about the dengue fever virus. There were four distinct agents that caused the disease—DEN 1, DEN 2, DEN 3, and DEN 4, all transmitted by mosquitoes. Once the holidays were over, she would call a buddy at the Centers for Disease Control and ask if he could send her some tissue with the virus so she could sequence it.

When she opened the refrigerator to determine how much room she had for new samples, the chill hit her, she wheezed a little, and she noticed that her heartbeat was irregular. Perhaps it was the toll of the investigation.

Or maybe it was a genuine problem. She often awoke from sleep with a strange flopping of her heart. She looked over at her sequencer. She could always test her own DNA to see if she had a genetic propensity to cardiac disease. But did she really want to know?

It slowly dawned on her that she could also test her dad's DNA. Perhaps, even if he hadn't been killed in Vietnam, he would have died young of an inherited cardiomyopathy. In a way, testing him would be a chicken's way out. If he didn't have the genetic mutation, then she couldn't have inherited a genetic predisposition to heart disease and the odd crackles in her EKG were nothing to worry about. Even if he *had* a genetic predisposition to heart disease, there would still be a 50 percent chance that she hadn't inherited it. If she tested her father's DNA, she could learn some information about her own risk without specifically having to stare into her own genetic crystal ball.

She cast her eye on the dish with the DNA sample labeled "ANB—Alexander Northfield Blake." Alex starting thinking about the sort of tests that she could run on her father's DNA. The heart genes, of course. Maybe Alzheimer's, too. She justified the quest by telling herself that if her dad were alive, she'd know what cards the genome had dealt him by seeing what symptoms he developed. Should she be gypped out of that information just because he died young?

She put the sample on the counter and prepared to layer it on a gene chip to run it through the sequencer. The photo of her father stared down at her from the laboratory shelf.

Then she put the DNA back in the fridge. She would not test her father's DNA. Troy was right. The dead should be honored, but allowed to rest in peace.

THAT EVENING, Alex hung the four angel ornaments she'd received from her dad off the dryer hoods in her living room. She'd stopped at the Duane Reade on the way home and bought a small live Christmas tree, already decorated. She put it on Luke's guitar stand, trying to convince herself that this wasn't pathetic.

The AFIP was closed the next day and she wasn't sure what she was going to do. Barbara and Lana were off in New York. Harding, who'd cooked more than one holiday meal for her on his houseboat, had booked a trip in the Bahamas for a fund-raising sail. Well, look at the bright side, she thought. She could get some rest, read a mystery, catch up on the medical journals that were piling up.

She slept in and was awakened by a 10:00 A.M. call on her cell phone, to which she'd rerouted calls from her office line.

"Are you alone today?" Michael asked.

Alex paused. "That's a pretty impertinent question."

"I mean, if you don't have plans for Christmas dinner yet, I'm laying on a big spread at my house."

Alex considered the invitation for a long moment while the telephone cackled. "Listen, I'm just in the middle of something. Can I call you right back?"

"Sure."

She hung up and sat on one of her dryer chairs. She pulled the stiff plastic bonnet over her head, as if to shut out the world while she thought this through. She felt comfortable with Michael, which must mean she had nothing to fear.

Then she gently berated herself. She was a crackerjack scientist and an increasingly good forensic investigator. But given her dating track record, she had no ability to make predictions about men.

She decided she would apply her best scientific logic to the situation. There was no record of him being near Lo Duoc. He'd just arrived in 1969—he had the lowest rank. How could he have ordered a massacre? And even if he'd gotten his hands on Mymy's skull in 1969, he would have brought it home at the end of his first tour of duty in 1970, not when he'd gone back in 1972.

Her rambling thoughts had reached a point where the scales of evidence weighed in Michael's favor. Content with that outcome, she dialed him back. "What time?"

"How about five P.M.? You can help me put the angel on the top of the tree and then we'll have a Christmas feast."

"What can I bring?"

"You're quite enough, just yourself."

When Alex hung up, she realized that there was something compelling out there in the forest. The hint of danger made it even more inviting.

Then she wondered if she was acting irresponsibly—not the first time in her life for that. Perhaps she shouldn't go out there without telling someone. She tried to think of who she could call who wouldn't talk her out of it. She knew that Barbara was in New York by now. She thought the best tack would be to leave a message on Barbara's machine at work saying she was on her way to see Carlisle. Alex was 99 percent sure nothing would happen to her out in the forest. But if danger did strike and Alex didn't return, someone at the AFIP would know where to start looking.

Alex donned black jeans and a red silk shirt, along with her favorite black Justin cowboy boots. She pulled out one of the bathroom drawers and found a free perfume sample that she'd gotten in the mail. "Presume," it was called. Well, she was certainly being presumptuous now.

The journey was familiar this time and the first twenty minutes passed by quickly. She was in the flow of the drive, listening to a rock station that mercifully wasn't playing Christmas tunes. She thought about how her musical choices had reverted back to the time prior to Luke. She'd put his CDs away on the back shelf in her pantry closet. He'd left her a few phone messages, but it seemed like every time she thought of calling him, he'd moved on to the next city of his tour, or she told herself she was too tired to get into a long conversation that filled him in on everything that was going on, including her near strangulation. How would she feel if he offered to fly home and take care of her? And how would she feel if he didn't?

When Alex arrived at Michael's, the gate was already open. She drove up to the house and he let her in. The living room had been transformed. Candles of different heights were lighted across the room, and at the far side facing the fireplace was a couch with a bow on it.

Michael noticed her puzzled look. "A present for you, of sorts. You didn't seem comfortable on the pillows when you were out here last."

Alex smiled. She was flattered that this handsome man was creating a space for her in his life. A new table in front of the couch was loaded with hors d'oeuvres—shrimp, tomato and mozzarella, melon and prosciutto. There was even a tin of Christmas cookies.

"Don't tell me you baked those?"

Michael shook his head. "Ellen made those for me."

Alex felt a moment of awkwardness. Ellen had probably made them hoping she'd be part of this scene. "Are you romantically involved with her?"

He looked surprised, as if he'd never considered it. "No, she's all business. She wouldn't cotton to a mongrel dog like me, never finished high school."

That wasn't the impression Ellen had given her. But, who knew? Some women had weird ideas about status. Unlike Alex, whose love life had included enough mongrel dogs to qualify as a pound.

She thought about the small, sad tree in her apartment and was glad she was here with Michael. He bent forward and filled a plate with food for her. She nibbled away and poured wine for them both.

They chatted about their families, movies they'd seen, worst Christmas presents they'd ever gotten. "A royal blue suit with short pants when I was seven," Michael said. "Mama must have gotten it on sale. I about died when she made me wear it to mass."

"*The Quotations of Chairman Mao* when I was that same age," Alex said, putting her empty plate down. "Not that it wasn't interesting reading, but I'd been hoping for a puppy."

Michael added a log to the fire.

"I'm sorry that the *Times* reported your connection with the skull," Alex said. "Just so you know, they didn't get that information from me."

"Hey, no worries. All that's happened so far is that a couple of old high school buddies called, told me they were impressed to see my name in print. I told them I was impressed they could read."

He poured more wine into her glass and asked, "Have you identified the men responsible for the massacre?"

"Not yet," she said.

"But you're the main link to a court-martial, right? Now that the letter is missing."

She put down her glass, shifting uneasily on the couch. "Whether I pursue it or not, they'll catch the guys."

He leaned forward. "Sometimes, Alex, it's better to let sleeping dogs lie."

Then he took Alex's hand and pulled her to a standing position. "Here's where I need your help."

She thought he was going to ask her to do something related to Lo Duoc, but instead he helped her into her coat and led her to his backyard.

Alex saw an incredible pine tree, maybe thirty feet tall, with strings of unlit lights all around it. "How did. . . . ?" she started to ask, and then noticed the cherry picker parked behind the tree. It had a seat in a metal box, like something from a carnival ride, big enough for two people.

Michael rolled right up to it and motioned her inside.

There was a picnic basket already there, with a champagne bottle poking out. Next to it was a basket of ornaments.

Alex sat down and Michael used his arms to lift himself out of the wheelchair and onto the seat next to her.

"You decorate, I'll drive," he said. He opened the champagne and poured a glass for her. After a toast, he put his arm around her, then whispered in her ear, "Just so you know, the break in my spine is at L 2."

Alex's cheeks turned pink. As a doctor, she knew exactly what that meant. His legs were paralyzed, but his accident had not affected his sexual abilities.

"Why, my good doctor," he said. "I believe I've made you blush."

He laughed and then nodded his head toward the basket. For the next fifteen minutes, she pulled ornaments out of the basket and hung them, one by one, on the giant tree as Michael propelled them up and around. Snow White and the Seven Dwarfs. A nutcracker. Snowflakes and stars. Even a Scrooge.

He handed her a box that had been shoved behind the seat. "For the top of the tree," Michael said.

Alex opened it. Instead of a blond angel, it was a carving of a Vietnamese woman.

"You're going to have to do the honors," he said.

The cherry picker couldn't quite reach the treetop without damaging the wider branches below. To put the woman on the treetop, Alex would have to stand and bend out of the metal box that held them. She stood up and looked down. This would be risky.

"Trust me," Michael said. "I'll hold on to you."

Michael moved the machine a few inches farther, but the lurch of the box nearly toppled the standing Alex. She turned to him, wondering if he'd done it deliberately to scare her.

"C'mon, honey," he goaded. "You're not afraid of a little danger, are you?" He put his right hand around her waist, fingers spanning the front of her jeans, up by the snap. As he put his left hand in place, she could feel a slight pressure of his fingers on her zipper. Whether from the champagne, the height, or his touch, she felt light-headed.

She turned to face him, which put her breasts at the height of his face. She reached for the carved woman he was holding, then turned back around. His hands had never left her body.

"Tallyho," she said. She bent completely forward at the waist. She held the treetop decoration with both her hands. Her safety was entirely in his hands. If he let go, she would topple to her death.

Her first pass did not get close enough. She stood back up straight, took a deep breath, and bent forward again. This time she stood on her toes, making her position even more perilous. She felt his left hand move slightly and then he took it away entirely. Only his right hand held her now. Her heart raced and she turned in panic at the thought he was letting go.

Instead, she saw that he was using his left hand to lift himself up, balancing against the metal rail. By thrusting himself forward a bit, he could hold her out closer to the treetop. She put the Vietnamese woman in place; then they both tumbled back to the seat.

"No limit to what we can do together," he said, brushing her hair back out of her eyes.

Alex did not speak. That moment of terror had tied a knot in her throat. She caught her breath, then chided herself for her overactive imagination.

He guided the cherry picker back around the tree and then down to the ground, next to his wheelchair. In an effortless maneuver, he thrust himself into the chair. She got out and walked a few feet back to admire their work. The tree was amazing.

"Wait till you see it lit up," he said. He started rolling back to the house, grabbing a log from the woodpile before he entered.

Back in the living room, he added the log to the fire, then stoked it. Alex sat down on the couch. He rolled his chair over and moved himself to the couch, sitting close to her.

Then he used a remote from the cocktail table to turn on the lights outside. Tens of thousands of tiny lights sparkled from the tree branches. A spotlight from the roof of the house illuminated the Vietnamese woman at the top of the tree.

He turned and kissed her. He caressed her hair, gently rubbed her cheek, and then moved his hands down toward her breasts. She moved his hand.

"Too much, too soon?" he asked.

She nodded.

"It's okay," he said, smoothing her hair with his right hand. "I'm a patient man."

He invited her into the dining room for dinner. After the meal, she said, "I can't thank you enough for everything—the tree, the food, even a couch."

Alex stood to leave.

"You forgot your final Christmas present," he said.

She looked at him quizzically.

"A rain check," he said.

CHAPTER THIRTY-NINE

THE NEXT day, December 26, Alex adorned her black turtleneck with a glowing necklace of tiny lighted champagne bottles. Lana had given it to her the previous year as a gift and she wanted to wear it to the AFIP holiday lunch that day. As was the tradition, Dan was taking about twenty of his team, including Barbara, Alex, Chuck, and Grant, out to a seafood restaurant in the District. They scheduled it every year on the week between Christmas and New Year's, so it didn't compete with family events. And they got to commiserate with each other over the fact that they generally had to work that week. Crime hit a high note over the holidays.

When she entered The Catch, she was taken aback by the way Dan was dressed. A navy blue business suit, starched white shirt, and yellow power tie. "What's with the disguise?" she asked him.

"Jillian's getting an award today at the National Press Club." Dan ran his thumb along his suit jacket collar, showing off the merchandise. "I'm trying to pass as a trophy husband."

"Jillian's crazy about you," Alex said. "She wouldn't care if you showed up in your skivvies."

"Truth be told," he said, "I wanted it to be her day. If I wear the uniform, people pay too much attention to me."

Over lunch, the group passed out the gag holiday presents

they'd bought each other. Earlier, they'd picked each other's names out of a hat and Alex had gotten Grant. She'd stopped to get him a T-shirt advertising the local YMCA. When he opened it, she couldn't resist saying, "To remind you of your nights at the clubs listening to the Village People."

Dan had drawn her name. She opened a package wrapped in goofy reindeer paper. It was a water pistol.

"Since you won't buy a real one," he said.

As he reached for his own package from Barbara, Alex noticed his cuff links—Semper Fi. He followed her gaze. "Jillian likes me to wear them. She says she wants the motto 'Always Faithful' to apply to me when she's on the road."

Alex didn't even stay around to watch Dan open his gift. Instead, she begged off and rushed back to the AFIP.

In her inner office, she reran the data about troop movements near Lo Duoc. She employed her new insight. The *S.F.* at the end of the letter was not the guy's initials. It stood for the Marine motto.

In the new run, there was only one Marine platoon that met the criteria of being near Lo Duoc and having a dengue victim: the 8th Battalion, 46th Marine Regiment. The one led by a twenty-four-year-old lieutenant, Nick Papparaplous.

With Chuck and the others still at the restaurant, she wondered how she could check his current whereabouts. She clicked on the virtual version of the Vietnam War Memorial and entered his name. He had not died in Vietnam. When Chuck returned, he would be able to look for a current driver's license and track his whereabouts with a Social Security number.

Alex paced her lab as she waited impatiently for the data guru's return. She wondered if he'd show up on one of the address Web sites or in a newspaper search. Then, thinking of how Troy had learned about her work at the World Trade Center site, she sat back down and Googled Nick.

And there he was.

The context was an article from three years earlier about Vietnam veterans, noting how many of them now worked with young people. They became high school teachers and school bus drivers and Scout Troop leaders. The reporter speculated that what drove them was a desire to give something back to society—and also to train each new generation to avoid the horrors of war.

Nick Papparaplous was a school bus driver for a junior high in Bridgeport, Connecticut.

Alex printed off the article and tracked Wiatt down in his office. She explained how she had deduced that he was the man in the letter. "Send someone to talk to him. I'm sure it's the right guy."

"Blake, the timing's all wrong. Even if you're right, we can't start a court-martial now."

She set her jaw. "You're sweeping this under the rug until after Cotter's ceremony?"

Wiatt angered. "You are done with the project. Finito. Take the next few days off, go sit on a beach someplace, I don't care. All you need to do is show up on the first with the skulls. I won't warn you again."

Alex gave a frustrated sigh on her way out of his office. "Happy New Year to you, too," she said.

CHAPTER FORTY

THE NEXT morning, Alex dressed for work, but then started throwing clothes into an overnight bag. Wiatt had practically ordered her to take time off and there was nothing more Dan needed from her on the Gladden case.

At Union Station, she caught a train to New York. She used her cell phone to make reservations at the Algonquin.

As the conductor punched her ticket, with the same funny little gadget used on trains for decades, she realized how much she fancied escaping into Manhattan's delicious anonymity.

Privacy had always been important to her. In grammar school, she'd rarely had friends over, wanting to keep her mother's depression a secret. She viewed personal information as a gift that people gave one another as a way to show trust and intimacy. But now her life had been splayed open, violated. Investigators had tromped through her apartment, confiscating pillows and Luke's guitar strap, snooping in drawers and closets, in the investigation of her attack. Someone, probably Grant, had described her apartment to other soldiers in the building. Now and then one of the nameless cloned men in uniform would hassle her, "Hey, girlie, how about giving me a permanent?"

When she got off the Metroliner at Penn Station in New York, she was in a cab riding to the hotel when she changed her destination. She headed to Grand Central Station and bought a ticket to Bridgeport, Connecticut.

ON THE train to Bridgeport, Alex started doubting her decision to rush off to find Nick Papparaplous. His current job as bus driver had made him seem safe, ordinary. But if he was the man who'd ordered a massacre in Vietnam, he could also have been the one who'd broken into her lab to get the letter. Alex shuddered as she followed her logic one step further. He might also want her dead to prevent her from testifying against him. Her fear began to work against her hope. She now started hoping this was all a case of mistaken identity.

But the trail was firm. He'd been a Marine posted near Lo Duoc at precisely the right time. Alex straightened her shoulders and sat erect in her train seat as the bedroom communities of New York commuters sped by outside of her window. How much danger could there be out here, where Starbucks and Gap stores dotted the horizon?

Her Bridgeport cab overshot the address, which was fine with her. She wanted to be able to claim she was at the wrong house if Nick looked too dangerous. She walked a half a block back to a small ranch house on a street of similar structures. Not like the glamorous Stamford or the intellectually vibrant New Haven, this section of Bridgeport was a conclave of the lower middle class.

When Alex knocked at the door, her heart raced and flopped in an irregular pattern. The door opened. Instead of the hard-bodied soldier she'd crazily imagined, a wheezy gray-haired man answered the door. She could tell he had emphysema, and maybe a heart condition. Not at all like the monster she'd pictured.

When Nick Papparaplous invited her in, he assumed that she was a friend of his daughter Bridget. But before he could call out to his daughter, Alex told him she was here to see him. He sat in the living room in a worn recliner covered in corduroy. A plastic container on the end table held this week's *TV Guide* and two remotes. A frame next to it held a photo of the face of a thin brunette, about Alex's age. Of course, the time line made sense.

She didn't know what reaction to expect, but she could not abide small talk at the moment. "I'm here to ask you about Lo Duoc."

"Don't know nothing about that place."

Well, Alex thought, he knew enough to know it was a place, not a person or a new soft drink or form of insurance she was selling. "Private Benjamin Lopata tells me otherwise."

"Benjie was a chickenshit coward. Besides, how's he talking to you? Voices from the grave? They're all gone now, 'cept me. I seen 'em on the Wall."

"Private Lopata wrote a letter. It's just come to light. It lays it all out. How you, Nick, gave the orders. How you burned the hootches. Shot at the civilians who ran out."

Nick covered his eyes with his palms, as if shutting out the scene. "No, that's not real. That's just the nightmare I get. How do you know about the nightmare?"

Alex sat quietly, then said, "Lots of men have nightmares about that war."

He put his hands on his lap and nodded. "I wanted to be like my old man. When I was a kid, I prayed that there'd be a war when I grew up. I wanted to prove I was as good as him."

"You didn't exactly get the sort of war you wished for, did you?"

"My old man made fun of me when I shipped out. Called Nam a pond of mosquitoes, a bullshit war."

"What happened once you were there?"

"CO told me not to give the formal count of how many POWs we'd caught before we took them up in a helicopter, but when we landed. Some of those North Vietnamese soldiers managed to get themselves pushed out of the copters. No one ever told us about something called the Geneva Accord."

Alex didn't like where this was going. It sounded too

much like Lieutenant Calley's defense that he was just following orders.

"When you got to Lo Duoc, you were in command. You weren't following orders there. You were giving them."

He started to cough, his emphysema kicking in with the stress of the memories. "At every stage of my life, I was just the sort of son the old man wanted. I shot the best, got the highest grades. And then we came to Lo Duoc. We were told to set fire to four huts that held Viet Cong supplies. We didn't know there were people in them."

"And when civilians and their children ran out, you ordered your men to fire on them."

He seemed shocked that she was describing the scene. "This wasn't like any war before. The Cong didn't wear uniforms. It wasn't like hitting a Nazi."

"But you didn't bother to find out, did you?"

His breath was shallow and labored. "In my nightmare, I'm willing to shoot those people, no matter who they were. After always doing everything right, I want to cover up the mistake."

He choked the final word as his labored cough shook his body.

A voice came from the other room. "Are you all right, Dad?"

A woman entered the room, the face in the photo. She had braces on her legs and severe scoliosis, curvature of the spine. Alex could tell from the laborious way she moved that she had a tethered spinal cord, which did not slide up and down with movement as it should because it was held in place by surrounding tissue. The doctor in Alex looked for the slight furrow in the skin along her neck that would indicate a shunt that drained the fluid collecting around her brain into the abdomen where it would pass harmlessly into her body.

Nick looked at Alex, seeing that she understood. It took Alex only an instant to figure out that the girl had spina bifida. And then she realized how the war had already punished

Lieutenant Papparaplous. Agent Orange could cause a child to be born with spina bifida.

"Your dad needs some rest, it seems," Alex said.

She turned to Nick and handed him her card. "I'd like you to talk to my boss about your dream."

He tipped his head in his daughter's direction. "No can do. I got responsibilities here."

The daughter used the crutches to move her braced legs with a surprising fluidity as she led Alex back to the door.

"It's nice you take care of your father," Alex said.

"He's the one who takes care of me. My mother left us right after I was born. I guess I wasn't the perfect baby doll that she had expected. Dad was the one who wouldn't give up on me, who refused to let the doctors put me in some state institution when I was a kid. He built parallel bars in the living room to teach me to walk, had special braces made. I'm who I am because of him."

As Alex said good-bye, she thought about what Papparaplous had said about not wanting to make a mistake. That philosophy in the hands of a scared soldier had led to a massacre. The same philosophy in the hands of a father had led to a miracle.

WHEN SHE arrived at the Algonquin, she'd had over an hour on the train to think about what she would do next about Nick Papparaplous. Her intense desire to find him had been satisfied. Her self-imposed timetable seemed to fade away a bit; it was clear he wasn't going anywhere. She called Barbara and told her what she'd learned.

"You can't just run off and compromise an investigation," Barbara scolded. "This 'Nick' person is probably lawyering up right now. There are rules that need to be followed."

"Barbara, the only rules I've run into so far are the ones that Wiatt declares. There's no way he's going to bring this guy to trial."

"I know how to work within the system. Promise me you'll stay out of it and I'll get someone in the JAG Corps to do the follow-up. Wiatt hasn't called me off of it yet."

"All right, all right. Now that I met him, I don't even know how I feel about it anymore. He's old, he's sick, he's taking care of his daughter. And he feels remorse."

"Now you're *defending* him?"

"It's complicated."

"Well, isn't everything?" Barbara said.

After they hung up, Alex decided to eat a late dinner at the Oak Room while listening to live cabaret. As the music washed over her, she thought about how Michael was now totally in the clear. She owed him an apology, even though she'd never voiced her doubts to him.

She went up to her room and called him. "I'd like to take you to dinner tomorrow night. When I drove out to your house that first time, I noticed an inn with a restaurant, near the Rampart River. How about eight o'clock?"

"Does this mean it's rain check time?"

"Not quite, but you'll get a good meal out of the deal."

"A meal it is. And maybe I can persuade you on the other."

CHAPTER FORTY-ONE

IN THE conference room the next afternoon, Dan handed Alex a photograph. "General Tran," he said. "I had someone follow the casket, find out about the man. He's the one who tried to kill you."

Alex played the scene in her apartment over in her mind. Then she looked again at the photo, which resembled the one of her father that graced her laboratory shelf. Young men, both of them, barely past boyhood, dragged into an upheaval of someone else's making. I'm sorry, General, she thought, that it had to end for you like this. It made him seem so much more human now that he had a name and a grave. Perhaps she would be less haunted with fear when she went home.

"What do you know about him?" Alex asked.

"Took a bullet in the American War. Worked for the Vietnamese government for the past fifteen years. Some sort of security job for the Ministry of the Interior."

Dan took the photo back. "I'm ready to close this case now. We know he was Gladden's killer—probably a revenge killing for leaking the oil report. We're pretty sure he went after you to keep the massacre under wraps."

"But how did he learn about the massacre?"

"We have no way of knowing. But this time next week, the

Trophy Skulls will be back in Vietnam and everything will be back to normal here."

"If you can call either of our lives normal," Alex said.

ALEX WAITED at the restaurant for an hour that night, but Michael never showed up. She tried his cell phone several times. She ordered appetizers when the waiter began to glare at her for taking up a seat without spending any money. But she couldn't bring herself to eat. Her emotions were a jumble. Did Michael feel she'd been jerking him around—and this was his way of getting back at her? She thought back to his voice the evening before. He certainly had sounded like he wanted to see her.

She left a big tip and retrieved her car. When she turned onto Rampart Road, she noticed a gaggle of police cars and an ambulance. With the crush of emergency vehicles, traffic slowed to a crawl. She slowed down to get herself within range of the speed limit and saw a Volkswagen EuroVan being pulled out of the Rampart River, which ran alongside the road. A closer look revealed it had West Virginia plates.

She turned the wheel sharply and deposited the car on the grass along the river. A police barricade already had been formed, and one of the officers shooed her away. She zipped open her fanny pack and pulled out an ID. "I'm a doctor."

The young cop glared at her for attempting to breach the line. "No one needing your services here, ma'am."

"The passenger, is he all right?"

"Whoever went down with the van hasn't turned up."

Alex stared at the water, willing him to surface. Then she realized how ludicrous her hopes were. A man with an L 2 spinal injury didn't have much of a chance when it came to a freezing winter river.

The van was lowered to the ground. The cops opened the passenger door, and water flooded out, with mangled vegetation and oval-shaped leaves from the river. Alex saw the drenched, stark silhouette of Michael's simple wheelchair. Staying about ten feet away at the insistence of the state police, she walked slowly to the other side of the van. Michael's soaked suit jacket was neatly hung across the back of the driver's seat, and there was a bouquet of flowers in the backseat. Tears formed in her eyes as she realized they were for her.

She couldn't see a briefcase, papers, or anything out of the ordinary. She stepped a bit closer and noticed the gouges in the driver's side door. Somebody had banged the hell out of the van. She looked down at the road. There were two sets of skid marks.

"Where's the other vehicle?" she asked the cop.

The detective gave a slow response. "We're asking that same question."

As he walked away to direct traffic, Alex pulled an evidence bag out of her fanny pack. She scraped some blackish or dark blue paint off the Volkswagen door that had been transferred to it in the accident. Please let it not be a Lincoln Town Car, Alex thought. In D.C., they were as common as Camrys and Accords were in the rest of the country. At 11:00 P.M., she personally drove to a hotshot chemist at Quantico who promised he'd have a fix on it by the next afternoon.

CHAPTER FORTY-TWO

ALEX MET Ellen Meyer at the office of Carlisle and Sons the next morning at 8:00. The state police had beat her there, and Ellen put her in the conference room while she finished giving a statement to the two men. Alex picked up each publication that was open on the table. A *Harvard Business Review*, with a Post-it on a page about South Asian management styles. Translations of poems by a Vietnamese writer and human rights activist, Nguyen Chi Thien.

> *There is nothing beautiful about my poetry*
> *It's like highway robbery, oppression, TB blood cough . . .*

Alex touched each object with reverence. They set the boundaries for Michael's last day. She wondered what he was thinking when he read that poem.

She looked up at the shelf. Books had been moved aside and the safe door was slightly ajar. She got up and opened it completely. The interior was empty, except for a few files, including one labeled "Photos." She took that file out and began to leaf through the photographs. The top one showed uniformed Americans with soldiers from the South Vietnamese Army. The next showed parajumper Michael dangling from a rope, trying to steady a badly wounded soldier who was being raised in a basketlike contraption into a copter.

From the angle of the photo, it had been taken from inside the copter. The photo caught a small slice of the profile of one of the other airmen. Alex's heart raced in recognition.

"What the hell are you doing?" asked Ellen, who stood in the doorway, having sent the officers on their way.

"It was open," Alex protested.

"No way. I haven't been in here this morning. Michael never—"

Alex looked down at the hardwood floor and then knelt and pointed out a spot. There was a brownish stain, still slightly wet. In the center were two leaves, with the same long oval shapes as the ones that had washed out of the van the night before.

Alex tipped her head back to address Ellen. "They've been dragging the river since dawn and they still haven't found the body. Is it possible he's still alive?"

Ellen considered the bare, open safe and then bent down to look at the leaves. Finally, she sat on the floor, too. "I have no idea, Alex. If anyone has nine lives, it's that man. The rest of his unit died in Vietnam. No one else could have survived that West Virginia car crash. Not to mention all those fights in bars and altercations with jealous husbands."

Alex unfolded her legs and rearranged herself on the floor. "If he made it out of the water, he would have needed help getting back here."

Alex and Ellen sat for a while lost in thought. Then Ellen stood up and Alex followed suit. "I'll check calls charged to his cell phone," Ellen said.

They moved into Ellen's office and she called the phone company. "I'm the managing partner of Carlisle and Sons, and we're investigating some calls made on one of our employees' cell phones. Can you give me the numbers called from the phone since five P.M. yesterday?"

Ellen gave the cell phone number and then started writing down the answers. The first number she listed was Alex's.

That's mine, Alex mouthed to Ellen. There was one other call, to a number in the District at 7:45 P.M., and no calls since then. The 7:45 call could have gone either way. It might have been moments before the accident, or moments after when—or if—Michael was getting out of the water.

The women were transfixed by the 202 number. Reverse directory pulled up nothing. When Ellen dialed it, the phone just rang. A subsequent call to the phone company found it was an unregistered cell phone, probably a disposable one.

QUANTICO REPORTED back that afternoon. Dark blue paint, from a Mercury Grand Marquis. It was the kind they used over bulletproof doors. A favorite of the diplomatic corps.

"It's got to be from the Vietnamese Embassy, what else could it be?" Alex said to Dan.

"Chuck, tell Alex how many embassies there are here in the District, almost all of which have bulletproof cars, often the Marquis."

Chuck, sitting at this computer station, tapped into a directory. "Who knew?" he said. "There are forty-one just on the two blocks known as Embassy Row."

Alex walked over and stood behind him. It was a daunting list. The diplomatic facilities on Massachusetts Avenue included everything from the British to the Brazilian embassies. Some of the countries had never even entered her thoughts before. Azerbaijan. Togo. Malawi. And this list didn't even include those embassies, like the Vietnamese one, that were on streets other than Mass Ave.

"But what other group would think they have a beef with Carlisle?"

"Do you know how many diplomats get into fender benders in the District?" asked Dan. "Especially those who drive on the left side in their home countries. The prime use of diplomatic immunity is for getting out of moving violations and rear enders."

"But this wasn't in the District," she said. "It was on a deserted stretch of road in Maryland. Call over for the police report. The skids suggest something intentional. We're not talking about a fender bender."

She bent down, so her face was inches from the seated Dan. "Are you saying we should just drop it? Pretend that a guy wasn't killed. Pretend that I didn't have a hand in getting him killed?" Alex could hardly recognize her own voice.

"Diplomatic immunity prevents us from going onto embassy property and checking out the cars," Dan said. "But I'll tell you what. At the White House on New Year's Day, when the ceremony takes place, I'll assign a couple guys to check the cars."

"Thanks," she said. Then she left to spend the rest of the day with someone who could understand her feelings.

"ANY SIGNS of him?" Alex asked Ellen when she returned to the office of Carlisle and Sons.

"No," said Ellen. "No movement at all in any of his accounts."

"The first time I came to the office, I noticed a lot of cash in the safe."

"Not only that, he's got a lot of people who owe him, in and out of various governments. But," Ellen added with a sigh, "he's also got a long list of enemies."

"Any worries one of them will come after you?"

"Nah, most of the people he's pissed off are from countries whose views of women make it hard for them to see me as a threat. They figure I'm either his secretary or his masseuse."

Alex remembered how pointedly Michael had referred to Ellen as his *partner*. "How can I help you? Did you call his family?"

"No family to speak of. I found this in the safe." She passed a sheaf of papers bound with pale blue backing over to Alex.

Michael's will.

"Look at the last page," said Ellen.

Alex's eyes teared up as she read his final wishes. He wanted to be cremated and have the ashes scattered in the countryside in Vietnam.

"He loved it there," said Ellen.

"I know."

"There's a group of them, guys who'd served there. They try to give back for what they did. They help work the land, build schools. Michael went over there every chance he got to help out."

"What do you think? Is he still alive?"

The color was returning to Ellen's cheeks as she formulated a plan. "I have no idea. But I know where to start to look."

THE NEXT day, Barbara entered Alex's laboratory. "I don't know how to tell you this," she said. "The man you linked to the massacre—"

"Nick Papparaplous?"

"He's dead."

Alex reached out to steady herself against the lab counter. She thought of his emphysema, his obvious ill health. She hoped her visit hadn't pushed him over the edge.

Barbara continued, "He was murdered."

"Oh no," Alex said, feeling a rush of fear. "What happened?"

"Somebody firebombed his house."

Alex gasped. "Is his daughter okay?"

Barbara nodded.

"Thank God," Alex said.

"He was home alone when it happened. They're sending the evidence to us."

"Why are we getting it?"

"We think there's a connection to the court-martial. Alex, the house was napalmed."

That evening, Alex looked for information about the fire on television and in the paper. The death didn't even make the news. If Barbara hadn't quietly been pursuing a court-martial, Alex wouldn't have even known about it.

At home that night, Alex couldn't shake the image in her mind of the man and his daughter. Could the Vietnamese have killed him for revenge? Or did someone in the U.S.

government kill him to sweep the Lo Duoc incident under the rug?

Alex knew that no matter who had thrown the jellied gasoline on the house, she herself was the person who had caused the murder. That night, fiery nightmares kept frightening her awake.

CHAPTER FORTY-THREE

ON NEW Year's Eve, Alex and Troy spent the afternoon in her laboratory preparing the skulls for their final journey. Along with a shipment of antibiotics, Alex was sending Dr. Kang information about the postings of all the soldiers who'd brought the skulls home. He'd start a national effort to connect the skulls to their families.

"It makes more sense," Alex said. "It's more poetic for these reunions to be fostered in Vietnam. I've always felt a little like I was trespassing, working on these skull so far from home."

Troy nodded and picked up each of the skulls in turn, placing each one in its own wooden box, lined in satin. Mini-caskets, Alex thought. As they arranged the skulls, Troy told Alex about some of the traditions of Tet, the Vietnamese New Year.

"Shortly before Tet," Troy said, "the Vietnamese bathe carefully to wash off the dirt of past missteps and misfortune. Then we pay tribute to the god Ong Tao, who on that night will go to heaven and report to the Jade Emperor about the moral conduct of each family during the past year."

Alex thought about the moral conduct of her family, the AFIP, during the past year. She'd killed for the first time and, even though it was in self-defense, she knew the action had changed her. She'd doubted the morals of her father, but her attempts to clear him had led to the murder of another woman's father. She needed to ask the Jade Emperor for lots of forgiveness, she feared.

"We'll celebrate once the ceremony is over," Troy said to Alex. He touched her on the shoulder and looked into her eyes. The physical contact was so unlike Troy that it sent a little jolt of electricity through her. He smiled at her. "You realize of course that in Vietnam New Year is not only a state holiday, but everybody's birthday."

"Even American blondes?"

"Ah, for you, Tet would be even more special, as everything is your first time."

THE NEXT morning, Alex searched her closet for something to wear. She pushed aside hangers of black pantsuits and black turtlenecks. Maybe that was why her social life was often so disastrous. Too much bad luck black.

Her closet inventory revealed only a few dresses. She pulled a royal blue one over her head and added a string of seed pearls around her neck. She slipped her feet into her only pair of high heels—black, strappy, and a relic of one of the few shopping-with-girlfriends experiences in her life. In her daily life, they seemed totally impractical. You couldn't hike or ride a motorcycle in them and they slowed you down when you ran.

The white Hummer limo picked her up at the AFIP and made its way to the Northeast entrance to the White House. The choice of vehicle was the result of long negotiation between Troy and Beatrix Graham. The White House nixed transporting the Trophy Skulls in a truck (not respectful enough) or an ambulance (too humanizing; the White House didn't want bystanders to think the United States had been holding actual soldiers hostage). Troy urged that the size, shape, and nature didn't matter at all. What was most important was the color. White, for mourning.

That's how Alex, Barbara, five young soldiers, a driver, and twenty skulls inside wooden boxes lined with plush satin had ended up in the interior of a thirty-one-foot Hummer limo. The car, whose normal run was for high school proms, smelled vaguely of corsages, J.Lo "Glow" perfume, beer, and teenage fumbling. Alex popped open the car's backseat CD player and found a Missy Elliott CD. Somehow the song "Lose Control" didn't seem appropriate for this morning's run.

Alex had been asked to take the lead in the handoff because a doctor in that role would emphasize the respect the U.S. government was according the skulls. She was glad to be front and center in the ceremony. She wanted to be the one presenting Mymy's skull to Binh, her mother. Barbara and the young soldiers would each be carrying two or more mini-caskets. Troy would come separately, after picking up Binh and the other Vietnamese civilians at the Mayflower Hotel.

The Vietnamese governmental officials would arrive in a more dramatic style. Assembly Member Huu Duoc Chugai and three staff members from the Ministry of the Interior had flown on a private Vietnamese jet to Andrews Air Force Base. After it landed, a Sikorsky UH-60 Black Hawk presidential helicopter would shuttle them directly to the White House lawn. They were bringing with them the remains of six American MIAs. David Braverman had disappeared after embarking on a five-aircraft attack against enemy surface-to-air missile sites in Thanh Hóa Province, North Vietnam. His were the only remains that had been easily identified by the Vietnamese. His dog tags had been found with his skull. After the handoff occurred, Alex would attempt to find useable DNA on the other remains to identify them and return them to their relatives.

The White House guest list had been carefully drawn to include equal numbers of American and Vietnamese guests. Alex was surprised that Vice President Shane hadn't tried to make more of the event. He hadn't invited anyone from the business community, surprising given his investment in Vietnam. The Americans attending the ceremony were simply civilians, people who kept vigil for the MIAs, who still prayed for the return of their husband, father, uncle, or son from Vietnam.

At the Northeast Gate, Alex and her companions filed out of the limo. Wearing a dress was a rare experience for her, and the high heels made her feel even more like a teenager going to a prom. The Northeast Gate security chief, a leathery-faced black man with a shock of short white hair, greeted Barbara with pleasure. He looked at the bars on her uniform, saluted, and said, "Well, Missy, you did all right for yourself. Now you're coming in the front door."

Barbara reached out to shake his hand. "Alex, this is Pug Davis; he's been working security practically since Abe Lincoln lived here."

Pug put his hand next to his mouth to shield what he was saying from the others and lowered his voice to talk to Alex. "Once, when she was late for Color Guard—"

"Or, in my case, the Colored Guard," joked Barbara.

"—I had to sneak the missy here in through the Marilyn Monroe entrance."

"Why, Mr. Davis, I didn't expect you to be the sort to kiss and tell . . . ," Barbara said.

Pug beamed at the unlikely possibility of kissing the lieutenant. He looked her over. "You are looking mighty fine these days, Lieutenant Missy," he said.

Davis waved them through, past the dozens of television camera operators on the lawn—networks, CNN, BBC, even a crew from Singapore. They were filming the arrival at the White House, but no reporters or cameras would be allowed into the ceremony itself.

The second gauntlet of security guards—Secret Service agents—was younger, more formal, and less friendly than Davis. They told Alex and her group to set down the wooden boxes and they patted each person down. The lead agent collected and tagged the weapons that the soldiers had donned that morning when they suited up in their dress uniforms. "You know the drill, boys," he said, pulling back his jacket to reveal his holster. "Only the Secret Service carries here."

Alex picked up her wooden box and prepared to put it on the metal detector conveyor belt before she walked through the arch of the detector. The head agent threw his body between her and the belt to stop her. "We've got orders from the top. No human remains are to go through the metal detector. It just wouldn't look right."

Beatrix Graham was waiting with a wheeled cart. She loaded the wooden boxes on the cart and asked a young man—presumably a White House aide—to push it.

The protocol maven apparently had taken Alex's color advice to heart. She was wearing a white suit despite the season. Alex looked at Beatrix's feet as she walked alongside the cart. It must have killed her to wear white shoes before Memorial Day.

ALEX TOOK one of the salmon canapés from the tray a uniformed maid thrust in front of her. As she bit into it, she noticed the taste of hard-boiled egg flecks in the dressing. She looked at her watch. It was 11:15 A.M. Would this still be considered breakfast?

She remembered how Troy had turned down eggs that morning at her apartment. There he was, the rational M.D., telling her not to have eggs in the morning on important days because it was unlucky.

Troy and his Vietnamese guests entered the room. Alex made a beeline to join him.

"Which one is Binh?" Alex whispered to him.

Troy made the introduction and Alex recognized the dignified woman from the long line of people she'd met in Lo Duoc.

"I have been honored to be in the presence of your daughter's bones," Alex said, holding down a button on her phone. The moment she stopped talking, the tiny speaker of the phone translated the words into Vietnamese.

Binh looked confused, but when Troy explained the device, her puzzlement turned to delight. Troy took the phone from Alex and showed Binh how it worked. Binh spoke rapidly and the phone translated. "You have taken my daughter from the black ocean of death to the comforting shore of her family. We are grateful."

Alex beamed at the woman. In her seventies, Binh was

accompanied by her father, who had to be at least ninety. Alex recognized him as the man with the goat. He looked tired from the journey, but nodded his head in agreement with Binh's expression of gratitude. Alex and Binh passed the phone back and forth as they continued their conversation. Binh trembled with excitement, her gaze drifting every few minutes toward the dais where the presentation would take place.

Binh's father nodded toward some chairs. Binh said, "My father needs to rest." She handed Alex back her phone and trailed after the older man.

Alex stood near Troy as he spoke in a quiet tone in his native language to an elderly Vietnamese woman, someone who was hoping the boxes would hold the spirit of her son. The woman scowled as she glanced at the most famous painting in the White House, Claude Monet's *Morning on the Seine*. Perhaps it reminded her too much of the lengthy French occupation of her country. She was drawn instead to Albert Bierstadt's luminous *Butterfly*.

Alex started walking toward the dais. "You're the woman who's been doing all that work to fix up the Vietnamese skulls," said an angry man in his seventies with cropped gray hair and the fit look of someone who still worked out. "What a waste. We should spend those bucks finding MIAs like my boy."

"I'm sorry to hear about your son," she said. "He served in Vietnam?"

The man's face reddened further as he raised his voice. "My son's still MIA there. We've been a military family for generations. You're too young to understand what that was like."

Alex bit her tongue. She did not bring up her dad, his dying outside Saigon. His death was not just some card she would play to ease her conversation with this jerk. Troy came to her rescue, pulling her away and telling her that the man was dealing with his pain the only way he knew, through anger. "Let's see if I can earn my grief counselor title," Troy said. He moved back over to the man and began talking to him in a calming voice. But the man lashed out loudly, "As far as I'm concerned, you're still the enemy."

A Secret Service agent took the man aside, and moved him into the adjacent library, where the skulls that were not part of the ceremony were stored.

Barbara was chatting with an African-American waiter, probably someone she had known from her Color Guard days. Troy drifted back toward his Vietnamese companions. Alex had already tried every hors d'oeuvre that had wandered past her and was getting bored. She found herself staring at various guests, trying to figure out their medical stories. One of the Vietnamese men, about her age, moved slowly, one leg slightly shorter than the other. Polio, she guessed. But even the Americans had their problems. Mrs. Braverman was overweight and, judging by the pulsing vein on her face, was exhibiting high blood pressure. One of the Secret Service agents, a handsome man in his forties, had pale blue eyes and dark hair with a discrete two-inch-wide patch of gray in the front. Alex knew it to be a sign of a genetic anomaly, Waardenburg syndrome. Most people with it were perfectly healthy. A few had symptoms of hearing loss.

At 11:45 A.M., Beatrix Graham started moving key people toward the raised dais. Alex, who would present Binh with the skull of her daughter. National Assembly Member Chugai, who would give Beverly Braverman the skull of her husband. Binh. Beverly. Beatrix gave them each a little colored slip of paper. "Look for the tape on the floor that matches your color," she said. "When the President arrives, keep your distance. If anyone gets too close to the President, other than when the Commander in Chief initiates a handshake, Secret Service is entitled to shoot you." At the end of the ceremony, the President would remain on the dais and, one by one, the participants in the gathering would be called up to have their photograph taken with him.

Troy must have advised on the colors. They were variations on red and yellow, the colors of the Vietnamese flag. Alex was surprised that Vice President Shane, who was standing at the edge of the crowd talking to the Bravermans' son, was not slated to be on the dais. He always thrust himself into the center of attention. And hadn't this whole hand-off been his idea?

Just then, Abby Shane entered the room. She wore a pale pink dress and a Jackie-style pillbox hat.

The crowd was small, fewer than fifty people, but all eyes turned to Abby as she kissed her husband and straightened his lapels. Alex thought it a bit odd that Abby had entered the room without a Secret Service man in tow. Then Alex realized that, unless the waiters were agents in disguise, the only Secret Service men she could identify were the one who had escorted the angry father into the adjoining room and the one with the blue eyes and tuft of gray hair.

Binh approached Alex and nodded her head toward the two boxes that were now displayed ceremoniously on the dais. She took Alex's hand and Alex helped her up the few inches up so that she could find her place on the dais and take a close look at the open box, at the face of her daughter. Binh looked at the open box, bent down, and kissed the skull's forehead. In her stilted English, she said, "Beautiful." As the tears ran down Binh's face, Troy stepped up on the dais to comfort the woman. Feeling as if she were interfering with a private moment, Alex glanced away and looked at the skull of the American pilot, MIA Braverman. This was her first chance to see it and, in a split second, she knew that something was very wrong. No way that skull matched someone who'd served in the war. The color was all wrong, and there were no pockmarks from the highly acidic Vietnamese soil. Sure, someone had tried to age it, maybe boiling it in tea leaves, but this was the skull of a man who had been killed in the past few days. Alex picked up the box to look at it more closely. In a flash, the Vice President was at her side.

"Something wrong?" he asked.

"This skull, it's not Braverman's."

"How can you be so sure?"

"Time of death is all wrong."

Vice President Shane thought for a moment, then brought his face closer to hers, speaking quietly. "What does it matter, really? What this family needs is closure. Don't dash their dreams here, Doctor."

Alex was still holding the box with the skull, and she realized that her arms were beginning to hurt. Then it dawned on her. "It weighs too much." Her voice became more adamant. "You need to have someone check out the box."

Shane looked at the clock. "Put the box back. I'll get the head of my Secret Service detail to look at it."

Alex put the mini-casket down. Shane nodded toward the tall man in the blue suit whom Alex had been staring at earlier, the one she suspected had Waardenburg syndrome. Shane began walking quickly toward the man. As the agent turned in front of a window, the light shone on his profile in a way that flattened his features. Alex recognized him as the man posing as a general on the AFIP videotape the night her laboratory was broken into.

Just then, President Cotter entered from a private anteroom. Alex moved toward him. It was two minutes to noon and Beatrix Graham was sending eye-daggers Alex's way since it was clear that she was the one holding up the ceremony. Ms. Graham ordered Troy down from the dais so that she could move Mrs. Braverman up there to join Binh.

Shane's wife grabbed his hand and urged him out of the room as his security chief walked quickly toward Alex, rather than the skull. Alex bounded toward the President. Something didn't add up—the agent, the skull. "Something's very wrong," she said to the Chief Executive, stopping him in his tracks. As she neared him, the agent unholstered his gun and pointed it at her. Binh picked up the box with her daughter's skull to look at it more closely. She stumbled slightly and, cradling the box, tripped off the stage.

Just as the clock struck twelve, the pseudo-Braverman skull exploded, creating a V-shaped wall of flames and propelling shrapnel across the room. The force of the explosion blew furniture into people and the fixtures in the room contorted into something out of a Dalí painting. Alex turned back toward the center of the room just as the ceiling started collapsing. She could hear Troy yell something in Vietnamese in

Binh's direction. And then, through the smoke and haze, she saw the blue-eyed agent shoot Troy through the chest. She yelped a wailing moan and started toward him, but the fire was consuming the room and the smoke filled her eyes. A large bookshelf toppled over, narrowly missing her leg. She moved forward, but tripped on a pile of books. The walls began to tumble.

Alex lay prone on the floor, in shock, with the President sprawled out behind her, blown back by the force of the explosion into the adjoining room. They were cut off from the rest of the people. She got up, lunged into the small room, and burned the palm and fingers of her right hand shutting the smoldering door behind them.

Her breath came in gasps as she considered the enormity of what was happening. An assassination attempt on the President. A murder by a Secret Service agent.

President Cotter was lying in a pool of his own blood. Alex knelt next to him, suspecting a fatal head wound. But when she wiped away the blood with her hand, she could see that there was just a small wound in his right temple, possibly from a metallic piece of the bomb itself. The main bleeding was from his left forearm, on which his head was resting. She eased him out of his jacket. The locator pin clinked against the legs of a chair as she tossed the jacket out of the way. Alex wanted to make a makeshift tourniquet with her panty hose, so she reached her right hand up under her dress to pull them down. But her burned hand was throbbing with a searing pain and she couldn't control its action. She switched to her left hand, yanked the stockings down, and, using her left hand and her teeth, knotted the nylons around President Cotter's upper arm.

He was in a haze of pain, on the verge of going into shock, but she could tell he recognized her. She knew the next few minutes could make a difference in whether he lived or died.

"I can help you," Alex said. "Stay with me, don't give in to it yet. Where are the medical supplies?"

He raised his head off the floor, spit out some blood, and

then half passed out. His eyes were slightly open, though, and he used his good arm to tap on the floor.

"Downstairs?" she asked.

His thumb came up to indicate she was on the right track.

Alex looked around the room. There was a private elevator in the corner. The temperature in the room was rising as the flames began to ravage the door she'd come through. She pulled the edges of the rug that the President had fallen on, in order to move his prone body to the elevator.

She knelt next to the President as the elevator descended. She was panicked and was talking rapidly, blah, blah, blah, just to try to keep him from drifting out of focus. When the elevator door opened in the basement, the evacuation clangs echoed through the deserted hall. Luckily there was a sign pointing her to the infirmary. She dragged the rug along the floor with the prone President on top. When she got there, the door was ajar. Thank God for the panic of an evacuation. She hadn't even considered what she might do if the place had been locked. After dragging him in, she locked the door behind them.

She found morphine, injected it into the President's buttocks. She had a brief giddy thought about how she had now seen the First Ass; then moved competently through her tasks. She bound the wound on his arm, cleaned the one on his face, and began throwing supplies into a pillowcase. She needed to get him out of here. Who knew what would blow next?

In her nervousness, she kept talking to him.

"Slow down," he said. The effort of even that one sentence was too taxing for him, and his eyes closed again.

Alex could hear footsteps in the hallway, two or three men, and the clear instructions coming through on a walkie-talkie. "Get the bastard," said the voice, with a Southern lilt. "Check the Rose Garden. If you don't find the body, then seek and destroy. Do you read me?"

The footsteps passed the door and then disappeared.

The President opened his eyes, his mind coming back online as the narcotic clicked in. He spoke slowly, with great effort. "Alert . . . Secret . . . Service."

Alex shook her head, and touched him soothingly on his good shoulder. "I don't know how to tell you, Mr. President, but I think they're the ones who are trying to kill you."

His eyes narrowed, trying to get his mind around this bit of information.

"Think about it. No one could get a bomb into the White House without someone on the inside. The Secret Service was giving the orders, letting the boxes through without passing the metal detector, making the decision not to use the dogs."

Cotter's eyes glazed over, the pain of his wounds merging with incomprehension as he tried to take it all in.

"We've got to get you out of the White House," Alex said, her own voice shaky. She stifled a cry of pain as she used an antibiotic rinse on her burned hand and wrapped it in gauze so it would be serviceable.

She opened a closet to see if they could throw something over their bloodied clothes.

Success. She pulled some green surgical scrubs over her clothes and then put a pair of the green pants over the President's pants while he was still lying on the floor. "Do you think you can get up?"

With her aid, he rolled onto his left shoulder, carefully avoiding putting pressure on his wounded left forearm. With his right hand, he grabbed the leg of the examination table and pulled himself to a sitting position. Then, nearly swooning to a fall, the shaky President stood up.

He leaned against the examination table as Alex helped put a doctor's green jacket over his shirt. Over his recognizable prematurely gray hair, she perched a surgical cap, shaped like a shower cap but in a gauzy material. With an extra tug, she pulled it down a tad farther so it covered the bloody dot of a wound on his temple.

He tried to walk, leaning against her. They wouldn't get very far this way.

Alex looked over at a large garbage can on wheels. She stuck the pillowcase of supplies into the can, and stuck a broom in as well. She now realized what the fashion consultants meant when they talked about the importance of accessorizing. Throw in a dustbin and they looked like cleaning people, rather than surgeons.

The President could lumber forward by pushing the rolling trash can, like an elderly person using a metal walker with wheels.

Alex put her mouth close to his ear so that he could hear her over the noisy evacuation siren. "Do you know where the Marilyn Monroe entrance is?"

He aimed the rolling can down a hallway as thin wisps of smoke showered down from the overhead ventilation grates. If the fire breaks through to this floor, Alex thought, we won't survive. The canisters of oxygen and other gasses in the medical suite—which in other circumstances could save the President's life—would explode and kill them.

Alex urged him on, her left hand on the small of his back, pushing slightly. But he stopped every few moments, unable to make it more than a few feet without a pause to catch his breath.

They rounded a corner and saw the busts of Winston Churchill and Dwight D. Eisenhower. Seconds later, the images of the two men shook wildly as a second explosion rang out. The medical suite exploded. Alex almost gave in to her terror, but now it was the President who pressed forward. He entered a number on the keypad of a door between the busts. As she helped Cotter maneuver the trash barrel through the door, the tottering Churchill bust crashed to the floor.

As she closed the door behind them, she could see they were in a storage room. Dusty desks and chairs, tables and beds, every conceivable type of furniture—ghosts of presidents past—were piled in precarious stacks around them. The jolt of the explosion a few seconds earlier had unleashed a century's worth of dust and knocked a sideboard directly in their path. It was lying on its rim, with its legs on the far side.

Alex bent to push it aside, then silently cursed the long-dead craftsman who had created this piece in heavy mahogany. With her left hand she tried to lift the rolling garbage can, the President's walker, over the sideboard. She didn't have enough strength in that arm to complete the maneuver. So she used both hands, crying through the pain of the weight of the can against her burned palm. She took care not to hit its wheels against the diamond-patterned inlaid border of the sideboard. She wondered if that was how people were judged in the afterlife—on what care they took with their words and deeds in their last moments.

She showed the President how to hold on to some shelving to the right of the fallen sideboard. If he could balance himself long enough, he could step, one foot in front of the other, around the furniture to the door on the far side of the room.

Amazingly, that door opened to the smell of fresh roses from a flower shop along a hallway. Alex could see a young woman inside, iPod connected to her ears, lovingly adding the finishing touches to an orchid and bird-of-paradise arrangement. The sheer normality of the scene stunned Alex, causing her not to notice a Secret Service agent heading their way from farther down the corridor. A crackle on his walkie-talkie when he was halfway toward them startled her. She peeked over her shoulder at him and this time it was the President who got them out of harm's way. He pressed digits on another keypad, causing a door on the wall near the florist to open.

"Hey wait," yelled the agent. But the door slammed behind them.

Cotter rolled the garbage can a few steps down the hallway, then crumpled into a sitting position, his back against the wall of the steel corridor that ran beneath the East Wing of the White House. Alex could tell by his confused look that the initial protective adrenaline was wearing off and his body was beginning to give in to his trauma.

He looked in the direction from which they'd come, as if he wanted to go back. "Sheila—," he started.

Alex bent toward him. "She and Matthew aren't there. They're visiting colleges, remember?" She reached out her left hand to him to help him up, but his deadweight merely caused her to lose her balance in her high heels and nearly land in his lap. So, instead, she held the trash can steady while he used his good arm to push himself off the floor slightly, lean into a squatting position, and thrust himself up, grabbing the hard plastic can.

At the end of the tunnel, they reached an elevator. Alex remembered the signs she'd seen in hotels warning against using elevators during a fire. But what did they have to lose? There was no place else to go and they were quite a ways from where they'd started out. She pushed the up button.

They rode up and exited into an office corridor. She held her right hand at her side so no one would notice the gauze. A few people were walking the halls, but no one paid any attention to the cleaning crew. Through a doorway at the end of the corridor, Alex could see the sun's rays shining in. They walked outside and Alex was amazed to see the White House. The tunnel had taken them right out through the Treasury Building.

There was no one on their side of the street. Everyone—including Alex's limo driver—had been drawn to the side with the closest view of the melee that was occurring at 1600 Pennsylvania Avenue. About a dozen American and Vietnamese guests were on the lawn, bleeding and crying, as ambulance medics triaged the wounded. Alex's heart raced as she scanned the emerging crowd, looking for Barbara. Was she safe? Alex tried to remember where Barbara was when the explosion occurred. On the far side of the room—that's right! Alex prayed that she was okay. Maybe she'd even left the building already.

Alex saw the white Hummer limo, keys still in the ignition. She guided Cotter into the back, where he lay across the leather banquette of seats along the side. She threw the pillowcase onto the passenger seat alongside of her and jumped into the driver's seat. She turned the ignition key and a Missy Elliott song croaked loudly through the speakers. She hit the stop button of the CD player at the same time she pressed on the gas. The limo raced past the television station vans that were parked around the corner from the White House.

She thought about where she'd take him. Who could she trust? The AFIP had been compromised by the break-in. The first thing any hospital would do would be to call the Secret Service. She needed time to think . . . and to start treating his trauma before he slipped into shock.

"I'll skip the 'your place or mine' discussion," she told him. "Yours is just a little too dangerous at the moment."

Fifteen minutes later, the most powerful man in the world was lying on a futon mattress in the bedroom of the Curl Up and Dye.

Alex pulled supplies out of the pillowcase, cursing her clumsiness from the limited use of her right hand. She grabbed a hypodermic needle, tubing, and a liter bag of IV fluid from the medical supplies she'd found and arranged a makeshift IV holder by hanging the bag from one of the drawer handles on the dresser next to the mattress. She took the President's blood pressure and was amazed that it was holding steady. That was a good sign. If he'd been bleeding profusely internally, the pressure would have dipped precipitously.

Alex walked back into the living room and dialed Dan. "I need to see you right away," she said. After the break-ins at her home and lab, she didn't want to take the risk the phone was being tapped.

"Okay, stop by the conference room."

"No, it can't wait," Alex said. "Can you come to the place where I found the wreath?"

He seemed to get that this was no routine call. "Ten-four."

Alex was starting to get chills. She wondered about her own blood pressure. She'd been closer to the explosion than Cotter and had fallen pretty hard. She pressed several places along her abdomen to see if the tenderness was accompanied by any swelling, blood pooling from internal bleeding, but didn't detect anything. Then she reentered the bedroom to care for her patient. She clicked on the television, but the assassination attempt had not yet hit the news.

When Dan arrived, she quickly filled him in on what had occurred at the White House and how she had recognized

the Secret Service agent from the AFIP tape. She explained
how she and the President had escaped.

Dan looked at her as if she'd grown a second head. "You
brought POTUS here? Holy shit!"

He and Alex entered the bedroom. The Chief Executive
lay prone on the futon, a trickle of blood pooling on the pillow. From Alex's small television, Vice President Shane's
slight West Virginia accent was calmly informing the nation
that the President had died. Abby Shane, her pink dress
smudged with blood, stood at his side. Where was the blood
from? Alex wondered. Abby and her husband had conve-
niently left the room before the explosion occurred.

The Shanes were standing in the State Dining Room,
where the luncheon in honor of the Vietnamese visitors was
supposed to have been held. Behind them was the carved
mantelpiece that had been unveiled by President John
Adams on his first day in the White House. It said, "May
none but honest and wise men ever rule under this roof."

Shane spoke somberly. "We are living through the
biggest tragedy that this nation has faced since the attack on
the World Trade Center. Using the façade of a return of MIA
remains, the Vietnamese have declared war on our nation,
striking at the heart of our government itself, and killing a
great leader."

He handed the mic to Abby, who was crying in an under-
stated way, just enough to tear up her eyes but not enough to
streak her mascara. That was a real trick, Alex thought. "Before President Cotter died, he said to tell his wife and son
that he loved them. And to tell the nation that they were in
good hands with my Tommy here."

Alex turned to Dan. "I was with the President from the
moment the explosion occurred. Either the Shanes think he's
dead under the rubble of the East Wing . . ."

"Or they're sure they're going to be able to finish him
off," Dan said.

"We've got to get him to a hospital," Alex said, "but we
need to make it appear that he's dead until we sort this out."

Dan got on the phone and paged Wiatt, who arranged an

ambulance to Walter Reed, the sister institution of the AFIP, which he controlled. Only Army docs with the highest level of security would be caring for the Chief Executive. They'd be restricted to the base—no phone calls out. Military special ops guys would stand guard; Secret Service would not be informed. Dan then called Grant and his team to guard Alex's house.

Dan turned to the President. "I'm going to the White House."

Cotter winced his eyes in pain. "Me, too," he said. He sat up straight, trying to look as much like a world leader as he could in his mock janitor outfit.

He used his good arm to prop himself up, but a wave of pain hit him and he vomited on Alex's gold and turquoise woven rug. He slumped back into a prone position. "Sorry," he said.

Alex moved toward Dan. "How will you get past the Secret Service?"

"The AFIP has jurisdiction over crimes involving the Executive Branch," explained Dan. "In a few minutes, I'll be up the Vice President's ass so far, I'll be giving him heartburn."

Alex walked Dan back through the living room on his way out. "You're not safe here alone," he said, handing her his .45 Beretta. "The Beretta's a little harder to shoot than a nine-millimeter, but it's got more force. You can kill with one shot."

She reached out with her right hand, but Dan realized that, between the burn and the clumsy-wrapped gauze, she wouldn't be able to handle the gun with that hand. He put the gun in her left hand instead. The barrel tipped down. She tried to remember what Barbara had told her about gripping hard and high.

"Dan, there's one more thing. Could you have someone move the Hummer limo that's double-parked?"

"You took a limo home?"

"Took a limo is right," Alex said. "I took it while the driver was looking the other way."

Dan shook his head. "Give me the keys. The last thing we need is for the local cops to come after you for carjacking."

Dan left and Alex, gun in hand, returned to the bedroom and sat down on the floor at the side of the futon. She put down the Beretta and reached over to feel the President's forehead. "You feel a little hot. I'd like to give you an antibiotic shot now. . . ."

She heard the apartment door open and assumed Dan had forgotten something. She chided herself for leaving the door unlocked and walked into the living room to greet Dan. The Secret Service agent with the gray forelock was gazing at her with his deep blue eyes. Aimed at her head was a .357-caliber Sig Sauer pistol.

She was frozen to the spot as he got ready for the fatal coup de grâce. But his body jerked in surprise as a weak voice from the next room called, "Dr. Blake." He grabbed Alex and spun her around, pointing the gun at the back of her head as he half pushed, half kicked her into the bedroom.

The sight of the President on the futon startled him, and he quickly aimed the gun at the prone man. Then he reconsidered and lowered the pistol to his side. "You're safe now, sir," he said to the President. "The girl here was the last of the conspirators. I'm just going to cuff her and then I'll get you home."

"Agent Moses?" the President asked. Alex could tell that the morphine was clicking in and he was disoriented. She tried to squirm out of Moses' grasp, but he wrenched her arms behind her. She could feel a light trickle of perspiration run down her neck.

Moses continued to talk soothingly to the President and the Commander in Chief began to nod in agreement. Alex interrupted, "Don't believe him. He may have tried to get you killed."

The President looked back and forth between them, trying to figure it out. His eyes were half closed and pain lined his face.

"If you're legit," she said to Moses, "let me go, because I need to give the President an injection."

Alex could feel Moses' grip tightening. He started moving

the gun toward her temple. A flash penetrated the sheet covering Cotter. "Bastard," said Cotter. Moses' shoulder erupted in blood and he dropped his weapon. Alex scrambled for it and held it on him.

The President moaned, then started shaking. The Beretta Dan had left slid out of the President's hand and he collapsed back on the futon. The President was going into a seizure. He must have a brain bleed, Alex thought. He needed an injection of phenobarbital or he'd risk a coma.

"Don't move," she said to Moses.

The Secret Service agent glared at her, his left hand raised to his shoulder, trying to stem the blood. She weighed her alternatives. The President desperately needed that injection. But she wasn't sure how to do it without taking her eyes—and the gun sight—off Moses.

For a moment, she thought of blasting him in the chest. Dan had told her that one shot could kill. But it had been one thing to strangle the man who was squeezing the life out of her. She couldn't bring herself to kill this man in cold blood. He wasn't a danger to them as long as she kept him in the gun's range.

She backed around the futon, so that she had a clear view of Moses, with the President and the futon between her and the Secret Service agent. She knelt down, the Sig still aimed at the intruder. She knew that if she started to work on the President she wouldn't be able to react as quickly to Moses' movements. The President's body shook, culminating in a grand mal seizure. She thrust herself toward the pillowcase full of supplies to pull out a syringe. In the millisecond that she had the gun off of Moses, he fled through the living room, with the creak of the entrance door squeaking behind him. Alex didn't even consider chasing him. She had her patient to attend to.

She injected the President with phenobarbital, holding her breath and praying that, on top of the morphine, it wouldn't slow his heart to the point that he wouldn't be able to hold on. Epinephrine for the heart was out of the question with these seizures.

Alex could hear the creak of wood as her front door opened. Thinking Moses had returned, she grabbed both guns and raced into the living room.

"Whoa," Grant said.

Alex had never been more pleased to see him. She uncurled her painful right hand from around the Beretta and set it down, along with the Sig, on the seat of one of the hair dryers. She explained what had happened and he radioed his men downstairs to chase after Moses. He would stay with Alex.

"POTUS himself," Grant said. "Got to be the most interesting guy you've ever had in your bedroom, Alex."

Alex thought of Karl the artist, Luke the bass player, and, more recently, a Vietnamese transplant searching for peace for his soul. "Not by a long shot, Grant. Not by a long shot."

CHAPTER FORTY-FOUR

ALEX BENT over the President in the ambulance. Wiatt wasn't taking any chances of leaking the news that the man was still alive. Wiatt's special operatives buddy Sergeant Derek Lander was driving. He and Grant had moved the President into the ambulance and then, after Alex had jumped into the back, started speeding through D.C. An Army doctor, Colonel Kevin Kellogg, started hooking up the First Patient to all manner of machines, including an EKG and EEG, while Alex explained—to him and, over the radio, to the waiting doctors at Walter Reed—exactly what she had done to him so far.

Kellogg nodded in approval. The President's breathing was shallow, but holding steady. He gave a weak groan as Kellogg, to Alex's surprise, pulled a stocking cap down over the President's head. In this frayed gray cap, the man on the stretcher looked nothing like a chief of state.

Now that Kellogg had attended to the President, he looked over at Alex. Her royal blue dress was splattered with the President's blood, IV fluid, and splotches of sweat. She'd put on a pair of cowboy boots as she left the apartment. "Quite a getup," he said.

"Not for long," she said. When Kellogg turned back toward his patient, she reached into the plastic bag into which she'd stuffed a change of clothes as they were leaving the house. Now that another doctor was focusing on the First Patient, she could finally change. She took a few steps behind the military doctor, took off her boots, and, left-handed, pulled a pair of jeans on under the dress.

She was about to pull off the dress and put on a turtleneck when she noticed Grant watching her in the rearview mirror from the front seat. Ah, Grant. She moved her finger back in a naughty-naughty sign, shook her head, and turned around to get some privacy while she completed her transformation. The ambulance whirled around a corner, and with her shirt halfway over her head, she banged against the wall of the ambulance. "Shit," she said.

Kellogg's eyes left the President for an instant. "You all right?" he said as she bounced back into a full standing position.

"Uh-huh," she mumbled through the fabric. With a final tug, she pulled the turtleneck into place, then sat and pulled on her boots.

Kellogg smiled and shook his head. "You got clearance for these sorts of maneuvers?" he asked her.

"Just getting ready for action," she said. She returned to his side, checking the President's vitals.

"He's holding steady," Kellogg said. Then he nodded at Alex with admiration. "For a girl in a torn blue dress, you're a helluva doctor."

"Never make it as a stripper, though," yelled Grant from the front. "No sense of balance."

A block from Walter Reed, Kellogg detached the President from the machines that had been reading his vitals. He'd be hooked to a better set soon enough. Outside the hospital, a phalanx of a dozen soldiers met the ambulance. They circled the stretcher with guns pointing outward. From a bird's-eye view, they looked like the spokes of a wheel. Alex and Kellogg had been pushed to the outside of the wheel, and they rushed through the line of soldiers yelling, "He needs us." Just inside the entrance to the hospital, the President had another seizure.

Keyed in by the radio transmission from the ambulance,

the first person they encountered, an Army doctor, injected the President with another antiseizure drug. Minutes later, a CAT scan of his head indicated that a tiny bit of shrapnel had entered his brain. It had caused some internal bleeding and the increased pressure could lead to a stroke. Army surgeons prepared to operate.

A medic noticed that Alex was holding her right hand limply. He had her remove the gauze and turn her palm up so that he could look at it. "That's a dangerous burn," he said. "You need to have it looked after."

He herded Alex into one of the ER stalls, those small compartments separated by curtains. The medic put a cold sterile cloth on her hand to dim the pain, then began the painful process of debriding the burn on her right hand to clean it so that it wouldn't become infected. He'd offered her Demerol for it, but Alex didn't want to space out now.

Until her tears started dripping down on the medic's hand, Alex didn't even realize she was crying. So much was happening so quickly. The medic put a Kleenex into her good hand, applied silver sulfadiazine to the wound, and added a sterile dressing. Then he went off, presumably to get a glimpse of the President. She used a paper towel from the dispenser over the cubicle's sink to wash her face. There were no mirrors here in the ER, but she could see the hollow look in her eyes reflected in the dispenser.

The adrenaline that had propelled her to this point was fizzling out of her. The President was now someone else's responsibility. For the first time since the explosion she could focus on her own thoughts. All at once, the scene in the White House flashed through her mind and she watched, in slow motion, as the bullet cut Troy down across the room from her. She saw him falling, falling, over and over, the startled look on his face imploring her. What is happening? he seemed to be asking Alex. His confused look cried out, It's not my time yet.

Alex's anger over Troy's murder was tinged with her fear about Barbara. With her good hand, she dialed Barbara's cell phone number.

"Credence Hospital, Five E Nurses' Station," said the voice on the other end. Alex almost hung up, thinking she had dialed a wrong number, but then she realized that Credence, the closest hospital to the White House, would be where the victims were taken. "Let me talk to Barbara Findlay, please."

"She's not available."

"Is she okay?

"Are you a family member?"

"I'm, uh, her cousin."

"You don't sound too certain and we're not allowed to give out health information to strangers."

"For Chrissakes, I called her cell phone number. I'm obviously close enough to her to have that number. What's happened to her?"

The nurse considered the logic of Alex's statement for a moment. "She's in surgery to have a bullet removed."

Alex gasped. "How bad is it?"

"I'm a nurse. We're not allowed to make a diagnosis."

Alex hung up. She looked at the clock. It was almost 3:00 P.M. on New Year's Day. Lana was at home where she expected her mother to return soon. Alex wanted to rush over immediately and be with her. But she knew she needed to stay and tell Wiatt and Dan what she knew about the White House bombing. Alex strained her thoughts to remember the name of the older woman who lived across the hall from Barbara. Maeve something. Worked at the reception desk of the Mayflower Hotel. Last name reminded her of a novel. What was it now? Yes! Maeve Chatterly. Alex called the hotel and Maeve agreed to stay with Lana once she got off work that night.

Then she fortified herself with a dreary cup of coffee from a vending machine. Her next call would be one of the hardest she would ever make.

She was met with a quiet sob on the other end. "Alex," Lana sniffed. "I turned on the news. They showed the White House explosion and people coming out. But I can't reach Mom. They didn't show Mom."

Alex's heart broke as she thought of a child getting the news like this. Because she was deaf, Lana wouldn't be able to hear Alex's soothing voice. All she would see, through her tears in an empty apartment, were the Times New Roman words that were the translations of what Alex said. Alex chose them carefully.

"Your mom is going to be fine," she said.

"But why isn't she answering? Why isn't she at home? Why didn't she call and tell me she was all right?"

"She got hurt and went to the hospital. But she's going to be all right. Remember how beat up I looked when I woke up in your room? I'm fine now and your mom is going to be fine, too."

Alex prayed that Barbara would recover and make those words come true.

"Can you come get me?"

"I'll come as soon as I can," Alex said. "Right now I'm helping to catch the people who planted the bomb. Mrs. Chatterly is going to stay with you tonight. But tomorrow at the latest, I promise I'll be there."

Alex hung up and walked to the nurses' station, figuring if she called Credence Hospital from an official Walter Reed number, she might get more details about her friend's condition. A television suspended from the ceiling showed footage of smoke and flames pouring from 1600 Pennsylvania Avenue. The image cut to a photo of the grief-stricken First Lady clinging to her sixteen-year-old son as they boarded a jet at Hanscom Air Force Base in Massachusetts to head home.

Grant walked up to Alex and pulled her away from the desk. "Wiatt wants to see us *now*."

CHAPTER FORTY-FIVE

WITH THE President in surgery, Wiatt had taken over a deserted wing of Walter Reed for both medical and forensic purposes. Equipment was brought in from throughout the hospital and laboratories so that once Cotter was out of surgery, he would be brought here for recovery. Next to the President's recovery room, Wiatt had ordered the four beds cleared out of a large room and replaced with two desks and a half-dozen chairs, a secure fax machine, two computers, and a base of telephones. This would be Wiatt's command center. A nearby room was fitted with similar equipment for Dan's team.

Alex heard Dan's steady voice over speakerphone in the command center. "The fire's out and we're in what's left of the East Room."

A grainy video of the scene came to life on the computer screen on Wiatt's desk. Wiatt, Alex, and Grant could see six AFIP investigators, led by Dan, working the scene. The rubble of the East Wing had buried most of the evidence and the water used to put out the fire had sloshed every other bit of evidence into a new position. Other than by eyewitness testimony—of one of the few people who had survived—there was little hope of figuring out who had been where when.

"If you can find pieces of the skull that contained the explosive," Alex told Dan, "I might be able to identify him to help you figure out who smuggled in the bomb."

An arm moved from under the fallen bookshelf.

"There's someone still alive in there," Alex shouted.

Dan and a warrant officer who'd accompanied him started unburying a man. His face was bloody, but Alex could recognize him. Braverman's son. A rescue team dashed in, put him on a gurney. Then an older man in a business suit came in, identified himself as the director of the Secret Service, and ordered Dan's underling to stop filming.

Dan looked like he was going to pull his weapon and shoot the guy then and there for interfering with his work. But instead he said calmly, "We've got jurisdiction here."

"And we've got you outnumbered." A dozen other Secret Service agents followed him into the room.

Dan put up a hand to signal them back. "Don't step on anything. This is a crime scene."

"On *our* turf," the director said.

"Your job is to protect the President and you did a pretty lousy job at that," Dan said. "I'm not gonna let you try your hand at forensics."

Alex was entirely focused on the scene unfolding at the White House. But her gaze moved away from Dan and toward the wall where Claude Monet's *Morning on the Seine* hung. The shimmering blue of the river was spotted with brownish splotches. Alex felt a spasm in her chest when she realized that the painting was covered with Troy's blood. He'd been standing in front of it when he was shot.

A Secret Service agent reached over to turn off the video camera. But Dan aimed his gun at him. "You've got thirty seconds to retreat," he said, "or I'm arresting you for interfering with a federal investigation."

Alex could see another Secret Service agent, about six feet behind Dan, unsnap his holster and slyly pull his gun out. She held her breath as he aimed it at Dan.

She turned to Wiatt to get him to do something, but he was placing a phone call.

"Stand down, both of you," Wiatt said to the screen. "I'm settling jurisdiction with Secretary Dunsfeld.

"Mr. Secretary," Wiatt said, when his call went through. He explained the situation evolving at the White House to the Secretary of the Treasury, emphasizing the need for military strength to solve this murder, implying that the Secret Service itself might be under suspicion, particularly if they kept the AFIP investigators out.

Secretary Dunsfeld protested mildly. He was an economics professor from a Midwest college who had been appointed to Cotter's cabinet a month earlier. The most exciting thing he'd done so far in office was sign his name to the new twenty-dollar bill. "You're making sense," he finally told Wiatt, who promptly patched him over to Dan's cell phone.

Dan handed the phone to the Secret Service director. Alex watched with interest as the man turned to the side to get more privacy, then ended the call with, "I understand, sir." He hung up the phone and called his men out of the room.

"Thanks, Colonel," Dan said to Wiatt. "Maybe now we can do our job."

The Secret Service men retreated and the AFIP investigators went back to work.

"Call me back when you've got something to report," Wiatt said, then severed the call and the video.

"Secretary Dunsfeld?" Grant asked Wiatt. "What's he got to do with the White House?"

"The Secretary of Treasury determines who guards the White House," Wiatt said. "Something to do with the Secret Service having jurisdiction over counterfeiting."

Grant and Alex mulled that over while Wiatt made another call, to the OR, to get an update on the President. Wiatt, whose face rarely betrayed emotion, seemed almost forlorn. Of course, Alex thought, this wasn't just about a case, or a national crisis—this was about his best friend from college, who might not live through the night.

Wiatt donned his soldier face again. "No change," he said.

The three sat in silence for a moment. Then Wiatt spoke

again. "Captain Pringle, I want you and Corporal Lawndale to go back over the guest list for the ceremony. We're looking for any red flags, anywhere."

"You got it," Grant said as he left the room.

Alex started pacing. The President was just an hour into a surgery that could take three hours or more. She worried whether she had done the right thing taking the President to her home. Had she saved his life—or hastened his death? Should she have taken him to a hospital straightaway?

As if reading her mind, Wiatt said, "Never second-guess yourself. You had to make a split-second decision and you acted upon the best information you had at the moment. You acted like a soldier, and I'm behind you one hundred percent."

Alex sat down. She motioned to the row of four televisions on the side wall, one for each of the patient beds that had, until a half hour earlier, graced the room. "Can I turn one of these on?" she asked.

"Hell, let's do them all." He tuned in ABC, NBC, FOX, and CNN.

Alex smiled. This was more like the boss she knew. He'd deliberately slighted CBS, which had treated him badly during the Tattoo Killer case.

She glanced from screen to screen as they ran without sound. CNN had called in the talking heads in force. Former President Bill Clinton was on-screen, feeling everybody's pain. ABC was showing the implosion of the East Wing. NBC that moment had a photo, from footage leading up to today's ceremony, of one of the Trophy Skulls. And FOX was showing a wall of reporters and photographers at what looked like an airport, probably Andrews Air Force Base. Wiatt turned up the sound. The blond female anchor intoned, "Sheila Cotter left D.C. as First Lady, and is returning a widow." The cameras panned over the rest of the press corps. There was some serious pushing and shoving going on, even though the First Lady wasn't scheduled to land for another hour at least. The anchor's voice continued, "Photographers from all over the world are jockeying for the photo of the returning widow for tomorrow's front page. But they may all be scooped by some unlikely competition." An inset photo showed a woman in her early twenties. "Meredith Hall, a freelance writer, accompanied Matthew Cotter and his mother to document his college interview trip for *Seventeen* magazine. Her photo may be the one that is linked forever with this tragic event."

Wiatt stared at the photograph that next flashed on the screen. The First Lady and her son were standing on the top steps of the Widener Library at Harvard when the news came. Hall had shot the photo from a distance, as if giving them their privacy. The First Lady looked fiercely noble, as if she were protecting her son with all her might. The handsome Matthew's perpetual tan had drained away, replaced with an unholy gray.

"I can't do this to her," Wiatt said, almost to himself.

"Do what?"

"Let her believe that her husband is dead. Deprive her of being with him in what may be his last moments."

"But once she finds out, how can we control who she tells?" Alex asked. "You were the one saying nobody outside this unit can know that Cotter's still alive. You'd be putting his life in jeopardy big-time." Alex couldn't believe that Wiatt was even suggesting this. Usually she was the one fighting to give weight to people's feelings and he was pressing for the good of the case. She was woozy enough from the day's experiences without having him do some sort of crazy role reversal on her.

"No, I think Sheila might be the key to our pulling the whole thing off. Think about it. It doesn't matter that Shane has assumed office. Nobody's going to accept him fully until there's proof that President Cotter is dead. Every reporter, every Secret Service agent, every conspiracy theorist has got their eye on the White House right now waiting for a body to be brought out."

"Yeah, so?"

"So we can have Dan bring back what appears to be the President, zipped in a body bag. And then bring Sheila here to pay her last respects. I can let her in on what is going on. For Chrissakes, I've known her since college. I went with her when she bought her first IUD before she made love to Cotter for the first time."

Yeah, Alex thought, I've definitely fallen through the rabbit hole this time. She wondered if Wiatt needed some sort of sedative. "And how does all this help us?"

"Sheila can make plans for a ceremony. She can say Cotter will lie in state for three days in the Capitol—closed casket of course because of the explosion. We can monitor how people react, figure out who isn't buying that Cotter is dead. If the Vice President is behind all this, it also gives us time to pin the murder attempt on him."

Alex pointed up at the scene of the press frenzy at the airport. "How will you swing a top secret chat with your old college shopping buddy?"

"Listen, that was on a need to know basis. If any of what I've told you here ever gets out, I'll not only fire your ass . . ."

Alex nodded. She didn't care to know what else he was threatening. She was too young to find herself buried in the Tomb of the Unknown Geneticist. She pointed again to the image on FOX. The blond anchor reported that Air Force One was operated by the Presidential Airlift Group, part of Air Mobility Command's 89th Airlift Wing, based at Andrews Air Force Base, Suitland, Maryland, where the plane was scheduled to land. "How are you going to run the gauntlet of reporters and photographers to get to the First Lady?"

"Oh, I'm not going to go to Sheila. She's going to come to me."

Alex looked at him as if he were crazy. Then she realized what he planned. She walked to the door. "I'll track down the President's pants."

It turned out that the clothes that had been removed from the President were hung up in the closet in his recovery room, right next door to where she and Wiatt were meeting.

She was back in just a few moments. Wiatt was on the phone and, from his side of the conversation, she could tell that he was convincing the manager of operations at Dulles to close down one runway. "No, sir," Wiatt told the man, "you are not in danger of attack. This is not another September eleventh. The White House was the sole target. We just need the runway for a military dignitary."

As Wiatt talked, Alex gingerly reached into the President's navy pinstripe pants and pulled out a wallet. He was a three-folder. People often asked the question of men, "Boxers or briefs?" But she felt that she could tell more about a man by what kind of wallet he carried, two-fold or three-fold. She definitely preferred the three-folders, who tended to be less traditional, sleeker.

Eel skin, it felt like. Soft to the touch, like all eel skin, but not bent out of shape yet. Still new. Maybe it was a Christmas present, maybe even from Matthew, whose sunny face smiled up from the clear plastic wallet insert. The thought of the care that might have gone into selecting such a present made her suddenly sad. Poor Matthew. He's flying back, thinking his father is dead. And soon that may be true.

She pulled out a white card and stared at the list of multi-digit numbers. She handed it to Wiatt. "How are you going to figure out which one relates to the plane?"

Wiatt ran his finger down the list. "This one," he said, pointing to the third one on the list. "It starts with VC-25A. That's the military's designation for Air Force One. Civilian flyers call it 28000, which is the tail number on it."

In less than two minutes, Wiatt was on the radio to the pilot commanding the plane carrying the First Lady Sheila Cotter and her son. By providing the magic numbers and a new set of coordinates, Wiatt caused the flight to be rerouted to Dulles. Sergeant Derek Lander, with three soldiers, was on his way to meet the First Lady.

Alex took the card back and reinserted it in the wallet. She marveled at how a small piece of paper could cause a presidential aircraft to be rerouted. What would happen if this wallet fell into the wrong hands?

"How are you going to get the First Lady away from her handlers?"

"Sergeant Major Lander was Special Forces with me. He'll know what to do."

CHAPTER FORTY-SIX

ALEX TOOK the first step in the deception Wiatt was planning. She entered a storeroom adjacent to Harding's morgue and requisitioned several body bags from the clerk. He put them on a cart for her so she could roll them out.

"Has the President's body been recovered yet?" he asked.

"They're still clearing the rubble."

"Any chance he's still alive? I heard they pulled some civilian out a couple of hours ago."

Alex chose her words carefully. She held up her bandaged hand. "I was at the ceremony. I saw the explosion."

The soldier looked at her with awe.

Alex continued. "If the President had survived, I'd know about it."

He put the requisition form on the counter. As she signed her name clumsily, she read the description of what she was taking. The military didn't call them body bags. They were "human remains pouches." Vinyl. Thirty-eight dollars each.

She nodded thanks to him and began to push the cart out of the room.

"One more thing, ma'am," he said to Alex's back.

Alex wondered if she'd misspoken or betrayed something in her tone. She tried to still any nervousness in her expression, then turned to face him.

"Yes, Corporal . . . ," she looked at the name stitched on his uniform, "Inlander."

"When they find the Commander in Chief, you'll need this." He handed her a triangle, blue with white stars. An American flag, she realized.

She'd never held a flag before. This one was slightly coarse cotton and she marveled at the stiff, precise points at the edges of its military folds.

She nodded. "You're absolutely right."

A half hour later, all the networks ran the same footage. Grant and Dan were lifting a heavy body bag with a flag into an ambulance. Beyond the White House fence, people's eyes grew large as they watched. Strangers turned to each other and fell into each other's arms, sobbing. The two men closed the ambulance door with reverence; then Grant cranked up the siren and sped off.

CHAPTER FORTY-SEVEN

"SO FAR, nothing's leaping out at me," Chuck said to Alex and Grant. They were in a room down the hallway from Wiatt's, with CNN blasting on a television set. "One of the American guests gave a lot of money to a white hate group that's off the grid in Montana, but that was a good ten years ago, and there's nothing to link that group to the White House attack. I can't find out much about the Vietnamese guests. Records aren't computerized, plus even simple documents like birth and marriage records were destroyed over there during all those wars."

"What about the government officials?" Alex said. "Surely, there's information about them."

"The only one with a lot of information is the member of the Qui Hoc, the National Assembly, Chugai. He's got a paper trail here from his Harvard Business School days. Dedicated student, high grades. He's even got a Web site over there."

Chuck keyed in the Web address and Alex walked around him to look at it. Photos of him with various world notables. Speeches extolling the virtues of patience and frugality. An animation of the billowing red flag of Vietnam, with its sparkling yellow star in the middle. She swore that, for a millisecond when the Web site home page first opened, Chugai's picture was in the center of the star. Subliminal advertising.

"Seems a little too me-me-me for a communist man of the people, no?"

"He obviously learned something for his $37,000-a-year Harvard tuition. Or should I say 618,862,000 Vietnamese dong?"

"A guy with aspirations like these doesn't seem the sort to put himself at risk as a suicide bomber," Alex said.

She stood behind him, reading the list of guests on his screen. She didn't see Moses' name.

"What about the Secret Service agents who were there?"

Grant said, "They've gone through loads of background checks to get the job."

"Humor me," she said. "Look for Moses."

Chuck displayed the file she requested.

"He's from Missouri," Alex said. "Isn't that where John Joseph Pershing was from?"

Grant walked over to her side. "Yeah, but Missouri's a big state."

Chuck zeroed in on a photo of Clive Moses.

"I'm sure he's the guy who broke into my lab," Alex said. "He looks just like the fake general on the tape."

Grant started to respond, but his attention was drawn to CNN. Alex and Chuck followed his gaze. The anchor was reporting that Shane had just appointed a new National Security Advisor, in preparation for declaring war on Vietnam. D.C. was in a state of panic. All the highways out of the city were jammed. Faced with the possibility that Vietnam was launching an assault on the United States, people were fleeing from the city that could be a prime target.

A photo of Troy, from his driver's license, appeared on the television screen. The anchorman said, "We believe now that this man entered the White House as a suicide bomber." The anchor said that, according to highly placed sources, Troy gave an order for a second bomb to be exploded seconds after the first one hit.

The CNN commentary was interrupted by a special broadcast from the Oval Office. Vice President Shane was denouncing the bombing as an act of war by Troy Nguyen on behalf of the Vietnamese government. Alex had to admit he sounded convincing. Why else would he have been willing to cut off diplomatic ties with the Vietnamese government and upset the deal struck between Vietnam and Westport Oil?

President Huac of Vietnam was denying any responsibility for the event. He was content to blame Troy as well. As he saw it, Troy was as much a traitor to the communist Vietnamese government as Troy's father, who had fought on the side of the South Vietnamese. Troy was Viet Kieu. A translator repeated President Huac's words: "Troy Nguyen was corrupted by American values. The violence of American television, of American aggression around the world, has come back to haunt the White House through the actions of an American citizen, Troy Nguyen."

Grant turned to Alex. "What if Troy was behind all this?"

"There's no way!" Alex said.

"Maybe that Secret Service guy came after you because he thought the two of you were in cahoots. After all, you were at the White House together."

"Troy's no killer," she said.

"Tell it to the special prosecutor," Grant said, holding his palm in the air to silence her. "Shane's about to appoint one to look into whether Troy had any co-conspirators." His voice got quiet. "You might want to watch your back, Alex. If President Cotter dies, it's not going to look so good that you spirited him out of the White House."

CHAPTER FORTY-EIGHT

WIATT AND Alex greeted Sheila and Matthew Cotter
when they were escorted by Sergeant Major Lander to
Wiatt's makeshift office a half hour later. With a little inter-
vention from the Secretary of the Treasury, Lander had managed to wrench the First Family away from the two Secret
Service men who'd accompanied them to Harvard. Wiatt
walked up to Matthew and put his hands on the boy's shoulders. At six foot four, Wiatt was five inches taller than the
President's son, and the image of them together made
Matthew look like a young child.

"Matthew, I am so sorry for what happened," Wiatt said.
"You know how much I valued your father's friendship and I
know how you've inherited all the best of both your parents.
You are going to get through this and be the man he always
imagined you would be."

The boy's mouth quivered in his grief-stricken face. Alex
wasn't sure whether those were exactly the words a boy his
age wanted to hear. But what else could be said at a time like
this?

Matthew just nodded, bravely holding back tears. Wiatt
bent slightly toward the boy. "I need to talk to your mother
alone for just a minute. Dr. Blake here will take you to get
something to drink."

Matthew looked panicked about leaving his mother. But

she kissed him on the forehead and asked him to bring her back a Coke. Alex thought about what a brilliant woman she was. She had given her child something to do for her. There was no way he would refuse that.

As they stepped into the hall, Matthew said, "Are you some sort of shrink who's supposed to figure out how fucked up I am right now?"

"No, I'm a geneticist."

He thought for a moment. "What did he say your name was?"

"Alex Blake." She held up her bandaged, burned hand to show him why she wasn't shaking.

"Oh, you're the lady who told Beatrix Graham off," he said.

"How'd you find out about that?"

"She's been wandering around in shock ever since," he said with a wisp of a smile. "She even forgot to tell me to change when I went out with lowrider pants. Honestly, she's worse than either of my parents." Matthew froze in place for a moment. Alex stopped walking, too. It was as if for a brief moment he'd felt his life was normal again. But Alex could tell that the word *parents* made him realize that he'd never use that term again. It would always be singular. Not plural. Despite her lecture to Wiatt about the importance of secrecy, it made her want to blurt out that his father was still alive.

They reached the Coke machine and Alex fished into her fanny pack for some quarters. But Matthew had his wallet out. A three-folder, she noted with a smile, eel skin like his dad's.

"What may I get you?" he asked. His composure and decency made her breath catch in her throat. Somehow that moment was as heartbreakingly moving as the tiny salute JFK Jr. mustered at his dad's funeral.

WHEN ALEX and the President's son returned to Wiatt's makeshift office, Wiatt turned the First Lady over to Alex and asked to speak to Matthew. He nodded to Alex, indicating he'd told the First Lady that her husband was still alive.

In the hallway, Sheila said, "You're the doctor who got him out?"

"I was with him for the first hour," Alex said. "A small bit of shrapnel lodged in his brain. The Army surgeon's done hundreds of these procedures."

"But neurosurgery is always a big risk."

"Anytime you operate on the brain, there are risks. But he's bleeding in a small, localized area. That type of injury has the best prognosis. For a little while afterward, he'll need phenytoin to control any seizures and a diuretic to prevent pressure in the brain. Full recovery should occur anywhere between a week and four weeks." Alex realized that she was presenting the best possible odds, realistic only if the surgery brought no surprises.

"I want to see him," Sheila said.

Alex hesitated. Wiatt hadn't given her any instructions about this and she couldn't quite open the door and ask him, in front of Matthew, whether it would be okay to go to the OR. Wiatt wasn't planning to tell Matthew that his dad was alive.

"You're worried I can't take it?" Sheila asked. "I was in Meridian, Mississippi, in 1964, nineteen years old when they found the bodies of Andrew Goodman, Michael Schwerner, and James Chaney. I'd gone down there to help Michael—Mickey—register people to vote."

Alex nodded. Two white civil rights workers from New York and a local black man who'd been killed by the Ku Klux Klan. "I remember reading that's what made you go to law school."

"Law school, clerking for Thurgood Marshall. My life was directed by that tragedy. I can handle the violence. But I wouldn't be able to forgive myself if I just looked away."

Alex thought for a moment. "I'll get you a set of scrubs."

DR. KEVIN KELLOGG was in the OR with two other surgeons, an anesthesiologist, and three nurses. He wasn't surprised to see Alex enter in scrubs, but his eyebrows raised above his mask when he realized who was following her.

The soft green eyes of the First Lady had graced too many magazine covers for him not to recognize them above her mask when she entered.

The two women stood back, not wanting to break the flow of activity that focused around the man on the table. Alex noticed the small, mobile MRI machine and the mounted CAT scan image of the President's preoperative bleed. The damage was about what she had guessed—a 60 percent or better chance of survival. The surgeon needed to treat the subdural hematoma by removing the blood to decrease the cranial pressure. Her attention turned to the drill placed on a cart. She hoped the First Lady wouldn't notice it. It's one thing to contemplate your husband's injury. It's another to try to fathom someone drilling into his skull toward his brain, the seat of his consciousness.

Kellogg was finishing up. After suturing the incision, he nodded to Sheila.

She moved toward her unconscious husband. She bent down and kissed his cheek, taking care to avoid the new scar, as if he could feel the pain. "I love you," she whispered. "Matthew and I are fine. We're right here, don't worry about us. Just take care of yourself."

Then the President's blood pressure dipped suddenly and a nurse hurried Sheila and Alex out of the room.

ON THE way back to Wiatt's office, Sheila asked Alex, "What happened just then. Is it normal?"

Alex considered her words carefully. "It happens in a lot of surgeries, but not all of them."

Sheila nodded. "I don't know how I can keep this from Matthew. If I let him continue to believe that his father is dead, how will he ever believe I'm telling him the truth in the future? *Trust. Honesty. Honor.* His dad and I raised him to live by those words."

"You've known Colonel Wiatt a long time and you trust him," Alex said. "He's out on a limb even letting you know the truth. We've got to make it seem like the President is dead for this plan to work."

"Right now I'm not thinking about him as the President. Right now, he's just Matthew's dad."

"WHAT HOTEL should the sergeant major take you to?" Wiatt asked when Sheila and Matthew prepared to leave.

"Was the residence at the White House damaged?"

"No," Wiatt said.

"Any chance of another attack on the White House?"

"No phoned-in threats, and the introduction of a skull with explosives was due to a major breach of security. My men have now taken over guard duty there."

"Then take me home. I've got a funeral to plan."

CHAPTER FORTY-NINE

IT WAS a little after 7:00 P.M. when Dan arrived at Alex's laboratory. He unwrapped a skull fragment, a piece of jaw with three teeth still attached. He pointed to the singed marks across the bottom. "This is how we know it housed the explosive. The other Trophy Skulls, unbelievably, were intact. And the rest of the charred bones we found were attached to bodies."

"Have they all been identified?" Alex asked. She gave a silent prayer of gratitude that Barbara had made it out alive, even if in precarious condition.

"We're matching the names of the living who are being treated at Credence with the guest list," he said. "Two of the people who died were from Vietnam—one was an eighty-year-old man, the father of a North Vietnamese soldier who was missing in action. The other was a thirty-year-old administrator from the Ministry of the Interior. The Vietnamese Embassy's pushing us pretty hard to get them the bodies ASAP, but I wanted Harding to take a look first, check for any evidence they might have been involved."

"Did you find any other bombs?" Alex asked, thinking of how the news anchor had reported that Troy had given the word for other bombs to be detonated.

Dan shook his head. "Negatory. It was like looking for weapons of mass destruction in Iraq."

Alex touched Dan's shoulder with her unscorched left hand. "You've got to talk Grant out of his cockamamie idea that Troy was involved."

"I don't believe Troy is good for it, either, but we've got to follow normal procedure to rule him out. Otherwise, the Secret Service would grab the case back, screaming cover-up."

"Why squander time on Troy when Agent Moses is still out there?" Alex said. "He was bleeding pretty badly from the shoulder when he left my apartment. He's going to have to get sewn up somewhere." Although, with the crazy way that this case was unfolding, Alex wondered if she really wanted him found. It was just her word against his that she wasn't the culprit. Unless the President survived surgery and backed up her story.

"We're doing everything that we can to track Moses," Dan said. "But he managed to slip through before we were on to him. At Credence Hospital, so many people were being treated for so many injuries from the explosion that nobody was bothering to check identity or insurance cards. Someone matching Moses' description just showed up there, had his wound treated and bandaged, got a shot of antibiotic, and left."

Alex's jaw dropped.

Dan nodded. "Yeah, it's bad. You may still be a target for him. And we don't know yet who else is in on it. I'd like to keep you in the building here tonight. It's too dangerous for you to go out until we track him down."

Dan left and Alex focused her attention on the skull fragment. You could tell a lot from the color of a skull, which was what tipped her off that something was amiss when she was at the White House. Whoever's jaw this was had died recently. It was indeed a Caucasian skull, but the bones in the vault of the cranium had not completely fused. That meant that it was from a young man, definitely not some MIA from the Vietnam War. She saw that one of the teeth had a partial crown, some real first-rate dental work. She used her cell phone to call Chuck and told him to search missing persons' files. He would be looking for someone between the ages of eighteen and twenty-five, probably not someone who had been missing long and living on the street. The other two teeth didn't show any decay or any sign of a poor diet. This boy had been killed recently and was the sort of person someone would have missed.

When she finished the call, she started to zip the phone back into her fanny pack. But then she remembered the function key for translating the Vietnamese language into English.

She tried to remember what Troy shouted just before he was killed. She closed her eyes and spoke. It was something long. It started like "chew." The phone spoke back, "All right, satisfactory." The phone's screen displayed the two languages. No, it was longer than that; maybe the phrase was *chew ac.* The phone flashed: "*chí ác,* very wicked."

She uttered a few more phrases to which the phone expressed confusion. "No such phrase. No such phrase."

What exactly was she trying to accomplish? she asked herself. And a thought snuck in, unbidden. What if Troy was responsible for the bomb? In his conversations with her, he couldn't have been clearer that both the United States and Vietnam had failed him. Maybe he'd just woken up one day and said, "To hell with them both."

But that didn't seem like the Troy that she knew. She didn't think he'd give up, take his own life, before he saw Lizzie again. It suddenly dawned on her. The lullaby he had sung to her, she bet he had sung it to Lizzie as a child. Her thoughts turned from sadness to anger. No, Troy had not been willing to die yet.

Alex tried harder to recall Troy's last words. He had seemed to be directing his comment to Mymy's mother. Now she remembered. It had sounded like "chewy canned something."

She spoke once more into the phone. "*Chú ý! cẩn thận!*" responded the screen. "Caution!"

Alex realized at once what had gone on. Troy had been reaching out toward Binh. He'd been warning her away from the falling bookshelf.

Now Alex knew that the investigators needed to talk to

Binh to corroborate this new evidence. Then they could focus solely on how Agent Clive Moses fit into the scheme, and how far up in the White House the conspiracy reached.

Alex's thoughts were interrupted by a strange blaring siren. She opened her laboratory door and a river of men in military uniforms flowed down the hall. Chuck was one of them. He stepped into her lab.

"The base has been activated," he said to her. "Shane is redeploying the soldiers."

"What does that mean?"

"Shane has ordered the men to California to prepare to ship out to Vietnam."

Gradually the implication of the order dawned on Alex. "We'll lose our protection here."

Chuck nodded. "Even though most of the men on the post have no idea that the President is here, we've had the benefit of a huge security force protecting the base from intruders. With the men reassigned by an order from the top, there will just be a few of us left. And those of us who remain will be declared AWOL."

Chuch had a solemn look on his face.

"You could be court-martialed for this?"

"Yes, ma'am. Wiatt's sent me to get you. He wants all of us in the wing with the President."

CHAPTER FIFTY

WIATT WAS pacing the hallway outside of Cotter's room, a .38 in his hand. Dan and Grant were in the adjoining room, passing out rifles, grenades, and other weapons to the half-dozen soldiers who had agreed to stay in the hallway to protect the President.

A nurse yelled out of Cotter's room and Wiatt entered.

He came into the adjoining room a few minutes later. "The President's come out of the anesthesia."

"That's great news," Alex said. "And now this whole mess can be cleared up. You can arrest Clive Moses."

Wiatt shook his head. "He can't remember anything that went on after the explosion."

"Oh crap," Alex said. "Anterograde amnesia. Maybe he'll get over it. A lot of trauma patients do," she said, trying to re-assure herself more than anyone else."

"The fact that Agent Moses hasn't surfaced yet tends to support your story," Dan said.

A story, Alex thought. Isn't a story something you just make up? "It's no story, Dan, it's the truth. Moses tried to kill me and the President."

"Alex, you haven't got the sort of battlefield training the rest of us do," Grant said. "When someone's got a gun pointed at you, you tend to get a little distracted and you can't correctly read all the cues."

"If he didn't feel he was in danger, President Cotter wouldn't have taken a shot at the guy. Or did I just make that up, too?"

Dan cleared his throat. "Actually we're having a hard time lifting his prints off the gun. You touched it after he did, no?"

Alex recalled how she had grabbed both guns when she thought she heard Moses coming back into the apartment. "What about the sheet? He was wrapped in it in the ambulance. You should be able to tell from the gunshot residue that the bullet came from the President."

"The sheet's nowhere to be found," Dan said. "We checked the laundry, the garbage. We're waiting for it to turn up on eBay."

"Wasn't everyone who is treating the President supposed to have the highest level of security clearance?"

Grant had trouble containing his anger. "Fuckin' A right!"

"We put the medical staff on lockdown." Dan said. "Opened a wing that was closed for renovation, cut all lines to the outside, confiscated cell phones. The orders are to keep the President alive and that's all they're going to be allowed to do. The last thing I need is someone calling *The National Enquirer* and selling their story. But when the Commander in Chief was first brought in, it was chaos. Doctors and nurses were running to the supply rooms and pharmacy, all over the hospital. Someone could have stuffed the sheet anywhere."

Alex gave a frustrated sigh. She'd read how, when President Abraham Lincoln was assassinated, half the White House staff pilfered souvenirs, some of which were later sold to museums. Linens, books, you name it. Hell, after Eva Perón died, a doctor started auctioning off blood he'd saved from her blood tests.

Alex sat on one of the stiff chairs for hospital visitors. From the chair's uncomfortable design, it was clear the hospital didn't want visitors staying too long.

Dan spoke first. "So far, there's no physical evidence that links the visiting Vietnamese to the explosion. The skull with the explosives in it—as Alex pointed out—is clearly a recently killed American."

"Could one of the visitors have offed him before the ceremony?" Grant asked.

Dan shook his head. "Timing's too tight. Assembly Member Chugai and the other government officials flew directly to Andrews and then helicoptered to the White House. The civilians arrived late the night before and all had dinner where they were staying, at the Mayflower Hotel."

"Nguyen met them there," Grant said. "He could have passed the skull to one of them or made a switch the following morning."

It pained Alex to hear Grant refer to him as Nguyen; he'd always called him Troy before.

Grant continued. "I talked to Nguyen's psychiatrist. He hadn't seen him for years—I guess the shrink stuff was part of his residency—but he had some interesting things to say."

"How did you get him to breach confidentiality?" Alex asked.

"Doctor-patient privilege has a resounding hole in it by the name of national security. Do you have any idea how many Dallas shrinks the FBI interviewed after JFK was shot?"

"Seems like a waste to me," Alex said. "If someone's planning to off the President, I doubt he's lying on a couch shooting the breeze with his therapist about it. Plus, what good is an opinion from a doctor Troy saw a couple of decades ago?"

"Dr. . . . uh . . ." Grant looked down at his papers. "Dr. Meserve said Troy had a lot of resentment at being brought to the United States and at the U.S. for costing his father his life."

Alex fell silent. It was similar to what Troy had told her. "He was just a kid when he came to the U.S.," she said. "In a very strange place. I was royally pissed, too, when my mother moved me around a lot as a child."

Grant continued. "And the people he worked with at NIH said he was frustrated that the U.S. wouldn't allow his sister to immigrate."

The scene of Troy being shot once again filled Alex's

thoughts. As horrible as it was, she hadn't even focused on the fact that it also meant that Lizzie would lose her last chance to leave Vietnam, her last chance to see her brother.

"Grant, you're twisting everything," Alex said. She thought of Troy's delicate hands soothing her that night at her apartment. "There's no way he's a killer. Look, it was pure coincidence that he even got assigned to be part of the Trophy Skulls team. His boss made him do it because he happened to be Vietnamese."

"Where'd you get that idea?"

Alex thought about the first day Troy had shown up at her lab. "That's what he, uh, told me."

"I called the head of psychiatry at the NIH. He says the idea was Troy's from the start—that Troy badgered him to be assigned to the Trophy Skulls, even threatened to quit if he wasn't detailed here. Why would Troy have been so hot to be part of this effort if he wasn't planning to use it for some sort of revenge?"

Alex considered the question. "Maybe he thought that if he was involved in some high-profile political endeavor, someone would begin to pay attention and help him get his sister back."

"If," Grant said, "there even is a sister."

CHAPTER FIFTY-ONE

FOR THE next hour, Alex watched as Wiatt prepared a dozen men to act as a command force, protecting the President. She even agreed to carry a gun herself. She was sitting uncomfortably in the command center when Dan summoned her and Grant to the autopsy suite.

Harding had the body of the young man on a table. His head was gone.

"Young delivery guy from Domino's Pizza went missing Sunday night on the way to a delivery in Dupont Circle," Dan explained. "The family he was scheduled to deliver to called in complaining because he never showed up. We combed the neighborhood of his last route. Didn't come up with anything, but we asked the District police to keep an eye open for the car. They found it in the parking garage at Dulles. Headless pizza guy in the trunk, floating in a pool of his own blood."

The corpse had a bruise on his lower back, consistent with a gun muzzle being shoved at him from behind. His hands had been cuffed with a cheap pair of handcuffs, like the kind you could get in any kinky sex shop in the District, or even at the more upscale Lovers Lane.

"Time of death is consistent with time of disappearance," Harding said, "a little after one A.M. Monday morning."

Grant processed these new facts. "Cause of death?"

"Piano wire around the neck."

"Where was Nguyen at the time?" Grant asked. Once he made his mind up about something, it was hard to dislodge the thought.

Alex spoke up. "He was at Dulles. The flight from Vietnam with the civilians was late and he was there to meet it. Where was Clive Moses?" Alex asked.

"We already checked the White House," Dan said. "He left a little after eleven P.M. And the couple with the parking spot next to his at the condo say they pulled in at two A.M. after a party and his Jeep still wasn't in its slot."

Alex glared triumphantly at Grant.

Dan caught her look. "It's not enough for a trial, Alex. I've got men interviewing people on the pizza guy's route to see if they noticed the Jeep or a guy with a bit of gray hair."

Alex nodded her head. "Piano wire's a tricky weapon of choice. Sure, it slices the victim, but it's hard to work, even in gloves, without slicing yourself in the process. Maybe I'll find a piece of Moses' DNA on it."

"Hard to believe that Moses—even if he were our guy—would leave any evidence that could be traced back to him," Grant said.

"Maybe," Alex said, "he's long gone. Maybe it was money that was the motivator here. He did his job and how he's spending the dough in a more suitable spot. Must get pretty wearing to always put your own needs second to those of the guy you're guarding."

Alex's analysis of the wire found no flecks of skin or blood other than the victim's. Instead, the wire had scratches along the section where the two ends had come together at the back of the man's neck.

"What do you make of this?" she asked Harding.

"Odd. Best I can figure, he was wearing some sort of metal gloves."

Alex turned to Grant. "Sounds like the sort of far out thing that you would design."

"Nah. My dad was a welder and he used metal mesh gloves all the time," Grant said. "I'll have my lab boys run tests on any metal transfer they find on the piano wire. If it's from a high-end metal glove, like the titanium mesh ones available only on the Web, there is some chance they can come up with a limited list of who bought them. More likely they're the sort that union guys use all the time."

"But," Harding said, "the piano wire's a different story."

"Surely there are millions of miles of piano wire sold each year," Alex said.

"Not like this," he said. "My wife Beverly used to play—with such enthusiasm that we frequently replaced the wire. Pianos built after the mid-1800s were larger in size and used a thicker wire, nearly five millimeters in diameter, with a high carbon content. This is less than half a millimeter and it's got some real wear. It comes from a piano that's got some age on it, maybe one of considerable value."

"In the District, you can arrange a kill for a carton of cigarettes," Grant said. "Why ruin a priceless antique to off a pizza guy?"

But Alex and Dan were thinking along the same lines. "Maybe it was a matter of using something handy," Dan said.

"Doesn't Vice President Shane have a piano in his office at the White House?" Alex asked, thinking back to the Barbara Walters interview with Abby.

Dan immediately responded, "Maybe we'll find it's out of tune."

As they were about to leave the autopsy suite, Chuck entered, with a troubled look on his face. "Shane appointed a new Secretary of Treasury," he said. "We're off the case and it's in the hands of the Secret Service." The AFIP guards that Dan had left at the White House had been forcibly removed.

"We've got to get back in there," Dan said.

"How about some sort of court order?" asked Chuck.

"Not enough time," said Dan.

"I think I know a way," said Alex.

CHAPTER FIFTY-TWO

ALEX, DAN, and Grant stood in the late evening darkness behind the Treasury Building. Grant, the king of devices, had a key card that he'd programmed to open any governmental door that needed to be swiped. "They've all contracted with the same vendor," he said. "It was a piece of cake to program in all the combinations."

Grant used the key to let them in through a side delivery door. Unlike the front and back entrances of the building, which had guards and metal detectors, there was no one guarding this entrance. Guards only attended it when a delivery was in process since they assumed no one could get past that door unless they opened it for them.

Once inside, they were counting on Alex to lead them back through the Marilyn Monroe entrance. She was dressed in a suit she had taken from Barbara's office. Her friend always kept one there for her court appearances. Shane was putting a new staff in place, getting rid of Cotter's as soon as possible, and Alex felt she might be able to blend in, looking like a new administrative assistant, if she wore the suit. Dan and Grant were dressed in suits, with curled wire earphones coming out of their ears, looking like Secret Service agents.

The pressure was on Alex to retrace her steps and find her way back into the White House. But as she walked down the hallway in Treasury, she realized she had no idea which direction to turn. After a few minutes' wandering, she came to the window that she remembered staring at the White House through. "This way," she said.

She found the elevator she'd used with the President. They took it down one floor. She located the door to the passageway between Treasury and the White House, and Grant used another device to override the keypad and cause the door to crack open. A dash through the deserted hallway with the florist shop led them to a second doorway through the storage room with all the furniture. Grant was a few feet in the lead, gun in front of him, when he veered sharply to the left and yelled, "Freeze!"

It took a few moments to ascertain that the man propped against the wall was already dead. The wall behind him was darkened with blood from a clean shot to the head, but his body had remained upright, wedged between two pieces of furniture.

Alex moved close to the man. "I recognize him. He's the other Secret Service man who was at the ceremony. I remember thinking it strange that there were just two of them."

"Could be he was in on it and then Moses got greedy," Dan said. He looked down at the man's feet and pointed to the spent .357 shell casing. Grant put gloves on, picked it up, and slipped it in an evidence bag.

Dan put his hand into the man's pocket and fished out his identification and key cards. "These may come in handy."

They continued through the storeroom, exiting next to the broken bust of Churchill. Dan, who'd had the run of the White House right after the explosion, knew exactly how to get to the Vice President's office. Now that they were in the White House proper, Grant turned his radio and Dan's to tap into the frequency on which the Secret Service was broadcasting. There was nothing suspicious about the commands that were coming across the airwaves—at least not yet.

Shane's former office was deserted. Alex closed the door behind them, shoved a rug near the door, and flicked on a desk lamp, hoping the rug would block light from escaping under the door. Dan opened the piano. It was indeed missing a wire. Grant plucked another wire out so they could compare their heft and carbon content back at the AFIP to determine if the wire used in the beheading had come from this instrument.

Alex and Grant prepared to leave, but Dan started opening drawers. She didn't want to make a noise by speaking, but she pointed to her watch. *We haven't got time,* Alex mouthed.

Dan was leafing through the drawers of a file cabinet. Grant started going through the compartments of the desk. Alex walked over to the window to close the curtains more tightly so that no one on watch outside would see the commotion inside. As she approached it, her shoe hit the window seat. The wood made a hollow noise. She picked up the upholstered bench of the window seat, revealing a storage space underneath. She pulled out a box that smelled faintly of incense. When she opened it, she found a skull. "Hello, Braverman," she said.

"The boxes must have been switched between the time the Vietnamese delegation entered the White House and the ceremony began," whispered Dan.

Just then, a crackling voice came across the radios that Dan and Grant wore. It said, "The tunnels have been compromised. Find the intruder."

Dan said, "Let's split up to make sure at least one of us gets out." He reached for the Braverman box from Alex. "I'll take this. It will be safer if you're not carrying anything suspicious."

"But—," she protested.

Dan took the box from her. "There's a greater chance for me to finagle getting this out. I've got the key card from the dead Secret Service agent. He was about my age and I might pass for him if I quickly flash ID."

A rapid fire series of orders came across the radio. The administrative night staff was being evacuated from the White House.

"They're gearing up for a firefight," said Grant, "getting the civilians off the grounds."

"Alex, you've got to try to head out with the crowd," Dan said. He handed her a yellow legal pad from Shane's desk.

Alex opened the door a crack and moved out of the room. She floated into a group of women who had been working late in the White House counsel's office. With her legal pad, she might be able to blend in.

They were headed toward the Northeast exit. One of the younger women was jittery. "Do you think it's another attack?" she asked Alex.

"No, President Shane seems to have things in control."

At the exit, the White House employees' briefcases and purses were being checked by guards.

Shit, thought Alex, thinking about the evidence collection kit she had in her fanny pack. How was she going to explain that? She looked at the three lines of employees, each moving toward a different guard. She tried to determine which guard it would be easier to get by. She picked the youngest one, who was the closest to her age.

The line moved slowly. The guard, a Secret Service agent in his early thirties, was searching the nervous younger woman. His Sig Sauer was on his hip within easy reach.

Alex stepped back, switching places with the woman behind her so she had a moment more to think. Then she heard a familiar voice speaking to the young guard.

"I'm here to relieve you," Dan said to him, flashing the dead agent's ID. "You're now part of the team guarding the Oval Office."

The agent didn't even question Dan. The new assignment was a promotion. When Alex stepped forward, Dan went through her bag. Then he told the people in his line to move over to one of the remaining lines. He walked out of the White House with Alex.

Enough people had cleared out of D.C. that the streets were eerily quiet. They walked down the block from the Treasury Building toward Dan's car, but D.C. police must have gotten word from the Secret Service. They'd set up a roadblock preventing vehicles from going in or out of a four-block radius around the White House. They wouldn't be able to retrieve the car. There were no cabs in sight.

Dan pulled a bow off a wreath in front of a closed souvenir

store. He stuck it on the wooden box he was carrying so that it looked like a holiday present. He took the radio earpiece out of his ear and tossed Alex's legal pad into a trash can. Then he took her hand. They took the escalator down to the subway looking like a holiday couple.

CHAPTER FIFTY-THREE

THERE WAS no one at the guard desk when Dan and Alex entered the AFIP. Dan handed her the wooden box with the Braverman skull and took his gun out of its holster. They took the tunnels under the AFIP to the command center at Walter Reed. The men who were protecting the President's wing were well trained and well armed, but they'd be easily outnumbered if the President's enemies realized he was there.

"Are you going to arrest Shane?" Alex asked Dan.

"Too many loose ends," he said.

"Like what?"

"No proof the skull was put in his office before the exchange. He could argue that someone else stashed it there afterward. He's been out of that office since assuming the presidency."

"Come to think of it," Alex said, "he moved into the Oval Office pretty quickly, considering the President's body wasn't found."

"Admittedly, but we haven't had time yet to go through the electronic records to see if anyone else entered the office since the ceremony. And we've got to figure out the motive. Why would Shane screw himself out of the oil deal?"

"You can't be serious," Alex said. "As President, he could make dozens of deals. Not to mention those speaker's fees and corporate board offers after he left office. And he's got a young wife. Don't you remember what Henry Kissinger said? Power is the ultimate aphrodisiac?"

"Listen, Alex, Shane's not exactly a flight risk. We've got to nail this right."

"Can't President Cotter do something?"

Wiatt entered the room. "He's in a coma."

A chill went through Alex. The lie that they were maintaining to further the investigation might soon be the truth.

"And," Wiatt continued, "Shane's scheduled to address Congress tomorrow morning to ask them to declare war."

Alex's mouth gaped open. "We've got to stop him," she said.

Her cell phone rang and she saw Barbara's home number. She moved into the hallway so she could take the call out of her colleagues' earshot.

Maeve Chatterly spoke. "You've got to come. Something's wrong with Lana."

Alex headed down the hallway that led to the ladies' room so her colleagues wouldn't realize she was leaving the building. Then she retraced her steps to the unguarded entrance, got in her T-Bird, and broke the speed limit on the way to see Lana.

Maeve opened the apartment door. "That poor child," she said, shaking her head. Alex heard screeching, plaintive wails coming from Lana's room. Alex ran through the tiny apartment and thrust open Lana's door.

The girl was shaking, trembling, jerking, as if she was wracked with pain. Alex put her arms around her young friend, but Lana strained against her and broke free. There was a manic anger in her eyes. Alex was consumed with worry. She put her hands on Lana's shoulders. "She's going to be all right. Your mom is going to be all right," she mouthed in a soothing mantra. But Lana ignored her. Instead, she thrust her arms up, breaking Alex's grip. She looked away.

Alex followed Lana's gaze and saw Lana's cell phone, shattered at the base of a wall. The wall wasn't looking too good, either. There was a hole in the plaster where Lana had apparently thrown the phone.

Alex moved so that she was again in front of Lana's face. She formed her words crisply so that Lana could make them out. "Lana. Sweetie. You have to listen to me."

Lana began signing wildly, but her trembling body caused her hands to career in odd ways. Even if Alex understood sign language, she was quite sure that she wouldn't have been able to follow what Lana was saying today.

The girl crumpled onto the bed in a torrent of tears. Alex sat next to her on the bed and pulled her close. She kissed the top of Lana's head and rocked her soothingly. Alex whispered, "It'll be okay." Then she realized that she'd been whispering into Lana's hair and, without being able to see her lips, Lana wouldn't have registered her words. But then again, words seemed pretty insubstantial at the moment.

Lana clung to her for a long time. A half hour passed with them in that position. Lana seemed exhausted.

Alex shifted her position, then got up and urged Lana to lie down. Lana tipped her body over and put her head on the pillow. Alex arranged her covers over her.

Tears rolled down Lana's cheeks. Her mouth was a gash of anguish. She spoke quietly. "I've been mad at my mom a lot, wishing she'd leave me alone. But now I don't want to be alone."

Alex smoothed the girl's hair.

"We had a fight yesterday morning. What if she dies before I can tell her I'm sorry?"

"Don't worry, your mom knows that you love her. We're all going to get through this. I promise."

She sat on the floor of Lana's room, next to her bed, until Lana fell asleep. Then she tiptoed out, thanked Mrs. Chatterly for staying with the girl, and hoped that Barbara's condition would allow her to make good on her word.

ALEX'S NEXT stop was Barbara's hospital room, which smelled of a curious mix of antiseptic and lilies. She was asleep, so Alex stepped into the room quietly and glanced at the card tucked into a small arrangement of tulips in a vase on the windowsill. Alex tiptoed over to read the card. They were from Pug Davis, the old White House guard.

Alex sat quietly in the chair next to the bed while her friend slept. A nurse came in and hung a new bag of intravenous fluid on the thin metal stand beside Barbara's bed. Then she jostled Barbara slightly so that she could take her patient's blood pressure and temperature.

"Alex," Barbara said quietly. "Is Lana okay?"

Alex paused a few seconds, then nodded. Well, it wasn't really lying if you didn't actually say it, was it? And Lana would be okay soon, Alex was sure, once she saw her mom.

The nurse handed Barbara a small cup of pills, along with a larger cup of water. Alex held her friend's wrist so she could look in the cup. She saw an antibiotic, a painkiller, a stool softener, a vitamin. The usual hospital admixture.

"The patient needs rest," the nurse told Alex. "I'm afraid you're going to have to leave."

Barbara spoke. "Actually, she's my doctor."

The nurse surveyed Alex's wayward blond curls, wrinkled turtleneck, and jeans. "I've heard that one before."

Alex zipped open her fanny pack and showed the nurse her ID.

"You should dress better," the nurse said.

Barbara smiled. "I've been telling her that for years."

After the nurse left, Alex sat on the chair next to Barbara.

"What's my prognosis?" Barbara asked. Her speech was slurred a little from the anesthesia. But even in a hospital gown after a daunting surgery, Barbara was her usual direct and efficient self.

"It was a close call," Alex said, and moved over and sat on the side of the bed. She gestured with her hands. "A bullet ricocheted off the mantelpiece, so it slowed a bit before it entered you from the back."

"I remember the noise and the pain, and felt myself falling. The only image in my mind was Lana's face. As an infant, at two, at four, when she first learned to ride a bike—

I never believed that malarkey about your life passing before your eyes but there it was. Then I went blank."

"Internal bleeding. You had a lot of it. Your blood pressure dipped so low they couldn't feel a pulse and almost left you for dead. But they got the bullet out, but stitched you up inside. There won't be any permanent damage."

Barbara considered that information and sighed. "When I was in the recovery room, it was strange. My thoughts of Lana picked up right where I'd left off. The bike, our first vacation together, her finally getting into a school where the other students and teachers didn't dwell on her disability, every Mother's Day card or candleholder she ever made for me, and then," Barbara shuddered, "how I felt when she was kidnapped last year."

Alex thought about that horrible day the previous June. Alex had rushed off in a panic to rescue Lana and the young girl had ended up saving Alex's life.

"But lately, I don't know how to mother her. It seems like she gets so angry at me."

Alex bent down and hugged Barbara, then said, "She's just a teenager, but she told me to tell you she's sorry. She's grown up a lot in the past couple hours."

DOWN THE hall from Barbara's hospital room, Assemblyman Chugai was in traction. The explosion had thrown him into a wall and he'd broken bones in his shoulder and neck, but not anything that would cause permanent damage. According to the nursing staff there, he wasn't exactly a model patient. The hallway was cluttered with chairs occupied by his Vietnamese security detail, guns propped in their laps. He complained about the hospital food and had his minions bring in French food for him once the tube down his throat had been removed and he was able to swallow again. And as Alex walked past the room after saying good-bye to Barbara, he was complaining yet again. He was yelling for a doctor who could speak proper French or English.

The Pakistani medical resident who had been treating him left the room in a fit. Chugai, a presidential candidate in

Vietnam, was used to demanding the best. The nurse who'd met Alex in Barbara's room looked at Alex imploringly as she walked down the hall. "Well, Doc," she said. "Can you get him to settle down while I get him more morphine and call the attending to ask him to drive in from home?"

Alex didn't have privileges at the hospital. She couldn't accept responsibility for his care. But he was a major link to the investigation. And she was extremely curious about what he had to say.

The nurse waved her toward the room, but she was stopped by one of the guards, who asked her to open up her fanny pack so that he could search it. She complied. He focused a lot of attention on the syringe she carried. She always had one on her, in a plastic package, to collect DNA. Wordlessly, he held it up to the light—probably, Alex thought, to make sure it didn't contain any liquid that might be injected into the Assemblyman to kill him. When he saw it was empty, he let her pass.

The system of metal weights and pulleys hovered above the bed like some out-of-control Erector set. Assemblyman Chugai's body was attached by metal cords to this hovering crane. He was immobilized in a prone position, with his head propped up slightly. In traction, he could not see her until she was directly in front of him. His startled eyes blinked rapidly when she came into his range of vision. A blonde with the wavy long hair and calming blue eyes.

"I must leave," he said. His feet and hands trembled as pain wracked his body. Even in pain, the traction kept most of his body immobile. "Get the plane."

"Assemblyman Chugai," Alex said. "The nurse will bring more painkillers in a moment." She looked at the EKG monitor. His heart was holding steady. "May I take your pulse?"

In his position, he couldn't nod his head. Words were an effort. Alex waited for a few seconds to see if he would otherwise indicate an objection. When he didn't, she pressed the fingertips of her right hand on his left wrist and counted. His pulse was running at 65. It would be fine to give him a little more painkiller without the danger of shutting down his heart. As she moved her hand away, he grabbed it. "The plane," he demanded.

She put her left hand over their locked hands to soothe him. "You're in no shape to fly right now."

"He's trying to kill me,"

"Who's trying to kill you?"

Chugai pulled his hand away, as if he were insulted to be in contact with someone who was so dense. "The Vice President," he said, as if talking to a witless child. As if that were obvious. Then he sank into his pillow, talking almost to himself. "All I did. The money. Sending the general. Losing the general."

Alex shuddered as it dawned on her that the man in the bed who looked like a broken puppet was the man who'd sent General Tran to kill her.

The nurse returned with the morphine. "Thanks, Dr. Blake."

Chugai heard the name and came to the same realization that Alex had. He lurched toward her in anger, then was pulled back to the bed by his restraints. He yelled in frustration and pain. The nurse approached him with the morphine.

"The plane," he yelled to his guards.

Two guards ran into the room. But, by then, the Assemblyman had fallen back into the bed in a drugged stupor.

CHAPTER FIFTY-FOUR

WHEN CHUGAI woke up a half hour later, Dan had joined Alex in the room. Dan knew he was on thin ice. Interrogating someone who was under the influence of a drug wasn't exactly kosher. But Assemblyman Chugai wasn't the fish they were after. It would be a nightmare to get him to trial in an American court. He was only an oracle who might finger the man running the country as a cold-blooded killer.

"Who are you?" Chugai asked Dan.

Alex listened silently from a chair on the side of the room, outside Chugai's line of vision.

"I'm your one chance to avoid rotting in an American jail." Dan stood next to the bed, an imposing figure in his full Marine regalia. Dan had changed into his dress uniform, replete with ribbons, thinking a warrior's garb might get a bigger rise from the National Assembly member.

Chugai smiled. "I have two words for you. *Diplomatic immunity.*"

"And I have three words for you. *Go fuck yourself.*"

Chugai reached over for the nurse call button to eject Dan from the room. But Dan had moved it out of reach.

He raised his voice and called out to his men in the hall.

"I'm afraid it's just us. Nobody's out there."

Confusion crossed Chugai's face. "How?"

"Seems like you've become a liability to your government.

Not to mention that your president is backing your opponent in the upcoming election. He was more than happy to demote you. You are no longer a diplomat; you're just some schmo. If you'd like me to translate, it means you are shit out of luck."

Chugai considered this new development, but still did not seem worried. "Harvard taught me that you need to let me consult a lawyer. You may go now. I'm not saying anything until I obtain legal counsel."

Instead, Dan walked toward the head of Chugai's bed. "It doesn't look good you being at the White House, bearing a skull that exploded. Forget the schmo bit, maybe I'll target you as an enemy combatant." Dan unsheathed a knife and ran the fingers of his right hand over the blade, feeling its sharp edge. Alex was too mesmerized to stand up and stop him.

"Are you crazy?" Chugai responded. "If I had desired to blow up the White House, I would not have put myself at risk."

Dan acted as if he hadn't heard. He took the point of the knife and inserted it into a screw on the traction apparatus, loosening a handle.

"As an enemy combatant, you deserve the same treatment you guys gave our Ambassador Pete Peterson when he was a POW. Just like those sadists who tied him like a rocking horse and then bounced on the rope until he'd pass out from the pain. He's still got those rope burns on his arm and his hands still go numb sometimes."

"That was my father's war. I was just a child."

Dan started turning the traction crank ever so slightly, which lifted Chugai's head an inch farther into the air. Chugai's eyes opened in terror as he realized that, with a few more cranks, the Marine standing in front of him could snap his neck.

"What is it that you want?" asked Chugai.

"Smart question. Just tell me about the deal between you and the Vice President."

AFTER HE'D learned what he needed, Dan marched into Barbara's room, woke her, and asked her to help draft the legal papers. He then went back to the AFIP to plan the next move. Alex stayed at the hospital with Barbara to act as a courier for the documents.

Barbara propped a laptop on her lap. As she wrote, a slender printer was spitting out papers on the bedside table that had previously held the plastic washbasin, Lubriderm hand cream, and other accoutrements of modern hospital life.

Barbara reached over for the newly printed pages and handed them to Alex. Articles of Impeachment of Vice President Shane to be tendered to the House of Representatives. Alex gave a low whistle. "Wow."

Apparently Vice President Shane and Assemblyman Chugai had cut an outrageous deal. Shane gave Chugai a major kickback for making sure the offshore drilling rights went to Westport and he arranged the high-profile White House handoff to give Chugai a lock on being elected Vietnam's next president. Whether Shane knew it or not, Chugai had ordered the death of Gladden for leaking the oil report to the Chinese before giving it to Westport. He'd also attempted to sign Alex's death warrant and might have succeeded were it not for Luke's lucky guitar strap. His deal with the Americans and his presidential bid would have blown up if she had unleashed an inquiry into an American massacre of Vietnamese citizens. There's where it got complicated. The wire that killed the pizza boy matched Shane's piano. But Chugai claimed to know nothing about the bombing. The way he told it, Shane had just gotten greedy. Thought he could get the money and the presidency. Shane left the East Room right before the bomb went off. He'd been willing to kill Chugai and anyone else who was left behind.

Alex looked over the charges. Graft, bribery, conspiracy to commit murder, treason. Violations of Article I, sections 2 and 3, of the Constitution, the commission of high crimes and misdemeanors. "Reads like something that would happen in some small dictatorship, not in a major world power."

"He's joining an illustrious group of politicians who've been impeached. Andrew Johnson . . ."

"Bill Clinton . . ."

"Not to mention Senator William Blount for plotting to help the British seize Florida and Louisiana in 1797."

"Don't tell me you learned that in law school."

"Hell, it's not even part of my job description now. It's just that Wiatt's trying to keep the whole operation secret until President Cotter returns from the dead and surprises the Vice President with a felony warrant."

Alex nodded. She knew the game plan. And she'd be right there when the dominoes started to tumble.

CHAPTER FIFTY-FIVE

WHEN ALEX entered the White House the next day at dusk, she didn't need to run the gauntlet of Secret Service agents at the door. A federal court order had replaced them with federal marshals so that Dan could serve the legal documents. This meant that her companions, Dan and six other officers, did not have to check their guns at the door. It also meant that Grant and another six men could roll the President in a wheelchair back into the White House the same way he had left—through the Marilyn Monroe entrance. Alex wondered if that entrance had seen this much high-level action since the Kennedy Administration.

Both groups met in the library in the West Wing. With Dan in the lead, they made their way to the Oval Office. Dan swung open the door, weapon drawn. The new President was behind his desk and Abby, wearing an extremely short low-cut black dress, was sitting on the corner of his desk.

"You are under arrest for treason, attempted murder, and conspiracy," Dan said to Shane. He nodded to two soldiers. "Cuff him."

"You can't send soldiers after me," Shane said firmly. "I'm the Commander in Chief."

The team of soldiers parted and Bradley Cotter stepped forward. An Army beret covered his surgical bandage. He'd left his wheelchair in the hallway and was using all his strength to stand tall. "Over my dead body," he said.

Alex winced. That was almost what had happened.

Shane looked like he'd seen a ghost. "You're alive," he said. The way he said it, Alex thought, he almost sounded happy.

Abby, though, slid off the desk and put her hands on her hips like a petulant child. "This can't be happening."

Grant admired the creamy tops of Abby's breasts in her low-cut dress until he caught Alex glaring at him.

"Thomas Malcolm Shane," boomed Dan's voice through the glorious acoustics of the Oval Office. "You have the right to remain silent. Anything you say can and will be used against you in a court of law. You have the right to speak to an attorney, and to have an attorney present during any questioning. If you cannot afford a lawyer, one will be provided for you at government expense."

Shane looked completely dumbfounded as he was cuffed. If the proof against him hadn't been so strong, Alex might have thought he was innocent.

Shane was protesting. "I might have bent the rules a little for Westport Oil. But I'd never try to kill the President."

Dan and the others hustled Shane out. Cotter walked over to his desk and sat down. He rubbed his hand over the polished wood of his desktop as if he had never expected to be here again.

"If you don't mind," President Cotter said to Alex and Abby. "They're bringing my family over now. I'd like to be alone with them."

Alex nodded. As the two women left the room, he called after Alex. "Dr. Blake, I can't thank you enough."

She turned back toward him and smiled. "Seeing you behind that desk again is thanks enough. Plus, you may not remember it, but you saved my life."

CHAPTER FIFTY-SIX

IN THE anteroom to the Oval Office, Abby bowed her head. When she raised it, a thin veil of tears clouded her eyes. "No more Camelot," she said.

Alex nodded. She didn't quite know what to say. She was actually beginning to feel a touch of sympathy for Abby for believing in the wrong man. Like so many women across time, she'd given her all to a particular man, but the expected payoff never occurred. Unless you count the chance to play Lady Di in third world hospitals.

Abby looked at Alex, sizing her up. "Think you can give me a lift home? Seems like time for me to start packing."

"Why not let Secret Service drive you?"

"You see anybody offering?"

Alex looked around. Abby was right. The Secret Service agents had been rounded up for questioning. The AFIP soldiers were focusing on the arrest of the Vice President.

Against her better judgment, Alex blurted, "Sure, why not?"

Abby gave her a devilish smile. "Can you pick me up at the West Wing gate? I don't want to ruin my hair in the rain." She looked at Alex's mop of long, untamed curls as if to signal that whatever happened to Alex's hair wouldn't matter a whit.

Alex sighed. Here she'd been feeling sorry for this

woman, but Abby wasn't exactly going coach class yet. "Okay, I'm driving an old T-Bird. How long do you need?"

"Just a few minutes, darlin'. I just need to make one phone call."

Twenty minutes later, Alex was fuming in the car and Abby had not yet emerged. She turned on her phone to call Barbara at the hospital and tell her the saga had ended, but before she could dial, she saw a figure in a long sweeping cape with a hood exiting the White House. Alex looked down at the mysterious figure's shoes. Stiletto high heels. It must be Abby, she thought.

Alex rolled down the passenger-side window, and reached her hand through the open space to grab the outside door handle. She could have gone out in the rain to open it limo-style for Abby, but she was too peeved by now. Then, upset with the pettiness of her feelings, she took a rag from the glove compartment and wiped the passenger seat to remove the traces of rain that had come through the open window.

She reached for her phone to turn it off, then realized her lunge for the window had knocked it between her bucket seat and the stick shift. Before she could retrieve it, Abby bounded into the car.

"Home, James," Abby said in the mock British voice of a movie character commanding her chauffeur.

"That's all well and good," Alex said, "but I have no idea where home is."

"Yeah, I figured you wouldn't. Everybody knows 1600 Pennsylvania Avenue, but do they give a shit where the Vice President and his wife live? No. I even had to shop for my own sheets."

Abby gave Alex directions. They moved away from the center of the city, out of view of the monuments, to a more run-down neighborhood. Geez, Alex thought, if this is where the Shanes were forced to live, then maybe Abby did have cause to complain.

Another few turns took them to the front of the parking garage of a decaying apartment building. Surely this couldn't be the Vice President's home. There were no guards, no cops.

She looked inquisitively at Abby. The woman shifted in her seat, and the cape parted slightly, revealing a metallic glow in her white-gloved hand. She had a gun pointed at Alex. "Now we wait."

Alex inhaled sharply. "How did . . . ?"

Abby smiled. "With all that attention to my husband, no one was covering the exits."

Alex sized up the situation.

"Don't think I won't use it. My daddy used to take me hunting."

Alex had no doubt that she was telling the truth.

"You never suspected, huh?"

Alex shook her head.

Abby laughed. "Shit, girl, didn't you ever own that Barbie game?"

Alex replied weakly, " 'We Girls Can Do Anything'?"

"Yeah."

Alex realized her one chance was to keep Abby talking. "I remember that the Doctor Barbie had a pink stethoscope, pink medical coat, and high heels."

"Don't knock it. You're pretty. You should dress better."

Alex thought it was ridiculous that they were discussing her fashion taste—or rather lack of it—just before she was going to be shot. She wished she had thought to write out a will. She hoped her mother knew to bury her like she lived, in a black turtleneck and jeans, rather than in one of those odd colorful dashikis her mother sometimes wore. "I guess I never was that type."

Abby continued. "Hey, don't knock it, honey. I learned early to work it—to get men to do what I wanted."

"You got the Vice President to put a bomb in the White House?"

Abby roared with laughter. "That old fart. He was only good for one thing. And it wasn't in the sack, either."

Alex still had her hand on the stick shift. She practically could reach out and touch the gun. But what would that get her? Dead.

She imperceptibly moved her hand down to her side of

the gearshift. The phone was out of sight between the shift and her seat. Maybe she could reach it and push one of the buttons to alert someone about her plight. Then she realized that was ridiculous. All that would happen would be that someone would pick up the phone on the other end, say hello, tip off Abby, and lead to her getting killed. Hmm, Alex thought, feeling a little less scared and more resigned to her fate. All roads seem to lead in the same direction. Chitty-chitty bang-bang.

Abby hardly seemed to notice Alex's silence. She was on a roll about her husband, gesturing with the little pistol. "Asshole had me sign a prenup, do you believe it? No way that I would get a cut of that black gold from Westport Oil. But he was my ticket. I was going to be the next Jackie O."

"I can't see you waiting around for eight years of two Cotter Administrations for that to happen," Alex said, her hand pressing down alongside her seat.

"No, ma'am," Abby said. "Do you know what the Vice President and his wife spend most of their time doing? Going to funerals of heads of state in countries that don't even have air-conditioning. A girl's got to move up from that, don't you agree?"

Alex nodded. "I can see how that would wear on a person."

"They can blather all they want about life beginning at forty. But I wasn't going to wait that long. And I was going to get the last laugh on the old fart."

A fizzle of excitement went through Alex. Her pointer finger, the one that tapped out the letter T for thymine when she was playing her silent symphony of the genetic code, had clicked the on button of the recording function of her phone. Abby might shoot her, but at least Dan might find the phone in her car and figure out whodunit.

"*You* were behind the bomb at the White House?"

Abby waved the gun at Alex. "Hey, show a little respect. Book smarts never gonna go as far as street smarts."

She continued. "Once Cotter was out of the way, I'd be First Lady, pure and simple. And once that was over, I didn't want to have to rely on some marriage to another old fart to make me rich, like Jackie and Aristotle Onassis. It came to me in China. I figured out a way to strike oil myself."

"What's China got to do with it?" Alex was glad Abby was a talker. No, even more than that, a braggart. The more she talked, the longer Alex would stay alive. Alex was half listening, but the forensic part of her thoughts was giving way to another voice in her head. She was making a list of all the things that she wished she'd done in her life. Tried hot air ballooning. Seen the pyramids. Gone to Ohio to spend this Christmas with her mother. Made a baby.

The oddness of that last thought jolted Alex back to attention and she focused once again on what Abby was saying. "I got the idea from Lil Wang, sort of. When we first met, she told me she thought her dad, the president of China, was a big hypocrite. Being nice to my asshole of a husband when all the while he knew that the recognition of Vietnam and the deal with Westport Oil would totally screw China. Turns out China's in worse shape than we are. More people, no domestic oil production. Totally dependent on foreign oil. Here, at least, we've got the Gulf Coast drilling back to what it was before Hurricane Katrina."

It sounded to Alex like Abby had picked up a bit of knowledge in her short tenure at Westport Oil. The saying "a little knowledge is a dangerous thing" seemed particularly appropriate here.

Abby continued, "A few drinks with Lil and we'd plotted it all out. I'd queer the deal with Vietnam and she'd make sure I got a cut of the Chinese oil deal."

"You don't exactly seem like the type who'd risk a manicure to wire a bomb."

"That's what I mean about working it, honey. Flash a little T and A and you can get any man to do anything. They're just big babies, you know."

"I'd ask for a refund from whoever was helping you. Cotter's still alive, and now you're not even the Second Lady anymore."

Abby jabbed the gun in Alex's ribs. "You think you're so

smart. You'll be six feet under and I'll be one of the richest women in the world."

Slowly it dawned on Alex what the state of play was now. "So your husband gets arrested, but Vietnam has already soured on the United States. The Westport Oil deal goes south, China gets the Phu Khanh reserves, and you ride off into the sunset with your accomplice?"

"Right you are, up to a point. As Mrs. Murphy told Mama when I was in preschool, Abby does not play well with others. I've got two loose ends to tie up—you and him. He's going to shoot you and then he's going to appear to commit suicide."

Alex was about to ask who "he" was when a Jeep pulled up alongside her car. The dark rain couldn't disguise the gray glare of his forelock. Agent Clive Moses got into the backseat of the car, pushing aside Alex's pile of medical journals to make space for himself.

"Hi, sweetie," Abby said to him.

"Drive," he ordered Alex. He pushed the button on a garage door opener. He ordered her to park inside the structure, close to the elevator.

When she turned off the motor, he exited the car, dragged her out, and cuffed her hands behind her. Alex groaned at the sharp pain as the metal roughly cut into her skin. She had an odd sensation that she would topple forward. The displacement of her arms behind her back made her feel off balance and vulnerable. Abby pulled the hood of her cape over her head. She got out of the car, told Clive that she'd missed him, and pushed the button on the elevator.

No one was inside the elevator as they hustled Alex in. Clive stood close behind Alex, hands on her shoulders, chin on the top of her head, looking like they were a romantic couple. Abby turned sideways, facing them, a small bulge in her cape concealing the gun. If anyone entered the elevator they wouldn't be able to see her face.

Clive pulled her arms behind her sharply, in an action that shot pain up through Alex's shoulder blades. The small trickle of a tear started to emerge from Alex's right eye. She brought her shoulder up and turned her head down to blot it, but that small action provoked Abby to poke the gun in her ribs.

The door opened to an empty hallway on the third floor. Clive shoved Alex harshly forward with his left hand. It hurt, but Alex's adrenaline was clicking in. She noted that he was favoring his left arm, undoubtedly because the President had wounded his right one. The thought of a small chink in his armor caused Alex to quell her fear for just an instant and let herself believe that she might have a chance to escape.

Clive used a key to open the door of an apartment on the third floor.

"See," Abby said. "I told you that renting this place was a great idea."

"And once we dump the girl, we can celebrate."

As they entered the living room, Alex saw a big bouquet of daisies on the table. Alex caught Abby wrinkling her nose, but Clive didn't notice. "Oh, honey, you shouldn't have," Abby said.

Alex knew that she meant that literally. She could tell that Abby considered herself more of the type for roses.

"You know you'll always be my Daisy Mae."

A fake, weary smile from Abby. The last thing she wanted was to be identified with some hillbilly.

As Abby held the gun on Alex, Clive turned the dinky radio to a soft jazz station and entered the kitchen, returning with a bottle of champagne. He popped the cork and filled a glass for himself and Abby. "To patriotism," he said.

The meaning was lost on Alex. "You blow up the White House and you make a toast to patriotism?" she asked.

Clive looked at Alex like his logic was impeccable. "Do you know what that SOB Cotter was planning to do? He was going to *forgive* Vietnam. That would demean everything our soldiers had fought for. It would be like inviting Osama bin Laden over to watch an NFL game with you."

Abby handed the gun to Clive. Alex focused her eyes on a single daisy and started counting the white petals. He kills me. He kills me not.

"Enough chewing the fat with the *doctor*." Abby said the last word in a mocking way. "Take her out."

"Right here?" Clive said. "It'll be too much of a mess."

"What's the big deal? There's no way to trace this place to us."

Alex spoke up. "Maybe not to her, there isn't. She's wearing gloves. But you've touched a dozen things since we got in here. The radio, the refrigerator, the glasses."

Abby glared at her and Alex was grateful that the gun had already changed hands. She was sure that if Abby still had it, she would be dead by now.

"I'll help you clean it up, Clive," Abby said.

He thought about it. "I'll take her into the bathroom and kill her in the tub. That way we can wash away the evidence. Once she's dead, we can dump the body someplace else."

Abby looked impatient, but knew it wasn't wise to argue with a man with a gun. "Whatever you say, honey."

Clive used the gun to prod Alex down the hall. "Clive, you're going to be the next to go," Alex said, once they were out of Abby's earshot.

"No way," he said, but the fingerprint comment had obviously unsettled him.

"Keep me alive long enough to let me tell you what I know."

They entered the bathroom. He held the gun on her and said, "Start talking."

"I've got some of it on tape, in the car," she said. "She didn't realize I was recording her. Get my cell phone from the car. It's jammed between the driver's seat and the stick shift. You can hear what she says about you and then I'll tell you the rest of her plans."

"Do you know where she's got the money?"

What money? Alex thought. But she answered emphatically, "Of course."

"Kneel down," he said.

Jesus, Mary, and Joseph, Alex thought. Kneeling in semi-prayer, she envisioned herself being shot, Mafia-style, in the head.

But instead, he uncuffed her hands and recuffed them in front of her around the pipe that led from the toilet to the wall.

Then he shot out the mirror, causing a loud crash of glass, to fool Abby into thinking that he'd killed Alex.

He put his finger to his lips and left the room.

Alex could hear Abby asking him, "Are we alone now?"

"You bet," he said.

Alex moved her cuffed hand down the curve of the toilet pipe to the metal supply valve that turned the water off. She pushed it roughly to the side, feeling a spike of pain in her burned hand. Then she used both her hands to start unscrewing the three-inch-wide metal ring that held the water supply pipe to the toilet tank. She turned and turned, but the rusted iron hardly budged.

"I've been fantasizing about getting you alone for so long," Abby was saying to Clive. "Why don't you put down that gun and come over here?"

Alex could sense that Clive was hesitating. "One last thing," he said. "I'm going to get a tarp from the car so that I can wrap her up."

The door shut behind him and she could hear the clink of the champagne bottle against a glass of Abby poured herself some more bubbly. Over the static sound of Abby changing radio stations, Alex could hear the woman giggle, "You're right. Just one last thing."

Alex shifted position so that she could put her feet against the wall to gain more purchase as she yanked at the pipe. She felt the metal ring move clockwise a quarter of an inch. In the other room, Abby changed the radio to a classic rock station. "I Can't Get No Satisfaction" blared out. Alex, frustrated, moved her right leg so that the cowboy boot left the wall. She positioned her foot over the pipe and started banging down on it, heel first, in annoyance. The loud music in the next room disguised her clanging, but the pipe ring didn't budge. She took a breath, tried to calm herself, and then came at the ring again with her hands.

The ring was cold against her unbandaged left hand and

only added to the chill she felt throughout her body. Sure, she had bought herself a little time. But even if Clive believed her and shot Abby before Abby could shoot him, that action would at most buy Alex just a few minutes to live. She'd be no use to Clive once he found out she knew nothing about the money.

Alex twisted and twisted and the metal ring moved slowly, barely half an inch. She could hear the apartment door open. Clive had entered the apartment, turned down the music, and pushed the play button on Alex's phone. His quick return indicated that he hadn't taken the time to listen to it in the garage. Alex continued to twist the metal ring as Abby's words came out of the precise, government-funded speaker designed by Grant. "Hey, show a little respect," the recorded Abby was saying.

"What the hell are you doing?" Abby asked Clive. In the background, a stadium rock song by Queen tinkled out of the hushed radio.

Alex pressed her shoulder against the porcelain toilet, pushed her feet against the wall, and yanked the ring like her life depended on it. Which it did. The ring spun around. She removed the three-inch section of pipe and a residue of foul-smelling rusty water flooded her jeans and the bathroom floor. She slid her cuffed hands up the stump of the pipe that was still attached to the wall and pulled them toward her through the three-inch opening. Grabbing the leg of the sink, she righted herself to a standing position.

She'd been so intent on the one task, she hadn't thought about what to do next. She picked up the small cylinder of metal that she had removed, stepped into the tub, and pulled the shower curtain across the bar to conceal herself. Maybe, just maybe, she would have a chance. She heard the tape in the other room. "It came to me in China," the Abby voice was saying. Alex thought of the permutations, the odds that a bookie would lay on how it would turn out. Math, like science, had always comforted Alex.

She played it out in her mind. Clive might shoot Abby, then come for her. Odds were maybe one in five that Alex would be able to overpower him. But, she thought, the odds tilted more in her favor, maybe even to sixty–forty, if Abby killed Clive. Abby might then leave the apartment without discovering that Alex was still alive.

Alex held her breath. Another minute or two and the tape would reach the point where Abby disclosed how she was going to off Clive. Alex exhaled sharply and moved her body into a warrior's stance. She strained to listen to the movements in the next room.

The radio static returned and the music changed to the soft jazz station that Clive had originally chosen. In a moment, it became clear that Abby was the one who had switched stations. "C'mon, honey," she was saying to Clive. "All that stuff on the tape is old news. Turn it off and come dance with me."

Alex could hear a slight *thwump* and surmised that it was Abby taking off her cape, dropping it to the ground. She thought of the low-cut tight black dress the woman was wearing. Don't fall for it, Clive, Alex thought. She felt like shouting to him, "Don't think with your dick! Keep the tape running!" But she knew that any noise from her would truncate those sixty-forty odds of survival to one in a million.

She could hear Abby, the real one, not the tape, saying, "Yeah, that's it, baby. Come to Momma."

Then a click and the tape was off.

Abby was working it, again.

ALEX COULD barely restrain herself from opening the bathroom door a crack to watch what was happening. The curiosity tugged at her as the events in the next room unfurled to decide her fate. She began a mantra. Curiosity killed the cat. Curiosity killed the cat. Her shoulder ached from her tense position. She relaxed her body for an instant. She wondered if this would be how she would spend the last moments of her life, in an ignoble bathtub, smelling like sewage water.

A sound of shattering glass. A scuffle. A gunshot. Then another. The sound of a body hitting the floor. Then silence.

Alex primed herself for action, trying to imagine who

was alive, and who was dead. Then she heard a female voice. "Good riddance."

Alex prayed that Abby would flee the apartment before anyone came to investigate the gunshot. But she had underestimated the woman's vanity. Alex heard steps coming her way. Abby wanted to check her makeup before she left.

Through a small tear in the shower curtain, Alex could see Abby's face reflected Picasso-style in the remaining shards of the broken mirror. Various pieces of the mirror had fallen out, so it was difficult to tell if Abby was still holding the gun. Her arm was reflected in one of the shards, but the piece of the mirror that would have reflected her gun hand was missing.

Abby turned sideways and Alex could see the gun. A second later, the curious Abby was using it to push aside the shower curtain. As the muzzle of the gun swept the plastic aside, Alex took aim with her cuffed hands and hit Abby's wrist with the metal pipe section with all her might. The gun dropped into the tub, but so did the pipe. Abby hardly missed a beat. She slugged Alex in the jaw, then grabbed for her throat. Alex tried to remove the tightening grip, but Abby's gloved fingers seemed to have rooted themselves in her skin, reawakening the vast pain Alex had felt when the general had tried to strangle her. Alex bent her head and butted Abby's in perfect soccer form. Abby released her grip and slugged Alex with all her might, bouncing Alex off the tiles at the back of the shower. Alex righted herself and rammed the metal connector between the cuffs under Abby's chin, knocking Abby off balance. The stiletto heels of Abby's designer shoes slid on the wet bathroom floor and she fell, hitting her head on the toilet. She was knocked out cold.

Alex knelt next to the body. Abby was coldcocked for sure, but still breathing. She was losing blood from a gash in her head, but not dramatically. Alex looked down at the woman's feet, at the high heels that had, in a perverse way, saved Alex's life. It reinforced Alex's notion that we girls could do anything better in cowboy boots.

Alex picked up the gun. Then she gingerly stepped out of the tub and over Abby's body and walked into the living room.

She surveyed Abby's handiwork. The woman had apparently hit Clive over the head with the champagne bottle while he was taking off his pants. He must still have had the gun at that point, judging by his position and the shot in the wall that he had automatically gotten off as he'd fallen. Then Abby must have grabbed the gun and finished him off.

Alex picked up her silent phone, sitting next to the daisies. She started to dial 911, then realized it would be difficult to explain her prints on a gun that had killed a Secret Service agent. Not to mention that she had no idea what address to give the cops or an ambulance. Instead, she dialed Dan, briefly explained the situation, and asked him to use the GPS on her phone to find her. Then she slid her right hand into the dead man's pants pockets, fumbled for the handcuffs key, and liberated her hands.

CHAPTER FIFTY-SEVEN

BY THE time Abby was arraigned, she'd gotten herself the king of criminal lawyers, Dennis Riordan. He'd obviously given her the Eliza Doolittle lecture. She was now looking quite the lady, almost like a nun, in high-necked blouses and long skirts. On the evening news, Alex watched Riordan announce that he'd filed a motion to suppress the tape. Alex gasped. Riordan asserted that Abby's privacy had been violated. A government official—that would be Alex—had taped her without a warrant. Abby might even sue the official in a civil suit for violation of a D.C. statute that prevented the taping of conversations unless both parties consented.

Son of a bitch, Alex thought. Then she revised her utterance. No, bitch of a bitch. Abby had sat in a car with a gun pointed at Alex and now she's the one claiming her rights were violated?

AT THE AFIP the next day, Dan told her he was pulling out all stops to find the account in which the Chinese had deposited Abby's down payment. "Don't worry," he said. "We're not going to let her walk."

At lunch, Grant was laying odds that, even with the best evidence inculpating Abby, she wouldn't do more than a few years' jail time, and probably in some comfy country club of a prison.

Alex sensed he was right. She could picture it. Abby would be out before her fortieth birthday. She'd probably even get her own TV show, like Martha Stewart.

In the ladies' room after lunch, Alex scrutinized herself in the mirror. She swept her hair up atop her head, curls framing her face softly, trying to achieve some shred of glamour. Perhaps she'd wear it like this to the party she was attending that night at L'Enfant Plaza Hotel. Maybe she should learn to "work it," like Abby.

Then she let her hair fall naturally, tumbling in disarray over her shoulders. She was happy with the type of "work" she did now. She went back to her lab to forge a new understanding of the infectious capability of dengue fever.

CHAPTER FIFTY-EIGHT

SO MANY dignitaries from foreign lands and citizens from across the country had flown to D.C. to attend Cotter's funeral that the President and First Lady decided to create an event to honor the visitors. Like a mini-inauguration, parties were being held in various conference centers and hotel ballrooms across the city. The First Lady and Matthew made it to every one of them. The President was still recovering from his surgery. His stealth return to the White House had taken a lot out of him. But he didn't want people to think he was not up to his presidential duties. So, whatever party his family went to, he appeared on a large screen via video hookup. He addressed each group and even took a few questions so that everyone would know that, mentally at least, he was firing on all cylinders, and they weren't just viewing some canned footage.

Dan, his wife Jillian, and Alex attended the party at the L'Enfant Plaza Hotel, which housed dignitaries from countries with names that started with E through I (Ecuador through Italy). They'd picked that party because Jillian wanted to show off her husband to some Israeli politicos. But, within a few minutes, she had left Dan and Alex alone and was talking animatedly with one of the politicians from Guatemala, trying to get the scoop on a potential new assignment. Then she disappeared altogether.

Dan didn't seem the least bit perturbed. Jillian, after all, was Jillian. He admired her independence.

Some of the diplomats were restless. Alex could hear one—from Guyana she gathered—saying, "I came to bury Cotter, not to praise him."

The orchestra struck up "Hail to the Chief." The lights dimmed further and the video screen lit up behind the stage. Alex and Dan faced the stage.

The musicians put down their instruments and walked out into the crowd so that they, too, could see the screen. A spotlight shone on the stage entrance and the First Lady and Matthew walked out on the stage to wild applause. Alex mused about how different Matthew looked now. He was back to his compelling, calm self, with perhaps a hint of a new maturity.

The transmission began and President Cotter addressed the group. He still had the surgical bandage around his head. People gasped as the camera panned to show that he was talking from the rubble of the East Room. "We stand here as a world united. In a time of tragedy, we have put aside differences to make this nation's Capitol a crucible of possibility. The damage in the East Room is a visual reminder of the traumas and trials faced each day by every nation, big and small, rich or poor. For some countries, the daily threats are violence and disease, for others it is men lost to war or children with no means of education. No nation has all the answers."

The President walked to the far side of the room and sat in a blue wing chair under the Monet. Alex could see that the walk was a struggle for him. She wondered how pale he was under all the layers of television makeup.

The President continued. "You have all honored me beyond measure by coming here. As I lay, thinking I was dying, I began to realize how often world leaders get caught up in inconsequential diplomacy rather than world-enhancing leadership. That's why, although you came for a funeral, I hope you will stay for a Summit. We must decide what the real priorities are for our world at this time."

Applause filled the room. Even the representative from Guyana was clapping enthusiastically. Onstage, Matthew was beaming, proud of his father. The First Lady came to the mic and said the President would be willing to take a few questions. The first three were spoken in excited utterances about the possibilities of global change. The last one was simple: "Is there any truth to the rumor you are planning to appoint a female Vice President?"

Cotter's tired eyes twinkled. "Let's just say that's not out of the realm of possibility. I'm here today because of the efforts of a female doctor and my amazing First Lady. And—let's face it—if a woman can almost bring down a President, it may be time to have a female Vice President to shore one up."

Laughter layered over the applause. Jillian appeared next to Dan and Alex. Alex said, "It's been great to see you both. I think I'll head home."

Jillian hugged her and said good-bye. As Alex walked away, Jillian dangled a room key in front of Dan. "Seems like the representative from Estonia had a little earthquake on his hands and hasn't made it yet. I talked the manager into giving us his keys."

Dan's step was jaunty as he let Jillian lead him to the elevator.

CHAPTER FIFTY-NINE

THE NEXT day Chuck was bleary-eyed from watching the dance of dots to determine who put the real Braverman skull into the Vice President's office. Shane was denying having done so, and Abby's confession to Alex provided support for his position. So far, neither Abby's nor Clive's dots had entered the office after the Vietnamese visitors had arrived. Alex stopped by to see how Chuck was doing. The combination of getting sued by Abby and nearly getting killed by her gave Alex more than a passing interest in how the evidence against Abby was mounting up.

That morning, Abby's lawyer disclosed his latest legal ploy. Since the President had announced at the party that a woman had almost brought him down, Riordan was claiming that Abby wouldn't be able to get a fair trial in the United States due to that public accusation. He'd filed a motion to change the venue of the trial to a South American country.

Great, Alex thought. He'd probably picked one without an extradition treaty. Abby could just walk out of the courtroom down there, pull her millions from the Chinese oil deal out of whatever bank they were stashed in, and live like a queen.

Chuck looked particularly frustrated as he went about his work. He closed his eyes and opened them again. "Even with my eyes closed, I still see spots."

Alex could see the time code at the bottom of the screen. Chuck was rerunning the data, starting from the morning of the ceremony. He pointed to a gray dot, number 345. "Agent Moses is right where he should be—in the Secret Service office at the White House. He came in around seven thirty that morning. He probably brought the skull with the explosive with him at that time."

Alex knew the President was gold number one. The Vice President and his wife, red dots one and two, had entered the White House around 8:00 that morning. They both went to the Vice President's office in the West Wing. Alex looked at the two red dots. For the first three or four minutes, they were about three feet apart; then they moved to another location and started moving ever so slightly up and down. Chuck started to fast forward, but Alex made him stop. "Things are getting mighty hot in there," Alex said.

She looked at their position in the office, recalling the layout of the office. It looked like the Vice President started out near the window. Then it dawned on her what they were doing next. From their location, Alex guessed that Abby was sitting on the desk and the Vice President was standing next to it. They were making love.

Then the Vice President went into the bathroom and Abby left his office. After that, Abby went into the East Room and he went toward the Northeast entrance. Alex looked at the time on the counter running across the bottom of the image. Eleven A.M., a few minutes before the dot representing the Vice President made his last trip to his office.

Alex thought about what she had been doing at 11:00 A.M. She had been in the East Room then and she didn't remember Abby being there. But she recalled seeing the Vice President standing in the center of the room, under the Bohemian crystal chandelier. She didn't remember him leaving a few minutes later.

As the images ran forward, dots five and six did not come back together until around 11:40. Alex remembered them both being in the East Room at that time. The dots intersected at the point that Abby had come in and kissed the Veep.

"Rewind to eight A.M.," she told Chuck. She pointed out the bouncing lovemaking dots to him and his cheeks reddened. "Now look at this," she said excitedly. "Here's where the Vice President's dot goes into the bathroom."

"Uh-huh," Chuck said tentatively, not knowing what she was getting at.

"Think about it. How likely is it that he would go to that bathroom and she would leave the office? Women are always the ones to jump up and pee after making love—after all, they have stuff oozing out of them. And Abby, particularly, is an egomaniac about her appearance. I'm sure that she must be the one who went to the bathroom."

"But the dots—," protested Chuck.

"Don't you get it? She switched the pins while they were making love—and then switched them back when she kissed him in the East Room."

Chuck thought about it. "You're probably right. But how are you going to prove it?"

AFTER THE explosion, the Vice President hadn't gone back to his own office. He'd chosen the more spacious Oval Office as his headquarters. And now he was the guest of a federal prison. When Cotter had returned to the White House for Shane's arrest, he'd spent a few minutes in the Oval Office, but he hadn't entered the Vice President's office, and he now was conducting state business from the Family Quarters. He needed to recuperate, plus he wanted to stay close to his son. The Chief Executive and First Lady did a television broadcast each night, though, to assure the public that state business was being attended to.

When Alex was swabbing the surface of the Vice President's desk, Sheila Cotter came to the door. "I heard you were here," the First Lady said.

"Any chance this evidence of coitus is from you and the President?" Then Alex bit her tongue. What kind of thing was that to say to the First Lady? Even if she did know the story of the woman's first IUD.

Sheila Cotter took it in good humor, though. "No, with

132 rooms in the White House, we just haven't made it to the Vice President's office yet."

Sheila watched from a distance as Alex did her work. She was hanging back, not wanting to mess up anything at a crime scene. Then she spoke again. "I've got some ideas for the East Room and I wanted you to be the first to know. Lyndon Baines Johnson signed the Civil Rights Act in that room. I want to make it a testimony to racial harmony. I've commissioned a mural of people's faces, from a rainbow of ethnic groups. I've asked that one of the faces be Troy Nguyen's."

Alex stopped what she was doing to consider the matter. Would Troy have liked that or would he not? He was uncomfortable with being the center of attention. Perhaps he'd been right, she hadn't paid enough attention during her psychiatry rotation. She should have known that, with his personality, he would be the last person to make himself a martyr with a suicide bomb. He wouldn't have wanted that measure of attention, alive or dead.

She was sure he wouldn't have wanted a portrait of just him, but in a sea of faces perhaps he'd feel a belonging that he hadn't felt in life. Perhaps his spirit would treasure a memorial to him at the place he died. "It's a lovely idea," Alex said.

THE SEMINAL and vaginal fluids were enough to establish the sexual encounter between Abby and Tommy Shane. But when she presented her conclusions to Dan, he said, "It's a great theory, but it's not enough. Sure, you can establish they made love, but nothing says that Abby switched the pins."

"What about the bathroom trip?"

"Defense lawyers will eat you alive on that one. They'll say a guy Shane's age is bound to have prostate problems, probably wakes up ten times a night to pee."

"But I saw him in the East Room at the time his dot went back into his office."

"Yeah, but we haven't got any reliable witnesses to back you up."

"What about Binh Trang?"

"She was helpful at verifying what Troy had said to her, but she'd only arrived in the U.S. the night before. She didn't even know what the Vice President looked like, let alone when he came into the room."

Alex looked crushed. But, of course, it made sense. She herself had no idea who the vice president of Vietnam was—or even if they had one.

"It was great detective work, Alex, and it will add to the final case. But we need a smoking gun to put the woman away. She's a real piece of work."

When Alex returned to her lab, she remembered the pink fiber that she had found. Perhaps that was linked to Abby in some way. Dan arranged for her to collect evidence in the Shanes' home and in Abby's private office. The official residence of the Vice President, at One Observatory Circle, in Washington, D.C., had been built in 1893 for the superintendent of the United States Naval Observatory. In 1974, it was taken over for the use of the Second Family. When she arrived there, Alex peered into Abby's closet. Abby cultivated the image of a bubblehead, but her dresses were carefully arranged by length and color. Her dressing room had bookshelves. Not the romance novels or chick lit Alex expected, but a garden of self-help, motivational, and business success books. Alex had to give Abby a little more credit. She was working it according to a master plan.

On the floor of Abby's dressing room lay a stunning rug that President Mubarak of Egypt had given the Cheneys when he had visited them. Its rose-colored fibers matched perfectly the one that Alex had found in her office. That tied Abby Shane, in some way, to the break-in at Alex's office. At the very least, it could be argued that Clive Moses had come to the AFIP to get the letter from the skull after getting orders from Abby. She'd probably planned to use it as a further weapon to queer the oil deal between the United States and the Vietnamese.

Abby could only use the letter as a last resort, though. How would she explain how it fell into her hands? Her plan must have called for Alex to keep pressure on the investigation.

On that hunch, Alex returned home for the quilt from her bedroom. When Cotter had shot Moses, the splatter from the Secret Service agent's shoulder had wet the quilt. Sure enough, when she analyzed it in her lab, the DNA matched that from the wreath planted to scare Alex into continuing her work on the massacre. Moses must have followed her to Carlisle and Sons when she first visited it, and duplicated her office and home keys then. The only way he could have known about the Lo Duoc affair at that time was through the President, the Vice President, or Abby, who'd been listening outside the Oval Office when Wiatt had brought the news.

Alex had now tied Moses to the break-in at her apartment and lab. But what good did that do? She still didn't have enough to put the noose around Abby's neck. For that, she'd need solid evidence of Abby's relationship with the Chinese.

THAT EVENING, CBS carried a special about the First Lady's plans for the East Room. The program alternated between historical footage, architectural plans, and an interview with the First Lady.

"This isn't the first devastation the room has suffered," the First Lady said. "In August 1814, when President James Madison ruled the country, invading British troops set fire to it, leaving only a burned-out shell."

When the room was rebuilt, each Administration added its touch. President Andrew Jackson installed glass chandeliers and two rows of spittoons. The room saw such a flow of visitors that a dozen years later a journalist opined that the chairs there would "disgrace a house of shame." During the Civil War, Union soldiers used the East Room as a bivouac.

"The most famous painting in the room was a full length portrait of George Washington," said the First Lady. "Dolley Madison had the foresight to remove it and hide it just before the British soldiers showed up. I'm afraid I wasn't that clever, just lucky. The portrait was on loan to the Freedom Museum in Chicago when the explosion occurred. It will be on display when the room reopens."

The teaser before the commercial showed a clip of

Matthew Cotter. Alex thought about the joy on the boy's face at the L'Enfant Plaza party after his father had resurfaced.

The show continued with a voiceover about how First Kids had used the East Room in the past. Theodore Roosevelt's kids roller-skated there. But Tad Lincoln took the prize for creativity. Abe Lincoln's son once rode into the East Room on a chair pulled by two goats.

Matthew Cotter was planning something much more practical. "When the plans to rebuild the East Room were first announced, I got calls from teens from other countries who had worked with me in Habitat for Humanity. A dozen of them are going to spend their spring breaks here, helping rebuild the room."

Alex smiled at his image on the screen. He was a good kid. His plan may not go over well with the unions, but what were they going to do, dump a Democratic President?

CHAPTER SIXTY

THE ATTEMPTED coup at the White House, the kickbacks to Vietnamese officials tendered by the Vice President, and the angry recriminations between Vietnam and the United States had demolished the Westport Oil deal over the Phu Khanh basin. But President Cotter was not about to let America's crude oil dependency fall victim to a political minefield not of his own making. His international popularity ratings were at an all-time high. When Cotter invited the presidents of China and Vietnam to the White House, they were in no position to refuse. Especially when Cotter informed the Vietnamese president that someone from his embassy had run Michael Carlisle off the road.

Due to the work of Ron Gladden and Cameron Alistair, all three leaders realized the incredible potential of the newly discovered oil field. But only Cotter had worked out a plan that would benefit them all. There was enough oil to meet the needs of both giants, China and the United States. And, by recouping the millions in graft paid to Chugai and his cronies in the Ministry of the Interior by Westport Oil and to Abby Shane by the Chinese, the respective players could offer an even higher price to the government of Vietnam. Win-win-win, Cotter told them. But to get to that point, the Chinese president would have to force his daughter to divulge where the money to Abby had been stashed.

After an intensive father-daughter talk, replete with raised voices about "losing face," Cotter—and, moments later, Dan—had the Ecuadorian bank account number where Abby's $15 million had been deposited. And damn if Jillian didn't know just the government official there who could make the connection between Abby and the money.

AT THE hospital, Barbara finished revising the list of charges against Abby just before Alex picked her up. After Alex dropped Barbara off at home to an ecstatic Lana, she went to the pharmacy to retrieve Barbara's antibiotics. The handsome blond pharmacist was there. "I haven't got anything for you," he said as Alex approached his counter.

"I'm picking up a prescription for my friend. It'll be under 'Findlay.' "

The pharmacist turned and found the bag in the "F" bin. He rotated back toward Alex and asked, "Is this the woman you sometimes come in with?"

Alex nodded.

"How come her husband didn't pick it up?"

Alex grinned. "She's not married."

The pharmacist grinned back. He came out from behind his counter and walked down the greeting card aisle. He picked a get well card off the shelf, took it back to the counter, and signed the card with his name and phone number. He stuck the card into the bag that held Barbara's pills. "Maybe, once she's up to going out again, you could serve as some sort of reference."

"What'll I say about you?"

"Was a fireman before I went to pharmacy school, love to cook, have season tickets to the Kennedy Center, have been known to send schmaltzy greeting cards, and," he smiled, "am crazy for a smart woman in uniform."

Alex smiled, took the bag, and said, "I'll see what I can do."

BARBARA SEEMED to be doing just fine when Alex dropped off the drugs and the card. Lana was fussing over her. She'd bought her mom magazines, set up a game of Monopoly, and arranged a snack tray with Barbara's laptop so that Barbara could work from her bed. That girl sure knew her mom. Lana had even forged a new candlestick for Barbara, a big heart with WELCOME HOME written on it.

When Alex got back to her apartment, she entered her code on the keypad. As she opened the door, a familiar voice called her name.

"Luke?" she said. The door swung open and he grabbed her around the waist, lifting her in the air. Then he put her down and stood behind her as she put her key inside the new lock to the inner door. He followed her inside, put his arms around her, and held her tightly. In the mirror in front of her she could see her own face and, reflecting back from the mirror on the opposite wall, she could see Luke. The way his head was bent, he couldn't tell that she was watching. A tear was rolling down his cheek.

She stepped back so she could look at him.

He used his right hand to brush his long brown hair away from his eyes and wipe the tear from his cheek. "You could have been killed," he said. "How come, when all this was happening, you never called me?"

Alex let out a sigh and then said quietly, "I wasn't sure if you'd come."

Luke looked hurt. Then he bent his head close to hers, and held her chin so that she would look right into his eyes.

"How did you find out about it?" she asked.

"Jillian called my hotel in Barcelona. She knows how stubborn you are, knew you'd never get in touch."

"Hotel?"

"Yeah, well, hell. I never did make it to Vanessa's."

Alex tried to suppress a little smile.

Luke continued, "You're a hard act to follow. All that time on the road, I missed you."

"How did Jillian find you? I had no idea when you'd be where."

He laughed. "Tracked me down through Interpol. You

know Jillian and her contacts. Sometimes I think the photo-journalist bit is just a cover."

Alex gave a mental note of thanks to her crazy Israeli friend. Then she took in the whole of Luke and looked over toward the bedroom. Enthusiastically, she uttered just two words: "Dare you."

THE NEXT morning, Alex awoke to the smell of coffee. She opened her eyes and noticed the disarray of the sheets, the clothes flung across the room. Luke was back. She lay in bed for a moment, trying to figure out how she felt about his return. She thought about their lovemaking the night before, gingerly gentle at first, then steamily exciting. All that and coffee, too. She definitely was glad the Lukester was back in residence.

She pulled a long T-shirt from the National Museum of Health and Medicine over her head and padded barefoot into the kitchen, where Luke was pouring milk into a bowl at the counter. Luke handed her a cup of coffee and motioned her to a chair. He then went back to the counter and mixed the contents of the bowl. "I went shopping this morning," he said.

"I can see that." A brown paper bag was on the counter, and every few minutes Luke would pull something else out of it.

She watched as he made French toast, which he topped with fresh raspberries and whipped cream. He joined her with the two plates on the table and handed her a postcard of the Casa Battló in Barcelona, which was designed by the surrealist architect Gaudí.

"If Gaudí were still alive," Luke said, "he'd probably have designed the Curl Up and Dye."

She stared at the surreal home, a mosaic masterpiece. Perhaps it was just the impact of the case, but, to her, the balconies looked like skulls and the pillars like bones.

She looked up at Luke and was happy to have a person of his energy and life in her home. "How'd you sleep?" she asked.

"With a very satisfied grin on my face, for sure," he said,

reaching across the table for her hand. "But my back's sore from the futon on the floor. How about if I use some of my tour money to buy you a proper bed?"

Alex considered the matter. She decided she was ready to face that choice now, especially with Luke's aid. She smiled at the thought of a mattress salesman watching them try it out. Ever so chastely, of course. "I've got an appointment this morning. How about meeting back here at two P.M.?"

"I've brought back some new CDs from Europe—perfect mood music for our using the whole weekend to break in the bed."

"Just so it's not Barcelona rock," Alex said.

Luke nodded his head. "Not my taste, either."

CHAPTER SIXTY-ONE

ALEX PARKED in front of Troy's building. She'd been there only once before, for their spur-of-the-moment dinner. She took a deep breath before entering the building, not quite sure that she was ready to enter a space so full of her friend's spirit.

She climbed the three flights of stairs, feeling Troy's presence grow. When she reached his door, excitement overtook her mourning. She knocked, and Lizzie opened the door.

Troy's sister was a slight woman with stunning blue-green eyes in her almond-colored face. She wore a white sarong which was a little too tight and short, perhaps because the genes from her American dad made her slightly taller than the average Vietnamese woman. When she turned to lead Alex into the apartment, Alex could see the tattoo on the back of her right shoulder. It was a caricature of Uncle Sam. In a noose. Alex could understand why Lizzie might have had a spot of trouble with immigration.

Lizzie motioned her to the couch, where she had set out a tea service. They both sat down. "I'm sorry," both said at precisely the same time, "for your loss." A small smile crossed both women's lips as they acknowledged each other's relationship with Troy. Then they sat silently for a moment, each lost in a memory of the man.

Alex raised the cup to her face and inhaled the smell of

the jasmine tea, a perfume inalterably associated with Troy. Lizzie was sipping hers, staring at the altar she'd made to her brother's memory on a bookshelf across from the couch. Alex's gaze focused on two small photos of Troy as a young boy. They were worn, tiny images, with gashlike lines through them where the photos had been folded or bent.

"I kept those photos with me, tucked in my clothes, close to my heart since the day he left," Lizzie said. "When my uncle took him away, I felt more of a loss than if my mother had gone. He *talked* to me, tried to explain things. She never did, not until the end."

Alex recognized the older Troy, her Troy, even in the images of him when he was eight. That earnestness. The maturity. Perhaps even a hint of his infuriating penchant for reducing the world to easy explanations. Well, Alex thought, Lord knows he needed some.

The two women faced each other—the fragile bond between them the shared feelings that they had for a man who was now dead. Lizzie was trembling slightly. Alex didn't know what the Vietnamese cultural rules were about touching. She wished for the hundredth time that day that Troy were here to welcome his sister. Then, as Lizzie began to sob and tears rolled down Alex's cheeks, Alex leaned forward on the couch and wrapped her arms around the slight woman. They stayed in that position for many heartbeats and a gallon of tears, until Lizzie pulled back and said, "I'm sorry, I haven't even thanked you for all you did to get me here."

"What Troy did, really," Alex said. He'd used everything within his power to bring Lizzie to the United States. When money and lawyers weren't enough, he'd inserted himself into the Trophy Skulls affair, hoping to get a fair hearing on the Lizzie matter from the leaders of Vietnam and the United States.

Lizzie looked around her new home, her mouth gaping open in wonder as she gazed at the cool forest green walls of the living room, the warm dark mahogany of the dining room table. She gently stroked the cushions of the couch, as if a rougher touch would somehow make this fantasy life disappear. She looked at Alex. "I always thought it would be my American father who would bring me to this country." She shook her head. "Instead, it was my Vietnamese brother."

Troy had never given up on getting his sister to the United States. Though he'd used most of his savings to set the wheels in motion to bring her to Washington, D.C., he'd been practical enough to have purchased mortgage insurance. The condo was now owned, free and clear, by his next of kin, Lizzie. And he had a modest governmental life insurance policy for which Lizzie was the beneficiary. But Alex fretted about how Lizzie would be able to afford to keep up the maintenance fees, taxes, and general living expenses when that money was depleted. Her English was good. Maybe Alex could help her get a job.

As if reading her thoughts, Lizzie reached into the pocket of her dress. "A man gave me a little book with my name on it. He told me that you would know what to do with it."

Lizzie passed it to Alex and she realized it was a savings account passbook from First American Bank here in D.C. She opened it and saw it was an account, in Lizzie's name, with $100,000 in it. "A man gave this to you?" Alex said with surprise. "What man?"

"He came to me in the camp the day before I left. He gave me chocolates and this. He was a man whose legs didn't work. He had a chair with wheels."

Alex's heart swelled. Michael. He was still alive. She sat silently for a moment, picturing him back in the country that he loved. She conjured up the image he had shared with her of Vietnamese women in thin boats picking lotuses. She felt giddy, thrilled for him.

"Did he have a woman with him?"

Lizzie nodded in surprise. "Yes, with gray hair."

Alex clapped. Ellen had found him. She thought of the two of them together. Maybe Carlisle would have a chance to create the "and Sons" for real.

Alex put the passbook on the table. She tapped the cover of it with her finger. "This is money," she said. "You'll be able to live well if you are careful with it."

Lizzie smiled, then stood up and walked back into the kitchen. She came back, not with more tea as Alex expected, but with two pairs of scissors and some white papers. "We must figure out what my brother needs in the next world," she said.

Alex reached for a pair, thought for a moment, and began clumsily chopping at the paper. Lizzie took the other scissors and, in a seemingly effortless series of turns and glides, transformed the white rectangle into a delicate fruit-bearing tree. "He'll need food and shade and beauty," she told Alex.

Alex labored on, while Lizzie clipped her paper with grace and determination. On Lizzie's side of the cocktail table, a stunning panorama was appearing. The tree. A gabled house. A violin—in case he wanted to take up music in the afterworld. Then Lizzie started cutting small rectangles. Alex wondered if she'd lost interest all of a sudden, but Lizzie explained, "He'll need money to buy things we haven't thought of."

Lizzie looked over at Alex's lopsided creation-in-progress, a strange combination of two semicircles on the bottom and some odd jutting structures on the top of one side. Eventually the outline of the item became recognizable.

"A motorcycle!" said Lizzie, smiling and clapping her hands.

Alex nodded. "He said he always wanted one." She propped it up, between the house and the fruit tree.

Then Alex reached over and took one of the money-shaped rectangles that Lizzie had created. She took scissors and cut one end of it so that it was book-shaped, rather than elongated like currency. She reached into her fanny pack and took out a pen. On the volume, she wrote a tiny title: "Trophy Skulls." She knew the inquisitive Troy would want to read it to find out how the story ended.

ACKNOWLEDGMENTS

WRITING A book is fun and terrifying at the same time. While some writers isolate themselves with their characters, I rely heavily on family, friends, and professional colleagues to help me through the process. Clem Ripley, Christopher Ripley, Lesa Andrews, Darren Stephens, Richard Fitzpatrick, Bob Gaensslen, Katharine Cluverius, and Kelley Ragland all contributed mightily to this book. I am also grateful to Paul Sledzik, who answered my first question about the Trophy Skulls by opening a drawer and putting one in my hands.

Not just individuals but also institutions played a role. By electing me an honorary fellow, the American College of Law and Medicine provided me with a set of colleagues with unparalleled skills in law and medicine. By asking me to speak on ethics at its annual meeting, the American Academy of Forensic Sciences exposed me to the cutting-edge technologies and policy issues within forensics. The Illinois Institute of Technology and its Chicago-Kent College of Law surrounded me with talented colleagues and students who undertake public interest projects around the world. I was aided mightily by IIT student Hoa Nguyen, who comes from Ho Chi Minh City; she instructed me on everything from Vietnam's contemporary perspectives on Americans to the taste and smell of durian fruit. And, in Chicago, I am lucky enough to be able to visit the National Vietnam Veterans

Art Museum as a place to reflect on the impact of war and the dignity of man.

Two amazing scientists, Dr. Minh Tran and Vinh Nguyen, took me behind closed doors at the Institute for Tropical Biology in Vietman and ushered me into a compelling visit to that incredible country. For those who can't make the trip themselves, David Lamb's *Vietnam, Now: A Reporter Returns* provides an unparalleled introduction.

One of the wonders of writing fiction is the incredible support you get from other writers. Eric Goodman and Mark Rosin have for decades been willing to act as gentle guides to the world of fiction. And I am enormously grateful to Michael, whose questions and insights over the past year have helped me to develop both as a lawyer and a writer.

Acknowledgments

Read on for the next book by

LORI ANDREWS

IMMUNITY

Coming soon in hardcover from
St. Martin's Minotaur

AFTER BAD booze in six bars, Castro's room at the Wanderlust Motel beckoned him like the arms of a lover. At four a.m., the Vegas Strip dazzled like a dowager's jewels in the distance, while the flickering neon on his hotel looked like a battered sequin on the pasties of an over-the-hill showgirl.

He scanned the area to make sure no one was lying in wait for him. A lot of guys wanted a pound of his flesh, payback for his past acts—or just the chance to treat someone like a punching bag to batten down their demons. His tired glance registered Lil Joe, a jittery speed freak who some nights had the fifteen dollars to rent a room, but more often just paced the broken sidewalk outside the motel. Lil Joe glared at him and paced backwards, away from Castro's six foot two, well-muscled frame. "Is cool. Is cool," said Joe through cracked lips.

A screeching car stopped at the end of the parking lot. The passenger door opened, followed by a scream and then a thump as the car sped away. Castro got to the spot in less than a minute. Looking at the body on the ground, he realized that being pushed from a moving car was the least of the girl's problems. Her clothes were torn, her face pummeled, and a large pool of blood was soaking through the crotch of her jeans.

As he bent down to feel for a pulse in her neck, she croaked weakly, "No more, stop it." Tears pouring down her cheek, she reached up and scratched his face with her broken nails.

Pinning her arm gently so she couldn't reach him, he said, "I'm not going to hurt you." But she didn't seem to hear him through her sobs. She curled into a fetal ball as he fished his cell phone out of his pocket. He was about to dial when he heard the click of a round being chambered behind him.

He put his arms out to his sides and slowly straightened up, cursing himself for not considering that the driver might park the car and double back. But when he turned his head, he saw the motel manager, a tough old broad pointing a Baretta 9mm.

"I didn't do it," he said.

He realized how bad this looked, what with the girl down and the scratches on his face. Lil Joe could alibi him, but the wiry junkie had slipped away. He pivoted slowly, keeping his hands up, cell phone pointed to the sky. He knew Ted would have handled it differently. Ted could sweet-talk any woman into doing anything. Ted had the gift of gab. Castro could only understand a woman after months or years in her arms.

His blue eyes blazed at the older woman. "Dolores," he said, "put down the gun and let me call nine-one-one." He said it calmly, watching her image strobe in and out in the flickering light of the Wanderlust sign. If she didn't lower the gun by the time he counted mentally to ten, he would pounce and break her arm.

Her gun went down. His fingers sped over the numbers and he gave their location to the emergency operator. As Dolores bent to soothe the scared teen, he dialed Ted. "We've got another one," he said. "I've got plates. Black Mercedes, FAN 231."

BY SEVEN a.m., the man who'd tossed her from the car was in custody. He'd stopped for a drink after his little errand, not even bothering to clean off the pool of blood from the passenger seat.

Ted and Castro watched his interrogation through the one-way glass in the Vegas police department where they were the DEA end of a joint LVPD/DEA investigation into a date rape drug simply called "J." The women who were slipped this beauty became sedated, then aroused, then psychotic. It pushed them further than anyone would have imagined, a sick game to the men who used it. But young girls were ending up mutilated or dead.

The driver—clearly not the sharpest knife in the drawer—claimed he was just helping out a friend at the Fantasy Resort on the Strip. "The girl was like that in the hotel room," he told the interrogator. "Woulda been bad for business to have her found there."

Through the glass, Castro could only see the back of the interrogator's head, but he could imagine his eyes rolling at that comment. The interrogator said, "So, Joey, you're telling me it's not bad for business to throw one of the guests out of a moving car?"

Joey sat up straight, as if offended by the question. "She wasn't no guest. A working girl like her booking a thousand-dollars-a-night room? Get real."

On the other side of the mirror, Castro thought about whether the owner of the Fantasy Resort, Frankie "the Bayonet" DiBondi, could be moving J. Why go for the piddly markup on a drug for lowlifes when you ran a legal brothel (a million a month declared on taxes, with an unimaginable sum socked away under the radar) and owned the hottest casino on the Strip (fifty million dollars annually with everyone from Bette Midler to Shakira wanting to play the five-thousand-seat showroom)?

"Why would the Bayonet move down the alphabet to J when he could make the big bucks moving H?" Castro said.

"We still need to get on his ass," Ted said. "If the drug made it inside the hotel, maybe someone there is dealing."

Castro nodded. If this had occurred under DiBondi's nose, what he did about it in the next twenty-four hours could tip them off to who was selling and, more importantly, who was producing the drug.

WHEN THEY reached the Fantasy Resort, it was barely nine a.m. Castro headed straight to the casino, the surest place to find DiBondi. The seventy-year-old don had a penthouse in the hotel, but was constantly in motion, greeting guests, throwing dinners for the headliners, and storming through the casino, watching the dealers to make sure they didn't dick with his money. Sure, he had state-of-the-art security and a slew of ex-cops on retainer, but he was old school.

At the bar in the main casino, Castro caught sight of DiBondi approaching a blond-haired man in his forties. Dressed in a navy suit with a prep school tie, the younger man stuck out in the casino, where the dress code encompassed either tuxedoed men escorting women in Cher-like beaded numbers or overweight Middle Americans in Bermuda shorts or sweatpants.

DiBondi put his arm around the blond man. But rather than buying him a drink, he steered the conservatively dressed man toward the exit. Castro moved into a flow of people headed out of the sumptuous breakfast buffet so that it wouldn't be so obvious he was trailing DiBondi. But he needed to stay close. A valet was turning over a Cadillac with the plates FAN OO1 to the older man. Castro needed to make sure he was back in his own car with Ted before the man hit the road.

DiBondi handed his keys over to the guy Castro pegged to be a businessman. That term in Vegas covered a lot of territory. The DEA agent didn't know what the connection might be to J, or even if there was any. Someone producing the drug would have known better than to show up at the casino dressed like that. And DiBondi wouldn't have been seen in public with him. But this was going down strangely enough to make them both persons of interest.

CASTRO'S WEARY body, which hadn't felt sleep for nearly two days, slumped over the wheel as DiBondi and his pal pulled into a gas station outside of Flagstaff, Arizona. It was their first stop since they'd left Vegas five hours earlier. Ted woke up as Castro eased on the brakes. "Fuck," Ted said. "Where the hell is he taking us?"

Castro didn't bother to respond. He switched positions with Ted and, once in the passenger seat, immediately fell asleep. When he next woke up, it was dusk and they were across the street from the Hotel La Fonda in Taos. He stepped out of the car, took a seat in the lobby, and surreptitiously snapped a photo of DiBondi's companion on his cell phone, transmitting the photo to DEA headquarters for identification.

He and Ted waited until the two men got in the elevator before they approached the desk themselves, checking in as a gay couple. Each of them had now gotten a good five hours' sleep and they were more than ready for whatever DiBondi had to dish out. Ted took Castro's hand as they waited for the elevator. Once inside, Castro let go and laughed. "Next time," he said, "remind me to get assigned a woman as a partner."

"Nah, you love me," said Ted. And he was right. He was Castro's closest friend.

In the room, Castro looked out the window and saw that the valet had not parked DiBondi's car. "Get ready to roll," he said to Ted as he grabbed a map from the desk. "They're just making a pit stop."

They took the stairs back down. Ted disappeared into the park across from the hotel for a moment, then got into the passenger seat of the car, just as DiBondi and his buddy were pulling out.

Castro's cell phone rang. "He's not in the system," the voice on the other end said. The photo didn't match any known felons or anyone with ties to the Mob.

"Much obliged," said Castro, who hung up and turned to his partner.

"I heard," Ted said.

"Doesn't seem like family either."

Ninety minutes later, the Cadillac turned onto an unpaved road.

"Think he made us?" Ted asked.

"Nah," Castro said, as he cut the headlights and followed the other car down the side road. The Cadillac was still traveling at highway speed, churning up dust and small pebbles. The road passed along the edge of a quarry that was dug down hundreds of feet. "What does the map say?"

Ted took out a pen-sized flashlight and looked at their map, shielding the light with his hand so it couldn't be seen from the other car. "Quarry for about a mile along the road, then the map is pretty much a blank for maybe ten miles."

"What's it called? Area fifty-one?"

"Nope, nothing on it but the initials RSV."

"Here, let me see." Castro eyed the map without slowing down and the car veered sharply to the right, bringing their right tires perilously close to the edge of the quarry.

"Shit, my man," said Ted, "pay attention. DiBondi's stopping."

Castro turned left and pulled the car behind a steam shovel. Ted pressed his night-vision binoculars against his face. Castro followed suit. DiBondi and his mystery driver had stopped about five hundred feet farther up the road. They were met by four men with long, black straight hair. Native Americans.

"RSV," Castro said. "Reservation."

They were tailing DiBondi because of his possible link to the new date rape drug. But they knew the Justice Department had been looking for a way to prove that the Mob was working its way into the Indian gaming industry, and now Castro and Ted were watching a possible connection unfold in front of them.

"Whatever tribe this is, it's not doing that well," Ted said. "Look at that wooden house. Pretty run-down."

Ted took his .38 out of the glove compartment. Castro already had his Sig Sauer in a holster under his windbreaker. They got out of the car and walked another hundred feet, but there wasn't enough cover for them to get closer.

Castro looked at the building, about eighty feet long and twenty feet wide. The arc-shaped roof had been created by bending a series of wooden poles and covering them with bark. He tried to remember something from his undergraduate class on Native American History at the University of Arizona. A longhouse. The four Native Americans had gone in, but left Frankie and his driver waiting at the door. Maybe they were deciding whether to invite the men from Vegas inside. Some longhouses were a big deal, males only, maybe some peyote and major decision-making. But wait, there was something going down. Some guy had shown up on horseback and was yelling. Castro raised his night-vision glasses. Guy was prepared for some sort of war dance for sure, blue stripe of paint across his nose. Chief War Paint jumped down and blocked DiBondi's path.

While the Indian was focused on DiBondi, his buddy was circling to the Indian's right, behind the horse. Castro expected the blond man to pull a gun and shoot the rider. Castro aimed his Sig Sauer at the driver's shoulder, but this would be a tough shot.

Suddenly Ted crumpled to the ground, and Castro dropped down, lunging toward his partner as he scanned the area for a sniper. Finding none, he looked at his friend, seeking out a wound. But Ted didn't seem to be bleeding anywhere other than his nose. A screechy, wheezing noise was coming from his mouth. Castro inched closer. Ted was shaking and his tongue was swollen. In the dark, Castro thought his eyes were playing tricks on him. His partner's face was swelling, distorting into some monstrous visage.

"Help," spat Ted through lips that were swelling so much they cracked. His eyelids swelled over his eyes. Blood from his nose clogged his mouth, silencing further speech.

Castro shoved his arms under his friend's, scraping his knuckles raw on the stones underneath Ted. He pulled Ted's distorted body over the gravel pathway back to the car. "Hang in there, buddy. Don't give up on me."

He lifted the man into the backseat, putting a backpack under his head so he wouldn't choke to death on his own blood. His friend was now shaking uncontrollably. He opened his blue lips in the shape of a scream, trying to suck in air around his swollen tongue.

Castro careened the car back onto the road. The tires churned up stones, but their patter on the road didn't disguise the sound of three gunshots coming from the direction of the longhouse and aimed at his speeding car.

ALEX STEPPED back from the gene sequencer and looked at the four-color quilt on the computer screen that represented the sequence of the glycoprotein gene of the dengue 2 virus. Call her macabre, but stripped down to its chemical bases—the red, blue, green, and orange representing the A, C, G, and T of the genetic code—the gene was quite beautiful.

She entered the genetic letters into a computer program and a swell of music filled the room. A professor at the School of the Art Institute of Chicago, Peter Gena, had created a formula for turning the genetic alphabet of deadly diseases into musical compositions. Gena used the gene sequences of HIV, measles, and polio as the basis for his songs. When Alex ran the program on the dengue sequence, jagged notes collided with each other, with an occasional soothing tonal switch. A chilling composition, fitting the high fatality rate of dengue fever, a Southeast Asian killer.

Alex, who'd earned an M.D. and Ph.D. in genetics at Columbia, had come to the Armed Forces Institute of Pathology—the AFIP—two years earlier to sequence the genomes of deadly epidemic diseases which the Department of Defense felt might be used in biowarfare against the United States. She also served on a government-wide commission led by the head of Homeland Security, Martin Kincade. The commission, populated with people from Homeland Security, the FBI, the CIA, Justice, and the National Institutes of Health, was charged with detecting emerging infections, analyzing the threat they posed, and initiating medical and social responses.

Her home institution, the AFIP, had lots more on its plate than addressing the possibility of bioterrorism. In fact, the traditional military men who worked alongside her viewed her work as marginal, rather like collecting primroses or trying to find life on other planets. They were trained to deal with immediate risks—targeting the enemy or capturing a killer.

Situated on one hundred and thirteen out-of-the-way acres in D.C. near the Maryland border, the semisecret AFIP oversaw forensic investigations in the United States and abroad involving the military and the Executive Branch. Congress also gave it a blank check to develop new technologies for national security, forensics, and traditional warfare. The AFIP's equivalent of James Bond's Q—Captain Grant Pringle—oversaw a bevy of researchers just a hallway away from her. But unlike his dapper British fictional counterpart, Pringle was an over-muscled weightlifter who'd grown up in Vegas.

Alex loved her work, but felt less thrilled about her workplace. She detested the military hierarchy, the baroque rules about secrecy, and the emotionless faces of many of the men she served alongside. Her natural response was to play the civilian card—coming to work each day in jeans and a turtleneck, letting her personal interests dictate which research she undertook, and finding enough ways to bend the rules that they seemed like overcooked linguini when she was done with them. Her best friend, Lieutenant Barbara Findlay, the general counsel of the AFIP, was often amused and occasionally infuriated by the way Alex maneuvered through the system. Alex kidded that she was Barbara's evil twin.

The music hit a particularly garish note, and Alex barely heard the knock on her lab door. She opened it and admitted Captain Randolph Stone, a pathologist from Walter Reed Hospital, part of the AFIP complex. She'd met him the previous month when she was asked to give a second opinion at the hospital.

"With that awful music pouring out of your lab, I felt sure you'd be applying electricity to a body with a jagged scar across his face," Stone said.

"Did you stop by to place an order? Bride of Frankenstein for you?"

"Hmm, clone of Angelina Jolie?"

"Take a number, buddy."

Stone smiled and leaned comfortably against a counter that held the bottles of the reagents Alex had used in this latest sequence run. He looked at Alex with the sort of glance she often got on the street from men who admired her package—the long blonde hair, the curve of her jeans and turtleneck over her five foot seven frame. Most of the men at the AFIP were beyond that. They treated her like one of the guys. All except for Captain Grant Pringle, who turned leering into an Olympic-level sport.

This new pathologist was around her age, mid-to-late thirties, with an engaging smile and sun-bleached blond hair that, while still short, was much longer than the buzz cuts she usually encountered in the building. He handed her a folder. "I'm here to ask you a favor."

She reached for the file. "Cloned girlfriend isn't enough?"

"Nah, I'm up to my eyeballs in autopsies and I just got a call asking if I could take this report over to DEA. There's no way I can leave the building right now."

Alex bristled. "Why not messenger it? Or use one of the eight hundred soldiers in the building?" It was bad enough her boss, Colonel Jack Wiatt, ordered her to do things that any lab tech could do. At least Wiatt was old enough to be her dad. But surfer guy here?

"Sorry, I should explain. It's a sensitive case. A DEA agent died yesterday in New Mexico while on the job. They've convened an investigation—brought in all the big boys—to see if he was using on the job. They want it brought over by a physician in case there are questions. You may not have noticed, but it's Sunday and there aren't exactly a lot of docs in the building."

Alex opened the folder and paged through the report. Honestly, she thought, sometimes she flew off the handle too quickly. It wouldn't exactly kill her to take a drive over to Arlington to drop this off. After all, Stone was doing a huge favor for her friend, AFIP pathologist Tom Harding, who was in Australia competing in a sailboat regatta. Stone was fitting in autopsies here at AFIP while running back and forth to Walter Reed for analyses of path samples in medical cases.

Alex looked down at the final line of the report. *Death consistent with cocaine overdose.* "I don't see any tox reports," she said.

"Body just came in this morning, lab results aren't back yet. But his nasal membranes were completely eroded, just like you see with the heavy users. And I found major organ failure—heart, kidneys."

Alex nodded. It was a beautiful April day, cherry blossoms in bloom, and she had a full tank of gas in her 1963 yellow T-bird. A little excursion might be nice. "What's the address?"

"DEA Headquarters is at 700 Army Navy Drive in Arlington."

Army Navy? thought Alex. She couldn't escape the military, even on this detour.

"Do you have a contact there?"

He moved toward her and opened the file to the second page. "Milford. He's the guy who requested the autopsy. Kept it out of the hands of the New Mexico medical examiner. Said the last thing DEA needed was publicity about their guy using coke on the job."

Alex and Stone walked out of the lab together. "Thanks, Alex," he said. "I owe you one."